# A German Winter

Jim McDermott

# The End

His head and gut tossed *Judas* between them, baiting the conscience he should have kicked into the ditch with his sense of duty. A man more at peace with war would have accepted that he was only a twitch of the bureaucratic machine, a hapless pawn, the innocent butt of orders from a place where troop movements were ordained by the million. But he was weak, stupid, someone who wore his good luck like a confession. It didn't so much invite guilt as help it on to a low roof, the better to jump on him.

Germany was over, finished. Less than a hundred kilometres to the east the Red Army was thrusting with appalling force into a corpse that twitched in imitation of life, its dead head dreaming on still, plotting, pretend-manoeuvring, imagining armies and throwing out diktats to reinforce them. In the city he'd fled the emptied barrel was being scraped frantically once more; anyone capable of fighting or of stopping a bullet that might otherwise find a more useful man - anyone, in fact, who bore no responsibility for the calamity that was upon them all – was front-line material now, prime slaughterhouse quality. He and the other invalids who staffed *LuftGeheimStelle IIb* had waited for days, knowing their turn must be coming. Their boss, Karl Krohne, had a horror of delivering bad news (a lamentable failing in a Luftwaffe officer), and was avoiding the office and the questions painted across every face. A few of them feared betrayal, that he was busily digging a private tunnel out of Berlin; but when he reappeared, Christ-like after three days and nights, he came carrying a small pile of envelopes, each containing a perfectly legitimate, counter-signed transfer order to somewhere other than a Front. Two of the younger men had refused the offer; they wanted to prove that they could fight still, even if the effort was pointless, a suicide posting. The rest of them hadn't cared to check the mouth of a horse that was offering a ride out of the apocalypse.

The transfers were treasonably agreeable. A one-handed, half-faced boy was stood down from his vital role of inventing paper air squadrons (to reassure the Allies that Germany had a Luftwaffe still) and punished with a posting to Flensburg II Passive Radar Station. Though pestered by the RAF, the station was only some ten kilometres from his family's farm, a curious coincidence. Another man, the department's sole broken-neck, had orders to accompany One-Hand as far as Schleswig but then to proceed further, to take up a liaison role in southern Denmark, where astonishingly few Luftwaffe personnel had managed to get themselves killed to date. Others were despatched variously to listening stations that could hear only the Reich's death-throes, supply depots supplying little or nothing and active airfields whose present inactivity was almost a declaration of surrender. Krohne wouldn't speak of his own arrangements, but bets were no longer being taken on a facility somewhere near Bamberg, where an accomplished adulterer would be well placed to seek out a fled wife whose family happened to live in that town.

Krohne's second-in-command, a man of troubled mind and much-altered flesh, sat in a train heading north to his childhood home, Usedom Island - specifically, to Garz air-station, which to his knowledge was no longer being made untidy by military aircraft. What his talents could bring to the establishment was something he intended to consider more carefully when his head cleared. For the moment he applied the lash, seeking absolution for seizing his chance at a time of universal disaster.

He indulged his torments in a crowded but quiet carriage. Almost to a man, the soldiers around him were sleeping, grateful for any loose time in which they weren't being deployed in front of massed Soviet tank formations. The few civilians who travelled with them were probably as weary but they remained fearfully awake, too aware that one boarded a train these days in the near-certain knowledge that it wouldn't proceed unhindered. Their collective will was almost palpable in the stale air, urging the locomotive to achieve more than a horse's pace, petitioning thin cloud cover to make a bomb-aimer's job more difficult than it presently was.

Other than an occasional murmur to bring a child into line there was no travellers' conversation to overhear, so he was able to examine his betrayal minutely. When they halted briefly at Neubrandenberg the gut twitched strongly and he almost decided to abandon the train and return to Berlin, to take his chances with a handful of ammunition and a shove towards the enemy. Unreasonably, however, the transfer order in his pocket didn't identify Garz as one of a number of options open to his discretion, so he was still in his seat when the train moved on again, northwards through Anklam and Western Pomerania's well-ordered fields. He tried to calm himself, to not obsessively re-visit the events that had brought him out of Berlin, to sleep. By eleven am they were on Usedom, turning eastwards towards the peninsula. The skies had cleared but the enemy was elsewhere and the sun was doing its best to arrange a half-pleasant day, the sort that tells lies about things not being all bad. His craven spirit took the offering gratefully, began to find brighter sides to his situation, to try to close the door on *Judas*.

The B-Uhr on his wrist made it two minutes before noon as the train squealed to a halt in a siding a few hundred metres out of Swinemünde's main station. Closer in, every track was blocked by more rolling stock than he'd ever seen outside Berlin or a forward marshalling zone. Refugees from East Prussia were pouring into the town, the first safe port west of the Russian advance, and everything that could be gathered to move them on was here, waiting only for orders to do the business. He was surprised that his own train had been allowed to proceed into this clench. Usually, it took a senior Party princeling or a large consignment of liberated artworks to get in the way of emergency dispersal plans.

His orders directed that he report to his new post by 4pm that day. From Swinemünde the journey to Garz would take no more than twenty minutes in a slow truck, so he had no need to join the general scramble to get out of the carriage and on to the tracks. The soldiers had only their kitbags and rifles to impede the flow, but the civilians (ignoring regulations against travelling with more than two items of luggage) seemed to be moving house and taking the walls with them. He sat patiently, shifting his knees whenever something threatened to remove them, peering into the outskirts of what had once been his hometown, recalling the layout of its pretty streets and parks, wondering if liquid distraction could be found here still.

When the carriage had emptied entirely he removed his bag from beneath the seat, taking care to preserve its precious contents, his farewell gift from the lads of *LuftGeheimStelle* IIb. On one knee, his head down, looking to ensure that nothing snagged on the way out, he had neither premonition nor warning of his latest piece of excellent, undeserved luck. He didn't see the pulse of flame that swept through the carriage, hardly felt the intense pressure build momentarily as energy concentrated massively in the confined space, and he paid no attention either to energy or space departing together, explosively. He was already somewhere else, floating.

Afterwards, memory kicked over the ashes and tried to reconstruct the evidence, but much was missing. He recalled regaining consciousness of sorts in a cramped, held position, trapped by the embrace of two (thankfully padded) seats attempting a consummation. He was aware that the blast had shredded his outer clothes and removed them almost entirely from his body, but only because the rescue crew that dragged him from the wreckage found a pair of trousers and a blanket for him, which would have been unnecessary otherwise. He also recollected the faces of his deliverers as they prised the seats from him, the comical manner in which they shaded from horror to relief as they realised that his quite startling injuries were old friends, not freshly gifted by the American Eighth Air Force. He was quite sure that most if not all the passengers who had shared the carriage with him had enjoyed the shittiest of luck, because their remains were laid out neatly upon the adjacent track, decently covered, by the time that he was extracted from the wreckage of what turned out to be only one of many destroyed trains in the yards of a smashed station in a near-obliterated town. What he couldn't recall, then or later, was the moment of wit, the only sentient movement in the sliding, derailing locomotion of his pounding head, that made him tell them that he could remember nothing, nothing at all.

Two days later, before suits from the Propaganda Ministry arrived to do a proper audit upon the raid, he discharged himself from the tent-field to which he and thousands of others had been brought. From a DRK orderly he had acquired an almost intact jacket, the former property of one of the thousands of poor bastards, evacuees, who had been crowded together in the town's spa gardens when approximately six hundred bomb-bays opened far above their heads. In a torn pocket he found the equally torn papers of one Gunter Probin, formerly a resident of Gdingen; these he presented at a vastly overworked *orpo* office that had been set up under canvas in an attempt to recapture thousands of fled or misplaced identities before the Regime lost its grip on them. Without troubling him with a single question, an *unterwachtmeister* issued a temporary travel permit noting that Herr Probin's ID card had been partially destroyed during the raid upon Swinemünde on 12 March 1945 and required renewal by 10 April, subject to the most severe penalties otherwise. He also became the owner of a pair of boots (two sizes too small) and ten reichsmarks, donations from one of the kindly souls sent by Ahlbeck Inner Mission to do their inconsequential best.

Usedom Island was home ground, and too dangerous now for a man whose papers said that he was someone else. He heard a rumour that relief transport was coming as close in to Swinemünde's western limits as the damage permitted, so he trudged bare-foot almost as far as Zirchow, where a makeshift hub had been set up. After a further six hours he and other nonessential personnel were allowed to board a line of wagons that might have seen previous service carrying the Prussian Army to Königgrätz. He found himself a corner and squatted unobtrusively, trying to be as forgettable to a passing glance as his face permitted. During the journey he opened his mouth only once, to ask their destination of one of the less alert guards. He got a single word, *Torgelow*.

He knew the town from his training days but it wouldn't do - there was a large Luftwaffe munitions base nearby, and his memorable face almost certainly would have excited memories. Within an hour of his convoy's arrival he was out on the road to Pasewalk, anonymous in a straggling line of refugees. Two days later he passed through Locknitz, head down, trying to be ignored by what seemed to be half the Wehrmacht, moving in the same direction. The only man who noticed his face was a private whose humanity, against all standing orders, had been retained. From this phenomenon he received some bread, which he stuffed into his mouth with an entirely authentic lack of dignity. It was probably what kept him on his feet for the next few kilometres, long enough to get to a place in which no one would think to look for him, a place where he might feel at least half at home for as long as it and he survived. It was a front-line town now, but he comforted himself that soon all German towns would be that. In the late afternoon of 16 March he stumbled into the western suburbs of the port of Stettin and found a DRK post where his bleeding feet were bandaged and his groaning stomach filled with something vile but wonderfully fatty. Its staff were very busy, sorting the civilian wounded from those who might be useful still. No one asked to see his papers before he slipped away.

In the following days he forgot about the *ordnungspolizei's* 10 April deadline. Even had he wanted to make Gunter Probin's resurrection official in a world in which officialdom was packing its bags and leaving no forwarding address his attention was devoted entirely to staying invisible and barely fed. He became part of a new breed of twentieth-century German, a grey wraith, wandering a ruined landscape that Breughel with a hangover could hardly have conceived, competing with rats for nourishment, feeding his thin blood and flesh to fleas. The matter of identity came to his distracted mind once more only on the day Third Panzer Army issued orders for the town's total evacuation. Naturally he didn't comply, and afterwards it hardly seemed worthwhile to make an effort to *be* someone. In any case, the Russians gave him a new ID card once they'd beaten, stripped, beaten, interrogated, beaten and rehabilitated the hell out of him for being in possession of a standard-issue Luftwaffe officer's wristwatch.

He should have traded it for food before the Reds moved into Stettin, but he'd become sentimental. Everything else - his Knight's Cross, Gold Wounds medal, that beautiful, unopened bottle of Albert Robin Cognac, two hundred cigarettes, his *soldbuch* and only spare pair of underpants - remained somewhere under the rubble of Swinemünde's atomized railyards, so the B-Uhr was all that remained to remind him of his part in an age of savagery. It almost got him killed, and then it saved his life. The Russian sergeant doing the beating was willing to end it for what he was assured had once been Generalfeldmarschall Erhard Milch's personal property, acquired by its present owner in a game of skat, somewhere in Belgium, a summer's evening, 1940. The Russian would have taken it anyway, but the lie flattered his taste in other men's watches and added a sliver of respectability to the theft. Even the Ivans felt better about tribute than plunder.

Ironically, it took much more effort to convince them of who he was, really was, having been caught with paper that quite definitely identified him as the unfortunate Herr Probin. It helped that he gave them his rank (who in their right mind would admit to such a thing unless it was the truth?), and no doubt the chaos that attends the death of nations made his strange story more plausible to them. Eventually they dusted him down and gave him a cloth to wipe away the blood; but before they could send him

East with most of the rest of the Wehrmacht his older wounds stood to attention and testified earnestly on his behalf.

Fischer, he told them - Otto Henry, Major, Luftwaffe. Discharged unfit, a very long time ago.

1

Before it became prudent to avoid the subject, the good people of the village of Bernhagen had often discussed the paths that had led them to be what they were, and what they might have been.

They were Pomeranian Germans of course, solidly so; but as folk sometimes said (usually after a drink or two), if a battle, treaty or strategic marriage had turned out differently they might have been Wends still, or Obodrites, or Danes, or Poles, or even Swedes. They were - despite the efforts of certain kings and emperors - Lutheran Protestants, yet their village stood hard by an impeccably Catholic region, and if one went back far enough their ancestors had resisted Christianity itself as strenuously as any who had survived the effort. So while Bernhageners felt as ordinary in their present skin as any folk, they were also quietly proud of the many pigments that shaded it.

They often spoke of those more epic times, when their province (or duchy, or kingdom, or something that was neither fish nor fowl – it had been all of them in turn) was a coveted prize, a clench in which the ambitions of too many protagonists had dashed and spilled. But as Prussia's grip became absolute the former marchland passed gradually into a quiet, parochial daze, content to have the world's excitements far elsewhere. By the time Germany came together, rural Pomerania was as sleepy a place as any could be and still have a heartbeat. One of Bernhagen's older residents, Monika Pohlitz, recalled that in her school days the place had lived so much in and of itself that their neighbours in Kürtow, Zampenhagen and Plantikow had been regarded as nigh-on ausländers, while any Bernhagener who travelled as far as the county seat of Naugard could expect to be pestered for the details as if he had been Marco Polo's wagon master. Elsewhere the world turned as it always had, and wars, revolutions and pogroms came, went or staggered on indecisively, but their part of Germany was done with all of that. The Baltic, once everyone's particular business, had become a pleasant backwater; the French bothered themselves now only with their eastern borders, Poles were cowed and divided and Scandinavians did whatever they did in their shrunken, icy world without troubling their warmer, richer neighbours. Little Bernhagen's pot of calm lay long undisturbed, and for that its citizens were very grateful.

Then came the First War, which gave Europe another taste of the seventeenth century. For a time it seemed that the Russian hordes would sweep across eastern Germany once more, but the Reich was defeated only in the west, and Pomerania was spared all but the loss of its sons (in Monika's case, her two younger brothers). Still, there was plenty of grief to share around and times were hard for many; demobbed soldiers couldn't find work, revolutionaries spoiled the cities and the nation's mighty industrial base collapsed almost to its pre-unification state. Pious Germans feared that God had abandoned them entirely, but if He couldn't provide jobs or a stable currency at least he blessed Bernhagen's crops, and no one in the village went hungry. Later, when the first National Socialists ran for local office, Monika turned out to listen to their harangues, decided that they were ill-bred louts, brash and ignorant, and firmly resisted the temptation to vote for them. Yet even she felt a certain satisfaction when they applied a stiff new broom to Weimar's dusty, degenerate closet and began to wipe away the shameful stain of 1918. As things got easier and the new Regime settled in, occasional half-whispered rumours drifted through the village, hinting at a much darker side to the men to whom Germany owed her recovering strength and self-respect; but as Bernhagen had no undesirable elements (and certainly no Jews, communists or known homosexuals), no one could say much about them, one way or the other.

Then almost without warning they had another big war on their hands, though this one went very well at first. Twelve men and boys from the village went off to fight; one was killed in Poland during the first weeks, but the others marched on in fine step through an astonishingly easy series of victories, a world from the gruelling, mud-drowned struggles that had torn the heart and spirit from the previous generation. Their families, pitied at first by other Bernhageners, began to receive regular treats from abroad, spoils from a growing number of nations that bowed speedily to the justice of German claims upon them. Monika had her first (and final) taste of duck confit courtesy of her best friend Kirsten's son Albert, who from his Paris posting sent home marvellous feats of cuisine. It was one fond recollection of several, but the good times passed much too quickly. In 1941 Albert went off to Greece and then Russia, where he found neither an obligingly disheartened enemy nor fine foods, and his letters – when he bothered to write - became strangely terse. Early the following year Kirsten received a black-edged card bearing the Führer's sincere thanks for her sacrifice. After that she stopped being much of a friend to anyone, and departed the world the same summer.

Another two years passed. All but three of those who had marched off to war were with God now, and Bernhagen had become a village haunted by its young ghosts. Farmers paused in their fields, lifted their eyes to heaven and asked how the land would be ploughed when they were gone; mothers regarded their daughters fearfully, wondering if they would be cursed to be like old Monika Pohlitz, childless and alone in their greying years for want of men to marry; and all the while the greasy, high-pitched voice on the radio proclaimed the continuing triumphs of German arms, though curiously they seemed to occur ever more closely to German soil.

And then a bleak time passed into a terrible one. At the beginning of 1945 the Soviets began to move their great armies westward across the river Vistula and into the German homelands. Tales of the casual murder and rape of civilians caught in their wide path drifted to Bernhagen, and villagers cursed their times, that such crimes could afflict a Christian nation. But soon the truth became too obvious to ignore - that what they had thought *casual* was rather the considered, decreed policy of the invaders, a strategy to annihilate or infect the entire population in revenge for the imagined crimes of the Wehrmacht. All the fears of Germans for what lay to the east were disinterred and roamed the land like the spirit of horrors past.

The first day that she heard guns over the eastern horizon Monika went to church to pray for the souls of those dead and soon to die. It was a very popish thing to do, but she felt that something should be said by someone as fortunate as herself for the many young souls they had lost. She asked for peace - at least in that other, looming world - and that there should be some meaning to what had ripped apart the present one. That her own time might be upon her was of no concern; she was eighty-three years old, tired, and had no great investment in a future that promised very little for Germans. If she felt anything for herself as she prayed it was only a tug in memory of her brothers, her friend Kirsten and the children she had never felt growing in her womb. She couldn't recall that she had ever before prayed from the heart, using her own words rather than those prescribed by the pastor, and it made her wonder if it was a sign of God's closing presence.

The next day the guns were louder still, and one of the old men who farmed a little to the north of the village told his neighbours that he had seen two tanks and a company of men advancing eastwards at dawn and then, a few hours later, a number of what he took to be the same men, without the machines, coming back again. He said that he was by no means a Clausewitz (Monika didn't understand the reference), but it seemed to him that the war couldn't be too distant now or going too well, and that wiser heads would probably be thinking of evacuating the village. Someone suggested they should consult their local lord, Albert, Ritter von Marienwalde, about what should be done. A message was sent, and the following day the reply came in the form of the gentleman himself, driving his landau and solitary horse. He assured them that he had been bombarding their *gauleiter* with requests for official instructions but as yet had not received even the courtesy of an acknowledgement. He intended therefore to prepare and lead the evacuation of his own village, and he suggested to the Bernhageners that they appoint a committee to organize an inventory of food supplies and transportation, and then to leave by smaller roads and make for a town west of the Oder. Don't go north, he told them - the Baltic coast was choked already with refugees fleeing from Konigsberg and Pillau, and the ports and railway stations were said to be overwhelmed. He most particularly urged them not to delay by even a single day. The more they needed to rush, to leave at a moment's notice, the harder it would be on the sick and elderly.

The old man who wasn't Clausewitz took very respectful exception to this. But towns are being bombed terribly, he said - surely, it would be better to put themselves at the mercy of other villagers, or to keep walking west until suitable accommodation could be arranged by the authorities? Marienwalde disagreed firmly. Yes, it was true that towns and cities were being bombed but much of it was indiscriminate, and as a beaten people they had to accept that all options had their dangers. As for remaining in the countryside, there wasn't and wouldn't ever be adequate provision made there for refugees. Every relief effort would be centralized, so that what food was available could find the most mouths. If you go to another village they will say truthfully that they have little enough for themselves; if you keep on walking then eventually you will fall down and die.

Marienwalde was known throughout western Pomerania for his wisdom, and even the old man who wasn't Clausewitz had to agree that they had little choice but to do as he advised. So that evening they elected a group of five men to organize the trek to the west. After some argument it was decided that their goal should be the town of Anklam. It was – or had been - a comfortably provided place, and if for some reason they weren't welcome there it was only a short further trek to Rügen Island, whose many large, empty resort hotels would surely provide adequate accommodation for them.

For two days the villagers prepared themselves. Carts were brought in from outlying farms, food stocks were placed in common and those with frail constitutions were allocated extra clothing. The postman's wife offered Monika her spare woollen coast but she declined it politely. She had good health still and was always warm enough after a little exercise - in any case, she didn't want anyone to think she might be a burden on their great trek. She packed only a few items for herself - photographs and mementoes of her parents and brothers - and then went back to their church and recovered the altar tablecloth, which she folded carefully and laid in her suitcase. If atheists were coming to Bernhagen, she wasn't going to leave her grandmother's finest embroidery for them to wipe their noses (or worse) upon.

Bernhagen's entire population departed together at dawn on a fine late winter's day, a convoy of thirty-nine wagons dragged by almost sixty old nags, with the healthier villagers walking behind, pushing handcarts stuffed with household goods. They noticed that a similar rumble from the south had joined the sound of guns to the east, and some of them began to be wonder if they had departed too late. In one of the rearmost wagons Monika tended her old schoolmistress Frau Beck, who was a short step both from her centenary year and the greatest human journey, and whose deliverance from the enemy could be at best a temporary blessing (every Bernhagener over the age of forty had been taught by her, so to have left her behind would have been like abandoning a parent or favourite dog). Neither lady heard the murmurs, the frightened speculations upon what would come next. Frau Beck's mind - wherever it was - could no longer be captured by earthly things, and Monika was straining to look back, giving all of her attention to her village, to the cradle in the farmhouse she could not remember and the grave in the churchyard she would now never occupy. And then, curiously, it was seized and carried far beyond the span of her own time here, to a final thought on the matter of belonging. The little roofs of Bernhagen, pushing timidly above the flat, fertile landscape, spoke to her of a place she had never seen yet never escaped and posed a question: whether the very first of her family to come here uncountable years earlier had held similar tears in their hearts for another, lost home.

## 2

The lame man paused at the shattered kerb and regarded the building directly across the broad, rubble-filled street. Less damaged than most German public buildings of the present age, it had been patchily re-roofed and re-glazed and seemed to be habitable once more. He assumed the Ivans or the Poles were inside, refitting, busily stripping out Gestapo preferences in wall-paint and office calendars and replacing them with those of NKVD or *Urząd Bezpieczeństwa*. The continuity would make a certain kind of person feel quite sentimental, he supposed.

An old woman passed by him, almost pushing him into the road with the over-weighted pram she struggled to keep in motion. It was full of the usual things, tokens of a life that had mutated with astonishing speed from a gentle downward slope to a daily leapfrog in which one's legs were always tied together. No doubt she would lose it all soon to one of the new owners of her world, who would point out that fascists hadn't bothered too much about property rights in the past and could hardly cite them now. And then she would cry, probably, and wonder how something like this could happen so casually, and look around for a policeman who wasn't there and wouldn't ever be, not for her, and say something to the effect that it wasn't *fair*. Germans were saying it a lot these days, not that it mattered. He wished her a good morning and helped her lift the pram across a line of stones that blocked her path. She neither returned his greeting nor offered thanks, as he had expected.

He had no idea why his feet had plotted a course to this spot. Old times' sakes weren't worth it even for the good times, and there was nothing of those in the building opposite. Perhaps, like the returning Jews who paid their respects to the hole on Grüne Schanze where the synagogue once stood, he was trying both to resurrect memories and bed them down. For the Jews they were happy ones, he imagined, or at least something better than what had followed. He couldn't say the same for himself. This was a place he had escaped rather than departed, an academy in which he'd learned all about what people could be when God looked the other way. But then, so too had many of the town's Jews.

He became aware that he had been standing still for several minutes. Soon, someone would notice and ask his business, or just smack his head and tell him to move on. What used to be taken for absent-mindedness or indolence was now officially symptomatic of hooliganism, or fifth-columnism, or some other 'ism for which the treatment was short and sharp. So he turned away without any sense of making a farewell and limped at a wounded pace down Augusta-Strasse to the steep drop of Admiral-Scheer-Strasse, past the pitted slope below Haken-Terrasse (where, during the first days of the occupation, the town's citizens had frantically dug out little caves in which to hide from the pillaging and mass rapes), down to the Bollwerk and the oily ships' graveyard of the Oder.

Occasionally, his rhythm faltered and he would pause briefly to stare down at his twin supports, trying out a hobble with each in turn to remind himself which was supposed to be lame. No one noticed, but that was the point of it - in a world of broken male bodies one more didn't register in strangers' minds. His other, real wounds were too singular, inviting attention he didn't want. A crippled leg was mundane, expected; it drew attention from everything else and people stopped looking. The rest was easy - his ragged clothes, surrender stoop and odour were universal stigmata, the adornments of defeat that all German-born Stettiners carried upon them. In that herd, to pass unnoticed one had only to move without vigour, to keep one's eyes averted, to seem an alien upon ground that had been home but was now something else.

At the river he turned south, making his *faux*-painful way towards Markt Platz where the *Jacobskirche*'s pastor, no longer having a church upon which to squander his time, supervised what was referred to as a soup stall but which more often than not had only black Russian bread to sustain its starving, non-paying customers. He didn't want to be late for whatever was available, but outside the Post Office he was stopped by a three-man patrol of the Polish Citizen's Militia who demanded to see his papers. He handed them over, smiling vaguely, his eyes squinting as if to make out something in the middle distance. The boy who took them could read German; surprised, he looked up from the ID card and almost came to attention. When he handed them back and explained it to his mates they laughed as they might at any poor joke. At least the *piss off* had no heat in it.

Today there was soup, the standard Soviet field ration variety, and he managed to finish all of it. About sixty ragged Stettiners joined him in the search for lumps of turnip, most of them standing as they ate, efficiently putting themselves outside the thin nutrition as quickly as possible. The pastor - a notorious optimist - had assembled his tiny choir, a mostly elderly female remnant of a once-proud choral tradition. Gamely, they did half-justice to the seasonal noise of *Gottes Sohn ist kommen*. A few Polish Catholics at the edge of the Platz paused to listen to its tuneful heresy, but the pleasure was largely lost upon the dour German Protestants whose souls Herr Bach had laboured to nourish. For them the time for higher forms of sustenance lay in the past or future, not now.

The *faux* lame man carefully wrapped his small piece of black bread, put it into a pocket and recalled suddenly that this was his first meal in almost two days. His appetite should have been stronger with the cold weather looming (it was going to be a bad winter, or so everyone's joints were saying), yet his stomach seemed to be satisfied with very little in it. According to his highly unscientific observations he now weighed about sixty kilos, which was almost fifteen fewer than just half a year ago. The aesthetic modifications he didn't care about (God knew, vanity hadn't been one of his vices for a long time), but he worried about what it might mean. A man with solid plans for a future would have been making more of an effort not to escape his trousers.

So he was considering the etiquette of asking for another helping of soup when he noticed that one of his fellow fine-diners was looking at him, paying *attention* in a manner quite uncharacteristic of a contemporary German. Had he been recognized? He'd long accepted that it would be a risk, even a likelihood - in a world in which crimes had been committed without reservation or discrimination it was hardly realistic to expect that all memories would or could blur. He tried to place the face, to extract it from ten thousand others. There was ... something, but before he could pin it down she had placed her empty bowl on the trestle table and walked over to him, putting herself close enough not to be overheard. Her coat smelled much as he imagined his did, but the rest was almost lovely.

'It's Herr Fischer?'

'Yes.'

'You arrested me.'

That was it, of course. 'When?'

'Sometime in '37, I don't remember.'

'And ...?'

'Six weeks, an *arbeitserziehungslager*.'

'Well, I'm ... sorry.' Pathetic, but what else could he say?

'It's alright. I'm still a great fuck, if you've got the money.' She smiled when she said it, and he forgot about *almost*. 'But I'm much cheaper now.'

## 3

She turned away, reaching for the glass on the table, and he took the opportunity to examine more of her. She was almost as thin as him, but her breasts and buttocks were full still, not half-emptied by a body turning in upon itself for nourishment. Only her ribs and pelvis - both more visible than fashion had once dictated - gave away something of the times, and he'd been distracted from both by the exquisite business of her lower belly. He touched her shoulder gently, anxious not to startle.

'You recognized me.'

She was savouring the sharp bite of slivovitz and didn't answer immediately. Two of her fingers wiggled; obediently, he fished a cigarette from beneath the pillow, lit and placed it between them, inhaling as it departed, enjoyed the aroma still. He had made a start on memorizing the lie of her muscles, the curve of her back, when she turned to him once more. Her gaze was forensic, and he was certain she was weighing the very many things that might have deterred a woman with expectations.

'It was luck, the way you were standing. I saw your good side, the old face.'

'Still, eight years. A good memory.'

'No, not really. It wasn't the arrest that did it.'

'What else?'

She made sure that his eyes were in hers when she said it. 'You shot my man. The jeweller's shop on Rosengarten-Strasse.'

He didn't need to search his memory. In six years as a *kripo* he had used his service pistol only the one time, on a misspent ejaculation named Erwin Boltze, a thug who hadn't so much committed offences as lived his life as one. His swansong had been a big move up professionally, a prank that had left the shop owner and his wife tortured and strangled for no better reason than their name - *Bluhm*. The perpetrator hadn't even cared to help himself to the inventory, and Fischer had been obliged to plant some gems in his pocket to make the shooting morally acceptable to his superiors. It was one of the few things he didn't look back upon with regret (other than that he had first offered Boltze the chance to surrender before putting one in his throat).

*Shit.*

'It's alright. Really, he was a pig.'

'He was your husband?'

She shrugged. 'I never had paper, but it's what he told the men he sold me to, his best customers, the ones who paid extra to fuck a man's wife while he watched. Sometimes he joined in, or took photographs.'

'That must have been ... difficult.'

'I wasn't a tart then, not by choice.'

'Why didn't you leave?' A stupid question, out before he could clamp his lips.

'Where would I go on broken legs?' She tossed her head, dismissing the idiocy graciously. 'You did me a favour.'

He doubted it. Her husband may have put her on her back in the first place but a *kripo*'s bullet had kept her there, a career-mattress for heaving sacks of perspiration. He wouldn't have been so forgiving.

She was giving him the physician's look again, and he felt the familiar throb of his wounds.

'You probably don't get many free ones anymore.'

He laughed. 'Not too many, no.'

'You don't mind?' Her hand touched the right, very wrong side of his face, stroking it from the hairline to his chin, auditing the hard, unpliable quality of dead men's flayed skin. It was an effort not to flinch. For her too, probably.

She moved to the shoulder, following the damage she couldn't see down his spine almost to the coccyx, where the unmutilated Otto resumed. He kept his eyes on the cigarette in her other hand, willing the thing to fall and distract her before she said it.

'You were lucky.'

He sighed. 'Very, yes.'

'No, I mean ...' she frowned, ' ... you got over it.'

"It's a work in hand.'

Her own hand moved swiftly, grabbed his cock and squeezed it. She giggled. 'This too.'

For a moment he wanted her again, but it passed. *One is good, two gluttony* as his mother used to say about ... cakes, probably. Besides, he didn't have the funds to find out whether he could be impressive.

Her hand lingered there, stroking. 'You were good.'

It was what whores said, of course. Still, he felt fairly pleased. As far as he could recall this was his first time since before he'd arrested her - eight years of abstinence, of carefully hoarded chastity, thrown away in an unthinking moment. He glanced at the cheap, battered man's watch on her wrist. In almost an unthinking hour, in fact. That made him feel even more fairly pleased, and he was moved to return the compliment.

'You're very lovely.'

She snorted and reached for what remained of the slivovitz. 'I always am, afterwards. How many of these do you have?'

The cigarette wriggled between two fingers. He glanced into the pack and offered it to her. 'Is this enough?'

'Of course.' Without checking the contents she leaned out of bed and placed it on to the coat and dress she had discarded. As she stretched to reach down her buttocks parted, giving him the deliberate view, a tender for future business.

'Can I wash somewhere?'

He'd worried that she might ask. He was lucky enough to have two rooms in a building with a roof still, courtesy of a landlady who'd known him from years ago and didn't mind getting her rent in potatoes. But it came with very few facilities, and a bathroom wasn't one of them. All he had for his modest needs was a tin bowl, propped in the corner beneath the three-legged table.

He pulled on his trousers, took the bowl downstairs to the courtyard and filled it from the pump. Aware that most of his wounds were showing he cringed slightly, trying to make himself inconspicuous while the water's thin, casual flow disobliged his strong desire to be indoors once more. As far as he could tell nothing twitched in any of the windows surrounding him, but then a lot of them no longer had the luxury of curtains, or glass. He thought of her upstairs in his bed - what she had done with him, indifferent to what he was - and wondered at the strange, twisted sliver of his psyche that could care still about what strangers thought that she didn't. Before the bowl had filled he was standing straight, exposed, almost willing an audience to take in the sights. An unfamiliar feeling, all of a piece with the day.

When he returned she was on the bed still, drawing upon the last of her cigarette. One leg was pulled up to her chest and wrapped by an arm; the other was half-bent and splayed, exposing her sex to him or anyone else who might have come through the door. He tried hard not to look, but her wide eyes followed his and eight years suddenly seemed like a tragic, wasted age.

When they were done a second time she hugged him tightly and kissed him on the lips. It wasn't what working girls did, and he assumed there was a reason. Most likely she had fled her latest pimp, lost a roof and was looking for temporary shelter, a needy girl deploying her only weapons upon an idiot mark. He had any number of ways ready to tell her no, you can't be serious; but when she made him wash her as she stood in the preposterously small tin bowl, her hand clutching his shoulder, squeezing it whenever he forgot to take his time, he didn't know what to think.

## 4

Her name was Marie-Therese Kuefer, a fact he discovered only on their third meeting, or assignation, or date. He had an ex-policeman's reluctance to demand personal details even after the hell of a re-introduction they'd given each other, and it became so obviously an issue that eventually she sat him down, took his hand, said it very carefully and asked if he wanted it spelled out for the charge sheet. He couldn't imagine how she'd kept a sense of humour.

Her papers said that she was thirty-nine years old, but she didn't think they were correct. Almost certainly she had been registered late, the fault of impoverished farm folks' larger preoccupations and a local pastor who awoke only for holidays, burials and the baptisms of those whose families could afford to put on a meal afterwards. Naturally, she'd left the farm just as soon as she could fuck a lift for herself, and as the driver's first stop that day had been Stettin it was here that she decided to make something of her mean, hopeful life.

But *something* usually requires good fortune, steady family or at least the beginnings of an education, so she was obliged to aim for less. She was willing enough to try, and worked hard at the sort of retail assistants' jobs that young, poorly schooled girls clutch to themselves until the right man comes along. God had fashioned her too prettily, however, and she wasn't allowed to wait for her elusive champion. At each new employment a foreman, under-manager or floor-supervisor availed himself of her secret places upon the offer of the slightest of advancements, and sometimes for nothing at all. Her compliance was a dismissible offence of course, and none of the few references she received were sufficiently effusive to secure something that might have had the makings of a career.

Factory work came next. It was hard, but at least it paid

decently and didn't require her legs to open on demand. That lasted only a while, until the unions colluded with the new regime to get women out of jobs that rightly belonged to men. Then she fell into a bad time, when successive lodgings were fled for want of rent money, her trim figure maintained by not eating very much, a time of wakening awareness that perhaps she had only one indisputably marketable quality. So it had seemed a blessing when Erwin Boltze noticed her, queuing at a soup kitchen next to a shop he had been planning to rob, and decided that she was good enough to be seen around one of the town's most up-and-coming fellows.

She had never been dined before, never kissed on the hand, never had sex with someone she'd wanted. It made her love him much too quickly, and when he took her back to his untidy but large apartment she did what was expected of her, inspecting it carefully, putting herself into it in her romantic mind's eye, noting exactly which parts could be improved with a woman's touch, telling him that she couldn't wait.

She had hardly made her mark upon their home when Boltze began to make his mark upon her, to improve her with a man's touch. At first it was only a little light bruising, and usually at the drunken end of a week to help him work its frustrations from under the skin. Then real improvements followed, the sort that counted as alterations, or remodellings. She became familiar with the day patients' department at the local hospital, and struck up a number of fleeting friendships with women who'd been similarly improved and needed bones resetting or skin stitched. It might almost have been a girls' club, except a lot of the members didn't stay around for too long, or retired prematurely to where no one could hurt them anymore. It was the way of things in any busy port, the price of cheap, strong drink in weary men's stomachs.

At some point she accepted that she was now a sort of wife, and assumed that this was how marriages went. She didn't blame

Boltze; he dealt with some mad people, hard sorts, and it was only natural that some of their edges rubbed off, tainting his many good qualities. She knew that she wasn't guiltless herself, that she had a loose tongue and probably should think more before using it, particularly when he came home late at night (or, more often, at dawn). For a while she made an effort, and it seemed to her that the improvements lessened in frequency and intensity when she did. Sex, which had become occasional, picked up once more, though not as before - it was more perfunctory now, as with animals, and didn't involve kissing or too many embraces afterwards. At first she quite enjoyed it, quite liked the game of pretending to be easy, a wicked woman. But when he started bringing home his drinking friends she understood her mistake.

The first time there was an excuse for it, of sorts. He and three strangers played cards one night in their apartment; there was plenty of alcohol available and she helped herself to it, laughing with them and sympathizing with the heavy losers (of whom Boltze was one). When the suggestion was made she assumed it to be a risqué joke, the sort of thing that was said when spirits soared and there was a pretty woman in the room. When she saw that her husband was serious and urged her on she decided that she didn't mind, though even then she knew that, really, it was the booze that wasn't minding. The other party - Ernst, she wasn't told his surname - was said to be *a lucky man*, and she realised that this wasn't anything to do with his very good fortune at cards. When they said it they winked at her, made gestures she couldn't fail to understand, and she laughed too, willing to seem like she wasn't at all prudish.

There wasn't any foreplay. The man she loved stood behind her, opened her blouse, lifted her skirt and pulled her pants aside to give them all a good first look at what they were going to see a great deal more of. They offered what they mistook to be compliments and rolled their eyes with roguish, comic appreciation, as if playing their part in an entertainment (which it was, of course). Then Ernst stood up and unbuttoned his fly, and it became very quiet in the room when they all saw just how grotesquely *lucky* he was.

He took her like a bitch, kneeling, while the others watched, their own smaller pricks in their hands, pulling energetically as her sand-dry vagina was ripped, her breasts tugged by hard hands. Thankfully, Ernst wasn't a long-distance man, and after only a few minutes she was able to stand, to go into the kitchen to wipe the blood from her thighs and the issue from her lower back, while the laughter started again in the sitting room and everyone complimented Ernst on his prowess.

The evening was such a tremendous success that it became a regular thing, though not always with the same players present. Soon, it wasn't just the one anymore, and not even one at a time, and Marie-Therese feared that she had begun to lose her mind. She knew that Boltze was taking money or favours from his guests and understood what that made her in their eyes, but that didn't nearly hurt so much as her husband's eager culpability, his obvious, priapic enjoyment as a succession of strangers' cocks thrust into the woman he alleged to care for. It removed something from within her, and she lost the strength even to resent her condition - she even felt a sort of dull gratitude that the beatings stopped once her true value to Boltze became apparent. She noticed too that he no longer wanted her for himself, that his gratification was now wholly detached, though always visible. He made a point of standing directly in front of her, letting her see him abuse himself as other men used her, flaunting the tumescent reminder of the strength of his affections for her.

As much as she had come to detest its every square metre, she rarely left the apartment anymore. She was sickened at the prospect of the knowing looks that would follow her down the street; certain that all of Stettin must know now of the depraved soirees of which she was the star, the resident act, the Whore of this Baltic Babylon. Her husband didn't seem to mind - or perhaps notice - her self-incarceration, and brought home food for them both when he was sober enough to remember. She saw much less of him now. He was increasingly distracted by his business arrangements (whatever they were) and made it clear to her that, as much as he loved to see them filled, her holes were the three least profitable sources of income in his expanding portfolio.

Without any understanding of Boltze's life outside their stifled domestic world, she had no way of anticipating what came next. The day it happened started as greyly as any other, without prospect of becoming less so. The neighbour who knocked on her door and then blurted the news was upset, the way that good people are when such things happen, and as old as she was she insisted on accompanying Marie-Therese to the Police Praesidium and standing beside her, holding her hand as she made the formal identification. The pretend wife stared at her false husband's body until they pulled the sheet over it once more and then asked them to point out who had done it. He was in a glass-partitioned office, speaking with others; he looked agitated, preoccupied, and didn't emerge to speak with her (though she knew that he'd been told she was there, that she'd asked about him). She saw him again, months later, when he arrested her and then testified at the brief hearing that took her off the streets for six weeks. He didn't recognize her, and she didn't remind him who she was or had been. By then she was much happier, living alone and dealing with life rather than being dragged beneath its wheels. Money wasn't any more of a problem than loneliness - in fact, once she came to understand that a man's only worthwhile quality was folded neatly in his wallet the one took care of the other. She was getting by, relying upon no one, looking for nothing more than what took care of practical things. Even her time in the *arbeitserziehungslager* wasn't too bad. The Regime punished prostitution, but whores were regarded as just about the least undesirable of the very many types who found themselves in such places, and she'd had the necessary skills to avoid a beating or worse.

Then the war came, which she really couldn't think of as a bad thing. The police were too understaffed, too busy elsewhere to bother her much, and men certainly didn't lose their appetites just because they were obliged to wear uniform. Until the final months she was as busy as she chose to be, and could afford all those commodities that had disappeared for people who lived in the regulated world. It was a pity it had ended the way it did, but if she'd learned anything it was that fresh starts happened if one's expectations were low enough. The rumour was that Russians were men, too.

The rapes were terrible of course, but it wasn't as though she could have expected anything better. After all, who would have dug out a little cave on the slopes below Haken-Terrasse for a girl like her?

## 5

They fell into a life that tested Fischer's self-respect severely. It would have been idiotic not to eat the food she brought home (as, rapidly, she came to regard his apartment), but its provenance was a slap to more than his face. That most of it was standard Soviet military issue - macaroni, soy flour, Mongolian tea, chicken fat - made any pretence ridiculous. It might as well have been labelled *Thanks for the fuck, darling* in Cyrillic.

She didn't try to avoid the subject or lower her eyes guiltily when he brooded about the men she'd been with. She laughed instead, said how ironic it was that he of all people should be enjoying - no, gorging himself upon - the fruits of immorality. He tried arguing the point on just one occasion; it went so badly he wanted to apologise for being unreasonable.

Her candid nature saw the matter unsentimentally. It was the times, the situation, she told him. They lived at the end of the world or its beginning, and everything that had been normal was now a memory, the sort of happy illusion that elderly folk cling to. They had to make do with what things were, not what they'd like them to be. He mustn't dwell upon it; things would get better.

He tried hard to be infected by hope, but it didn't take. This was a place in which anticipation came as purple did to a blind man, and with equal utility. Even the Russians seemed to be unsure of Stettin and what to do with it. When they marched in the previous April they had decreed that the town was to be a part of the new Poland rather than the old Germany but then booted out its new Polish mayor, installed first one and then a second German communist and then changed their minds once more and settled for a joint administration in which the former deadly enemies faced each other across a council table. Finally, in June, they dismissed the German element and proclaimed that there was to be a purely Polish regime after all - but only for *most* of Stettin. The Red Army retained control of its security zones on the river and harbour areas (the town was the official port of departure for the booty they were pillaging from Western Pomerania and Silesia), so even a short walk could leave Stettiners in some confusion as to which bit of Europe they were currently inhabiting. Meanwhile, the worst sort of Poles were flooding into the spaces left by fleeing Germans, fighting off the ones that tried to return to their homes and losing few opportunities to encourage those who remained to leave also. It had become almost impossible for German householders to prove ownership of the property they occupied and largely unnecessary for Poles to attempt the same. Assaults were frequent and unpunished; a prudent German apologised for a beating rather than made a fuss about it, and quietly comforted his wife and daughters when they were dragged into cellars and outraged. In the previous July about 80,000 native Stettiners had remained in or returned to the town (down from a quarter of a million in normal times); now, six months later, they were probably fewer than half that number. The intervening months had brought starvation, typhus, occasional forced labour - to help bring in a potato harvest of which they were allowed little share - and the first stirrings of a 'voluntary' repatriation scheme that would herd German families into the western suburb of Scheune, on to trains and sent them West with no provision made for their arrival at journey's end. If there were spoors of *better things* in any of that, he couldn't see them.

When he went on about it she shrugged, smiled, told him that he was right but it was what they had. The old times were gone, and only a furious churn remained from which anything might emerge. Of course it would be best to be prepared, but as they had no idea what it was they should prepare for they had to live as they must. All they could do was to take no risks, offend no one and definitely make no eye contact in the street. They had to be like Jews, until it was safe not to be once more.

When, finally, he forced himself to ask the question, she told him that she was renting herself only to Russian officers. They preferred women who cared to be discreet and uninfected, and were willing to be courteous, or at least correct, to those they wanted more than the one time. There was no point offering herself to the few remaining German men in Stettin - they had nothing with which to buy her, and Polish men saw no need to pay for sex with German women (nor even to ask permission beforehand). At least her regulars could be persuaded to offer a little protection, to let it be known that she wasn't fair game to anyone seeking private reparations. And she reminded him that roubles were strong currency in a world turned on its head - not that she didn't dream of dollars and what they could do with them, naturally.

He found her matter-of-fact monologues strangely comforting. They put the brake upon his obsessive analysis of their prospects and forced him to consider today as more than a high fence to be leapt into tomorrow. But the matter of his passive, parasitical role in their relationship was harder to put aside. In post-war Stettin his only talent was useless - the Poles were putting together their own police force, and crimes committed against the German population didn't count as such. His sense of being a spare part left over from a reassembled engine had been well developed even before Marie-Therese's arrival. It wasn't eased by her willing assumption of the breadwinner's role.

Desperate for distraction, he put the word around their building and its neighbours that a former *kripo* had the time and inclination to help out for little or no recompense. No doubt the last was his strongest selling point, and gradually people who had once regarded Authority as the spine in their lives came to his apartment with a variety of problems, many of which were far beyond his ability to alleviate. The most common supplication was upon the point of a son, a father or husband, missing since the Red Army dipped its toes in the Vistula at the start of the present, terrifying year. He went to Soviet military headquarters, requested forms, was laughed at, cursed, slapped, and, eventually, obliged. He assisted old women, wives and daughters to complete applications both to the military authorities and International Red Cross and submitted them with no confidence that they would travel further than the nearest incinerator. The gratitude he earned for this, the trust in his ability to move immoveable objects, made him feel worse than if he had attempted nothing.

He joined a most optimistic body - his street's German Residents' Committee - and helped to prepare several petitions to the local Polish State Repatriation Authority requesting that certified legal documentation issued during what was referred to circumspectly as the *previous regime* be acknowledged when considering property disputes. Probably, these were of even less use than his efforts to find the town's lost sons, but at least he was paid in potatoes and cigarettes for his time. His most recent job - a formal request, drafted in English, that Frau Wilhelmina Kuhn in his building's basement apartment be allowed to join her sister in Munich - had actually been successful (the town council rarely made a problem about departing *schwabs*) and paid what in better times might have been called dividends. The old lady's nephew, a career petty criminal turned people's hero, directed him by way of thanks to a rumour of an elusive trunk, reputed to be stuffed with fine foods, the booty of some general officer who had fled the advancing Soviet Front in the final days. He found it within hours, supporting a stack of rubble in the corner of a building in Albrecht-Strasse that had served temporarily as an officer's club during the early months of 1945. The 'fine foods' were two hundred *eiserne* portions (early 1945 vintage), hard tack and canned meat that hadn't found its way to the Front before the Front found its way to Stettin. With the nephew's assistance (cheerily, he'd told Fischer 'call me Earl' and then demanded half the booty), he transferred his share to two hessian sacks under cover of night and brought them safely to his private bank vault - the space beneath his iron bed. He had no intention of using any of it other than as currency.

The vacated Kuhn apartment was immediately occupied by two Polish families, which put the rest of the building on notice. The new tenants didn't go out of their way to let Germans know what they thought of them, but nor did they excuse their creeping annexation of the former *hausmeister*'s rooms and the rest of the ground floor, or the defiantly loud manner in which they asserted their presence among the enemy. Fischer, being as it were an almost semi-official presence by now, was sent downstairs to complain about the noise and what odours suggested was a tannery business they'd set up in the basement. When he returned to his apartment, Marie-Therese expertly stemmed the arterial flow of blood from his nose and lectured him once more upon the virtues of invisibility.

It was a curious time, and he worried that he was surrendering to a way of life that held out no promise of anything good. He wondered if this was how the Jews had felt in their ghettoes, having reached a debased, desperate condition that nevertheless could count as existence for as long as they were permitted to have it still. The irony of the analogy didn't escape him; it stoked his fear that there was an element of deliberation in their treatment, a trial run at a more lasting solution to the new administration's German Problem. Already, the town council had banned his compatriots from working in shops and restaurants, which brought memories of 1933 flooding back. Some of his building's tenants began to whisper of a *pogrom*, and though few thought that the Poles would go so far as to crib Himmler's methods it was obvious that tenderness and natural justice weren't likely to be much in evidence. Stettin was finished; Szczecin was rising from its shattered bowels, and the new place would have no more room for Germans than the old one had had for Poles. The town stood upon - was part of - too violent a fault-line in both nations' histories.

He tried to keep these black thoughts buried. Without their

speaking of it, his relationship with Marie-Therese had become a relief from life as it was. Like teenagers, they set aside special days in which to do nothing, to indulge in fantasy vacations in which a locked door and closed curtains set the bounds of the world, with an occasional tin of oily fish serving for the feast upon their private tropical beach. Sometimes she asked her clients (she forbade him to call them *tricks*) to pay in vodka, a commodity so readily available to Russian officers as to represent hardly any payment at all. When she brought home a bottle their escape was near complete - an easy, blurred few hours taking pleasure from each other's company, conversation and bodies, pretending to be safely elsewhere, ignoring the random gunfire that punctuated the nights in their near-lawless town.

It seemed to him that she was happy, or at least not looking for something more or other than this. He envied her small expectations, her ability to banish reality, and began to try to play the game. When (usually at the lower end of a bottle) they talked of the future, it was in deliberately confined terms - finding a better place to live, more regular work for him, less for her - that wilfully avoided the pregnant questions of *when* and *where*.

But the world pressed hard upon their pretences. The northern suburb of Zabelsdorf in which their apartment stood had been designated a 'German Protection Area' by the Soviets. Naturally, that had been a fantasy since the town's native administration had been kicked out, yet even though the district had been officially renamed *Niebuszewo* its population remained predominantly Stettiner. Elsewhere, things moved more quickly as the New Year arrived. Several intact blocks in the district west of the old Artillery and Pioneer kasernes were allocated arbitrarily to Poles, their existing tenants given less than two days to pack up and get out, and neither compensation nor alternative accommodation were offered. Less than a fortnight later, it was the turn of the streets around what had been Kaiser-Wilhelm-Platz (now *Plac Grundwalzski*), much closer to Fischer's home. He watched these initiatives carefully, poring over a large-scale map of old Stettin to get a sense of the strategy, a hint of when it might be their turn.

Worse, the Soviets - any ten of whom the remaining German residents would have preferred as neighbours to a single Pole - were content to sit back and let it happen. The old folk in Fischer's building began to talk of going west, and having half-formed an intention became quite enthusiastic about what they'd find there. Most of them wanted to keep going, to cross overcrowded Mecklenburg and get to the British Zone. No one thought much about the Americans. They had the best resources and occupied the most pleasant parts of the former Reich, but stories of their vindictiveness to former National Socialists (and in the Amis' eyes, *all* Germans were that) made people nervous about the welcome they could expect. At least the British were willing to start again, to draw a line beneath their two nations' unnatural enmity. That's what folk were saying, anyway.

He talked a lot to Marie-Therese about Berlin, his old home. It was their logical sanctuary if things went badly but she wouldn't consider it - t*oo much competition*, she argued, and reminded him how many more Germans were starving in the capital than here in Stettin, or Szczecin, or whatever it would be called tomorrow. He didn't press the point. Usually, she was right about everything except *what next*, and on that she wouldn't form an opinion.

But the building slowly emptied of its old German residents, and even the streets of Zabelsdorf began to fill with Poles. Twice in the same week, Marie-Therese came home in tears, trying to play down to Fischer what he feared had been rape but turned out to be casual kicks from passing strangers who objected to her presence in *their* town. She dismissed them as hints that she wasn't going to take, but Fischer knew what hints could become if ignored. For the first time in years he had more than himself to worry about, and to make up for it he worried at a forced march's pace. He asked her to consider not working for a while, just until they could see more clearly where things were going. He tried to bribe her, suggested that if he traded some of his hoard of *eiserne* portions they could lock the door, close the curtains and spend a debauched fortnight together in Rio, or Amalfi. She hugged him and said that it was a fine idea, the way people do when they mean of course not, don't be unreal.

He feared they were becoming creatures fallen into resin - held fast, slowly succumbing to something they had no ability to change and with no strength of desire to escape. As in dreams, he knew that something had to be done yet allowed himself always to be distracted, and did nothing. People fled, or starved, or succumbed to disease, kicks or bullets, and the two residents of Haydn-Strasse 43/13 went on as if time could be suspended selectively for the sake of those who had taken more than their share of life's cruelty and earned a little saving grace. They held on to each other and by frayed straps to what they hoped was an immutable present, but the passage of days ground inexorably, carrying away shards of the familiar like small stones caught in tank tracks creeping towards an unknowable New World.

At the end of the first week of February 1946, the straps parted.

## 6

Carefully, Monika smoothed out the altar tablecloth, counting the stains upon it and trying to contain an anger that wouldn't fade. She reminded herself that God provided and man accepted, and if things had turned much for the worse then they had to be taken for what they were. For herself, she was old and so could look upon her present state with a certain detachment, perhaps even gratitude that its difficulties were almost passed. But it was different for others, particularly the young. The fire through which they all had passed left much more terrible scars upon those who had hopes of the world still.

She had not expected to lose her virginity at the age of eighty-one, but far better that than at thirteen, as had two of their village's girls, *used* repeatedly by Soviet soldiers come looking for diversion. For her it had been merely degradation - humiliating, a little painful and even ridiculous that healthy young men should satisfy themselves upon her tired, unappealing body. But for the children it was an ending, an excision; they survived in body only, mute and unmoved even by the desperate love of mothers who had been violated beside them in a stinking cow barn, their bridal suite. It was spots of their innocent blood that Monika counted upon the altar cloth, marks of stigmata that held not even the small consolation of meaning.

She prayed a great deal for their recovery, without hope that such a pain could be soothed. After the soldiers went away one of the girls' fathers, a crippled veteran, had limped into the woods and killed himself with a paring knife, penance for his failure to be a man to his women. Neighbours had comforted and then restrained his wife, watched her constantly until it became clear that she had quite lost her mind. Soon afterwards she died too, without need of a reason. The world had gone mad and was taking good folk with it.

Some villagers believed that they shouldn't have returned to Bernhagen, but what choice had they been given? Like so many other refugees their plans had been built partly upon idle assumptions and the rest upon air. Their little exodus hadn't reached poor, smashed Anklam or Rügen before they were turned back by their own soldiers, berating them angrily for blocking the roads, for trying to escape the Front without prior evacuation orders. Already half-dead from hunger and lack of sleep they had been made to retrace their trek, back towards the war. At Torgelow they stopped to bury Frau Beck, who by God's mercy had been too far removed from life to understand what it had become. Then, outside Falkenwalde, they lost three old men in an air raid, strafed at the road's edge by brave young fighter pilots (one of their village's most prominent aviation experts claimed confidently that they had been Americans, but Monika knew that his head had been buried as deeply in grass as her own while it happened). Others - sick, confused or hopeful of other destinations - wandered away at night or fell behind and then away, and by the time the convoy straggled back into Bernhagen they were fewer than three hundred. A few hours after that the Russians arrived, and what remained of their world was consumed in horror.

And yet, as bitterly as Monika tried to deny it, things could have been worse still. They owed a debt of many lives to old Albert, Ritter von Marienwalde, whose own trek, like theirs, had been turned around. At home once more he had immediately put himself to the ancient printing press he kept in his smallest barn and despatched his healthier tenants to post notices in all the other villages of his patrimony. Bernhagen's weary travellers had returned to find one pinned to the church door, and in the brief time allowed them before the Russians came had obeyed its every letter.

Destroy any papers that link you to the regime, it told them - Party membership cards, your daughters' *Bund Deutscher Mädel* certificates and uniforms, anything that betrays your sons' enrolment in the *Hitler Jugend* - it doesn't matter that you participated unwillingly, without choice, the Soviets won't care. Don't conceal your possessions, other than a little food; if pillagers need to search they will certainly use force to make you reveal your hiding places. Don't try to resist mere robbery, nor even look the thieves in the eye; if they get what they want they may leave it at that. Those of you who have potato crops (all Bernhagen's farmers did, naturally), empty your illicit spirits into the streams; whatever enemy soldiers intend to do will be made ten times more terrible if they are drunk. And above all, the notice said, destroy this notice immediately.

So, even as Monika prayed for the souls of their recent dead and the minds of their recently raped, she gave grudging thanks also for the small mercies that Bernhageners had received. Stories of mass killings elsewhere, of grotesque games played by the conquerors upon innocent German civilians, had circulated like fire in a wind, and no one disbelieved them or thought them embellished in the retelling. What had happened here was tragic but within the bounds of what imagination told them had to be borne by the defeated. Given time it might hurt less, even if it couldn't be forgotten.

Monika's personal penance for surviving (she really *was* becoming a papist) was her daily unfolding of the altar tablecloth. She had decided that, as obscene as its stains were, she wouldn't ever try to remove them. They commemorated an event that shouldn't be forgotten, a chastisement to any future pastor who might boldly preach the necessity of war to his congregation. Besides, it was a delicate cloth, and all she had by way of detergent was a half-cup of Henkel's coal extract that she intended to use upon herself when the smell became distracting. She would wait for better weather and then put it away somewhere safe - a hole in a field, perhaps - until the foreigners went away.

And yet they remained, though the war was over. Someone

had told her that Bernhagen was no longer in Germany but Poland, which was ridiculous - it hadn't been Polish since the thirteenth century, and history couldn't simply be bartered away. Many people were on the move and boundaries were less fixed now, but great wars and upheavals did that, and it took time for things to return to normal. She reassured herself and others that they had to be patient, that the Authorities would re-establish order eventually.

For the moment a few Poles, farmers, had moved into the village and occupied empty houses, the homes of those missing or lost on the great, failed trek. No one objected because the newcomers were armed and had the support of the Russians, and anyway, it was really the business of those whose property was sequestered. Of course no one spoke to the new arrivals, and so far they had made only a little trouble. A few weeks earlier, one or more of them had put up a sign at the western edge of the village bearing just one word - *Ostrzyca*. The villagers were puzzled by this and wondered what it meant. Someone suggested that it was a family name; that the sign was there to let other, arriving Poles know that they had taken up residence in Bernhagen. But surely the eight families who had moved in already didn't share the same surname, someone else argued. And that was the moment when everyone present realised what the sign *meant*. After dark the same evening two men pulled it down and threw it into the stream. It hadn't been replaced since.

Russian patrols still passed through the village occasionally, but there was no reprise of the crimes committed previously. No one could say that these were the same soldiers, because memories of the trauma were fragmented and confused even for the wisest heads, and the many non-Europeans among them shared the same nondescript yet vicious look that didn't encourage a lingering glance. The villagers acted very respectfully towards them, taking great care not to give any offence (though what might be considered offensive by these strange creatures was a mystery to decent folk). There was a rumour that the

*Landrat* of Naugard County and other important local officials had been arrested soon after the surrender and sent east for special treatment, or as an example, or as hostages to some purpose. One of the village's constitutional experts explained that this was against the Geneva Convention and other international law, but when he said it he was told to keep his opinion to himself, and certainly not express it loud enough for their unwelcome guests to overhear. As someone else pointed out, when millions of armed men occupied you, you didn't have a say about what laws said or didn't say.

In late autumn a group of armed men, Poles in some sort of uniform, came to the village and robbed its German inhabitants with brutal efficiency. The few crops that had been scraped from the dirt that year were *requisitioned* (they used the German term familiarly, so Bernhageners assumed that theirs wasn't the first village to be stripped this way), and then German homes were *inspected* to ensure that weapons were not being hoarded in anticipation of an uprising. Beds, linen, chairs, picture frames, utensils and other dangerous ordnance were removed and no receipts offered; cleverly, Monika managed to preserve the altar tablecloth by putting it back upon its table and facing down two young men who came to the church with the intention of plundering its fittings. Fortunately, their native piety (or decent upbringings) made them nervous of offending even a Protestant God, and they satisfied themselves with some battered pewter.

Soon after that, Bernhagen's resident Poles departed hurriedly when the undernourished, lice-ridden bodies of their German neighbours began to exhibit symptoms of typhus. Almost a hundred villagers managed to die in time to avoid the winter, which, though relatively mild, carried off a further fifty. By mid-January 1946, Monika - who had long since achieved a perfect state of acceptance of her imminent death - was the only surviving Bernhagener over the age of seventy, and most of the younger ones were unquiet spirits, wandering aimlessly between days in as many layers of clothes and rags as they possessed. No one could recall their last proper meal; nourishment came to them now as it did to all scavengers, as fortunate discoveries in the woods or ditches, thrust into mouths without the formalities of cleaning, plucking or pealing. They fell into such a state of want that even the Poles who returned tentatively with the frost sometimes risked their health to brew a large pot of thin broth and leave it at the church for their undead neighbours. It was during one such act of mercy in February 1946 that they placed a piece of paper upon the altar table and weighted it with a stone. One of the mute girls, she whose parents had died so cruelly, brought it to Monika and sat upon the low window ledge in her sitting room as the old woman read it. The text was badly phrased and difficult to understand, but when she was done Monika went to all the other houses in the village that still sheltered Germans and told them to come to church for something to eat.

She read it to them slowly as they shared out and devoured their broth. It was an official notice, announcing that a conference of Allied Powers had decided to implement measures recognizing previous agreements with regard to displaced populations. After several minutes' pause while people argued about the meaning of 'displaced', Monika continued. To this effect, all German nationals presently residing in areas east of a boundary delineated by the rivers Oder and Neisse were to be relocated to the west. It concluded with a short, bald statement that arrangements would be made to facilitate matters in due course. The document was stamped, and although no one present recognized the frank its impressive design stifled any suspicions of its authenticity.

When Monika had finished reading, a farmer's widow raised her hand timidly. 'But ... *we're* to the east of the Oder.'

Their expert on international law had died during the typhus outbreak, so no one could speak to the legality of the order. A few of them declared the thing to be impossible, a fantasy, something made up by the Poles to scare a few more Germans into fleeing their homes. Only few months earlier Monika would have agreed with them, but now she could see its ominous logic. She had tried to convince herself that at worst this part of Europe was going to be as it had been before the great Confessional War, a splintered confusion of peoples huddling within tiny enclaves, the whole a patchwork of insignificant political states. But folk had got used to calling themselves Germans, or Poles, or whatever else, and if the rulers of the new world had decided to refashion its face and move or create entirely new polities, who could argue or resist? After all, hadn't the Führer attempted something similar with only the power of one nation behind him?

She didn't say any of this aloud. She had never believed that she could convince others by the force of her opinion, nor had ever wanted to. So she let them argue on, the ones who urged a new trek immediately against those who believed they should encase their feet in concrete and die resisting this foul diktat. It didn't matter, nothing of what a Pomeranian German believed or said mattered anymore; whatever was going to happen would do so despite them, or at best with their acquiescence. She neither despaired nor hoped for anything; she regretted only that she hadn't yet died, that God seemed to have afflicted her with robust health so that she could be a witness to every terminal convulsion of her age, to the end of Germany itself.

## 7

He wasn't allowed time to compose himself or let shock lay on its numbing hand. He was offered only a terse explanation, a few moments to scramble into outdoor clothes and then the Russian officer - a lieutenant - drove him to the Soviet military hospital in a battered GAZ, to a mortuary where her body was laid out among several others, all young, all male. No formal identification was required of him; they knew precisely who she was and asked only that he take possession of her purse and confirm by his signature that it contained thirty roubles and other, unspecified necessities of a life that had ended abruptly at some point between 10pm and 2am the previous night. His hand shook badly as he complied.

The lieutenant's manner was almost brutally matter-of-fact, and Fischer could see that he was uncomfortable. He wondered if he was one of them, her *regulars*.

'Why here?'

The Russian shrugged. 'She was found on Berg-Strasse by one of our patrols. Otherwise ...'

Otherwise she would have been allowed to rot until the rains swept her liquefied remains into the Oder. A German corpse would be regarded by the town's new administration as no more than a potential hazard to Polish pedestrians, like rubble, fissures or dog shit. But litter of any description wasn't allowed to disfigure the ground directly outside Soviet military headquarters in Stettin, a scoured antipode to the broken landscape its creators now administered.

The officer coughed and rubbed his nose with a finger, bracing himself to give the details.

'Her neck is broken, cleanly. She wouldn't have known much about it.'

Apart from the Slavic roll of his consonants he spoke perfect German, the sort that requires time spent among natives rather than just an excellent teacher. He knew how to inflect to indicate emotion correctly, without emphasis. It sounded like regret.

The head was turned to one side, an unnaturally acute angle. Hair and clothes were damp still, the cheap blouse and skirt beyond a steam press's ability to put right (it had rained heavily the previous evening, and he had sat there, oblivious to what was happening, worried only that she might take cold on her way home). Her only piece of jewellery - a ring set with a chipped amethyst of minute proportions - was on its usual finger still, the only *usual* thing he was trying not to see.

His dulled, stupid mind was suspended between two places, unable to reach either. During the short journey from Zabelsdorf he had fought the familiar feeling, the screen falling between the living and the dead as if the essence of her had been excised and placed at a remove. The time they'd spent together building their hopeful, make-believe existence was folding already into a composite plane from which memory removed data like a needle from a recording - imperfectly, warped by a tiny but unbridgeable distance. He couldn't say that it was an ex-*kripo*'s armour or his native inhumanity, but by the time her body was uncovered it was working upon him, trying to make it less than ...

*Less than ten weeks. Don't call it love.*

He turned away and swallowed before it became something else. 'She was at your headquarters. Last night, before ...'

'Shut up.' The lieutenant nodded at the bored orderly who had brought out the object. The man dragged the sheet back over it and shuffled off to deal with his more regular clientele.

'Sit down.'

There was a bench against the wall behind them, beneath a sign that Fischer couldn't read but almost certainly had something to do with vigilance - in any case it exhorted, as Soviet messages did. He obeyed, and got out what he needed to say before the Russian could set more rules.

'The address on her ID card is out of date but you knew where to come. And you wouldn't have brought a German corpse in *here* if she'd died in a sentry box, not unless there was a damn good reason for it. You know her, and what she does.'

The Russian had lit a cigarette for himself without offering the pack. He drew deeply and blew the smoke upward, away from them both.

'Actually, I don't. Your address was given to me, as were instructions to bring you.'

'By whom?'

'Don't be silly.' The Russian shifted, offered a hand. 'Zarubin, Sergei.'

'Otto Fischer.'

'Yes, I know. Formerly Major Fischer, Luftwaffe Counter-Intelligence, East. Prior to that, the war reporters' unit in Berlin. Active service in *Fallschirmjäger 1*, rank of hauptmann, terminated abruptly sometime early in 1942 courtesy of my compatriots. And further back still a *kriminalkommissar*, right here at Stettin. Most recently, a man who tracked down a monster in a nation full of similar and removed it. This is what I adore about Germans - you keep such *complete* records.'

Fischer's stomach contracted violently. His mind stumbled badly, refused to make a start on alibis, mitigations or the sort of blunt denial that might fool a blockhead long enough for him to make a break for the west, or the river at least. He realised that he was gaping, and closed his mouth. There was nothing he could say, no hope of passing off his record as mistaken identity or a clerical misplacement. He knew enough of Soviet policy regarding captured enemy combatants to catch his first scent of pine needles, snow, the spa diet of 700 calories a day.

'Am I detained?'

'Why should you be?' The Russian was smiling, enjoying the moment. It told Fischer that his reaction had been comically obvious.

'German officers must be interrogated, surely?'

'You'd imagine so, wouldn't you? But here's the thing - any attempt to extract what you know would almost certainly give you an idea of the extent to which we not only penetrated Luftwaffe Intelligence but fed disinformation to you in quite startling quantities. Oh God, I seem to have let it slip anyway. Well, spilt milk, eh? We *know* what you were and what you knew, Major. Let's leave it in the ground.'

Lieutenant Zarubin seemed delighted to have such an obliging foil for his wit, and Fischer indulged him - it gave him time to herd his scattered thoughts, to try to find the point on a fogged horizon where this was going. Even if his head was of no value to the Soviets the rest of him should have been on the way East as a matter of course, to join the millions of his compatriots in the gulags. Former intelligence operatives - however comprehensively duped by their counterparts - were the cream of potential resistance in occupied territory, and any conqueror worth the name treated them as a doctor would a virus. So this reprieve, or implied mercy, or game, meant something.

'What do you want?'

'For myself, nothing at all. In fact, my feeling is that this is almost certainly a mistake, but being only a scum-fuck lieutenant I have no say. What *someone* wants is to give this sordid business more attention than it deserves.'

'Attention?'

'Consideration, then, when even a passing glance would be excessive. To me, it risks offering a minor comedy the chance to become Shakespearean. Or perhaps Hollywood? We commence with a corpse after all, and I don't believe the Bard ever did that.'

With the first cigarette still glowing in his mouth, the Russian removed another and lit it. This time he recalled his manners and offered the pack. Fischer shook his head, though he'd hardly noticed the gesture. He was trying to think of her as *her* still, not as the cold, shrouded meat from which he was averting his eyes.

The orderly was several metres away, tending to his other guests' comforts, but Zarubin kept his voice low. 'Obviously, this isn't a crime unless we say it is. Unfortunately, one of us has said precisely that. So what do we do?'

'Investigate it?'

'Don't be absurd.'

'Ignore it then.'

'That would be my choice, certainly. But ...'

Fischer tried to apply himself to *But*. Marie-Therese had been murdered, for what reason he couldn't say. The culprit was a German, or a Russian, or a Pole, or one of a number of less well-represented minorities in the town. It seemed to him that a German was the least likely prospect, not only because there were so few males remaining but those who did had hardly the strength to molest a dormouse. In any case, would their *someone* believe that such a man could be followed and apprehended when so many Germans were leaving the town - dead, expelled or fled - each day? If a Russian were responsible, wouldn't his own people be chasing him - if, that is, a whore's death was considered sufficient reason for anyone to climb out of an armchair to avenge? The third possibility was that it had been a Pole. He considered that, how it might be problematic for everyone. Obviously, the killer's own folk wouldn't go after him for the sake of a dead German tart, even though they had the town's only functioning police force. In any case, the Soviets might be sensitive about jurisdiction, the potential for clashes between those who believed they now owned the town and its real masters. If - for whatever reason - *someone* could declare an interest in finding her killer, might he prefer to maintain a fiction of being disinterested?

'You think he's Polish?'

Zarubin shrugged. '*I* don't think anything, it isn't my business. I just want to stop it becoming so.'

'Who are you?'

The Russian smiled, tapped the side of his nose with a finger.

'NKVD?'

'Here, talking to foreigners rather than shooting them?'

'NKGB? SMERSH?'

'You might say I'm a student of Anti-Soviet Agitation.'

'Polish or German?'

'What's the difference? Now, don't ask for help, because you won't get any. Don't say that you're working for us, because you're not. Don't try to be too clever, or aggressive, or *visible*. Find your lover's murderer. That's all.'

'And then?'

'Then kill him. Or hand him to us, quietly. After that, if you have any sense you'll leave, go West.' The Lieutenant stood up. 'You'll be meeting *someone* tomorrow, at 9am. He wants to see you, to see who you are. Come to the Administration building, the Bellevue-Strasse entrance.'

Fischer stared down at his hands. He wanted only to mourn, to let grief do what it did. He was being offered something he didn't remotely need – a measure of retribution, an anaesthetic for certain wounds, applied in this case to an amputation. Whatever lay before him now was a foreign place in which he had no part, no investment of hope or interest. In a seethe of a town, a hive of ambitions and fears all looking to something whose form was as yet indistinct he was becalmed, sinking, finished with it. He really didn't care who had killed Marie-Therese, only that she had died. Her killer had a motive, an itch, an agenda or a compulsion that satisfied itself in atrocity, and he had no mind either to see it continue or end, because his own ending was here, indelibly written, certified upon a form for form's sake and placed upon the emptied form of the first woman he had ever ...

'Hamlet.'

The Lieutenant had picked up his cap and was signalling to the orderly that he was finished with the *thing*. The noise made him pause. 'What?'

'Hamlet. It commences with a ghost.'

'But not a corpse.'

'Isn't a ghost a corpse with unfinished business?'

Zarubin laughed again, an infectious noise, entirely at odds with what he was.

'If it is, this continent requires the mother of all exorcisms.

His obvious first need was for some decent clothes, so he went to Grossmann, Zabelsdorf's sole remaining professional tailor. He made the decision reluctantly, fearing it to be a bad, dangerous one. Though German himself, Herr Grossmann was not over-fond of other Germans. Like all returned Jews (there was no other kind, naturally), he had acquired an unreasonable dislike for the race that quite overcame his desire to part them from their money. But he had no love for Poles either, and now that they were top dogs here he allowed himself - just - to do business with the defeated party, so as to rub the nose of one into the shit while climbing into the nostrils of the other.

Grossmann and his two sons had returned to their hometown from England, to which they had fled back in 1938, taking the hint after exuberant National Socialists smashed the windows of their fine premises on Turner-Strasse. These days, most Jews in Pomerania were survivors from the camps, *Bricha*, passing through on their way to the not-quite-as-yet Promised Land. But the Grossmanns were here to stay, to give the finger to everyone who hated Jews because they were Jews. In both Stettin and Szczecin this was a large constituency, so the finger was very busy. The family resided at their modest new business premises in order to be available to offer discouragement to anyone thinking of reprising *Kristallnacht*. To that end they had acquired a reasonably comprehensive arsenal, as most folk in that part of town were aware – though not, evidently, all. A few weeks earlier, some fellow with unresolved feelings had turned up with friends and attacked the front door with an axe. He managed to land a few good blows before old Grossmann emerged and shot him cleanly through the head. The friends had departed promptly but their dead comrade's blood lay on the stoop still, and whenever it rained Grossmann came outside and placed a bowl over the stain to preserve it. It was an advertisement, good for business.

At least four bolts slid back noisily before the battered door opened and a solidly built young man filled the space he'd made. Fischer wasted a polite *good morning* on the scowl.

'I'm looking for a suit.'

The young man didn't blink. 'Fuck off, *shkutz*.'

'I have money. Look'

Fischer opened his bag and removed an *eiserne* portion. 'Twenty-five, for something that won't embarrass me.'

Grossmann junior sniffed, took the ration and examined the tin carefully, looking for tell-tale punctures. He tossed his head and Fischer opened the bag, giving him a good view of the rest.

'All 1945, all intact.'

'*Grosskampfpackungen* would have been better.'

'And *foie gras*, I expect. This is what I have.'

The young man turned and went indoors. Fischer followed him into a room bisected by iron bars extending from the ceiling to a counter running the entire length of the long axis. Behind them, racks of clothes disappearing into the unlit rear like an army awaiting its bodies. An older man stood on the other side of the barrier, his sleeves rolled up, arms crossed, eyes fixed firmly on the trade.

'What is it, Ephraim?'

'Foreskin needs a suit.'

'Well, he has to be buried in *something*.'

Ephraim snorted and pushed the *eiserne* portion through the bars. 'For iron rations, he says. Twenty-five.'

'Now that … ' The elder Grossmann released an arm and

stabbed a finger at Fischer, '... is respectful. He brings us proper currency, not some pitiful heirloom I couldn't pass off to a Tartar. What sort of suit would the gentleman be looking for?'

'Something that fits reasonably, that's it.'

'Passing ourselves off, are we?' Grossmann pushed his face into the bars and stared into Fischer's. 'But not as a film star.'

'Max Schreck, maybe. Hard-wearing, if possible.'

The tailor pursed his lips and sized up the object at a glance. 'Medium build, very *average*. Good.'

'My waistline isn't what it was.'

'We've taken in all our trousers, naturally. Emaciation is *a la mode* this season.'

Grossmann disappeared into his racks and re-emerged almost immediately with a dark blue French serge two-piece, double-breasted. He placed it on the counter and smoothed the fabric lovingly with his hand. 'Top Party quality, no holes, guaranteed.' He looked up and shrugged, pantomime Jew-style. 'The pig blew out his brains, so there was a little matter of matter on one of the shoulders. But it cleaned up nicely.'

'Anyone I know?'

'If you did you'd be with him now, I expect.'

'May I try it?'

'I regret, no changing rooms.'

'Just the jacket, then.'

Fischer removed Herr Probin's sad bequest and took its replacement through the bars. The fabric was smooth, quite exquisitely of a lost age, and when he put it on there was little sense of its weight. Hardly a bespoke fit, but for once he felt almost old-time human.

Grossmann regarded the result with deep distaste. He lifted the sample *eiserne* portion with a finger and thumb as if it were primed to explode. 'Thirty-five, and I'll find you a shirt and tie.' He leaned forward, looked down. 'And something that won't disgrace your feet.'

## 9

Lieutenant Zarubin was waiting on the steps of the Bellevue-Strasse entrance, leaning comfortably against the decorative stone archway, smoking a filtered cigarette. Directly in front of him two sentries stood stiffly to attention in the heroic, spine-stretching Red Army manner, assault rifles clutched in both hands, eyes unblinkingly daring the sky to start something. Through the gate Fischer could see Soviet military vehicles parked in lines across the former kaserne's parade ground. It underlined the seamless shift of power, the world become another in a bewildering moment, and his sense of wandering into a bad mistake intensified.

Zarubin waved casually, as if he'd caught sight of a dear friend across a crowded bar. 'Nice suit, Major.'

Fischer winced. The previous evening he had visited the town's only remaining steam bath for native Stettiners and scraped off the patina of months. Now, shaved and dressed in Grossmann's finest, he gave the impression of a man with business in hand, someone who could cast a shadow still. He wondered if he'd made more of an effort than was sensible. Few Germans dressed this well these days unless they had an engagement before an Allied tribunal.

They shook hands formally and entered the kaserne. Fischer didn't get a second glance from any of the Red Army personnel they passed on the way to a large office on the first floor. For once his face wasn't out of place, or at least not a circus exhibit for a curious crowd. Either this had been a hard-fighting unit or it was presently a convalescent formation, easing its broken men back to something like fitness.

What he assumed to be an adjutant of sorts sprang to her

feet as they entered an outer office and threw an impressive salute at Zarubin, who returned it with something disgracefully slack. She went through a door and bawled his name. He turned and shrugged apologetically, and Fischer felt the surviving hair on the back of his neck come to attention. In his experience, people who tried too hard to be one of you usually weren't, remotely.

They were ushered into a commandant's office, a heavily wooded affair that a platoon would need a day to polish. Behind a massive desk sat a uniform with a Soviet General's red tabs, but it was filled by what might have been mistaken for a Junker nobleman, complete to the startling duelling scar that ran across and did no favours for his nose. The apparition laughed (which spoiled the illusion) and said something. Fischer turned to Zarubin.

'The General asks if you share a skin specialist.'

'I don't think mine admitted to a specialism.'

Zarubin translated. It earned another laugh and a brief mime that indicated some sort of unlucky brotherhood between the General and his visitor. Fischer nodded as if he got the joke, though a large office and a senior officer's uniform weren't the sort of misfortune he'd been most familiar with. But perhaps *that* was the joke.

The older man's gaiety dissolved in a moment, shading to what appeared to be marrow-deep sorrow. It wasn't clear whether this was a Russian being Russian or an attempt to emphasise something across the barrier of language. The text took a while to deliver.

Zarubin coughed. 'The General expresses his sincere sympathy for your loss. He wishes you to know that he knew Fraulein Kuefer in a strictly proper manner. He is aware that the nature of her profession makes such a claim seem ... *implausible*, but please be assured that he has only a fatherly interest in bringing to justice the creature who attacked her. He asks what lines of enquiry you propose to follow.'

'She died yesterday. I haven't begun to think about what I'm going to do.'

'No, of course not. But we should prefer that you keep us informed of your intended approach, when this becomes clear.'

'You mean, how will I question Poles and not get at least kicked for it?'

Zarubin translated. The General, smiling again, nodded vigorously.

Fischer really hadn't given any thought to it (grief's selfish demands had entirely pushed aside the practicalities). He searched for a bauble that would satisfy them for the moment.

'I know a boy who deals with them. He can arrange something, an introduction.'

It was weak, and 'Earl' Kuhn wasn't going to be happy when he got the good news. But if it turned out to be the dead end Fischer anticipated they would have to drop the thing and leave him to mourn.

Zarubin gave the General the plan, and this started a conversation in which their reluctant German guest played a piece of furniture. From the tone of the exchanges it didn't seem that the Lieutenant was displaying the respect due to a (much) senior officer, but then Fischer wasn't too familiar with Red Army protocol. He knew there'd been a period immediately following the Revolution when all ranks had addressed each other as 'mate' or similar.

At one point the General's voice rose, and Zarubin discreetly mimed with a hand to bring it down again. *That*, Fischer was sure, was not in regulations. He also heard something that rang a distant bell.

'What did you call him?'

Zarubin broke off and turned. The expression on his face was damnably guileless.

'*Dyadya*. Uncle.'

A pfennig dropped loudly, and only Fischer's present state of distraction kept his pulse steady. An initiative taken up by someone from an organization that never bothered itself with less than ten thousand casualties; a family matter disguised as some sort of Red Army business involving the murder of a prostitute; a culprit who was almost certainly able to kill a German with impunity (hell, who couldn't these days?); a crime - *possibly* a crime - that no other German dare investigate. It only required that he be smeared with bear grease and commence his efforts in a police kennels to make this the dream assignment.

The General turned abruptly and spoke directly to Fischer. Zarubin cleared his throat twice in the time it took to get out, in a way that suggested he wanted earnestly to stop the flow. When it was done it took a definite prod from the old man to have it translated, and Fischer knew that he was getting only the bones.

'While ... while the Soviet authorities cannot be seen to be in any way complicit with your efforts, you may request practical assistance that does not implicate them. Obviously, this *assistance* will take the form of monies ...'

The General opened a drawer in his desk, removed something and threw it at Fischer. It fell towards his right side and his bad hand failed him. He stooped to pick up the small bundle from the carpet. Its outer layer was a ten dollar bill, US. The General spoke again, briefly, and laughed. This time, even Zarubin smiled slightly.

'He says good German dollars, made in Philadelphia. Do you

have any questions?'

## 10

In a remarkably well-stocked cellar in one of the less
damaged properties on Schwartzkopff-Strasse, Fischer tried to
listen politely to what he assumed to be several black gentlemen
laying in to a musical composition. The pianist, their leader, was
clearly a master of his instrument, though the notes emerged in
combinations that spoke little to conventional melodies. His small
ensemble followed gamely and almost in syncopation. Some
might have called it noise; others – perhaps - *art*.

He was no expert, but the gramophone appeared to be an
expensive model, impeccably maintained. The inner face of its lid
carried an image of an attentive little dog, so he deduced that it
was of either American or British manufacture. He couldn't
imagine how it had escaped the Ivans' attention. In the initial
period of pillaging musical boxes had been higher on their booty
list than what lay between German women's legs.

'They're really breaking it down!'

'Very nice, yes.'

Earl Kuhn regarded Fischer with unaffected disappointment.
'This really is marvellous, you know.'

'In what way?'

'It has *soul*.'

'Has it?'

The younger man's eyes went to the ceiling, and he recited
what might have been a prayer by way of explanation.

'The transportation of the Negro from his natural habitat to
the Americas nurtured a profound melancholia. This, and his

primeval sensing of natural rhythms, creates an expression of feeling in music that's fundamentally emotional, rather than a sterile outpouring of intellect. Which is why all black men in America understand the *soul* of music.'

'And why you are Earl.'

'The prophet of modern jazz! I would have preferred 'Fatha', his *nickname,* but we Germans pronounce it very badly, as Brooklyners do.'

Earl Kuhn (his given name was Adolph, so the *nom de jazz* hardly required explanation) shrugged regretfully. He was a slight young man, prematurely balding from the top. To Fischer he seemed entirely inoffensive, but against nature and much-discredited phrenological theories he had cornered the town's cigarette trade between its native citizens and Red Army personnel. Rumours persisted of a stalled train north of Gotzlow during the finals days of the war, a swift extraction of its cargo by a gang of adolescents, a brief chase offered by soldiers whose minds were on anything but protecting a general's retirement fund. A lot was going on back then so it might have been true, but all that anyone knew for sure was that as most native Stettiners had become much poorer Earl Kuhn had moved up in the world without stepping on dangerous toes. His mild demeanour was a natural advantage; he also lived modestly, put on no airs and played the *Klostermayr* occasionally, helping out desperate cases with donations of food or firewood. No one had a bad word for him that they cared to share. For Fischer, it was enough that he had as many contacts as cigarettes, and that they spread far beyond Zabelsdorf.

"I didn't know that Stettin had *swing boys.*'

'It did, for almost three months! We played records, danced after a fashion, defaced some walls, acted like top men. Then a local *HJ* squad tried to use our heads for footballs, and after that 'Stapo organized a trip to the camps.'

'Were there many of you?

'Yeah, eight.' Kuhn didn't seem to regret the experience; perhaps the ordeal had tempered the steel of his spiritual negro-hood. He looked up, hopefully. 'So, dollars you said?'

The bundle was produced. 'One hundred.'

'Pick a bill.'

At random, Fischer selected one from the middle of his thin roll. Kuhn held it up to the light and examined it expertly, then licked two fingers and rubbed the fabric between them as he held it to his ear.

Fischer was curious, given the source of his windfall. 'Is it real?'

'Probably. The serial letter matches its year and mint location, which is good. You wouldn't believe how many fakes fall down on the obvious things. I'd need chemicals to be certain. Who gave it to you?'

'The Russians.'

Kuhn's eyebrows rose. 'Well, *very* probably, then. The Ivans couldn't make this sort of stuff in a century. If it *is* bad it was made by Germans, but I haven't seen any in circulation.'

'Will it be enough?'

'In Stettin? You could buy anything, anybody or both with a hundred dollars American.'

'I don't know if I can get more, so I need to be thrifty.'

'Let me have just this one for now.' Kuhn pocketed the bill. 'It's enough to get attention.'

Fischer didn't mind losing the money (it wasn't his, after all), but giving it to Kuhn was putting the thing in motion. His best-trained nerves twitched.

'You know these people well?'

'A couple of them, guys who don't hate Germans enough to pass up a deal.'

'Who are they?'

'Who do you think? Professional types who came here to stake out a territory even before we surrendered. Cigarettes smugglers, thieves, recovery agents, the usual dregs.'

'Recovery agents?'

'Yeah, their boys steal German property and then they 'find' it and sell it back to the poor bastards. It's good trade, particularly in documents.'

'So they're not really a part of Polish society here?'

'The decent Poles suffer them much as we do. Like I said, the dregs.'

'And you do business with them?'

Kuhn shrugged. 'Mostly introductions for people wanting their fancy goods returned. The occasional sale, if I get lucky. I cleared out a few of the wrecks a while back. They were happy to take almost everything I had.'

Before the surrender, Red Army Artillery and Allied bombers had sunk virtually everything that once had floated in the Oder. For months after the ceasefire the hulks had been largely untouched. An enterprising man, one with nerve, an intact boat and a carrion bird's instincts, would have given himself a head start in building a post-apocalyptic business.

'Alright. How will we do it?'

'One fellow, he's well connected, knows some police and Ivans as well, I think. He doesn't get too crazy like some of his competition - no disappearings, killings or maimings, and he doesn't mind *schwabs* too much. In fact he speaks German like me, almost. I'll push the bill his way, tell him there's more for the right sort of information. But ...'

'What?'

'That's the thing. What *is* the right information?'

Fischer considered it. The man he was looking for almost certainly wasn't a client, unless Marie-Therese had tried to over-charge drastically or threatened to tell his wife, and he was certain she hadn't been that sort of girl. So either the culprit knew her and had some other, specific reason to kill her, or he was the sort who did it for the act itself, to satisfy a need. Either way, the clues wouldn't be flagging themselves.

'Your man probably isn't going to be too much use to me. But he may be able to point to someone in the local administration.'

'Town Hall? They'd sooner dump him in the river than give him a nod as he walked by.'

'Really. Those respectable gentlemen, even the career *kozis* that Moscow parachuted in, need smokes, whisky and truffles. What's the point of power if you can't taste it? And who else supplies it anymore? Is *Dienemann's* still pulling them in? *Ufa Palast* doing any business these days?'

Kuhn grinned, pulled a face.

'What I want is someone he's into on a regular basis, one of his best customers. And make it clear that all I want is to talk, very privately.'

## 11

Despair came soon, and hard. He tried to take an hour's rest and slept for twelve, without relief. When he awoke from a particularly foul dream, reality returned like a wall falling upon glass. He got up, opened a bottle of cheap Romanian brandy (something he and Marie-Therese had been saving to celebrate a good day that never arrived), went back to bed and didn't stop until the surface bisected the label. It was just what he needed, a further depressant. He didn't ruin its effects with breakfast.

Puking took his mind off everything that wasn't puking, but only for a few minutes. Washing himself consumed a further five, which left only the rest of his life to occupy with things that weren't the smell, touch, taste or company of her. Staring at the wall didn't help so he dressed, pulled on his overcoat (an old Luftwaffe item, stripped of its trims) and went for a walk.

It was raining - cold, pitiless sleet that went some way to scraping Stettin off the shortlist of the world's most desirable locations. He walked south and east, deliberately pointing himself at the heart of the new Szczecin. Soon, he was in territory he hadn't visited since the day she'd re-entered his life, and it was difficult to shut out memories of the intervening weeks. He tried to concentrate instead on the changes, the heavy hints that the end of German days was upon them. Every strasse was now a roughly re-painted *ulica* and all allees *alejas*; Kronenhof had become *Wyzwolenia*, Augusta *Mazowiecka*, the badly damaged Bollwerk resurrected as a *bulwar* and Adolph Hitler Platz reincarnated as *Plac Stefana Batorego* (a real wiping of Teutonic noses, that). In several places where the lie of ruins required clues as to their former situation the new names confused him further and he actually lost his way. It was all strange yet familiarly so, an absurdity that pinned the age precisely. Nations had once fought for castles, lands, river-navigation and subject populations; now, it was a matter of rubble, all apparently worth seizing and renaming in memory of men who wouldn't have squatted to shit upon any of it.

His only pleasure of the day was to find the old Helios cinema almost intact still, though it was closed and heavily boarded up. It had been one of his regular nights out in the old days, with or without a girl to squeeze in the dark. For six weeks during 1937 he had been on sick leave with a brutally inflamed testicle and had made the Helios a nightly treat, a half-kilometre hobble from his old apartment on Beringer-Strasse to worship Lillian Harvey and Zarah Leander in the company of dozens of not-quite similarly disordered groins. He was surprised now at how he felt about it. He'd never before allocated any of his Stettin memories to the *fond* column, and it made him wonder whether his head could be trusted still.

At the corner of what used to be Falkenwalder-Strasse and Philipp-Strasse a young Polish man took a moment to tell him to fuck off to Germany. He smiled politely and raised his cap. The man flushed and said something else (in his own language this time) which didn't sound like an apology. A fist clenched to emphasise the point but it stayed down. Its owner wore office clothes, so either he was too genteel to obey the heart's yearnings or he didn't need the mess on his suit. Fischer nodded to his new friend and walked on quickly. A parting shot followed him up Falkenwalder-Strasse - a curse probably, or directions to a nearby terminus with services to the west.

He didn't pause again until he had returned to the thin safety of Zabelsdorf, and it was only there that it occurred to him that he had not seen a single, obviously German face south of the so-called 'protection' area. In a matter of weeks, intimidation, force or self-preservation had removed the centuries' old heart of the town and transplanted its Slavic successor (the Poles would call it a restoration, probably). If he was going to do this thing he would be monstrously visible.

In the hallway of his apartment building Earl Kuhn and a

large dog were blocking the foot of the stairs. He knew immediately that it was Earl's dog because it wore a tie - a wide, garish thing with a geometric pattern, fastened so as to leave sufficient length for its wearer to sit upon (or, presumably, trip over). The rest of the animal was more conventionally canine, of indiscriminate though heroic parentage. Its wide, open-mouthed smile hosted more and larger teeth than a Tarzan feature, and Fischer suspected that he was in the presence of at least part of Kuhn's otherwise inexplicably absent bodyguard. A man wouldn't want to pull a sideways glance with this thing in the room.

Kuhn grabbed a handful of fur and squeezed affectionately. 'Her name's Beulah May Annan. I bought her from an Ivan before she became sausages.'

The bushy tail did a single sweep at the name but the eyes remained fixed upon Fischer. He found her attention span disconcerting. It was as if she couldn't decide whether he was a potential threat to her lunch ticket or lunch itself.

'You'll be alright if you lose the coat. Uniforms make her nervous, I don't know why.' Kuhn smiled as people do when heartily enjoying the naked fear of others. Fischer took the suggestion very slowly, dropping the garment on to the hall floor. Beulah May bounded to her feet, barked once (a mezzo, if not contralto) and promptly sat upon the threat. Her tail didn't stop this time.

'Good girl.' Fischer made the statement without conviction either of its accuracy or power to keep him from a new round of mutilations. But Beulah May surprised him, leaning forward slightly to lick his bad hand. Like most women she seemed to take shallow endearments at face value.

'An unusual name.'

Kuhn pulled her tail playfully. 'After the Chicago Jazz Killer. Actually, the lady was acquitted, so perhaps she wasn't. But it suits, don't you think?'

'Without doubt.'

'A dog is a very *good* idea. She's such excellent company, never complains about the shit I feed her and knows as much about the business as me.'

'Really?'

Kuhn looked up seriously. 'Oh yes. She can smell out the rubbish in bad cigarettes or spot an armpit bulge in a moment. I couldn't manage without her. Anyway, it's arranged, tomorrow, 2pm. I'll take you.'

'Who am I seeing?'

'My guy first. He wants to make sure he's not being *set up*.'

Kuhn used the English term and raised his eyebrows slightly, as if there were some doubt about it.

'*Set up* for what? I'm going to rob him?'

'It's a trade that relies upon no trust whatsoever. You can't be surprised?'

'So how will he be convinced? Don't dollars do it?'

'Of course. But he wants to know that he's not getting more than that.'

Fischer sighed. 'Alright.'

'There's something else.' Earl Kuhn looked uncomfortably at his large friend. 'Really, I wouldn't ask, but ...'

'You're not serious?'

'It's that I have to leave town for the night, a shipment. She isn't good in the dark with strangers. The last time she almost killed a guy.'

Beulah May collapsed to a prone position, pressing Fischer's foot into service as a pillow. He didn't pull it away or nudge her head by way of a hint. Kuhn stood and handed him a package.

'I've brought horsemeat, so you'll both have supper. She prefers hers warmed up a little, if that's ok?'

12

Kuhn returned late the following morning. The apartment's two occupants sat in its small bay window, watching him stoop-shuffle the length of Carla-Strasse, casting studiously nonchalant glances to left and right. A welcoming rumble fired up in the bitch's throat but subsided when Fischer put his hand on the back of her neck and pulled gently at the coiled muscle. It was a trick he'd discovered the previous evening when he took her downstairs to drink at the water-pump. The two Polish families whose claim upon the courtyard was making such visits difficult for the German tenants had scattered like chaff when Beulah May outlined her own territorial ambitions. Fischer, grabbing desperately at her neck as she lunged for fresh meat, had been astonished by her immediate, lamb-like compliance. He wondered if he'd missed a similar trick with girls generally.

'She hates Poles', said Kuhn cheerfully. 'As a pup she must have eaten one that disagreed with her. It's why we can't take her with us today.'

He placed his package on the small coffee table at which Fischer and Marie-Therese had taken their more formal meals, opened it, removed a pack of Lucky Strikes and held it out for Beulah May's opinion. She sniffed and blinked but raised no objections.

Kuhn handed the pack and one more to Fischer. 'Here, it's good currency.'

'Thanks. I thought you dealt only with Russians?'

'I couldn't make a living that way. I've got a mate in the west, he trades Red Army memorabilia to the Brits and Amis. They can't get enough of it. This time it was campaign medals, but we could sell them a fucking T34 if we wanted to.' He pursed his lips, weighing the options. 'Ammunition might be difficult.'

'A useful friend.'

'Yeah. It was him who first introduced me to our guy, the one you'll meet today.'

'Where?'

'Pelzer-Strasse, the Castle.'

'It's a shell.'

Kuhn grinned. 'He has a nice view of it from across the street.'

The castle of the dukes of Pomerania had been almost obliterated during one of 1944's air-raids, but some of the old five-storey merchants' houses on the opposite side of Pelzer-Strasse were intact still. It had been the town's prime residential address before the bombing, and everyone knew its ruins would be some of the first to be restored. The new administration was already making noises about the castle, built originally by the almost-Polish Gryfici dynasty and a headlining opportunity to whitewash over the intervening German centuries. Anything on Pelzer-Strasse was a good long-term investment.

They locked Beulah May in Fischer's apartment and walked the two kilometres to the castle. Many of the town's new citizens were out of doors already, absorbing the day's meagre ration of vitamin D. A few stared briefly at the two unkempt Germans but no one tried to make anything of it. Kuhn seemed not to notice the attention; he chatted away about his business, the altered landmarks, his ambition to head west eventually and open a record store somewhere nice, Heidelberg perhaps, though it was heaving with fucking Americans, and ...

Fischer had hardly been listening, but the profanity grazed

something in his inner ear. 'I thought you liked Americans?'

Kuhn shrugged. 'I love American culture. I just hate Americans. The way they treat us you'd think we'd screwed their grandmothers. Why the fuck is that? Did *we* declare war on *them*? (*yes*, murmured Fischer, unheard) Did a single German bomb ever fall on America? Why are the Brits and even the Ivans getting over it while the Amis stay biblical about us?'

'They don't see shades of grey. And there was that business in Belgium.'

'What?'

'During Operation *Watch on the Rhine*. Some Waffen SS units couldn't be bothered to take prisoners. They lined up about eighty GIs. It caused bad blood.'

'*Eighty*? That's it? The Amis shot prisoners all the time!'

'Yes, but they won. It's like absolution.'

'Bastards. What about the British Zone? Any nice towns there still?'

They turned the corner into Pelzer-Strasse. On any other day Fischer might not have noticed, but several men, all handy-looking fellows loitering too casually in doorways, made the hairs on his neck come to attention.

Kuhn grabbed his arm. 'It's cool.'

Fischer had no idea what *cool* was for bad or good, but none of the Muscle seemed to object to their presence. A couple of them called out to Kuhn by name. He replied in Polish, something witty, and they laughed. One of the larger ones slowly prised his back from a wall and intercepted them. Kuhn came to a halt in front of him and looked up like a climber weighing the challenge from base camp.

The mountain nodded. 'Hey, Earl.'

'Hey, Wojciech. What's the news?'

'Nothing much.'

'We've got an appointment with your man. We're a little early.'

'Fine, he likes to be ahead of himself. Go up.'

They entered number 13, a building large enough to be an apartment block but which was in fact a single house. Kuhn led the way up three unlit flights, knocked on a door and walked in without waiting for an invitation. Fischer followed into a large, under-furnished room with carved architraves, an ornate ceiling rose that missed its centrepiece and a bare wooden floor that must once have been polished. Its boards were broad and even, well laid, flush with each other still, and their colour matched an old, high Pomeranian fireplace precisely.

Fischer glanced around. A large walnut bookcase, built into and covering almost one entire wall, held not a single book, while an impressive dining table, large enough to accommodate a council-sized feast, hosted a total of three small chairs that seemed to have been recovered from a bombsite. The two corners of the room flanking the fireplace were busier; each was stacked almost to the ceiling with cartons, several bearing US Quartermaster Corps 92G stamps. The only other impediment to a clear run from one wall to another was a solitary leather chair, its back presented to them. From its right side a burnished, golden object protruded a few centimetres.

An old, half-lost memory stirred. He took two steps toward the chair and looked down upon a trombone in immaculate condition, lying on several sheets of music. He opened his mouth but the question died as he turned back towards Kuhn and saw the third man in the room, his back pressed against the wall in the space behind the door. His mouth was open too, but he recovered himself before Fischer could do the same.

'Hello, Hauptmann.'

'It's … never mind. Hello, Mazur.'

Achym Mazur, former cigarette czar of Trassenheide, the only man ever to have made a half-decent living from the wrong side of a labour camp fence, thought about it for a moment and then smiled broadly. 'Welcome to Poland.'

## 13

Tea was served in tiny china cups. Their waiter was Wojciech, who moved as comfortably as a porpoise in a corset stuffed with its cousins' bones. With an absurd flourish, his little finger (larger than any of Fischer's) pointed outwards at a delicate angle as he transferred the crockery from his tray. The last of them he knocked slightly against the edge of the table, spilling hot liquid on to his hand.

'Fuck!'

'It's fine, Wojciech', Mazur said mildly, in German. 'Have we any *butterkuchen* for our guests?'

'No.'

'What about *paczki*?'

'Plenty.'

'Fine. We'll have those, then.'

'When in Poland, eh?' said Kuhn, and laughed.

Fischer took a sip from his cup as he hunted desperately for the right etiquette to resuscitate an awkward relationship. He recalled vaguely that at one point he had threatened Mazur with time in a worse camp than Trassenheide (even). Or had it been summary execution? A bluff, obviously, but that sort of thing tended to stick in minds. He hoped the Pole's memory of their final meeting was a little fresher.

Before he could make a start Mazur replaced his own cup on the table, leaned forward and tapped the enemy's knee.

'Well, Hauptmann. The world's turned shitty, eh?'

'Just Fischer. It *was* Major; now it's nothing.'

'Oh, I couldn't. Call a German by its name and you start thinking of it as human. Makes it harder to kill eventually, like with a piglet.'

Kuhn laughed again, easily. He really did find it funny.

'Achym's taking the piss. He actually likes *schwabs*, thinks every home should have one.'

Fischer watched both men working the routine and wondered if this was how it might turn out eventually - two nations reconciled by the refusal of their citizens to take anything seriously. It didn't seem likely.

He was nudged unceremoniously. Wojciech had returned with a plate of dainties. Another thick finger, ornamented with a thicker gold ring and an impeccably manicured fingernail, stabbed at the choice.

'Chocolate, curd, *budyn*.'

'Thank you, no.' A sugar bombardment upon his serially-empty belly would probably send him into a diabetic coma.

Mazur and Kuhn helped themselves and for a minute nothing more was said. Fischer used the pause to examine their host. He was heavier now that the standard labour camp diet had been abandoned in favour of calories, and his complexion was much improved. The grey striped pyjamas affected by Trassenheide's inmates had been swapped for a black crew-neck sweater and matching leather jacket. They gave him something of a louche air that his industrial demolition of a fancy cake only partly traduced.

Mazur noticed the up-and-down he was getting, gripped a lapel and grinned, letting crumbs fall on to his chin. '*Maquis* chic, the modern Pole's first choice.'

'Very elegant. Can you help?'

The smile disappeared. 'Difficult, Hauptmann. I'm on a wire here. My lads won't be happy if I do anything to get us noticed by the straights.'

'I need an introduction, that's all. To someone who keeps an ear open.'

'You don't understand; an introduction might just be the thing to do it. This ... ' his hand swept the room, but Fischer sensed he meant something more than their immediate surroundings, ' ... is temporary, good while it lasts and then it's over and we get out, quickly. You too, if you're smart.'

Kuhn nodded sagely. 'It's a sweet deal right now.'

'Yeah, but now is *now*. Soon it'll be like the rest of Josefland, a soulless, enterprise-free zone. At the moment they're too busy sorting out the basic stuff – food, power, roads and getting the Hermans out of New Poland. But we're stage two - the naughty boys, the dealers, the reason they call Szczecin the *Wild West*. They'll get 'round to us sooner or later, and I'd hate to make it *sooner* by inviting attention. What if I find you a guy and the first thing that comes to his mind is why the fuck did that bastard Achym pick on *me*, one of his best customers? How many upright Poles in this town do you think want to *see* a German, much less get the full interview?'

Fischer stared down at his cup. He recognized it as Dresdner without needing to see the underside. Its pattern had been a bestseller pre-war, something Schumann had been dragged from the grave to endorse.

'What if it's a business the Ivans want settled, quickly?'

Mazur laughed. 'Oh, fine! Lots of Poles will want to oblige in *that* case.'

'Why wouldn't they? You can pretend all you want that Stettin's Polish, but as long as the Red Army's sitting in the docks it's just a dream. You want to give them more excuses to stay?'

'I've never met a Russian I couldn't bribe, so personally I hope the fuckers stay forever. In any case, you'll need to tell me more about what *something* is.'

It had been coming for almost two days now. Kuhn hadn't asked, just assumed that it wasn't his business (to Fischer it was one of the boy's more admirable qualities). He should have thought of something plausible, but it was a matter about which he hadn't wished to think at all.

'Someone was killed, murdered. They want it sorted out. I think it has the potential to embarrass them - at least, one or two of them.'

'Who? I mean, who died?'

'It's better you don't know. Really, would you want the Ivans to know you have something on them?'

Mazur pursed his lips, weighing the utility of pressing for useful information against the definite disadvantage of being found face down in the Oder with the back of his head missing. He shrugged. 'Why you? They can't rate retired German cops as better than their own?'

'I think they're worried that a Pole did it. If they investigate it looks political. Obviously, they don't trust another Pole to do it.'

'And if was a Russian, they'd be down on ... ' Mazur's eyes widened. 'Fuck! The dead guy's a German!'

Fischer shrugged.

'Why would they care, for God's sake?'

The only plausible lie came to him suddenly. '*She* was one of their own, a *kozi*. You can see why they don't want to upset their pet Poles by stirring things directly. If they were all Comintern back in Moscow, one of them could be the culprit.'

Mazur smiled. He seemed to be entranced by a vista of stabbed backs. 'You've drawn the latrine detail with this one, Hauptmann! All right, I think I know someone who can help, if help's the word. I'll see to it.' The Pole regarded Fischer critically. 'You'll need to freshen up if you're going to deal with the Straights. A suit, perhaps?'

'I have one. From Grossmann.'

'Well then, you're set. Nothing like a Grossmann for making a man look more than he is.'

If it took the right clothes to impress, that was fine with Fischer. He much preferred to deal with people who'd tasted enough of life's pleasures to fear losing them. 'Your fellow; who is he?'

Mazur's mouth twisted apologetically. 'He's more of an *it*, to tell the truth.'

## 14

Kuhn seemed pleased with how the meeting had gone. He was cradling a bottle of Lamb's Navy Rum in one of his coat pockets, Mazur's way of telling him no offence. Fischer said nothing to interrupt the apparently limitless flow of his chatter. Most of it was about the Poles, and he badly needed some perspective.

'They're not a *gang*. I mean, sure, Achym makes most of the decisions, but only because he's the one with the contacts, which means he's got the best chance of finding the profits. But they're not the Mazur *gang*. If they call themselves anything it's the Castle boys, but then only to put space between them and the crews who run Pommerensdorf, or Torney, or Lastadie. I mean, who'd want to step into the firing line by putting their own name to a social problem?'

'Isn't Lastadie in the Ivans' Control Zone?'

'Yeah, but they buy stuff from the gangs. Look, Achym was right about *now*. Town Hall's police force is still pathetic, but you know as well as anyone that they're dragging in as many Polish settlers as possible to make a fact that can't be unmade. It's like a reservoir that's still filling, and until it does there'll be pickings on the beach. I reckon we've got another two, three months and then it's over - goodbye to me, you and any other German who imagines he can stay or return, *and* to any Pole who thinks he can make up his own rules. So if you do something to bring it on, you'll get the last thing you need - more enemies. You dig?'

They leaned on one of the few undamaged sections of railing overlooking the Oder, directly opposite Silberwiese's shattered warehouses and wharfs. The river below them was a succession of shoals created by Allied bombing and Soviet shelling

- demolished bridges, collapsed river frontages and capsized vessels all leeched into the water like a succession of half-piers going from nowhere to nowhere else. The *Bahnhofsbrücke*, once as pretty and as memorable as London's Tower Bridge, now served as a fine reef for any fish stupid enough to have stayed around, and only its submerged bascule section was doing in death what it had done throughout its working life - allowing a narrow passage for river traffic. The place was a bottleneck, just another of the very many reasons why the town had little access to food six months after the end of hostilities.

Two Germans shouldn't have been this far south, deep in the new Szczecin, but one didn't care and the other couldn't think of a good reason to put it off any longer. Fischer watched the greasy swell rise over and then re-expose the bow of a half-beached barge that had once been named *Kriemhilde* (that was a guess; it actually admitted only to - *emhilde*) He wondered if she'd been a mother, wife or sweetheart, and whether the Poles would raise her or just send down a diver to daub on a Slavic identity she could rot with. The streets weren't safe from the future; why should wreckage be?

'Earl, if it's up to me this business is going to be a quicker, neater failure than a Polish cavalry charge. I'll ask a few questions, apologize for any inconvenience caused and then go back to the Russians with wide open arms and a *well, I tried* expression on my stupid face. It won't stir things.'

'What you said, about her being one of them. Was she?'

Kuhn hadn't known Marie-Therese other than as one of his more regular cigarette buyers, but he knew how she'd earned the means to pay for them.

'No, but don't say anything about that. I don't want people to know I'm doing this because she was my ...' he couldn't think of a term that didn't sound ridiculous. 'They wouldn't help if that's all she was.'

'No. They say they're a romantic race, but that's shit, like with the Russians. What is it with Slavs that makes them want to be French?'

'History, like how it is with us and other people's property.'

Kuhn grinned. 'So I've just been expressing a racial imperative?'

'Exactly; you're a dupe, not a fascist.'

A four-man patrol of Szczecin's fledgling militia was approaching from the south, their attention obviously on the two Germans. Kuhn straightened quickly, waved at one of them and had a pack of his Lucky Strikes ready. He got a nod from his friend; the others stared, saying nothing even as they each took a cigarette and graciously accepted a light. Nervously, Kuhn said something in Polish. The stares swerved in formation to Fischer.

'I told them you were police here in Stettin, one of the good guys. Said you got out in '37 because you didn't like the work back then.'

All true enough, but it was exactly what someone *would* say these days, when not a single German admitted to ever having had time for National Socialism. He wished that Kuhn had talked about the weather instead.

Their corporal, or whatever he was that his two stripes signified, pointed his cigarette at Fischer and asked something. Kuhn's anxiety ratcheted up visibly. 'He wants to know how many Poles you fucked up, back then.'

'Tell him hardly any, which is how many Poles lived in Stettin back then. When they broke up bars we put them in the cells and then straight back on to their ships the next morning. German crap was what we had and dealt with, mainly. And the Jews, obviously.'

Two of the Poles smirked. Their corporal took a drag on his smoke, dropped it and stubbed it out, said something short and sweet. The fourth man, Kuhn's friend, didn't look too friendly anymore, and Fischer knew immediately how he'd misjudged it. The patrol moved off. Kuhn got several nods by way of a goodbye, Fischer the same hostile glance.

'He's ...'

'Jewish. *Shit*.'

'It's ok, he isn't so proud or stupid that he admits to it. The poor fucker spent a year under a bed, three years in the forests and then emerged into what he hoped was a new world, only it isn't. I got him the papers that turned Amoz into Andrzej, so he's sweet.'

'Why isn't he in Palestine?'

'Flies, heat, camel shit, hairy girls - what you'd expect.'

'Does he have a thing still for the wrong sort of German?'

'As much as the next Jew. But you aren't. Wrong that is, not unless there's a career you haven't mentioned. You'll be fine. That face of yours is gold - I mean, one glance at it and people need a reason not to pity you. I wish I could buy one for myself.'

'Apply to the Russians.' Fischer began to feel a little easier. True, he'd had Kuhn to smooth the way this time, but at least he knew now that it was possible still for a German to move around freely below Zabelsdorf. He made a mental note always to carry good quality cigarettes. The suit he decided to leave on its hanger for most of now on. Poles were very comfortable with reminders of how things had turned out for Germans, so for one of them to be well-dressed and seemingly solvent would be like a slap in the mouth.

'Earl, do I *look* German?'

'In that coat? Sure. Who else would think Luftwaffe was the present fashion?'

'No, physically I mean.'

Kuhn took a step back and examined him as if they had met for the first time.

'No, but you don't *not* look German either. It's those wounds again - you could be anyone, really. What hair you've got is cut a little short for a healthy Pole's taste, if that's what you're asking. I'd either grow it out or shave it off. Plenty of them lost their hair in '44 when we stopped feeding them. The rest of you says that you didn't have an easy war, so it's credible. A shame you don't do the language.'

They watched the river for a few minutes more, until rain started to break up its surface. Kuhn didn't like getting wet; he suddenly recalled that Beulah May became skittish when she hadn't been fed, so they headed north along the Bollwerk, collars up, caps pulled down. The road had just curved to the west and departed the river, becoming what used to be Blumen-Strasse, when a well-dressed woman holding an umbrella crossed the road and came straight up to them.

'German?'

This time it didn't seem too dangerous to admit it. Fischer nodded.

'Please, you must go now. Home.'

They usually put more venom into it. And she seemed upset rather than angry, as if they'd trampled soil on to a favourite carpet. Kuhn smiled and said something vaguely apologetic in Polish. She chattered briefly, waving a hand, and as colour filled her face it drained entirely from Kuhn's. Fischer caught only one word, *Gumieñce*. He knew it; it used to be …

Kuhn grabbed his arm and dragged him away, towards what they thought of as home still. 'They're killing Germans, she said. At Scheune station, today.'

15

What remained of the apartment building's residents' association had organized a public meeting. Prudently, it wasn't actually held in public but in the inner courtyard of one of the larger, more ruinous properties on Industrie-Strasse. An old lady who lived directly beneath Fischer told him about it. She repeated more or less what the Polish lady had told them and then begged Fischer to attend on behalf of her failing hips. They arrived as the association's envoy, lately returned from Scheune, was giving the facts.

The death toll was two, with a third man wounded but expected to live. A Polish squad had dragged someone from the train and told him that he had been recognized as someone who'd done some bad things back in '39. The accused party had only begun to enter a plea when one of his accusers shot him in the head. Two would-be evacuees close by tried to intervene; one obviously had worse luck than his mate. The rest of the hopeful passengers were then allowed to finish embarking without further outrage, and the train departed west.

Fischer held up his hand quickly when their informant (a former town councillor) invited questions.

'Who were they?'

The man shrugged. 'They didn't identify themselves. *UB*, perhaps.'

It seemed likely. Interior Ministry thugs tried more or less constantly to get a reaction that would give them an excuse to wade in (not that they minded shooting other Poles, if Germans weren't handy). It was an ugly incident, but at least they'd had a sort of excuse for it this time. Three months earlier their colleagues had turned out in force at Scheune to discourage German refugees from the East who intended to make a new home in Stettin. When they discovered that there were Kolbergers among them they decided to commemorate the heavy Polish losses suffered during that town's siege in the last days of the war. By the time they'd tired of the entertainment, German bodies had littered the platform.

A few more hands went up. Someone from the back of the crowd shouted out the obvious question.

'Was he guilty?'

Their eyewitness shrugged. It was as likely as not, and immaterial except to the dead man. The Poles had wanted to send a message- *you aren't getting out quickly enough, please try harder, thank you*.

Kuhn sighed. 'It could have been worse.'

'It will be.'

'Yeah. I really should liquidize my assets and think about Heidelberg. You?

Fischer almost laughed. 'Assets won't be a problem.'

Someone behind them was making a fuss and getting a lot of agreement.

'They'll either shoot us all or put us into a camp and let us starve, like at Lamsdorf!'

The ex-councillor was trying to cool them down, but this explosion had been waiting for a combustible moment for months now. They were some of the final ten thousand Germans in the town, who had seen every bitter price being exacted for something they hadn't done, or wanted, or even agreed with. Fischer could almost smell the concentrated essence of victimhood's twisted logic - finally, they had it, absolute proof of what a certain Austrian gentleman had claimed all along, that Germany was surrounded by natural enemies who should have been dealt with before they could exercise their vicious predilections. *If only they hadn't treated the Poles so leniently! If only they'd hadn't behaved so well in the east, and given the Ivans a taste of what suffering could be! Isn't this always the way, when a civilized nation faces barbarians?*

'Fucking idiots.' Kuhn took Fischer's arm. 'Come on. We don't want to be here if *UB* get a sniff of it.'

He was right - a mob would be just the sort of excuse they'd need to finish off the job, and there were enough Poles in Zebelsdorf now to slip the word to the wrong people. Fischer allowed himself to be dragged away, but at the archway through into Industrie-Strasse he paused. Kuhn turned to him. 'What?'

'Your whistle, give it to me.'

Kuhn had only one means of recapturing Beulah May once she had set a course to somewhere inconvenient, a standard referee's device.

'What for?'

'If *UB* or the citizens' militia find this lot here then it's up for all of us, not just the idiots.'

He took it and blew three short, piercing blasts There was a deathly silence in the courtyard and then, as Fischer and Kuhn stood back against opposite walls, a rush of bodies all trying to be somewhere else, quickly. The old ones were the last out; Fischer held up a hand to reassure those who seemed closest to an aneurism.

'Please, we've just heard that some militia may be coming, but there's plenty of time yet. Don't worry, and mind yourselves.'

Obediently, they slowed and shuffled out without pushing. An old lady, recognizing the responsible authority, took Fischer's sleeve.

'Excuse me. Weren't they going to serve soup after the talk?'

'No, mother, not today. Earl?'

Kuhn's eyes went up to the archway's curved ceiling. He put a hand into a pocket and removed two pieces of *zwieback* - treats for his flatmate - and held them out to the old lady. She stared for a moment and sniffed. 'With these teeth? You can't be serious!'

She shuffled on, morosely. Kuhn pulled a face at her back. 'If they'd been sugared I'd have lost fingers, probably.'

'The elderly have a right to be miserable.'

'Don't they! A friend got a note to me from Aunt Wilhelmina, to say she's safely with her sister in Munich. She tells me to thank you for what you did. The rest is the terrible weather, the awful food, the German girls who whore themselves to the Amis, how she misses home, and on, and on, and on. I don't believe she's ever been happier.'

They returned to Fischer's apartment. Beulah May had relieved herself generously on the floor and made a bed of the ragged torn sofa, which, on other days, hosted his tiny collection of books. Half the library lay in dog piss, fermenting gently. For a moment Fischer thought he spotted a condom in the middle of a dry patch, but a closer look reassured him that it was the skin of the pea-sausage he'd intended to have for this and the next evenings' suppers.

Kuhn glanced down ruefully. 'She likes *erbsenwurst*. After any sort of meat it's her favourite. You shouldn't leave food around.'

'I didn't *leave* it anywhere. It was pillaged!'

'Yes, well. Come on, darling.'

When they were gone Fischer spent some time cleaning the mess and then took to the sofa with what remained of his bottle of preferred nourishment. Grief and the dullness that came with it had been blurring things, but he was beginning to see what was wrong with his situation. He was relying upon other people for everything - introductions, information, his personal safety even - that once he'd have had a grip upon. There was no part of what he was about to do that he could verify independently, anticipate or avoid. A child walking into the school gates for the first time would have been no less helpless or trusting to the goodwill of others to make it through to the closing bell. There was no sure footing here, no support to the rear.

This put him in an excellent mood, one that a half bottle of raw Romanian brandy couldn't begin to dent. To torture himself further he recovered Marie-Therese's bag from the bedroom and emptied it on to the sofa, pretending that his search for evidence began here. He knew perfectly well what he would notice first, and being proved correct didn't lessen the pain. They were her only pair of silk pants, always worn to the job but never afterwards when alien fluids filled her and might leave an indelible stain. They were neatly folded still; she had been coming home to him, unbearably used, her sex uncovered to the cold, when she died.

There was also an old brooch (her grandmother's), two condoms, the thirty roubles that Zarubin had demanded he count and sign for, a pill box, toothbrush and a small bottle containing clear fluid that Fischer was almost certain was a mild disinfectant. For a moment he didn't recognize the final item. It was old, worn almost to a nondescript state, and in a woman's purse or bag so expected an object that his attention had almost passed over it. He held it up to the light, and his sense of pained boredom evaporated. It was a hollow brass button, slightly more than a centimetre in diameter, with an almost invisible motif in its centre - a five-point star, enclosing a hammer and sickle.

Zarubin or one of his lackeys must have seen the thing yet they hadn't removed it, a palpable clue. Even it were an innocent memento that Marie-Therese had kept to recall one of her nicer fucks, wouldn't their instincts have told them that no suspicion at all was better than a faint one? Or - and this made no sense at all - had they *put* it there? If they suspected a Russian culprit he would have been chased or ignored by his own people, not gifted to a German amateur. And if they *didn't* suspect one of their own, why plant the thing? This wasn't an oversight, or something of no consequence; Fischer was reasonably certain that only officers in the Red Army wore embossed tunic buttons; that those of lower ranks were plain. It shouldn't have been there, he shouldn't have seen it. Therefore, he was being worked.

And then there were the two larger *whys*. The first was of no consequence to him. There had always been any number of reasons why a man would kill an attractive woman; it only concerned him that the thing had been done and to her, not whatever motive had moved the bastard. The other *why* was the important matter. Why did a Russian General – someone whose soul, if it was mirrored by the face, was harder than Siberian bedrock - want this resolved? In Fischer's experience even cultured, recognizably human general officers reserved their maudlin moments for old battles and older school songs, and held women in slightly less regard than they did their favourite adjutants. He wasn't even sure he'd been given the correct story - Zarubin might have translated faithfully or offered an entirely different version to the one that had left the old man's lips. If uncle or nephew really had some sort of resolution in mind, it was either to cover their arses or kick someone else's. At least, that's what the bottle was telling Fischer, and bad brandy rarely lied.

After an hour of this mental twitching he felt more exhausted, more vulnerable, than he could recall. He replaced everything except the button and her silk pants, put the latter beneath the pillow on her side of his now too-large bed and lay down. The light had faded almost to dusk; there had been no electricity in the building for three weeks now and the cold had a wet, bone-penetrating quality that added ten years to the way a body felt. He pulled the tattered eiderdown over his body, closing his eyes against a bad day and his mind against the worse that would be tomorrow.

## 16

The orphaned girl - Erika - came to keep company with Monika most days now. She had nothing to say of course, but she seemed content enough to sit upon the window seat and listen to stories of Bernhagen in the old days while they knitted new pieces from unravelled clothing. Mostly, Monika spoke of her own family, but on two occasions she tentatively introduced a fond anecdote about Erika's parents to coax out a reaction. If there was any she didn't see it; the girl's head stayed down both times, her frown unwavering upon the needles, a quiet, endless non-tune vibrating between her lips.

They made mittens and scarves (Erika applied herself to the latter, her skills not extending much beyond terminating one line and starting another), which they exchanged for food. Though the language barrier kept them from mixing much, not all the Polish families who had come to the village treated their German neighbours badly, and some were willing to trade their surplus potatoes, cabbages and seed for useful commodities. This had ignited something of a crafts renaissance among the original inhabitants, who set themselves to darning, knitting, whittling, shoeing (horse and man) and generally odd-jobbing their way through the lean months in the hope that summer might bring some unforeseeable change in fortune. Strangely, no one complained about being obliged to follow these almost menial pursuits. After weeks of anxiety, inaction and pointless speculation about the future, busyness that had any sort of real purpose was a tonic for their shredded morale.

Bernhagen was gradually filling with immigrants. No Germans had yet been forced to abandon their homes, though they lived in fewer dwellings now. Without anything being said, extended families had returned to their nests, to keep warm more cheaply and effectively and to make sure that their siblings, children, nephews or nieces weren't eating better than they. Monika had no family so she lived alone still, and resisted the occasional offer to share with someone who doubtless would be less tidy or organized than she. Even so, she enjoyed Erika's visits, her silent company. It warmed her, took her mind from what was coming, and sometimes made her feel that she was doing a very little to keep the girl in this world.

Few Germans passed through the village from elsewhere, so there was no news or rumours of when the ordained exodus would begin. Some Bernhageners comforted themselves that the longer it was postponed the less likely it was to happen at all. But even as they said it there was the look, the nervous *shy* about broaching the subject at all, as if to do so would bring it on. Two villagers who spoke Polish tried to find out if the newcomers knew any more than they, but all they got for their efforts were shrugs. Great men had spoken, but no one seemed to know how or when their wishes would be put into motion.

As the weeks passed fewer armed men came through Bernhagen, and those that did contented themselves now with a gruff, inconsiderate manner towards the German villagers. There were no more assaults, much less the thefts, rapes and worse that stained the first few weeks of the defeat. One of the villagers, a pious man, suggested that they might hold a service of thanksgiving for this blessing, but he was silenced quickly by several very good reasons why this was a bad idea. They had no pastor, no music, no way of knowing whether they had reached a permanently happier state or a brief pause, a calm between prevailing tempests, and to pretend otherwise was almost certainly going to bring bad luck. Monika, whose nature was calm and forgiving usually, asked him sharply whether he had information that God was done testing Germans as he had the Israelites, and if so, why hadn't he thought to share it with them? She regretted it afterwards, but with one fearful eye upon all their horizons she quite forgot to apologize.

When winter's frosts eased a little, the few remaining German farmers went to see their Polish colleagues to discuss how the land would be apportioned for crops. Some of the newcomers wanted to take everything for themselves, but the wiser ones resisted; they were too few as yet to work the all fields without help, and a man who knew the land intimately was worth three younger, stronger men. So after some argument in was decided that, for this year only, Poles and Germans would work together and share the produce. It was a hopeful sign to many of Bernhagen's native residents that old enmities could be put aside for the common good, but others (including Monika) weren't so sure. In this new world, a German had little redress if someone decided to break an agreement once the hard work had been done. Everyone knew the stories of folk being herded out of Stettin the previous summer, ordinary men and women with no experience of farming, to dig out a harvest that they hadn't been allowed to share. Why should it be different in little Bernhagen?

It preyed upon Monika's conscience that she had become one of the village's foremost pessimists - a certain, sure harbour for anyone wanting the worst possible view of things. She found it perverse that, as her old body refused to be bowed or beaten by the privations that had carried off much stronger, younger folk, her mind had pushed out all hope and anticipation of better times and shut the door upon them. She couldn't say why it had happened. Perhaps the prospect of little Erika, knitting every day in her window seat, kept war's cruelties too clearly recalled. Or was it the toll of her self-imposed duty of recording every death and disappearance of the folk she had grown up and old with, the lengthening list of names, birth and death dates in the back of the psalm book that had passed down the generations of her family since the first years of the German Reformation, her personal testament to the ending of Bernhagen? Whatever the cause, she felt more and more detached from the blessings that she had known formerly, as if they had passed not just into memory but history itself, never to be recovered.

So when some of the German villagers began to take refuge in the old days she joined them, hoping to reawaken some sense of comfort from familiar things. They met in the school hall on warmer evenings and talked about their families - not those recently passed away but their ancestors, as far back as each of them could recall. Amon Stemper, who had been a librarian in Swinemünde between the wars and so had access to local records, could speak confidently of his kin's arrival in the area during the Great Elector's reign. This ignited much rueful discussion on the treacheries of Prussia's so-called allies (particularly the French) and gave everyone a pleasant glow of shared injustice. Another villager, Ellie Bontecou, became very excited as Amon spoke and left the hall abruptly. She returned with a book in which was pressed an ancient passport, acknowledging that her great-great-great-great grandfather, Louis Fabian Bontecou, was a good Protestant fleeing persecution in France and authorising him to settle and conduct his bootmaker's trade in the Electorate. It was dated June 1687.

To folk whose sense of their roots had been slipping badly for months now, these were wonderful comforts. Others spoke of more recent arrivals, farming families arriving from the west after the *Fürstenbund*, or during the *Vormärz*, or even after the 1870 war; but no one looked down upon his neighbour for being a callow *arriviste*, or sat upon his or her own, more ancient lineage. Everything offered was taken gratefully, to be added to the shared store of belonging.

Monika said nothing about her own family until the evening she was asked to speak, and then it was impossible to resist. She had hoped that she would be overlooked, a silent witness rather than a participant; but of all people it was Erika who waved a hand when a contribution was requested and then pointed triumphantly to her knitting companion.

Accepting the inevitable, Monika whispered to Erika, asking her to bring her psalm book to the hall. This was so like the prelude to Ellie Bontecou's surprise that a ripple of excitement passed around their small group. While the girl was on her errand, Monika told them that she had a fairly good knowledge of her family back to the days of Frederick William III, but only a single piece of information regarding older times. The way she said it, offhandedly, deflated expectations a little, and by the time that Erika returned there was a sort of murmur in the hall that hinted at attentions wandering.

Monika took her psalm book and held open the frontispiece. It stated that it had been printed at the sign of the Red Horse, Zurich, in 1529. Above it, an intricate woodcut depicted a pope with the head of a fox, besieged in his pulpit by a righteous crowd of Protestants, and, above that, a neat hand-written inscription: *Albert Pohlitz, Bernhagen, 1538.* This drew a gasp of amazement from all present except Monika herself and Erika (who had seen it already but didn't find it particularly interesting, she being very young and unburdened by all but the recent past). And then Monika turned the page, back from the frontispiece to the inner cover of the book. There, a sort of mirror to her forlorn list of the village's recent dead at the book's end, was a faded, roughly written genealogy of the Pohlitz-Ehlke, Ehlke-Maronn and Maronn-Bröcker families prior to the sixteenth-century. The very top entry noted the marriage of Abel Maronn to Mathilde Bröcker, sanctified by a priest at Stettin 'in the year that German rights came to the city.'

Each of the villagers in the hall took the book and read this list in turn. Most were impressed by the detail but a little unsure of what it meant. When it was Amon Stemper's turn he peered at the book closely, the old script, the archaic language, and then he looked up, astonished.

'But ... that was the year Twelve Hundred and Thirty-Seven.'

Monika held her sinful pride firmly in check and nodded. 'The Duke Barnim, before Bernhagen was ever here.'

They all stared at her mutely, reverently, and suddenly she wished she had stayed at home that evening. It wasn't in her nature to seek attention, much less to lay claim to any pre-eminence, and now they were regarding her not so much as a fellow-villager as the village's soul made flesh. She took back her psalm book and shrugged.

'I don't know when my family came to Bernhagen. Perhaps they were farming here as it was built, or moved from Stettin much later. No one can say.'

Ellie Bontecou had been squinting at the ceiling, her lips moving slightly, but now she spoke in a hushed voice. 'Seven hundred and nine years!'

The rest of them bowed their heads as if a Catholic priest had raised a host, and Monika, seeing where this was going, groaned quietly to herself. Whatever was coming - a mass evacuation, more trouble from armed gangs, a plague of in-growing toenails - they would now ask her opinion, her advice upon what they should do. It was what Bernhageners had always done, to identify a figure of moral authority and cling to him or her for dear life. For years it had been their pastor, until he decided to walk away from everything at the start of 1945 (the rumour was that he had fled west to relations in Hesse, but no one had heard anything since). Then, in turn, their self-proclaimed experts had filled the role, but expertise usually comes to older men, and none had lasted long enough to make his mark as a prophet. As one of the few educated villagers alive still, Amon Stemper had been the latest idol raised from the clay, and now, as Monika looked at him, she was certain she could see relief as well as awe in his face as he considered the prospect of relinquishing his unwanted eminence.

'Monika?'

One of the younger women, a war widow who was struggling and failing to fill her husband's boots around their farm, raised a finger respectfully.

'What is it, Margret?'

'Do you think it will happen?'

There it was, her first engagement as seer, as she hadn't even been given a chance to leave the hall. She opened her mouth with nothing yet in mind to fill it, and before she could think of a vaguely reassuring form of words Erika was on her feet, her own mouth open, struggling to recall how words were formed.

'Monika says that Germans are finished here, and they'd all better get used to it.'

## 17

He was up before light and bathed in water that required cracking. When his fingers regained some feeling he put on his shirt, tie and Grossmann, and checked the result in the bedroom mirror. Even with the waist of his trousers taken in there was little about the suit that suggested it had been made for a man of his reduced physique. He decided that it made him look vaguely American, of a particular fashion he had always regarded as faintly ridiculous (no doubt Kuhn would think it a sharp look). At least his wounds helped, as if stamping a certificate that explained the hollowness.

He was about to leave when a wave of dizziness blurred his vision, and he had to steady himself against a table until it passed. After a moment's struggle with his inner fool he stumbled to the bedroom and extracted a single pack from his precious horde of *eiserne* portions. It was an effort to open it, as much for the loss it represented as the strength of the oiled paper seal.

There was no label to identify the contents of the 200-gram tin of pressed meat, but he would have taken pot luck on the prospect of one of Beulah May's cousins. It opened easily, untainted, the contents immediately identifiable as *labkaus*, corned beef. To his wasted palate it was ambrosia, and his intention of rationing it across two meals dissolved. He ate everything, wiping the fat crust from the corners of the can with a finger and smearing it on to the four rye crackers that comprised the remainder of his soldier's emergency ration. Whatever nutrition it held could hardly have penetrated his stomach wall in so short a time, but a warm core was spreading filigrees out into his numbed body before the last mouthful was consumed.

He washed his hands under the water pump in the courtyard and went out on to Carla-Strasse to await his visitor at the edge of a pavement. It was an iron day, carrying a standard ration of cold; everything was grey, uniform cloud-cover daubing a new coat of it upon the existing shades. With no human movement visible it might have been a still from a film reel depicting a vast turn-of-the-century slum clearance plan, half started and then cancelled for want of sufficient vision, or cash, or enthusiasm. It made him wonder why he'd become stubborn about *here* and not Montevideo or Capri.

He was still thinking about warmth and sand when Achym Mazur came to a clumsy halt in front of him. The Pole was powering the front end of a Gitane in-tandem bicycle, and dressed for it even to the floppy flat cap and scarf. He gave Fischer's summer suit a doubtful glance.

'God, it's cold! You don't mind?'

Fischer gazed, equally doubtfully, at the rear saddle he was expected to occupy. While he had as yet no great sentimental fondness for his Grossmann it had been expensive, and he was fairly certain that its creator hadn't envisaged cycle sports. Naively, he'd assumed that a mobster would care for his image sufficiently to have run to the cost of a motorcar.

His expression must have said the same thing. Mazur shrugged. 'Fuel, Hauptman. The Russians don't care to share it, not at a sane price. In any case, it's mostly downhill on the way there.'

About halfway during their hurtle towards Stettin's centre, Fischer realised how clever Mazur's strategy was. One couldn't ask questions or gauge a face for a reaction on a bicycle - in fact, the experience removed all desire to do either. He clung on grimly, comforted only by the likelihood that the pilot would die at least a half-moment before his passenger should one of Stettin's many potholes or bomb craters leap out in front of them.

Thankfully, the brakes were well maintained, and Mazur

applied them sensibly, in good time and not too severely. Their careen slowed to a cruise as they entered Paraden-Platz, and much to Fischer's relief they came to a halt in front of the former General Landschaft Bank without need of legs flung out as extemporary anchors. He climbed off immediately and tried to stretch some feeling back into his groin.

'Your contact works here?'

Mazur parked their mount carefully against the monumental stone pediment and placed a red-bordered Cyrillic notice in the front basket.

'First floor, the relocation office  - a grand title for a fucking calamity.'

'The Getting Poles In and Throwing Germans Out Department?'

'Yeah. The problem is, most decent Poles don't want to come and the Germans don't want to go.' Mazur grinned. 'And the Poles they *do* persuade to make the effort take one look at the Poles already here ...' he slapped his chest, ' ... and fuck smartly off, back to where they came from.'

"It's hardly easier for Germans.'

'No, and it won't be. An empty Szczecin, or one crawling with head lice like me, is better than the slightest hint of old Stettin. This can't be western Poland if you *schwabs* are still here, can it?' Mazur took his arm. 'The hair, by the way - it's a good idea.'

When he'd wakened that morning, and before he could think too much about it, Fischer had taken Earl Kuhn's advice and shaved his head. It wasn't a great loss; since his minor *contretemps* with burning aviation fuel the right side had been able to grow no more than a few irregular patches, which the healthy part only made more notable. And Kuhn was right - he didn't look German anymore. Now, he was just an anonymous Middle European whose luck extended only to his fine tailoring.

They entered the former bank. It appeared currently to be an asylum, a holding area for extremely fraught temperaments. He didn't know whether this was typical of Polish office culture generally or the aftermath of a demonic visitation. Everyone appeared to be shouting - at each other, into telephones, at God and His Works, the walls - and the quantity of loose paper in free motion reminded him of the Reich's last days, the burning time. He deeply appreciated the confusion. It almost guaranteed that he wouldn't be noticed.

One man paused to draw breath when Mazur stepped in front of him. They shook hands and something passed from one to the other. A nod sent them on, through the bustle and into an inner hallway with two flights of stairs, left and right, disappearing upward.

Only one obvious thing was missing. 'Don't they have guards?'

'To guard *what*, the filing system they don't have yet?'

On the first floor noise was muted somewhat by the panels between individual offices, but still Fischer was reminded of a divisional headquarters only now learning of a previous day's withdrawal. He followed Mazur's confident path towards the further end of a corridor, all the while conscious of the growing distance between himself and the safer outdoors. The Pole stopped at a door, gave it a shave-and-a-haircut knock and strode in as he would into his grandmother's kitchen. Fischer remained in the corridor, the remaining few hairs on his neck trying to stand to attention.

The conversation was in Polish, and hardly audible above the general buzz. It had a quality of urgency, or at least *stress*, that surprised him. He'd prepared himself for abuse, or amusement, and certainly failure; he hadn't imagined that any Pole in Stettin would regard the matter as something to get worked up about.

Mazur emerged from the office and waved Fischer in. He managed to whisper something by way of forewarning. It sounded like *displacement officer*, but was framed almost as a question and he couldn't be sure.

The only chair in the room was occupied by a middle-aged man, a bland presence in a similar suit who probably would have been rendered invisible by the day's grey light were he out of doors. The face was regular, unmemorable, neither pleasingly ugly nor handsome, more a template than something that mirrored the soul. Fischer had a *kripo*'s habit of forming first impressions, but it was difficult here. In a crowd of three this fellow would disappear.

Comrade Template looked up from papers on his desk. A slightly querulous expression made the blandness untidy momentarily, as if it were responding to a slug that had unexpectedly oozed between naked toes. To Fischer it seemed counterfeit, rehearsed.

'This is the man?'

An unnecessary question, posed entirely for effect. Why would a Pole speak in German to ask something of fellow Pole otherwise?

'Who else would it be?' Mazur put some weariness into it, to let his friend know that the desk didn't impress him.

'I don't like Germans.'

'Who does?'

'So I don't see why I should need to speak to one.'

'You *know* why. Don't tease.'

Fischer felt a sudden affinity with the room's wallpaper. Perhaps he needn't have attended until the proprieties of communicating with a fascist had been resolved. He yawned, noisily, and didn't trouble to cover his mouth. Grey eyes regarded him peevishly.

'What does he want, then?'

'*He* wants information on criminals,' said Fischer. 'Polish criminals, in Szczecin.

'This is the Relocation Office, not the Police Praesidium.'

'Poles who come to this town for legitimate reasons must apply to you people, yes?'

'The honest ones ...'

'And if anything bad then happens to these nice folk they go to Augusta-Strasse - sorry, to *ulica Malapolska* - to talk to a policeman. Only there aren't any. You have what, a hundred, to keep this town in order? So they come away disappointed. Who else do they know to speak to *officially* here? Probably only the nice men who directed them to an empty German apartment on the very day they arrived. That would be you, I think.'

Template grimaced slightly. 'I don't speak to the ...' he looked enquiringly at Mazur.

'Public?'

'Yes. My job is to help arrange the transformation of this historic Polish City, not concern myself with the raw matter.'

'Of course. But if one of your people hears bad stories I expect you get to know about it?'

'Possibly.'

Well, that's all I want. To know whether the good Poles have been saying things about bad ones.'

'I find it distasteful that you should have any concern about Poles, no matter what their crimes. But I suppose … what sort of *things*?'

'Anyone who's been attacking women, hurting or molesting them.'

'Other than theft, it's probably the most prevalent crime.'

'I imagine so. But the more violent cases would be notable, wouldn't they? Particularly the ones that don't involve robbery also.'

That raised a smirk. 'But this is a German woman you're concerned about, surely? As I understand it, many Poles regard their bodies as reparations.'

Furious, Fischer glanced at Mazur, who wore a betraying quality of innocence. 'That's true, yes. But she wasn't *just* a German woman, otherwise I wouldn't be doing this. I can't say much more, but I doubt that her nationality got her killed. It's to everyone's advantage if we can find the man or men who did it.'

'Where did it happen?

'In the Soviet Control Zone, near the kaserne.'

'Well, then, no Pole would be there, it's restricted. You're looking for a Russian - a Tartar, probably. Everyone knows those beasts will do anything to anyone.'

'It's possible, yes. But even Tartars aren't permitted to wander the streets alone after dark. This is Poland, and Red Army personnel are subject to military discipline now that permission to rape and pillage freely has been rescinded.'

'A German, then.' The Pole smirked. 'I *know* you bastards

are good at murder.'

'How many male Germans remain here? And with the strength still to be a menace? Again, it's a possibility, but not likely. On the other hand this town is full of Polish males, many of whom came here looking for trouble or a quick profit. You can make a guess at the odds, surely?'

There was a long pause. Some papers on the desk suddenly became very interesting. Fischer waited for the routine to play out.

A sigh. 'Very well. I've been told that it's better to get this thing resolved quickly, so ...'

Fischer lifted a finger, as a schoolboy might when he didn't quite get something. 'May I ask who said that?'

The Pole looked blankly at him. 'The Russians, of course.'

'Which of them?'

'I don't know. Ask *him*.'

Fischer glanced at Mazur once more, and saw only mild indifference. The young man didn't seem to be capable of embarrassment. Fischer nodded at Template.

'Thank you for your help, sir.'

## 18

Out on Paraden-Platz (now *aleja Niepoleglosci*, according to a hand-daubed sign nearby), Mazur passed a small tin of pilchards to Fischer, who pocketed it without thanks. The young man's face was open; he was slightly puzzled, as if required to explain a prevalence of rain in March. 'Of *course* I told the Russians. I do business with them. If I can't trust most of the Poles in this town, who else would I keep sweet?'

'Was it Zarubin?'

'I don't know. Is that his name? Tall guy, too smooth and pretty to be regular Army?'

'You went to him?'

Mazur laughed. 'I don't do that. Being in the Control Zone isn't good for trade or teeth. He found me.'

Fischer wasn't aware of having been followed since his visit to the General's office, but that meant little. Perhaps it had been Earl Kuhn, offered no sort of choice. He wasn't sure if it mattered either way, but it added to his sense of being dragged along.

'Who was that? The displacement fellow?'

'My good mate Piotr.'

'He didn't seem like a friend.'

'He's a swine, but I don't discriminate with customers.'

'Cigarettes?'

'He doesn't smoke.'

'He can't eat much. Alcohol then?'

'I don't believe so.'

'What else do you have that he'd want?'

Mazur tapped his nose and then began to untie the chain that held his in-tandem to the General Landschaft building. 'Piotr has unusual tastes. They got him into a lot of trouble before the war, apparently. But who am I to judge? I just supply the product.'

'You're a pimp!'

The young Pole's face was comic-hurt. 'I've *never* done that sort of thing! Running girls is trouble, trouble, trouble. You've got to keep them sweet, fight off the competition, pay for rents and doctors' fees and still not mind being called a louse every day. Why would I put myself through that? Product is best when it doesn't have a mouth or temper.'

'So what does he want?'

Mazur glanced around quickly to confirm that no ears were handy. 'Little boys. Specifically, little boys with no clothes on, either alone or being friendly with what look to be fond uncles.'

'Pornography?'

'Is that what they call it?'

'Where on earth do you find the stuff?'

'An ex-policeman needs to ask? Perversion's always big business. The war got in the way for a while but the supply's still there.' Mazur's eyes lit up. 'Most of it's German, naturally. You'd be surprised how many of the uncles start off in a nice black or brown uniform before getting down to it. Hell, perhaps it's the military memorabilia that Piotr's really interested in. Either way, he could hardly refuse when I asked the favour. We Poles have strong views about cocks not being pushed up our sons. Do you want a lift home?'

'No thank you. The suit ...'

'Fine. Try not to open your mouth until Zabelsdorf.'

Fischer watched until Mazur disappeared into the thin traffic at the foot of what had been Kaiser-Wilhelm-Strasse. The urge to return to the relative comfort of his apartment almost overcame his intention to make a first survey of the crime scene, but the *locus in quo* was a straight line to the south, too convenient to put off. The problem – his problem - was the *locus* itself. Marie-Therese had been found on Berg-Strasse, just too far into the Soviet Control Zone for a German (even a German in a nice French suit) to wander unchallenged. Zarubin had pointed him at this business without supplying any sort of authority to pass unhindered, and his single experience of a Soviet prison cell didn't leave him keen for more.

At the corner of Albrecht-Strasse two women were selling apples. They looked to be poor, bruised things (the apples too), but no one complained about quality anymore. Fischer crossed the road to the makeshift stall, pointed at one of the two boxes holding the produce and asked the price. They didn't speak German, but recognised it at once. One of the women pulled her face and waved him away as she might a fly. He took his precious roll of dollars from his pocket, peeled off a five and offered it, sweeping a hand to indicate that he wanted an entire box. Her eyes widened. The other woman snatched the note and held it closely to her face for a moment before jabbering something that sounded much too eager to be a negotiation. He took a chance and picked up his purchase. They both smiled at him, the way that seems safest when confronted by a dangerous lunatic.

He cradled the box in one arm and continued southwards. There was little human traffic on this once-major thoroughfare, and it thinned further as he approached the Control Zone. He crossed no obvious boundary and saw no guards, but the Polish presence seemed suddenly to have melted away like *succubi* before a crucifix. He walked slowly but confidently, taking care not to glance around, trying to give an impression of a man who knew exactly where he was going.

He made it to Berg-Strasse without meeting a single Russian soldier. To his left, the wall of the former kaserne loomed; to his right, a lower wall without a single opening ran the entire length of the block. He couldn't recall having been this way during his *kripo* days, but nothing about the visible stonework hinted at recent alterations or additions. Even the bombs and artillery had managed to miss this short stretch.

He took a second, longer look. A thought had only just made a start on surfacing when a shout, far too close to his ear not to terrify him, put an end to the day's manoeuvres. Before he could turn around a boot had done its best to pass through his arse and a hand slapped his head with damaging force. He jabbered something, tried to smile stupidly. There were three of them, though thankfully only one was scowling in the regulation Red Army manner. The other two pushed him playfully between them, almost dislodging his apples. He offered the box, said the same word, *puzhalsta* - please - over and over, and almost let the relief show when one of them snatched it from him. His recompense was another kick, but he'd expected that. When the shove came he took it gratefully and ran, comically, with little steps. Their jeers followed him almost a block up Linden-Strasse.

The thought caught up with him when he slowed, and if it had been any business other than this he might have felt at least a small sense of satisfaction. But every time he tried to work it out, to put himself into it as any good *kripo* would, he saw only her face passing from life to death, and that killed any urge to congratulate himself. Still, at least he knew something now. Wherever Marie-Therese had died, it hadn't been on Berg-Strasse.

19

Piotr Sasala stared at his office door for almost half an hour after his unwelcome guests departed. The interview hadn't gone at all as he had hoped. A supplicant German should have been entertainment, an excellent opportunity to rub its nose in the New Order's brown end. But the expected deference, the self-debasement, hadn't occurred. Worse, his supposed friend Achym Mazur had acted like it was the occupation still and played the blue-police stooge to his fucking *kripo* master. It was upsetting, and Piotr most decidedly didn't enjoy being upset.

He had no choice in the matter, obviously. His balls were in Mazur's tight grip, and the friendly way he'd been assured that there was no question a certain secret would ever come out had been quite terrifying. In just two days, a pleasantly discreet, cash-based arrangement had mutated into a whip and dog-collar affair, and Piotr was in no doubt as to who wore the latter. His only comfort was that neither of them would survive a loose mouth.

He tried to be calm, to think about what to do next. It didn't seem to be dangerous to give the *schwab* what he wanted, if that was all it was going to be. He had lied, of course; everyone in the building had heard the stories - how could they have avoided them when people came here, begging in loud voices for something to be done as if this office were some sort of kommandatur? It surely wouldn't be any trouble to speak to a few of his colleagues and collect their experiences. He could pass on the information quickly and forget about it, if they let him - if they didn't continue to dangle his *interests* like a sword above his head.

Piotr could never harm a child. He was quite certain about that. In fact, the thought of a physical act involving himself and another human being of any age or sex was quite repulsive to him. But the depiction of it, between a young boy and an older man particularly, quite overwhelmed his senses. He didn't need a psychoanalyst to tell him that this was the tainted legacy of his own experience as a child; that no matter how distressing the recollection of his older cousin's games their mark lay deeply upon him still. It was why, as the memories had faded to something less visceral, he had found the need to freshen them at a remove.

He wasn't stupid. He knew that to chase his needs would put him into the hands of the wrong people, make him vulnerable. Perhaps if the times had been more settled he wouldn't dared have embark upon such a dangerous course. But in a world in which the obscene acts of men were stacked in piles waiting to be disarmed, dismantled and scattered, his own, modest needs had seemed inconsequential - invisible, almost. He wanted only to observe, not to participate. Really, what was his crime?

It was an effort to quell the familiar sense of injustice. *The Russians have demanded that this happen*, he told himself. Well, that was what Achym had said, so it could be the truth or a lie - either way, it wasn't the kind of thing you tossed a coin about. Like every other good Pole, Piotr wanted the Red Army removed as soon as possible so that they could get on with building their nation. They had all taken the measure of Comrade Josef, who pretended fraternal love but found any number of ways to twist an agreement, to postpone an arrangement, to slide the knife into his friends as readily as he would a rabid dog. It was going to take patience and forbearance; with idiot Home Army hold-outs threatening to carry on their resistance from the forests it was necessary that no one further offend the Russians while they were here. As an official and a good communist, Piotr had a regrettable duty of compliance.

It was just a pity about the timing. In two weeks' time there would have been no 'investigation', because by then no Germans would have remained in Szczecin.

## 20

Senior Lieutenant Sergei Aleksandrovich Zarubin's stare addressed itself to the wall of the office, and then to the pistol on his desk. It passed between them every few minutes, swapping views without appreciating either, lost to a third, unseen object - himself. He was wondering whether he was capable of following through a thing that required a degree of iron, and his audit was inconclusive. When circumstances required he could be as stern or pitiless as the next fellow at 2nd Directorate NKGB, but on the whole he felt more comfortable when not arresting, interrogating or executing enemies of the state. Naturally, he didn't make a point of advertising this, but he wondered sometimes if some subtle manifestation of his better nature had suggested the wrong sort of virtues to his superiors and throttled his prospects for promotion. Certainly, he'd never been one for shouting prescribed Party slogans when putting bullets into the backs of heads.

He suspected that the NKGB's ideal type was a hybrid of himself and his uncle, a composite creature having more brains than a stoat yet retaining the beast's cheerful ferocity. It probably existed somewhere, though he'd never met it. As with most other Soviet institutions one could never discern a recruitment strategy, an effort to find a single sort of right man. He'd known dolts and adepts share the same offices, fools and wise men the same tables in committee, thugs and academics the same front-line responsibility for preserving the Revolution. His own place in all of this was as hard to make out now as it had been on the day in January 1939 when his transfer from Signals Corps had been authorized. Since then he had worked hard, and well, and progressed very little. Some of his fellow virgins from that time, men whose abilities could be measured in millimetres, now occupied far loftier perches than him in the People's Commissariat for State Security and took considerable pleasure in observing the fact on occasions when their company couldn't be avoided. His lips had never found the right arses, for sure.

*Never mind.*

He stared once more at the wall opposite, a structure that was doing its best to stir his resentment. It was painted the same shade of dull green that had raced ahead of him since his schooldays, waiting upon every vertical surface to lower his spirits, to help him contemplate his career and where it wasn't going. He'd speculated that there was a single, vast factory somewhere that churned it out, its order books comfortably maintained by what appeared to be a universally drab bureaucratic taste. There was no logic to its popularity that he could see; it neither improved bare plaster, calmed the spirits nor enhanced whatever furniture one tried to conceal it with. And it was hell to remove blood stains from.

He allowed himself a sigh, the day's full ration. He *wanted* to have the sort of consistently remorseless nature that attracted the right sort of attention - to be NKGB's version of Blokhin, perhaps, or even Beria (though without the monster's taste for little girls). Career paths in his business were definitely best cleared with limitless energy, a gun and a handy talent for making absurd accusations stick. But an inconvenient part of him couldn't overlook the truth – that it was all absurd posturing, a lie, an ordained process understood by victim and executioner alike. They were required to be actors upon a butcher's stage, and he had no natural talent for it.

He found it easier to remind himself that life just wasn't just. The Deserving often didn't deserve what they got or get what they deserved; fairness and mortality didn't mix in water or anything else. The immovability of this truth was comforting, and it had allowed his persisting lieutenancy not to be a constant needle in the groin. He envied few men their better fortune, and didn't even jibe at his present lack of resources (a single secretary and a driver, when some 6,000 Soviet military personnel were presently encamped in and around Stettin, doing very little) or his ill-defined mission to subvert subversives in what appeared to be Poland's new colon while most of the rest of NKGB and NKVD were colluding enthusiastically – and profitably - in the stripping-out of Germany. There were worse things, if not places, to be.

He was almost grateful to his new employee for illustrating the point so graphically. Whatever God or Fate Otto Fischer had offended, the price had been cruelly overpaid. Zarubin seen similar wounds before of course - who could be present at a massed tank battle and not have? But Fischer was a corpse that moved still, that carried the same hopeful anticipation of future days as everyone else. *Poor bastard* had been Zarubin's initial, uncharacteristic reaction when the apartment door opened, and only strong self-discipline had kept his regulation bored expression in place. The physical damage was one thing the file had missed, or overlooked. Still, he was glad he'd read it through carefully before introducing himself. One wouldn't have put the career with that face, or half-face.

It was going to be - it already *was* - a gamble, and Sergei Aleksandrovich Zarubin wasn't a gambling man usually. On the available evidence Fischer might be good enough to carry through this thing, and that wasn't necessarily the point of it. On the other hand he might blunder badly and wake the beast, and that would be very bad, worse – perhaps - than success. There was too much that might go wrong for Zarubin not to be nervous, not to feel as if he were waltzing across a minefield on borrowed legs. But Stettin, or Szczecin, had at least one sublime quality - it was a wild place, disassembled and formless, emptied yet full of opportunities, where a degree of boldness might at a stroke re-propel an intelligent young man's prospects for advancement. The serendipity of the thought cheered him slightly. He was, after all, employing what appeared to be the ultimate resurrection to make it happen.

## 21

Two days after his visit to the relocation office, Fischer lost his home and was displaced from Stettin. At dawn the militia came to Haydn-Strasse and emptied three full blocks of their remaining Germans, who were allowed a full fifteen minutes to pack their meagre personal belongings (but not furniture) before being herded to Scheune Station. Without hurrying, Fischer collected his worldly estate - eighty-five American dollars, a deceased prostitute's handbag and sixty-four *eiserne* rations – and placed it in an old kitbag before putting himself among his fellow ex-tenants on the pavement outside. For a further ten, unscheduled minutes three old women surrounded a Polish militiaman and distracted him at some length with their opinion of the situation. Then they all learned to shuffle almost in step.

A locomotive with eight carriages was waiting for them at Scheune. There was no trouble, no further arguments; a sense of resignation hung like a pall above the expellees, who queued where they were told to queue, mutely took their allocation of bread and water and boarded silently when the whistles blew. Fischer grabbed half a seat for himself in the middle of the train and leaned his head against the window, to give it a chance to catch up with events.

The rail line crossed the new international border about eight kilometres west of the town, just south of what used to be the village of Köstin. For the moment the checkpoint consisted of a hut on the Polish side (the Germans were understandably less enthusiastic about recognizing it as a border) to shelter the solitary guard who monitored traffic, usually with little more than a nod to the drivers as they passed by. Today, however, the train slowed and halted a few metres from Germany in a stand-off with a tree-truck, braced by piled stonework, lying across and blocking the line. Behind it, three civilians, a makeshift *orpo* (he wore an armband, no uniform) and a Russian officer waited, all but the last with folded arms.

Fischer couldn't overhear the conversation that gradually heated over the next half-hour, but he imagined it had something to do with notifications and egregious surprises. Several times, one party or the other made supplications to the Russian, whose brief appeared to comprise whatever a shrug could convey. As the ambient temperature rose also, the atmosphere in the carriages slowly became restive. Cat-calls and jeers interrupted the conference, which itself had degenerated into half-shouted statements of intent. Eventually, a truckload of *orpo* reinforcements arrived on the German side of the border and deployed across the track, raising the potential for a brawl to that of an *incident*. The final blow to Szczecin Town Council's master plan was a light rain shower which allowed the militiamen to re-board the train for consultations without seeming entirely craven. Hurriedly, they considered alterative crossing points, were disabused about each by the driver, and then threw in the towel. By midday the exodus had reversed itself to Scheune, where the passengers dispersed without more hindrance than an occasional, desultory kick and went off to check whether they had homes still.

Fischer wasn't one of the lucky ones. Already, every floor of his former apartment building was full of chattering Polish families, busily laying claim to the largest rooms and best views. A glance told him that these weren't the tough, lawless sorts who had flooded into Stettin almost before the surrender; they seemed ordinary, decent folk - easterners, probably, refugees from Ukraine who had grasped a second chance, a cherry from the turd of their lives to date. He had had no intention of arguing his claims, but seeing them order their new situation with such desperate energy made him realise just how much of his own was now slung over his shoulder. He withdrew quietly, still unnoticed, and went to give Earl Kuhn the good news.

Schwartzkopff-Strasse lay outside the first day's clearance zone. A few of its German residents were on the street, whispering to each other, digesting the news about the expulsions. Fischer excused himself to two who blocked the top of the stairs that descended to Kuhn's cellar and watched them move away hurriedly when Beulah May's best killer voice challenged the rap on its door. Kuhn opened it a fraction and then widely. He was wearing badly-holed underpants and a pair of socks beneath an open bathrobe.

He listened to Fischer's report without interrupting, yawning at the kettle as he filled it. If he was worried by the prospect of his own removal it didn't show.

'You've just experienced the problem.'

'Which one?'

'They want all Germans out of Stettin but no one's yet volunteered to take us. Shoving us over the border to Mecklenburg would be easiest, but it's just about full to the brim with refugees already, and the Russians want rid of those too. There's the port of course, but loading folk on to a ship and casting them adrift is against at least some of that international law the new Polish Government want recognition from. What's left is to line us up against a wall, and they can't do that either. They need to bribe the right parties to take us, but the parties don't exist yet.'

'They could just not feed us, not give us access to what enters the town. In a few months typhus or scurvy will have done for everyone.'

Kuhn shrugged. 'But they're impatient. Besides, disease doesn't mind which nation it buggers, does it? We're a problem, alright.'

Fischer rubbed the hard bone of Beulah May's forehead. 'It took almost a century to get the Slavs out of Stettin, did you know that?'

'When?'

'The twelfth I think, or thirteenth.'

'Well then I wouldn't, would I? Coffee?'

Fischer drank slowly, trying to find the best way to raise a difficult matter. Before he reached the dregs Kuhn put down his own cup, scratched his balls ostentatiously and sighed.

'You'd better stay here for now.'

'Thanks, Earl. I can pay the rent in dollars.'

'Nah. You can wash up, I hate doing that. And complaining about the music is forbidden, right?'

'Fine.'

'We'll get you a mattress. I've only got the two, and Beulah May's not going to give up hers for free.'

Fischer suppressed a shudder. He had no desire to test the theory that human and dog parasites were entirely different species. She probably felt the same way.

'I'm wondering if it was a coincidence.'

'What?'

'Yesterday I had Mazur pressure a Pole in the town's administration to help find a potential murderer, perhaps another Pole. Today they did their best to expel everyone in my building.'

Kuhn shook his head. 'It was just shitty luck. That's their other problem - they don't know who we are, can't place German names to properties. The town's *volkscartei* records went up the day before Third Panzer Army withdrew.'

'I didn't know that. The Praesidium doesn't seem badly damaged.'

'A Pioneer squad organized a bonfire on Behr-Negendank-Strasse just before the Reds took the town. I was one of three passers-by they pressed into helping them. Two hours of hard manual labour, up to my arse in other folks' business, and then I got a pack of cigarettes and instructions to fuck off smartly. I've thought a lot about it since, how strange it was.'

'What?'

'The Reich turning up with kerosene, inviting me to make myself invisible.'

If it had been another day Fischer might have laughed. Kuhn offered him a Lucky Strike. 'So what will you do now?'

'I'll wait for Mazur's friend to get me some names. After that, I don't know. It depends on who the names are.'

'They won't be anyone the Poles mind losing.'

'No, probably not.'

'So it could be a waste of time.'

'Almost certainly. But then the Russians will have to let go of it.'

'I wonder why they're bothering at all?'

Fischer scratched the fur cliff in front of him. 'It's the only thing that's keeping me interested. Why does *anyone* care? Germans in this town have been dying like mayflies for the past year. Those that haven't are being shovelled on to boats and trains, or they're stumbling westwards without bothering anyone. So what is it about a whore - a German whore - that's giving the Russians such an itch?'

Kuhn looked as if he didn't want to say it. 'Love? Someone fell for her?'

'I know, it's possible. But wouldn't a man in love take on the business himself, rather than leave it to her boyfriend? Wouldn't *he* want revenge?'

A low, threatening rumble rose from Beulah May's gut as shadow passed momentarily across the only one of the cellar's three high-set windows that wasn't boarded. The old iron gate at the top of the outside steps groaned. Fischer grabbed a handful of neck while Kuhn went to the door. He opened it a few centimetres only and kept it there, so it was obvious that the visitor was a Pole. The whispered conversation lasted perhaps two minutes. Fischer didn't catch a word of it over the noise of the canine motor idling under his hand, but Kuhn was smiling slightly when he closed the door.

'Business?'

'Yep, wholesale. They're having a football match!'

'Who?'

'A Red Army eleven and the new locals, an exhibition match to demonstrate their fraternal feelings. Just down the road, at Nemitz Sportsplatz.'

'Cigarettes?'

'God, yes. You can't have a game without a wracking chorus from the terraces. I'll get a couple of lads to help. We could clear my entire stock in ninety minutes.'

'Why have they given it to you?'

'Supply, probably. Achym's sells everything he gets to the Straights at Town Hall, so he couldn't manage the extra business. He'll get ten percent of what I take and put it around that I'm not to be bothered.' Kuhn shrugged. 'It's sweet.'

'A bit too close for comfort.' The sportplatz was less than a half-kilometre from Kuhn's cellar. If the Polish side got hammered it might be very bad news for the local residents.

'It's going to happen sooner or later. At least we have warning of this one.'

'When?

'In five days. They were going to do it tomorrow, but Wladislaw says the Ivans are bringing in some guy from Vienna, a sergeant who used to play for Spartak.'

'What do the Americans call that?'

Kuhn grinned. 'A ringer. There must be money moving on the result.'

'Not much of a ringer, if the Poles know already.'

'Yeah, well, they're probably scouring Poland right now, trying to find Kuchar and get him back into kit.'

'Who?'

Kuhn looked disappointed. 'Only superman, a God. Weren't you interested in the game, Otto?'

'I used to work for 'Soccer' Felix Linnemann. What do you think?'

They ate before dusk, so that the cellar wouldn't need to advertise its stock through a lit window. Fischer offered his *eiserne* portions but Kuhn waved them away and produced four of his own. He opened them, reserved the beef ones for himself and his new lodger and mashed the two horsemeat portions into their biscuits for Beulah May. He put her bowl into the cellar's far corner and almost sprinted back to the table

'You'd better get yours down before she's finished. She begs like a fucking *zigi*.'

Fischer obeyed but hardly tasted it this time. It had been necessary - prudent - to mislead Earl Kuhn. The day's upheavals had taken his mind from it, but there was something else that interested him about Marie-Therese's death. If it was just a killing, a casual murder, why had she then been moved - and to a place where the killer might have expected to be discovered while executing the manoeuvre?

Kuhn belched, sighed and threw his cigarettes on to the table. Having finished her supper and checked the table for seconds, Beulah May was scratching at the door and turning hopefully every few swipes to check whether the hint was being taken. Fischer watched her until he realised that he was on the end of more than one meaningful stare.

'She only needs to go as far as it takes to squeeze out a good shit. You don't mind?'

Later, Fischer discovered that he minded very much. Gripping the broad end of her jazz tie he took her as far as Nemitz cemetery, trusting to the probability that even the town's worst Polish elements wouldn't hang around several thousand departed Germans. In one of the eastern sections he allowed himself to be dragged on a course that would have evaded the *Scharnhorst* as Beulah May checked for dog-piss telegrams. A particularly violent twitch pulled him all the way over to a grave in a section that almost entirely lacked headstones. An old woman lay across it, as dead as what lay beneath. He switched on his borrowed torch and examined the scene in a moment before returning to the safer dark. From the evidence of the small wooden cross upon which one of her hands rested he surmised that she was Frau Gartner, wife of Hans, who had gone to his eternal reward on 2 October 1936, aged 77 years.

*Lucky man*, thought Fischer - unlike his spouse, whose skin, even several days dead, bore the wafer-like brand of severe malnutrition. Unless the cold got her first it would have been a cruel, lingering death, the sort that lays on every reminder of what dying is. He experienced a sudden, profoundly sincere wish that she'd gone west, packed whatever she had owned still and fled before winter set in. The town's new rulers, delighted to have one less Stettiner on their hands, probably would have sent an official to pay the fare to Lübeck and help her on to the train, had she asked. But Hans was here, not there, departed from all things except her heart.

It went against every instinct to leave her decomposing on that moist plot, but Fischer couldn't think of anything he might have done that wouldn't have seemed a further desecration.

## 22

Achym Mazur didn't often think about life. As much as it shoved him in the one direction the view to the front was always opaque. Experience had taught him nothing; it was hindsight dressed as wisdom, bruises disguised as marks of understanding. He'd given up trying to see any plan, much less to tweak it. If life was a river's flow (as his mother used to say) it was best to let go of the oars, settle back and hope for nothing jagged beneath the waterline.

So on occasions when someone started a conversation with *if life has taught me anything ...* he tended to walk away, or change the subject quickly, or tell them not to talk out of their fundament. If they were friends or customers he made the concession and pretended to be joking when he said it, but that was as polite as he was prepared to be. If your own life couldn't teach you anything, what was the point of being uplifted by someone else's delusions?

But sometimes - today, for example - it wasn't sensible to do anything but stand quietly, attentively even, while your intelligence was being abused. It seemed to be something about seizing the moment, or turning adversity into advantage, or not letting opportunities slide, or ... he struggled to keep the appropriate expression on his face (a polite smile and raised eyebrows) while the stuff washed over him. That it was delivered in a deadly monotone didn't make the ordeal easier to bear, or that the font of wisdom was a frog-eyed apparatchik whose sense of his own importance was only slightly less than that of a certain Austrian gentleman, recently deceased and much missed by some German folk hereabouts. But there was gold buried somewhere in this drivel, so Achym kept the face where it was and wished a salt-bath upon his tormentor's haemorrhoids.

He became aware suddenly of a pause, and he hoped he hadn't missed its start, hadn't been smiling at nothing for more than a moment or two. A faint memory of an upward note lingered, which hinted at a question. There was only one plausible technique for dealing with this sort of thing, and he glanced quickly at his watch. 'Was that twelve o'clock?'

Frog-Eyes blinked, an unattractive sight. 'I didn't hear anything.'

'Oh, sorry. You were saying?'

'I asked whether you wanted it, and if you could handle it.'

'Yes, and probably. But tell me more.'

Achym admired the speed of his thinking. He'd left just enough doubt there to encourage the bastard to walk away if *it* turned out to be stolen munitions or ladies' underwear. The first would put him into competition with too many crazy men; the other simply didn't have a market anymore. Or *yet*, he couldn't say.

'I'm responsible for all purchases by the Administration. We contract with the Russians, who control the supply of course. But their stock control is very poor, and often we don't get what we order. One suspects corruption, naturally, but it may be mere incompetence, or sloppy handling. The thing is, while they never do anything about it, they don't challenge our claims either.'

'So you could tell them they've short-changed you even if they haven't. And then keep the difference.'

That got a smug little smile. 'Exactly. But I can't deal with this on my own. We'll need quite a few reliable men. It isn't exactly like diverting diamonds, is it?'

'And you're offering ...?'

'Ten percent. After all, it's my risk ...'

'Forty. It's mine too, if I'm caught. And I expect it's my pocket that's going to be paying for the labour?'

'It will only be *manual* labour. You need pay very little.'

'Not if the goods are hot. Reliable men, as you put it, are just the sort who can smell a deal a kilometre away, and they won't settle for a pat on the back. If you can't manage forty, I won't be doing it. Sorry.'

The familiar puzzlement spread slowly across the fat face. He'd had it all worked out beforehand, a clever little racket that stupid, greedy Achym Mazur would be eager to get in on upon set terms. But like all amateurs he'd commenced with what he wanted from it and then worked the logic to fit.

'But it's as good as gold! Everyone needs it, the winter being what it is, and stocks are never going to be adequate, not with the Russians taking most of it for themselves.'

*Coal.* Achym relaxed a little. It wasn't something he'd ever dealt in, but the bastard was right, it was a must-have product. The new Poland had inherited almost all of Silesia's vast coalfields, but the infrastructure was smashed, and a lot of what they were managing to get out of the ground was being requisitioned as war reparations (a case of Poland getting the shop and the Soviets the sweets). Anyone who diverted part of the supply wouldn't have to worry about finding a market for it. Of course, it would risk putting both the town's administration *and* the Ivans on his back, and Achym wished suddenly that he'd asked for fifty percent.

'Where would we grab it? The marshalling yards?'

The yards to the south of Szczecin's central rail station had been turned into a vast coal depot, the exit point for shipments to Konigsberg (or whatever the Russians were calling it these days). But they were solidly within the Control Zone, and Achym for one had no intention of tiptoeing into that wasps' nest with a coal sack over his shoulder.

'No, of course not, that would be suicide. But I'm not saying more until we have an arrangement. I'll go to twenty.'

'This isn't an Arab fucking *souq*. Forty, or no deal. Not thirty-six or thirty-eight. Forty.'

Frog-Eyes pretended to think about it, but Achym knew he was there already. The man didn't know any of the really bad types in town and didn't want to; he came to Pelzer-Strasse to buy cigarettes and the occasional leg of stolen pork, but that was as close to the underbelly as he'd dared tread. Achym was his only contact in a world in which a man's station above ground was at best an irrelevance, at worst an incitement. Finding the right partner for wrong stuff was tricky - make a bad choice and the only cut you'd take from the deal would be the sort that a doctor searched for between cold ribs.

'Alright, but you need to put up your share of the finance for the first load.' Frog-Eyes smirked. 'Forty percent, obviously.'

'For how much product?'

'Between two and three tonnes. Never more than that, we can't risk attention. But it's regular, every three weeks.'

There - the genius had told Achym not only the source of the coal but where they would be diverting it. The Ivans shipped out twice each week, the same two Russian freighters loaded to the deck-line, playing relay across the southern Baltic. But many of the river vessels bringing coal north to meet that rendezvous were Polish. There was one particular lighter, a Szczecin vessel that somehow had survived Allied bombs and Red Army artillery, which went south to Silesia and returned every three weeks. Achym knew this because he had a contact on board who brought him cheap *Bystrica* and *Detva* brand cigarettes, smuggled through

Wroclaw from Czechoslovakia. Frog Eyes was bribing someone - almost certainly the lighter's captain - and dressing it up as a patriotic reallocation of their nation's natural resources. It wouldn't be too difficult to put in at one of the many wharves along the Oder south of the town - probably at Gryfino - and extract a few tonnes while the crew fixed their eyes firmly on the river's opposite bank.

'How much do you need?'

'It depends. If we pay roubles or złotys, much more than if we had dollars.'

'And dollars?'

'A hundred would do it. So if you can get hold of forty …'

Achym didn't think to ask where this upright local official was going to find his share. No doubt the budget of some half-resurrected utility would be tweaked for a few days, the sleight hidden somewhere in the books. It wasn't so much the fact of it he despised as the self-righteous aura that hung over the trough. The new Poland was shaping up to be very much like the old, where business had been done principally with the finger, the nose and a tarpaulin-covered truck bearing official plates. At least Achym was honest about his chronic distaste for honesty.

'I can. When?'

'Two days. I'll let my man know.'

## 23

In a slightly damaged office in the spa quarter of
Swinemünde - *Świnoujście*, to most of its more recent inhabitants
- a military gentleman wrote a letter to an old friend. He had
received quite astonishing information anonymously and wasn't
sure if it could be trusted. If it was accurate he needed to be
involved; if not, it was important not to offend. So he began with
a few reminiscences of the times he and his friend had seen
together, the changes both wondrous and terrible that had
marked their lives. He was careful to play up their part in the
events he recounted, perhaps more so than memory told him was
accurate, but he wanted to put his correspondent in a good (or at
least amenable) mood before he came to the difficult point.

The meat of the matter he laid out frankly and concisely. He
was careful not to frame it either as a request or an ultimatum,
only to state what he believed to be the facts and then to put his
case regarding them, the part he saw himself playing, the piece he
hoped to take from the profits. He concluded with his sincere
good wishes for his friend's health and prospects, but when he
reread the letter he decided to begin again and omit this last
sentiment. It read too much like the sort of threat with which
they'd all become familiar.

When it was done he sealed the letter, placed it in the
official bag and then dismissed the business from his mind. The
last was easy, because he had much else to think about. His new
posting was a sensitive one, requiring a degree of tact that did not
come naturally to him. One could hardly blame the other party for
being bruised about how things had turned out, but hadn't it
always been this way in this place - too many claims for the land
to support, too many tribes calling it their promised home? No
doubt it would all turn again in time - time, and blood, were all

they had too much of.

So now he was a diplomat (of sorts)), a man whose job it was to explain realities in ways that wounded the least. It wasn't a comfortable task; for the past thirty years, seeing another point of view hadn't been in vogue much, and accommodating it - if only superficially - would have been close to heresy, a guaranteed ticket to a place where the notion could be kicked out of a head. If only his father had lived to see how things had changed - it would have made him laugh, or cry, to see the convolutions one went through to avoid rubbing noses in too much shit.

During the next few days he didn't think about the letter or its reception, and it was only when he received a reply that he was forced to consider what should come next. He read it through four times, trying to spot a mood, a subtle indication of what his friend was thinking (though subtlety hadn't ever been one of the man's vices); but the content was agreeable enough, with several droll references to the near-misses they'd had, the farm girls they'd violated, the villages they'd burned back when that sort of thing needed to be done. The matter itself was hardly mentioned, though the invitation spoke to it of course. It surprised him that his friend was making an effort to be discreet, but he liked the suggestion. It wasn't as though they could afford to be relaxed about this sort of business.

He replied immediately, agreeing to it. His excuse to his own people came to mind easily, and it was plausible - he was a liaison officer after all, and there were any number of people with whom he needed to liaise. He announced it with a shrug to show that it was a pain in the arse, but what could he do? They laughed, told him not to be too soft with the bastards, to hurry home as soon as possible.

He ordered a staff car and made sure that he got the Packard and his choice of driver - a former adjutant, faithful like a dog, who had done some things and seen much more. It felt like the old days, the two of them together, and they were both almost smiling as they departed the town, taking the Wolin Road, passing the bottle between them occasionally to give the car's heater a helping hand. The view added to the pleasure of it - the day itself, the neatly ordered fields and broad waterways, the slight otherness of foreign parts that gave a man a sense of being half out of himself. So his mood was already fine, when, at midday, they found a farmhouse just north of Goleniów (his map referred to it still as Gollnow), where they ate cabbage soup and black bread at a table under a tree and overpaid only a little for it. They sat too long there, talking about their wars, but he'd studied the rendezvous on his map and knew they wouldn't be late. It was an hour's journey at most, an easy drive down a good road. The most difficult part would be the final half kilometre.

But even that wasn't a problem. A clever fellow had hung a Red Army car pennant on a telegraph pole at the roadside, and they turned left there, into the woods. The Packard's suspension didn't like the rutted track, but another set of wheels had already smoothed out the worst of it. They came to a halt in a small clearing, a mini-cathedral created by overhanging branches, dappled by sunlight.

His friend was waiting, out of his car already, smoking – the usual shitty Mongolian weed, no doubt. He patted his driver's shoulder, told him to wait and climbed out. The ground was wet here and his boots were almost new, but it didn't bother him. In fact, he was a little pleased that he could demonstrate how, even after all this time and acquired layers of rank, he didn't care too much for appearances.

They embraced, and he knew immediately that he'd done a stupid thing, had pushed his way far too clumsily into a delicate matter. There was something stiff and matter-of-fact about the grip, as if it wanted both to hold him yet keep him a fraction away from the old intimacy, to make what needed to be done a little less difficult. He noticed for the first time that his friend's driver was out of the car, leaning casually against it but keeping the other vehicle front and centre in his vision. It was ridiculous, and he wanted to say something to convey that it was alright, that he understood perfectly, that it wasn't something to feel bad about. But when his friend released him and looked into his face he smiled as if it the words been said already. Forty years, you get to know a man.

He turned to his own driver and waved him away, back down the track. The man had probably worked it out for himself, because the car began to reverse almost immediately. He waited until it had disappeared and then turned back to his friend. He felt strong, clear-minded, almost in control.

'It's a beautiful day, Feodor. Let's walk a little.'

## 24

'You want me to *invest*?'

Mazur shrugged as if it was no great matter, but he looked uncomfortable.

'You'll be committing your cash for two, three days at most, and the return's going to be at least a hundred percent. You could use the money, surely?'

'No, absolutely not, and don't tell me anymore about it. I don't want someone with fists to be able to work it out of me, later.'

Fischer wondered how badly business was going, that Mazur needed to seek funds from the enemy. Or was he being clever, tapping a source that had no redress should the *opportunity* turn out to be a pig? Perhaps he was speaking to every German he could find before they were kicked out of Stettin - perhaps *this* was the opportunity, a final skimming of soon-to-be refugees' assets. He had no gold teeth, but he could feel them aching slightly in anticipation.

Mazur was breathing hard, thinking about what to try next. Fischer wagged a finger in his face.

'And don't *think*. I'm not going to say yes.'

'Ach! Look, this thing needs dollars, and you're the only guy I know in Szczecin with dollars. Can I buy them from you? I'll give you the commercial rate, plus ten percent.'

'In what, roubles? No thank you. Anyway, how the hell would you establish a rate? The Ivans print money like it's going out of fashion.'

'Ten for one! I'll give you ten for one!' Mazur hated haggling on the wrong end of a need; he had no feel for it, no face to hide what he was thinking.

'That might buy me as much bread as dollars would, but it wouldn't buy people, or influence.'

'Fuck your mother!'

This was the most enjoyment Fischer had tasted in the past week, and he almost wanted it to continue. But Mazur was useful to him, and no one whipped a good pony for no reason.

'I'll *lend* it to you, at ten percent. But you repay in dollars or sterling, in five days.'

Mazur thought it about for almost a fraction of a second. 'Good, definitely! You'll get forty-four dollars or ...' he closed his eyes, ' ... um ...'

'Never mind. I'll trust you.' Fischer pulled his bundle from a pocket and peeled off four ten-notes. The Pole took them with thumb and finger, reverently, and squinted closely. 'Aren't they beautiful? What number president was Hamilton?'

'I don't believe he ever *was* a president. He invented their money.'

'A holy man, then.' Mazur removed a leather wallet and inserted the bills as if they were communion wafers. 'Still, it's a pity. You'd have made a quick profit.'

'A very dirty one, no doubt.'

'Slightly soiled at most, Hauptmann. Would you like a drink?'

'Only if it damages liver tissue.'

They drank slivovitz from small crystal glasses. Mazur's 'office' remained largely unfurnished, but commodities had moved both in and out since Fischer had visited last. All the US PX rations had disappeared, their space beside the chimneypiece taken by military boots, dozens of pairs, kept with their partners by tied laces but piled haphazardly, like the aftermath of a battle that had gone very badly for one side. The fine dining table at which they sat was stacked with detergent cartons, a French brand, and a neat pyramid of tuna cans. It was all exactly what a disaster area like Stettin was going to need badly.

Mazur caught Fischer's glance as it took in the tuna. 'Would you ...?'

'No, thank you. When will your man Piotr be able to give me names?'

'It's only been two days. I'll squeeze him a little tomorrow, at least get him to give a date. What other enquiries are you making?'

'None. This is my first and only effort.'

'The Ivans won't like that. When they hold up a hoop they expect a man to jump.'

'I'll jump alright, probably to Lübeck on the next ship out of here. Let them follow me to the British Zone.'

Mazur pulled a sour face. 'Don't go *there*, Hauptmann, it's a bad place for Germans. Here, the Poles hate you, that's understandable enough; but a good, hard kick up the arse and most of them are satisfied. The Russians actually like you, even after all this recent shit - it's probably Karl Marx or Frederick the Great, but I think they want to *be* Germans, deep down. The British, they just despise you. They're very correct about it, naturally, but you'll be treated at as if you occupy the underside of a shoe, and Germans aren't used to that. A mate of mine, a kid on Rügen, he thought he'd be clever and get out before the Reds arrived. So he jumped a lift from fishermen all the way to

Fehmarn and surrendered to the Tommies. He wasn't beaten, starved, accused of anything or locked up for more than six weeks, but as soon as he could he headed back east again. He told me he'd been treated like a much-loved family turd.'

Fischer had stopped listening at Rügen, when something else snatched his attention. The last time he'd seen Mazur in that other world, a small boat had been carrying him off towards the island with ...

'How was it? Rügen, I mean.'

The Pole shrugged. 'We ate, didn't get mistreated. I found work on a gang rebuilding a beach bulwark. *She* cleaned hotel rooms that never saw a guest. It wasn't too bad. You did us a good turn.'

'Did she ever say anything about me?'

'Not a word.'

The way Mazur said it - too quickly, like he'd expected it and was looking forward to giving the news - was a slap to the face. At least Fischer could scratch an entry from the ledger, a debt he couldn't ever satisfy.

'What happened to her?'

'Before it ended she got news from home that her parents were dead, so she went west to try to find her brother. I wanted to go too - you know how I felt about her. But there are only so many times a guy can take that sick look before he gets the message. I haven't heard anything since. Don't worry, she'll be fine if she finds him. Rocket-scientist-resistance-heroes are always welcome somewhere, right?'

Fischer took it as a symptom of his emotional immaturity that even recalling her made him feel as though he were betraying the memory of Marie-Therese. He waited until Mazur had refilled his glass and then drained it in one go, stood up and nodded at the room's far corner.

'What does a pair of those boots cost?'

'To you? Nothing. Make sure you take a half-size too large, so you can wear two pairs of socks.'

It was the slivovitz or the casual solicitude acting upon the rest like a detonator, but Fischer felt a sudden, urgent need to run away, to hide and cry until his guts were emptied. He went over to the pile and took his time, his face safely toward the wall as he lifted and discarded the wrong sizes, keeping his mouth closed, trying to choke it off. Behind him, Mazur had picked up his trombone and was moving tentatively up and down a scale, a lugubrious, chastising noise. It didn't help.

The right pair came to hand, eventually. They were German-made, standard Wehrmacht issue. For a moment he was squeamish about their provenance, but the treads had nothing on their odometer, and as far as he knew even the Russians didn't strip boots from the men they herded into captivity.

Mazur put down the instrument carefully and poured two more glasses. 'You'll want this.'

It was a kind thought. Fischer let the fiery liquid catch in his throat, coughed and spluttered, giving his eyes an excuse for their redness. The Pole turned to the window, pretending not to notice.

'When I came here from Rügen I couldn't sleep for the first week. I thought it was nerves, or my being unfamiliar with the place. But really it was the strangeness in my head, trying to get used to the prospect of having initiative. I couldn't take *ordinary*, the fact that every day was going to come and go like the one before it without someone telling me what to do or else. It's fucking unsettling, choice.'

'Like parole?'

'Yeah. I suppose in your case it's much worse - you lost, and it's only half-over or half-started. Getting out of here, back to Germany, might not be a bad thing. At least you'd be sharing the shit.'

'My head says this *is* Germany still. That's part of what's wrong.'

'Well now you know how it is for Poles. We've had that feeling for so long it's passed in mothers' milk. Even this so-called victory's another kick up the arse. We get Pomerania and Silesia but, whoops, lose the East. It's always the way with Poland. If it isn't the fucking Swedes it's the fucking Austrians. If it isn't the fucking Austrians it's the fucking Germans. If it isn't the fucking Germans it's the fucking Russians. And if it isn't the fucking Russians - and it usually is - it's all the fuckers together.'

Fischer found it difficult to laugh and remain miserable. He told himself that he was one of a hundred million souls afflicted by the same foul luck; that Marie-Therese had seen it before him, the new world for which you braced yourself only a little and complained quietly; that he not only had a new, free pair of boots but also the option of putting them on and walking westward for just a few kilometres to where a German might find a future still. It was a choice, and not all choices were poisonous. He tugged at the laces, trying to loosen their tight knots.

'This wonderful investment - it's not boots, is it?'

Mazur laughed. 'In a demobilization market? I can hardly give them away.'

## 25

Piotr Sasala was becoming a worried man. He had lived with a degree of anxiety for years now, but that was only natural. Like anyone who feared exposure he hoped - expected - it would never happen, and so the threat only ever pressed unbearably in the sleepless early hours. But now he was drawing eyes to himself, inviting fingers to point.

He hadn't thought the business through. Imagining a question was much easier than putting it, particularly *this* question. The most likely answer was going to be *why do you ask?* and he could hardly say he was idly interested, or that he was conducting a survey into local criminal elements' preferred mode of killing women. It had to be plausible, enough to be dismissed from mind immediately.

His best idea was to claim that he had received word from the east that Szczecin was getting a bad reputation, that displacement officers were finding it hard to convince decent Poles to come here for fear of their lives and property. It had the advantage of being both the truth and difficult to verify. If challenged, he could always admit that the evidence was anecdotal, but that, with the Russians still apparently having half a mind to leave a mixed Polish-German population here, it would be mad not to remove any potential obstacles to clearing the town as quickly as possible. This struck him as a clever argument, one that obliged a patriotic fellow to tell what he knew. He rehearsed it silently, moulding it to a smooth credibility, to the point at which he'd be able to get it out easily, without stammering.

But it didn't work as he had hoped. He began with his more voluble colleagues, the sort who didn't need an excuse to empty their heads. But gossip wasn't going to be good enough for Mazur and the German, and hearing the same story told five wildly different ways was discouraging. So he decided to make it a *strategic* matter - to approach certain members of the administration whose concerns extended beyond the movement of paper around a desk - men who mixed with members of the Council and could drop hints of the effect that the town's lawless reputation was having upon their intentions for it. Again, this seemed to Piotr to be a very clever idea. If he was ignored he had risked nothing; but if it moved the Council to consider the situation his name would be remembered, and something worthwhile would have come out of this bothersome exercise.

It went terribly wrong. To begin with, the men he approached were so senior that the smooth, credible delivery failed him completely. Some of them demanded to know the precise sources of his information, and he was obliged to be evasive. Two of them were so immediately, eagerly interested that he knew they intended to snatch the business from him and put their names to it, and he hardly knew what to say. Most worrying were the openly hostile reactions, variations on *who the hell did he think he was* to be asking such a question? It dawned upon him then that the worst sort of Poles in this town might have bought some powerful friends who would be pleased to report back that a certain Piotr Sasala was sticking his pasty face into some very wrong places and should be strenuously discouraged. He cursed Achym Mazur for pushing him out of the trench like this.

It was a relief when Mayor's Zaremba's office contacted him and asked if he could make himself available for a meeting. It would give him a connection at least, perhaps provide a degree of safety by association. If they were dragging him to Town Hall only to tell him to stop his enquiries, he'd happily oblige and apologize for making trouble. There would be nothing that Mazur could say about that. Then again, perhaps they were impressed by his initiative and wanted him to pursue the matter officially. But he didn't allow himself to hope too hard. After how things had gone he no longer had the composure be optimistic about things.

Then he got the telephone call. Don't worry, he was told - it's an informal matter, just a chat about what he'd heard. That made him feel a little easier, even though he was going to have to make up whatever he said to them. At least it would be off his chest, and anyway, everyone knew that women weren't safe in Szczecin, not unless they went around accompanied by a man. It hardly mattered that so few of them were Polish (because of course so few Polish women had chosen to settle here as yet). Even a German had a right not to be molested. Well, officially.

So he forced himself to be cheerful, put on his best suit and went for the interview. It didn't last long. Afterwards, as he sat on the train for Poznań and his new, much less attractive job, trying desperately to think it through, to find some cause for hope about what was coming, he could hardly recall what had been said. All that remained in his head were the cold faces, the stark ultimatum and the expensive illustrated books that they'd found beneath his bed, brought to the office and spread out on the desk in front of him, their beautiful content despoiled by the hot coffee they slowly, deliberately poured on to them once he'd said yes, of course he'd go.

## 26

When Fischer returned to Schwartzkopff-Strasse, Beulah May was scratching the cellar door, whining to be let out. He took her down the street, let her douse the pavement and then returned the long way to stretch her legs, a circular route via Stoewer-Strasse. Earl Kuhn was waiting for them on the pavement outside their home, prone and bleeding.

It was difficult to examine the patient with the dog trying to climb on to them both, and muffled gasps discouraged a straight lift-and-over-the-shoulder. Fischer opened Kuhn's coat and pulled up a sweat-drenched shirt. The skin was soft, discoloured, already swelling.

Gently, he helped his landlord to his knees and then his feet, acting the crutch as they moved tectonically down the five steps to the cellar. The door was self-locking; the injured man leaned back against it and waved towards one of the darker corners. On the second attempt he managed a croak.

'Pecithin.'

Fischer found a medical kit stocked to support a trauma ward, opened a bottle and counted out five pills. Kuhn leaned painfully against the sink, sipping them down with water while Fischer lifted his shirt again and checked his back. There were no bruises here, which cheered him considerably. At least they hadn't gone for the kidneys.

The blood was from the nose only, and with a cloth they stemmed the flow in two minutes. Then it was a matter of removing Kuhn's clothes, which took longer than it would from a stiff corpse.

'It was the Nemitz boys.' Kuhn's voice was flat, nasal, as if pushed up from the gut. 'Bastards.'

'So it was just a kicking?'

'Yeah. Sorry to disappoint you.'

'You need a doctor.'

'I need a yacht, too. What are the chances? You'll have to strap me up.'

The fact that Kuhn had managed to enter the cellar upright probably meant that he had no serious internal injuries, but *probably* wasn't any sort of diagnosis. Fischer retrieved a bandage from the kit and wound it tightly around the purpling torso while its owner ran through a catalogue of noises.

The physician pinned his work and stood back. 'Now, breathe a few times. As deeply as you can.'

Kuhn did so, shallowly at first but them full gulps. There were no whistles or echoes.

'Now spit in the sink, four times at least.'

The first gob was bloody, the second slightly so. The rest was clear.

'Well, your lungs aren't punctured. What they've done to your liver we won't know until you shit.'

'Then I'll try not to shit. Get the brandy, will you?'

'That isn't a good idea.'

'Neither is life. Go on, Otto, be a good fellow. And light me a choker. And feed her if you would, because I can't bend down.'

While he was about his chores Fischer considered the possibilities. Kuhn appeared to be doing the same. He had managed to lower himself on to the sofa and was staring at the wall, anaesthetizing himself alternatively from left and right hands.

'Where did they do it?'

'At the allotments on Hermann-Strasse.'

'Is it this football business? Are you competition?'

Kuhn shook his head. 'They don't do cigarettes. With them it's extortion and theft mainly.'

'Have you ever dealt with them?'

'Only as a go-between for recoveries. I never asked anything for it.'

It didn't make sense. Even if they were the sort of Poles who wanted Germans out as quickly as possible, they'd need Kuhn to be the last man gone if he was acting as their agent.

'Were you robbed?'

'All I was carrying was that pack of Lucky Strikes. They didn't touch them.'

'Then this was a job. They did it for someone else.'

'Yep.'

'How many enemies do you have?'

Slowly, Kuhn laid down on the sofa, curled like a foetus. 'I don't. I get on with everyone and those I don't I keep well away from. I pay asking prices, sell at modest mark-ups and I haven't fucked anyone's wife or daughter. Not for a long time, anyway.'

'Could we bribe them to tell us who paid for it?'

'Dangerously unethical.'

'Beat it out of one of them?'

'Difficult. They hang together like bats.'

'It worries me that they'll do it again.'

'I don't think they will. I begged them to stop, and when they didn't I offered something.'

'What?'

'An address, an easy mark.'

Fischer suppressed the sour feeling in his gut. A man had no right to judge when he didn't know what he'd do in such a situation.

'Who's the unlucky man?'

Eyes closed, his face pressed against a half glass of brandy, Earl Kuhn grinned sleepily. 'Grossmann. And sons.'

27

'He's gone?'

Mazur nodded. 'Vanished. I spoke to three guys in his office. None of them have seen him since they went home the night before last, so I went to his apartment. It's locked up, but I got in through a window. I doubt there was ever much in there, but it's gone now.'

Fischer leaned on the low stone balustrade on Haken-Terrasse, looking down on the Oder. On the far side of Schlachterwiese a tug was pulling a Russian freighter out of its makeshift mooring on the Dunzig canal, probably another consignment of machine-tools pillaged from formerly German factories before the Poles could lay claim to them. A few seagulls circled above the vessels with doomed optimism. No one was throwing away edible things anymore. If a bird wanted to eat these days it was best to go straight for the eyes.

He'd walked here from Zabelsdorf with a tiny hope that there would be just enough news to put an end to his pretend investigation, but this was worse than being handed a strong lead. Earl Kuhn had been beaten up and Mazur's tame pervert Piotr expertly disappeared, the one within twenty-four hours of the other, and a fellow didn't need to be a mathematician to find the common denominator. He put his hand into a pocket and found the roll. 'I need a gun. Something small but useful.'

Mazur shrugged. 'No problem. Twenty dollars, I'll deduct it from what I owe you. A hundred rounds ok?'

'Yes. Has anyone threatened you? Said *anything* at all with a sideways look?'

'Not for more than a month, and that was a

misunderstanding about rent.' Mazur grinned. 'Our landlord wanted to pile it on, but as it happened Wojciech managed to negotiate a reduction.'

'How many men do you have?'

'None. We're a fraternal commune, not a hierarchy. But if someone came after me they'd have to speak to my fourteen brothers. Fifteen, if you count Wojciech as two.'

'Good. But watch yourself. Whatever this is it isn't insignificant, not with ...'

For a moment he'd been tempted to tell Mazur about the General and the real reason he was chasing Marie-Therese's killer. But if he offended *that* constituency a hundred bullets wouldn't be nearly enough.

The Pole seemed not to have noticed the slip. 'I think it's you who should be worried. The atmosphere in this town isn't good, but it's going to get a lot worse soon.'

'Why?'

'Did you know they've taken a census? A national one. It won't be published for a while, but a guy at Town Hall's been involved with the people and he's seen their data. He told me it shows a slight reduction in the number of Poles in Poland since 1939. Have a guess.'

'I really couldn't.'

'Ten to twelve million. A lot of them have migrated west or been caught in what used to be Poland but isn't anymore. But for the rest, about half the total, they only have one explanation. *This* you'll be able to guess.'

'Adolph.'

Mazur's finger made a gun and pointed at Fischer's heart.

'What makes the cream even more sour is that the same census counted over two million Germans here still, where they've no right to be, rubbing in the fact of it.'

No one needed an excuse for what had been done to Stettin's native population over the past year; but if someone wanted it to make it even uglier this was the perfect justification.

'And it isn't just you *schwabs* who are going to pick up the bill. The guy at Town Hall tells me there's a plan.'

'A plan?'

'I knew you'd be surprised. Plans aren't very Polish, are they? But it's been decided that new Poland's going to be very different than the old. He says we've been fools, tolerating minorities who've had loyalties to anything but their homeland. Every time we've gone to war or tried to fight off a partition we've had a clutch of ready-made fifth columns waiting to help the other bastards. So in future we're not going to have any - minorities, I mean. Obviously, there'll be plenty of bastards still.'

'Difficult to organize. We tried that, remember?'

'Yeah, well, you've already done the business with most of our Jews, but those that managed to hide it out are going to find that life hasn't got any better. It's the same with Ukrainians and Lithuanians - if they didn't fight for us in 1939 why the hell should we be nice to them now? And let's not even mention the few gypsies who evaded your boys, they won't even be head-counted as humans. Believe me, in a few years' time, we'll be as pure as you ever tried to make Germany.'

'The war's not over.'

'Shit, isn't it? Everyone congratulated themselves on how it was only Germans who were insane, that the rest of us were marching into a bright new world. But that brightness, it's nothing but detonations. Everyone's scrambling to repay old debts and grudges while they can, and when it's over we'll all still be whores, sucking either Cossack or American cock. Fuck them all, I'm off to New Zealand.'

'Would they have you?'

'Me? Not a hope. But they'd welcome Jerzy Tarnowski with a bouquet of roses. He fought in Spitfires, got wounded three times.'

'You bought his papers.'

'Very cheaply. His injuries have a taste for whisky, but he makes do with slivovitz.'

'When?'

''When I have enough to buy a sheep farm and hire a couple of hands to do the unpleasant bit. I'll sit on my veranda all day, drinking beer, watching them tend the flocks like I was *ziemianie*. I'll even have a knout to let them know who's boss.'

The tug had pulled the freighter almost as far as the northern tip of Schlachterwiese and into the Oder proper. Dispassionately, Fischer watched their progress, half hoping that the starboard correction wouldn't happen in time, that the freighter's prow would drive into the silt banks almost clogging the river at that point. But the pilot knew his business, and eased his charge expertly into the narrow dredged passage hard against the ruined railhead wharfs. A cheery toot from his horn rubbed in the fact-on-the-water - another load of war booty safely dispatched to Uncle Joe.

Mazur flicked his stub down the slope. 'I don't have any more pets in the town's administration. So this business you're on, I can't see what else I can do.'

Fischer couldn't see what anyone could do. He couldn't talk to the Russians, some of who (for reasons far beyond his understanding) wanted *this business* resolved. He certainly couldn't approach the town's fledgling police department, who wouldn't have a file on it anyway but would be happy to kick him for his impudence in raising the matter. He couldn't wander around Stettin questioning ordinary Poles because he didn't speak the language, and in any case so very few of them counted as ordinary in the accepted sense. Potentially, their women would give the most sympathetic ear to his story, but almost the only Polish women in the town were wives of army or police personnel, and he was fairly sure that he didn't want to offend the local military. So who remained? The vanishing German minority with whom Marie-Therese - a shunned whore - had never mixed, the semi-feral Polish gangsters that made even Mazur and his boys seem apostles of rectitude, and ...

'Jesus.'

'I definitely can't offer an introduction to *that* party.'

He'd been staring at it for days, something so familiar to him that it had been as invisible as the blood spots on his chest. He'd spent years down among them, trying to keep a peace that went against all natural law, getting beaten occasionally (once so badly that his balls had almost cleared the Oder in a clean arc), thrusting the iron fist of National Socialist justice under the noses of men who'd promptly blown them on it and invited him to proceed elsewhere, quickly.

Most of them must have died or fled, but he knew that the Russians were using some still as forced labour - they had no choice, with the river so damaged, full of wrecks, collapsed buildings and virgin silt. Who else knew it as they did?

'Mazur, do you deal with anyone who works in the docks or port? For the Ivans I mean?'

'Hauptmann, it's a remarkable coincidence that you should ask me that.'

## 28

Someone had given it a name - the Battle of Wussowerstrasse - though the blood could hardly have dried on its cobbles yet. No doubt the surviving Nemitz boys would think of something different, if they ever got around to commemorating it. Five of them had died in a terrific exchange of gunfire lasting less than thirty seconds, so *battle* was overstating it a little. But it was the first triumph of German Jews in - well, no one could quite say how long, so it was going to be remembered.

The victors had a single casualty, Herr Grossmann's youngest son Rafael, who took a bullet in the shoulder - a nice, clean, uncomplicated passage straight through and out the other side. Earl Kuhn brought his medical kit and fixed it nicely at no charge, though Grossmann felt that he owed the boy something already, he being the one to have warned them beforehand of a rumour regarding the Nemitz gang. But Kuhn wouldn't take money or even a suit for his trouble, so the old man shook his hand and silently scratched a new entry in his tiny list of human *goyim*.

Fischer heard the story from Kuhn, who hardly tried not to preen himself on the brilliant success of his strategy.

'The fucking idiots stood in the middle of the street, firing from the hip, cowboy-style. Old Grossmann and his boys put them down like ducks. They used scatterguns, hardly had to aim.'

'And you just happened to be close by, with your medical supplies?'

Kuhn grinned. 'I waited around the corner for five minutes after the last shot. Then it was *Oh my goodness, Herr Grossmann, I heard and came as quickly as I could!* You know what the best of this is?'

'That you didn't get the Grossmanns slaughtered?'

'Well, yes. But no, that half of Zabelsdorf's shouting them up as German heroes! The same pricks who used to swear they'd never known a Jew, they all crowded 'round, patting Grossmann on the back, making him blush with the stuff they were saying. He's their new Siegfried!'

Kuhn's own injuries made him wince as the belly strained his ribcage, but tears of laughter kept coming. 'It's a pity ... a pity the Führer's not here to hand the old man his Knight's Cross!'

As clever as the business had been, Fischer wondered if wasn't a bad mistake. The Poles at Town Hall would be as happy as Kuhn to hear of the Nemitz boys' fate, but they didn't see the gangs and the remaining Germans as being separate problems. Gun battles in broad daylight amounted to pebbles thrown against Zaremba's window, a spur to get his organized expulsion right next time. When Marie-Therese said that it was best to be like Jews in this place, she probably hadn't been thinking of the Grossmanns.

He didn't share his thoughts with Kuhn. The boy deserved a good day after the kicking he'd taken and before what he needed to hear.

'Earl, do you have any protection, apart from Beulah May?'

Kuhn's face fell. 'Why, what now?'

'I don't think the Nemitz gang came after you. It was a warning to me, through you. I don't know what it was about, and until I do I wouldn't want to bring it on again, or worse. In any case, I'll find somewhere else to sleep.'

'Don't do that, she'll miss you! Anyway, there are only three Nemitz boys breathing still, so they won't be a problem.'

'There are other gangs in Stettin who'll take money to do

this sort of thing.'

Kuhn sighed. 'I had a few mates, but they went west last year before the Ivans found out who they were and got around to shooting them.'

'What had they done?'

'It's what they believed in. They were Fourth Internationalists, the purest niggers of politics.'

'All of them?'

'Yeah, all six. They were probably one hundred percent of the surviving German sub-species. I was just a bourgeois fucker - that's what they told me - but they tolerated me for cigarettes' sake.'

'How did National Socialism miss them?'

'One was a farmer, the rest miners, so none were drafted. And they all made an effort not to talk politics until proletarian internationalism spreads further than Avenida Viena.'

'That may take time.'

'Well, they were pricks, but decent ones.'

'Weapons, then?'

Painfully, Kuhn got to his feet and shuffled to a pile of wooden boxes and crates that almost blocked the short hallway connecting the living area to the closet-with-a-sink he called a kitchen. 'Help me move these.'

The bottom crate was a standard *Heer* medium arms container. Kuhn lifted the lid and stood back, giving a clear view of three MP-40s, an StG44, an MG-42 and two Browning HPs. Apart from pure astonishment, Fischer felt a sudden pang that only two hours earlier he'd parted with twenty dollars for the battered

FN1910 that sat in his pocket, probably the one that had started its career ventilating Franz and Mrs Ferdinand.

'You have ammunition for these?'

Kuhn shrugged. 'Sure. About a minute's worth for the Bonesaw. For the rest, plenty.'

A minute's supply of ammunition for an MG-42 was at least twelve hundred rounds.

'What are you, the official Resistance?'

'It was an opportunity, that's all. The day Third Panzer Army withdrew they sent a squad to blow what was left of the Bahnhofsbrücke and block the river. When they parked their gear by the station ruins and crossed the road to do the business we just grabbed it and walked away. And then the lads got out of Stettin too quickly to take their share with them.'

'Christ, Earl, you can't be caught with an arsenal. They'll hang you from a wire and call it an anti-terrorist campaign.'

'I thought I might sell it all as a single lot, but the right buyer never came along. Don't worry; when I leave town for good I'll rig the cellar. No one's going to find anything.'

It was becoming an urban tradition for the less forgiving Stettiners - on the tragic day they were obliged to pack a suitcase and headed for Scheune, a few moments spent dousing their homes with kerosene lifted spirits considerably. What came next was a matter of personal taste; some struck a match immediately, others left it as a sort of housewarming present for the Polish family that would replace them.

'Anyway, you'd be wise to load one of those Brownings and keep it with you. It might save your ribs further grief.'

'I'll do that, Otto. But you'll stay, won't you? Until we all have to go?'

'I'll stay until *I* have to go. It may not be the same day.'

'Good.'

Kuhn seemed relieved. The town's Germans were short of a great number of commodities, but nothing so much as human company. They had become a colony of widows, orphans and recluses, their front doors the bulwark between semi-existence and a world that was moving somewhere without them. When you came to that state, hearing a voice other than the one in your head was as nourishing as bread.

The Grossmann shootout had distracted Fischer from the important business. 'I have a date tonight, Earl. You had no plans to dump that monster on me, I hope?'

'No. Can you tell me about it?'

'Not yet. I should be back within two days, so don't fire through the door when I knock. And for God's sake don't shout 'breakfast'.'

'Don't worry; she loves you enough to make me jealous. But if it's going to be dangerous you should take your own advice.'

Fischer removed the FN1910 from his pocket and held it out for inspection. Kuhn stared at the object, appalled. 'Christ! It doesn't matter where you point that thing, if you pull the trigger it'll kill you. Take one of mine, at least they were made in living memory.'

'I don't intend to use it.'

'Well, don't let the bad guy get a good look unless you intend to disarm with humour.'

'There shouldn't be any trouble, not tonight. It's business, a toe in the water. Do you have any roubles?'

'Yeah, lots. What do you want?'

'To bribe two or three fellows, possibly. No one important.'

Kuhn pushed his hand into the gap at the back of his sofa and withdrew a large roll of currency. 'Fifty should do it, then. Give me five dollars.'

It was too generous, but Fischer didn't argue. He did the swap, put on his new boots, his cap and overcoat and extracted an *eiserne* portion from his kitbag.

Kuhn seemed surprised. 'It's early, isn't it?' The clock on his wall (an old railways fixture, too large for its present setting) was a minute from three o'clock, and there was too much daylight still for the sort of business he was used to transacting.

'Not if I'm to get to Greifenhagen.'

'Why the hell would you go there?'

'To pick up sailors.'

## 29

'It's Lübeck.'

'Lübeck? I don't know anyone in Lübeck.'

'Where *is* Lübeck? Is it Germany still?'

'It's in Schleswig-Holstein. It's where those ships sank last year and all the poor people drowned.'

'So many ships sank last year. I don't recall.'

Amon Stemper cleared his throat. 'It was the leading Hanse town for centuries, a beautiful place.' He paused. 'It *was* a beautiful place. I heard a lecture there before the war, at the *rathaus*. The British run it now, of course.'

'Well, I don't want to go there. Can we refuse, do you think?'

'Certainly, if you don't mind being ignored, or worse.'

Most of Bernhagen's Germans had come to the school hall to talk about the notice, which had been delivered and pinned to the church door by two Poles who had arrived in a car and which, therefore, was understood to be official. So far, the discussion has consisted of a series of plaintive comments upon its injustice, none of which caused disagreement. No one wanted to begin the matter of what came next, but almost everyone who said something did so with one eye upon Monika Pohlitz as if to coax out an opinion - or, better, a pronouncement.

Monika had no idea what they expected of her. The notice was precise and admirably clear, allowing as much interpretation as a signpost listing a single destination (which it was, of course). The doubtful matter – though again, clearly stated - was *when*. It might be as early as 10 April or as late as 24 May, and if one chose to argue the merits or otherwise of a particular day between the two, well then. She wasn't going to offer an opinion because she had none; it was going to happen when the Poles in this state (or *voivodeship* as it was now) either decided or managed to arrange it, and nothing that an old lady thought about the business was going to influence their efforts. The only choice left to Bernhageners was how they would play their part.

They and other non-Poles in the district were required to assemble at the city of Stettin (graciously, the notice employed the German name, so as to prevent confusion) a week after receiving a definitive date for their departure to the west. A military detachment would arrive on the specified day, present its credentials and offer protection during the journey, but all other arrangements were the responsibility of the evacuees. From this, even the most obtuse villager had already deduced that, absent a fleet of motor coaches or the horses they had eaten since their return from the great trek of the previous year, a walking holiday was in prospect.

A few made complaints about this, until Monika reminded them that others had much further to come than they, and on worse roads than those that lay between Bernhagen and Stettin. They had eighty kilometres to walk at worst, and most of it upon a metalled surface. Their trek of the previous year had been four times that, there and back, and undertaken in the middle of air raids and other calamities. Don't complain, she told them, or God would give them good reason for it.

It was a fair censure and the more resented for it, but God and Monika Pohlitz together were more than the bravest soul dare take issue with. So attention turned to the general injustice of their situation, the cultural blight that must fall upon Pomerania with only Slavs to occupy it and the prospects of finding adequate means of living in Lübeck (or wherever they would finally come to rest). Someone whose cousin had been a merchant seaman between the wars spoke confidently of British decency and undoubted sense of fair play towards their German subjects, but it didn't need Monika to throw out *Hamburg* and *Dresden* to quash hopes in that respect. Whatever was coming couldn't be anticipated on the evidence of past times. Folk had been changed by the war - yes, even Germans - and not for the better. Perhaps the British would be gentler masters than the Russians (God knew, they could hardly be worse), but what reason had they to be decent, much less fair?

These reflections made everyone present very gloomy, until Amon Semper stood up to offer one of his inspiring talks, the sort he used to deliver twice or three times a year in that very hall, and usually on matters of civil engineering or the Scriptures. He pointed out that they all had had a terrible year, and for folk in a dolour it was natural to forget that the world would turn into light once more, eventually. It was true they were being evicted from their homeland and into a future without present promise. But he exhorted them to think of the Germans who had first come here all those centuries ago (at this he held out a hand, palm upwards, towards Monika) and the dangers they had faced then. At least Bernhageners were being sent to live among their own kind, Christian folk, who, even if they had little more than they needed themselves, would surely offer some comfort. And whatever the British had become, was it in their interests to accept so many refugees from the East if they weren't prepared to feed them? If that were their intention, wouldn't they just tell the Russians to keep everyone and let them die at home, in bed? It didn't make sense; it wouldn't happen. They might not find much in Lübeck, but they would find something

It was the most common sense anyone could recall hearing, and if it didn't quite cheer hearts it took the edge off sharper fears. Monika entertained a brief hope that Amon's performance – one that had contradicted her own, at least in spirit - would be enough for him to reclaim his village seer's crown; but when he sat down and the others had finished nodding approvingly they turned to her once more to hear what would or should come next. She was seven hundred and nine years old (or her blood line was, at least that, indisputably) and somehow she had cured little Erika's muteness. A minor thing like an exodus couldn't possibly be beyond her.

She rubbed her eyes and spoke without looking up. 'We'll talk to the Poles here, tell them we'll leave everything in good order in our houses if they can help us with food and clothing, especially shoes. Start thinking now about what to take with you. I mean, it should be as little but as useful as possible. We don't know whether we'll be travelling from Stettin by ship or rail, but in either case it shouldn't be more than two days' journey, so we should be concentrating most of all upon the walk from here to the port. Anything that isn't jewellery or photographs or letters will be too big to carry, so that's something else you might trade to the Poles. But don't go to them on your own. We should make a list of what we have and arrange a meeting, otherwise you might just be robbed. I'll think some more about this.'

Reverently, Monika's audience - her congregation - considered her words. A woman's hand rose at the back. 'What about our papers? Some of us lost them last year. Will they take us in if we don't have the proper documents?'

Amon Stemper spoke while Monika was considering this. 'Of course they will. How many millions of Germans don't have papers anymore?'

It was a good point, and it brought home to everyone (if they needed reminding) how different this new world was, a world in which a person could *be* someone still without his or her *volkscartei* data. It was both liberating and terrifying, a measure of how far they had passed into a sort of freedom or chaos.

Monika stood and leaned on Erika, her willing crutch, for support. 'How many of you know your birthdates?' she asked.

The murmur suggested that more or less everyone was comfortably certain of that event.

'Well then, the diocese should be able to find your register entries if they exist still. If they don't, Amon's right - the authorities will have to take your word and provide new papers, or admit that officially you don't exist. They can't do that, of course.'

'But what shall we do there? In Lübeck?'

It was a hundred questions masquerading as one, and no one noticed who had spoken because it had been at the front of all their minds. What would farmers, old people and children do in a strange, already overcrowded land where they would be accepted only reluctantly? Would there be work for those who could work, and help for those who could not? And in a place that wasn't really Germany anymore but a group of colonies administered by the Allies, would being a German count for much, even to other Germans? Who could they trust, other than their fellow Bernhageners?

Monika sighed. Whatever she told them might displace what their hearts told them already - that they were going to find destitution, or succour, or something between the two, and that no one could know which it was going to be. So she said what sensible seers always said at times of upheaval, of loss, of fears for whatever lay ahead. It was cowardly, but the burden she had taken up unwillingly was pressing far too heavily upon her old shoulders.

'God will provide.'

30

The Oder here was as Fischer recalled from better days, clean, broad and smooth, catching the best of the day's last light from the west. He breathed in the fresh, cold air deeply, trying to flush a year's worth of Stettin's corpse-foetor from his lungs. Old memories surfaced like eels chasing flies - the girls he had rowed on this stretch; the drunken bulls' outings on hired barges that resulted – miraculously – in no drownings; a picnic during a family holiday in 1920, his mother sat on the bank in her only decent frock, laughing helplessly at his father's impersonation of an Olympic swimmer, drowning.

The fat Pole in the leather coat wasn't happy and didn't care to hide it. He'd been glaring back and forth between Fischer and Mazur since they put off from Pommerensdorf almost an hour earlier, twitching to say something but kept polite by his proximity to the younger man's three large accomplices. Fischer assumed that he was the Plan and Mazur the Money, and that the elements weren't yet mixing in the correct proportions. A mildly amusing *frisson*, but it didn't interest him nearly as much as the miracle of blue water, green fields, no ruins.

The Pole's valve blew just south of Ferdinandstein. He leaned forward and hissed too loudly not to be overheard. *'Dlaczego on tu jest?'*

Mazur glanced at Fischer and shrugged. *'Nie martw się, to nie ma nic wspólnego z naszym biznesie.'*

'Tell him I'm nothing to do with your arrangement.'

One of the hard fellows in the boat laughed. 'There's a fucking echo,' he grunted in German.

Mazur had mentioned something of the deal (it could hardly

be kept secret if Fischer was going to be stood over them while they loaded coal). It sounded like a good thing if they managed to keep it quiet - a steady income flow with almost laudable motives if you took the view that it was Polish coal and not war booty. Of course, it would only reach Polish hearths at a price, but to Fischer (a member of a sub-species for whom coal and Fabergé eggs were equally obtainable) the injustice didn't seem too pitiable.

At a little before ten o'clock, lit only by a half-moon, they put it at Greifenhagen's northernmost wharf, a facility that Allied bombers had somehow overlooked. The coal lighter was moored there already, almost invisible against a backdrop of warehouses. Their boat's pilot exposed a lantern for a moment and then recovered it. The reply shone equally briefly from one of four portholes in the lighter's hull. They moored alongside her, almost hidden from the wharf by the height of her deck. Her name, badly scoured and faded, was *Beatrycze*.

Two heads appeared over the rail, reasonably distinct against the sky, and the end of a rope ladder fell into the boat, only just missing one of Mazur's men. He remained in the boat, holding fast upon it; the others climbed quickly. The Plan remained seated at the stern, nervously scanning the river and what he could see of the dock, no doubt wishing now that he'd delegated his role. Fischer grabbed the ladder and pulled himself clumsily up to the lighter's handrail. The big fellow who'd laughed earlier took a fistful of collar and dragged him easily over it.

'Quietly, *dupek*. Stop using your fucking knees.'

A pulley had been rigged on deck, directly above one of the hold's hatches. Mazur and the rest of his men were gathered around it, peering down. Beside them, a large, older man in a peacoat lit a cigarette and hissed something into the hold. Fischer glanced at the wharf, as nervous now as the Plan. He knew that the Russians had relinquished control of this stretch of the Oder to the Poles the previous month, but that didn't mean they'd left entirely, or that its new owners were completely incompetent.

The transfer began immediately. Already bagged, coal was hoisted to the deck and manhandled over the rail into the boat. It was a slower job than the lighter's crew might have made of it, but much quieter also. Mazur didn't dirty his own hands; he and the sailor stood against the dockside rail watching out for port police, and when Fischer was sure that everyone else was too busy to notice he joined them.

In Polish, Mazur introduced him and asked the question. At first the sailor (from the man's age and demeanour, Fischer was fairly sure he was the lighter's Captain) didn't understand, but then he went across to the hatch and called down quietly. A head appeared like a badger's from a sett, and the crewman joined them on deck.

'Miron.' A hint of a smile flashed in the dark, and the man gave a short, polite bow.

Mazur shook his hand and whispered '*Czy mówisz po niemucku*?'

'Very well, yes, for twenty years now. My wife is German.'

Fischer held out his own hand and introduced himself. The Pole didn't hesitate. 'What do you want, boss?'

'You work in the Soviet Control Zone at Ste ... Szczecin?'

'Couldn't unload coal there if I didn't.'

'No, of course not. There are Germans still, working there?'

'About fifty, maybe sixty. The assistant port manager and two pilots; the rest are dockers and rail-head loaders.'

I assume they're confined?'

'Yes, it's a shame. They live with their families, in old warehouses in Drzetowa - Bredow, you would say. They get fed enough and they have proper rooms for modesty, but it's still a prison and these are civilians.'

'But during the day they work outside? The pilots take boats up and down the river?'

'To the north, obviously. The port manager, I think he organizes the dredging. It's becoming urgent.'

'I want to be taken into the Control Zone. Ask your captain if he'll do it for fifty roubles. Or I can give him ten dollars American.'

Miron translated. 'He says twenty roubles and the ten dollars, and we'll put you right into the Vulcan yards. But you find your own way out.'

'Yes, good.'

The loading was finished. Silently, the boarders went over the side. Mazur was the last, pausing only to pass something to the captain, take a package from Miron and pat Fischer's shoulder. Ten seconds later the smugglers' boat cast off. They stood at the rail, crew and German stowaway, watching it drift slowly downstream until it disappeared beneath the opposite bank's tree line.

In the tiny cabin the captain lit a small lantern and almost dropped it when he got his first clear glimpse of Fischer's face.

'*Chrystus! Nie wychodzi na brzeg, aż Szczecinie.*'

Miron was staring too, horrified by the view. 'He says you must stay on the boat tonight. You don't mind?'

'It would be stupid not to. I'm not easily forgotten.'

'We go on shore now. I'll make you a bed.'

The cot was small but comfortable, and the gentle sway of the lighter's hull worked more effectively than a cosh. Fischer ate a piece of rye bread and was asleep within minutes of being abandoned. He passed the night hours in a near-coma, tormented by none of the dreams that had followed him since Marie-Therese's death. When he awoke it was almost dawn. There was movement on deck already, a low hum of conversation too distant for him to identify the language.

Miron brought down a sticky confection and a mug of something that smelled almost like coffee. The Pole's eyes were hollow, darkened by the pain of not being able to sleep off the previous night's damage. His breath was pure fermented plum, probably flammable still, and Fischer had to force himself not to recoil.

'When do we cast off?'

Miron burped and swallowed hard. 'Ten minutes ago. Five more and you can go on deck if you like. But when we drop down to Klucz you come inside and stay, ok?'

'Fine.'

It was a bright morning, the first in several days. For the next hour Fischer leaned on the rail, putting his face into the rising sun, feeling the same quiet euphoria as in the previous evening, the novelty of clean air and a world that had begun to forget war. He almost regretted that he was moving back into what was familiar; found it easier to imagine that Stettin lay on a different continent than just over their placid, bucolic horizon.

At ten he was invited to eat with the crew. There were seven of them; one nodded as he sat down, the others looked somewhere else or straight through him, uncurious or indifferent to their supercargo. Afterwards, he offered around his pack of Lucky Strikes and was relieved when no one made a point of refusing. The last thing he needed was a crewmate who despised Germans enough to betray him to the other great enemy.

At midday they docked on the western bank, next to

Stettin's marshalling yards. Fischer remained in the cabin, squatting on its floor while the cargo was unloaded. He'd worried that vessels entering the Control Zone would be searched or at least inspected, but no Russians boarded them. When the hold was emptied the captain went onshore to deal with the paperwork and returned with a bottle of vodka. He looked as relieved as his passenger felt.

'*Odbieramy stali teraz z doku Vulcan.*'

Fischer got the one word, which was enough. The captain stared at him for a moment, turned and shouted something. Miron entered the cabin, carrying one of the crew's heaving leathers that covered the shoulders and head, protecting the wearer against coal dust.

'You wear this when you go ashore, so no one gets to see your face. Don't worry, it's a common thing in the yards, they use them to carry steel also.'

'Steel?'

Miron shrugged. 'Of course. What you Germans are there for, to dismantle everything. We take some of it south now, to be re-smelted.'

A few days before the Red Army took Stettin, Fischer had been in Bredow searching for food and had seen what war had done to the Vulcan yards. The massive lattices that once had framed the great ships as they rose slowly upward from their keels had become a single, vast, twisted skeleton, fallen into and covering the pens - thousands of tonnes of metalwork fused into itself and anything solid that it had touched. He couldn't begin to imagine the effort required to remove it all.

The captain insisted that he remain on the cabin floor as the lighter moved beneath the high ground of the Oder's west bank, but when the Bollwerk snaked inland at its northernmost point he was allowed out on to the deck. Directly ahead, the southern tip of Bredower Werder loomed, its shattered warehouses removed already and the ground cleared. As Fischer absorbed the changes the lighter's prow turned almost imperceptibly to port, keeping their course in the main channel of the Oder. The opposite, west bank had been hit hard early in the previous year; there, wreckage remained extensive and extended well inland from the wharves, a wasteland across which he couldn't see a single human movement in almost half a kilometre's passage.

Miron nudged his shoulder and pointed ahead. 'Vulcan.'

The yards' collapsed steel superstructure dominated the view still, but the sections that had fallen into the river were gone, a clean amputation to allow vessels to dock at the mouth of the pens once more. The lighter slowed and approached a short jetty. Its crew, who had been scouring the hold since leaving the marshalling yards dock, came on deck. Four of them were carrying loading leathers.

'The captain thought you might need more camouflage. At least until you're off the boat and can't be traced to us.'

Miron laughed as he said it, the way a man does when admitting an embarrassing truth. Fischer put on his leather and allowed the Pole to adjust it. The front acted as a cowl, protruding several inches over his face, keeping it nicely in shadow.

'Are there guards here?'

'Yes, but only to bring and take home the Germans. In the hours between they're usually at the *obwody* – the, um, the yard perimeter, making sure that no one tries to walk away or get in. They don't often oversee the work, but you need to wait until dark before you leave.'

The crew went ashore in a line, Fischer in the middle of the other cowls. There was no one on the wharf, though faint sounds of industry carried from the basin. A load of dismantled steel scaffolding was stacked against a half-ruined wall, and the Poles and Fischer waited by it while the captain went to announce their arrival. He returned in ten minutes with another, obviously German fellow, thick-set and dirty, with tattoos commemorating an extended family that ran up both arms. But he had anxious eyes and a gait that suggested both familiarity with the terrain and absolute deference to a man carrying a correctly stamped piece of paper. The captain waved Fischer to one side and left them together. He didn't offer a hand or say goodbye.

The introduction came as readily as if it had been dragged to the man's mouth and shoved out into driving sleet. 'Gottlieb.'

'Fischer.'

'He said you wanted to talk.'

'You understand Polish?'

Gottlieb's mouth twisted. 'It's necessary, these days.'

'I'm trying to get information. It isn't sensitive, and it gets no one into trouble. Perhaps you might know someone who can help me?'

Fischer was used to stares, but this one wasn't a reaction to his face or lack of it, and he realised that he was confronting one of the World's new usages. They were speaking the same language with almost identical inflections, yet the easy familiarity of compatriots was missing. Germany was nothing but an ideal once more, a re-fragmented racial pot divided between proper nations. Each of its divisions was no more bound to the next than to its masters; identity and loyalty extended no further than the hearth. Why should one German trust another's word, even when he spoke it as you did?

Gottlieb pulled on his cigarette and blew to one side without taking his eyes from Fischer. 'What's it about?'

'At the moment you're clearing bomb damage from the yards, I understand?'

'Yeah.'

'But you also load ships here?'

'It's what we all did, before ...'

'The Russians take materiel out of this port, to send home?

'It's no secret.'

'No. I'm interested in the vessels that dock here, and what ...'

Gottlieb's eyebrows rose slightly. Slowly, he shook his head. 'Better not to ask, mate.'

'But you know something?'

'No, I don't. I make sure that I don't, and when I'm really sure I get someone to punch me in the face to remind me to stay sure.'

'I can pay ...'

'There isn't enough cash in Pomerania, and I wouldn't have the chance to spend it anyway. You'd better fuck off before the guards do a sweep.'

'All right. Wait ...' Fischer had no further card to play, but to come to this place so easily and get nothing was maddening. 'Would any of your friends be willing to talk to me?'

'Not if they *are* my friends, because if one of us gets caught everyone suffers for it.'

And their families too, obviously. Fed and housed by the Russians, they enjoyed a quality of life that every other German in this town would envy. But it was a fraught, dangerous existence, and Fischer could imagine how small an infraction it would need to be to bring everything down on their heads. Gottlieb would be a fool to speak to him or anyone else.

'Well, thank you. I won't come again.' He held out his right hand. Gottlieb looked before he grasped it, winced and took it as gently as if it were his infant daughter's.

'Don't use a gate. You know that, right?'

Fischer nodded. 'I'll wait until dark and go over a wall.'

'Good.'

Gottlieb released his grip and didn't walk away. It might have been the hand or the face, but something had stirred a near-set crust. 'I can't, really.'

'I know, it's fine. What I said about no one getting into trouble - that was shit, probably.'

'Yeah. It wasn't a request for ships' registrations, was it?'

'No.'

'So it's about what they're carrying.'

'Possibly, I'm not sure. It's just an idea. I'm not interested in coal, or metal, or plant and machinery.'

Gottlieb couldn't drag his eyes from Fischer's face. 'If it's people, the Ivans don't take them through here.'

'No, I don't suppose they do.'

The eyes narrowed further.

'As I say, it's fine. You can't put your folk at risk.'

The other man took out his cigarettes and offered the pack. Fischer took one, lit them both and forced himself not to say another word while Gottlieb examined every line, scar and badly-healed stitch-mark in front of him. The foul tobacco scoured the burn tissue in his throat but he neither coughed nor swallowed it away. The gaze became almost difficult to bear but he held it without trying to give the impression he was trying to effect a grip, a moral headlock. It all slowed time immensely.

Eventually, Gottlieb sighed. It didn't sound like surrender; more a small satisfaction at having reached a point not clearly seen until now.

'Money won't do it. Something else, perhaps.'

## 31

Earl Kuhn was nervous, and uncomfortable. For once it wasn't only for his own skin, but that was hardly the point. If his guts were correct then the shit would fall just as if he were the target of it.

Beulah May's nose caught the exposed nerve-endings. She whined at him every few minutes and stared pointedly at her sofa bed, which had been dragged directly in front of the door. Kuhn had also covered the only window, so the kerosene lamp had to be in use constantly. For months he had intended to go outside and check the view inside when it was lit, to see whether shapes could be discerned sufficiently to aim at through the coarse sheet. He wished now that he'd done it, rather than put it off with iron indiscipline.

Fischer had said that he would be gone for a night, possibly two. It was now the second evening so nothing was necessarily amiss, but Kuhn disliked not having a grip on plans, not to mention stratagems. The Russian had warned him that he shouldn't interfere beyond helping with arrangements, and while he had tried to comply he wasn't sure that making room for Fischer at *Chez Kuhn* didn't count as *beyond.* In his line of work risks couldn't be avoided, but provoking a guy who had a hundred divisions in his pocket was a bad idea. And what, he'd taken to wondering, constituted provocation? Was it knowing too much, or not enough?

*Let me know if he discovers something.* What did that mean? When you weren't trusted with a story how did you know when it got to the interesting bit? He could imagine himself blurting out *something* and it ringing the wrong bell in the Ivan's head - *Oh dear, the schwab shouldn't have got wind of that. Pity, he seemed like a nice boy.* And what if he heard nothing that was worth passing on? Was haplessness a shooting offence in this arrangement?

There was also the moral issue. How could Kuhn look himself in the mirror, much less meet his customers' eyes, knowing that he'd become an informer, a ... (gratefully, he drew upon the impressive American lexicon of betrayal) rat, a snitch, a stool pigeon, a fink? His business was built upon a tiny but precious degree of trust — trust that mutual self-interest would keep both parties from sliding a blade where it wasn't welcome. If it became known that he was either in the Russians' pocket or bending over to accommodate a comradely fist his commercial goodwill was going to vanish faster than a fart in a stiff breeze.

He stared into large, troubled eyes and wished for a dog's uncomplicated life. You slept, ate, got walked, relieved yourself and that was it. If you weren't lucky enough to be owned you killed things until a soft touch came along and took responsibility for rations. Best of all, you didn't know enough to be worried. If he dragged Beulah May's sofa back to its usual place, hummed a tune and rubbed her head she'd forget all about what it was that was niggling under her fur. He sighed, a long one this time. She switched her weight between front legs and whined again.

He had cleaned and loaded both his Brownings that morning, and the prospect of them on the table had reassured him almost until midday, when he recalled that what counted as firepower against a Polish gang wouldn't necessarily impress a Soviet Shock Army. The Russian didn't look the type to take risks. He'd probably assume Kuhn was of the calibre of German they'd dealt with on the eastern Front, the sort who needed shooting twice to stop. It wasn't likely he'd just send a couple of bored *soldats* to do the job. They weren't short of men.

What made it worse was that he couldn't really blame anyone or anything other than his shitty luck. He couldn't even throw the rock at his so-called mate Mazur, who must have been the one to spill it to the Russian. After all, he - Kuhn - had been the one to start it all, to go to the Pole and ask him to help with

Fischer's little matter. If Mazur had covered his arse by passing it on, well, it's probably what he would have done himself.

He didn't mind dealing with Ivans, usually. Most of them were straightforward types, and if they tried to stiff you their eyes always gave it away. He'd often wanted to take advantage of that, to finish off a trade by suggesting a game of cards. The ones he did business with were always armed, however, so it hadn't seemed sensible. This one, the officer, he wasn't like them. His eyes didn't say anything at all, and if he had emotions they were folded neatly on a shelf somewhere, probably back in Moscow. They'd had a single conversation, a simple exchange of information and a request for more, and it had been polite, civilized and thoroughly bowel-scouring. Kuhn was reminded of the 'stapo who'd arrested him back in '43 for his anti-social hooliganism, a friendly sort who hadn't used harsh language or insults, who'd helped him back to his feet every time he'd knocked him down and gone out of his way not to do too much to the face. At the end, when they packed him off for the standard six-week spell in an *arbeitserziehungslager*, Kuhn had been abjectly grateful for the quality of attention he'd received and convinced to the deepest part of his soul that he could never go through anything like it again. The Russian hadn't needed to ask twice.

When the light faded he covered the window, lit the lamp, wrapped the Brownings and returned them to their case. He just might, in an extremity, be capable of putting the barrel of one of them into his mouth and pulling the trigger, but he was certain he wouldn't be so stupid as to use them against anyone else. He might miss and make a guy angry enough to earn some very special treatment, the sort that required a small room, a sloping floor and a sluice hole at its lowest point. If it came to it, it would better to do nothing, to put up his hands, keep still and let them get their aim right the first time.

He ate at six, and tried to see things more clearly. He

reminded himself that he hadn't indulged this much self-pity since the day after his release from the *arbeitserziehungslager*, when an imagined friend had taken exception to his return to Stettin and beaten him up for reassembling his stall in the town's black market. On top of several weeks' strenuous official abuse it had been the last straw, almost; but the death of his tormentor during an air raid soon afterwards had cheered him considerably, and then the war's end had opened up a slew of new possibilities for which he'd had little competition. The lesson here was that things always seemed worse than they were.

While he was feeling a little better about *things* he thought about his options. The decent thing would be to tell Fischer, and possibly the sensible one, too. As an ex-*kripo* he was used to thinking around corners, to smelling rats (as a Yank *kripo* would surely put it) in rose gardens. Kuhn wasn't dumb, but nor was he familiar with professional levels of duplicity. His habitual problems were more straightforward, usually to be faced down with a rueful smile, a big dog or a small bribe. In any case, having someone else know what he knew felt like insurance, or at least company.

So he had almost decided to admit his sin when a knock on the door made him curse his stupidity for having reinterred the Brownings. Beulah May barked once, without intent, and her tail told him to relax. When he opened the door Fischer swayed for a moment and then fell inside, and the whole matter of ratting, or squealing, or finking passed entirely from mind.

## 32

Senior Lieutenant Zarubin waved a finger at the sergeant. The man was good but too enthusiastic; once he started he seemed not to know how to stop, and there was no point to just letting him carry on until he became too tired. The object of his undivided attention would almost certainly be dead by then.

The sergeant (an Azerbaijani with no apparent neck) straightened stiffly, though the finger hadn't constituted any sort of formal command. The object between them coughed, spattering the floor, and wriggled slightly in his chair. He was an older fellow, a veteran of the Revolution, tough as frozen boot soles, and Zarubin didn't think he was going to talk, not this way. But he was obliged to follow the proper forms, even if it wasted time he'd rather have used to better effect.

He offered the obligatory cigarette, but the fellow didn't raise his head. He'd lost a couple of teeth already, and the bruise on his temple suggested that concussion was going to slow things down further. It was inconvenient, but Zarubin was determined not to rush things. This had to be done right, by whatever imaginary regulations covered the interrogation of Red Army personnel, because he'd fought to bring the business within his jurisdiction when clearly it wasn't. That was a wrong step, and another one (not to mention a wrong outcome) would be just the stick that NKVD needed to impale an insolent young poacher.

'A drink of water for our guest, Ahmadov.'

The sergeant's face suggested that he considered this a very bad idea, but he poured a beaker and thrust it under the man's face. He managed a few gulps before falling back, head up, and Zarubin had to cough hastily before the brute took this as an invitation to begin the afternoon session prematurely.

The trouble with beatings like this was that it became

difficult to spot subtle reactions to questions, and if things went too far the questions became pointless anyway. The man's face was so bruised already that any faint hint of awareness, a moment's betrayal in the eyes, was hidden beneath expanding blood vessels. Zarubin wished that he could have taken over the interrogation entirely and conducted it his own way from the start, but junior officers of whatever department didn't get to set their terms on a matter like this. He was lucky enough to have kept it from being known generally, which would have been an end to everything. Still, he needed more than what he had.

The sergeant was waiting. Zarubin glanced down once more at his handiwork. It was all going to the unimaginative, standard plan. When the fellow could no longer move anything except his fingers they'd get him to sign the confession that had been drafted and typed already, hold a swift hearing, put one in the back of what remained of his head and close another file.

'Ahmadov, would you arrange for someone to bring a cup of tea for me, please?'

He couldn't be sure whether it was the request or the polite manner in which it had been made that more astonished the sergeant, but his eyebrows almost touched the hairline across the simian slope that separated them. For a moment the mouth twitched as if it were about to question the order (*what a beating that would be* thought Zarubin, wistfully), but the Azerbaijani slowly roll down his sleeves, put on his tunic and fastened it. Zarubin smiled encouragingly to further dislocate the man's composure and held the door open for him. The canteen was three floors above them, at the other, west end of the Praesidium. Even if the sergeant just gave the order and came straight back, he'd be elsewhere for two or three minutes. If he did the dutiful thing and waited for the tea, perhaps ten.

The footsteps hadn't quite faded when Zarubin made a start.

'Vassily Ivanovich, I won't lie - there's no chance you're not guilty, even if you aren't. You know how it is. You and the General went for a drive, he disappeared and you turned up fifty kilometres from your post with the keys to the car you signed for in your pocket. The car they found in Szczecin Lagoon, in four metres of water. They don't need it to be any more straightforward.

'But this business isn't necessary. I need just one thing and then we write a new confession, in which you admit that you took your old friend to the Lagoon and helped him do what he wanted. Since the war ended he'd been adrift, lost, an old fighting soldier confined to an office, obliged to be nice to the same Polish bastards who made him look such a dick back in '20. He'd had enough; he'd served the Revolution well and did more than his share and it was his time, so you and he had a nice drive to the water. You had a drink or two and a couple of *blini*, you talked over the old days and then he asked his oldest, best comrade to help him over the fence into Valhalla, and you couldn't decently refuse. But then you panicked and ran - it's only natural, knowing that you had no more chance of walking away from it than a dead Pharaoh's favourite dog. Now you want us to know the truth, so the General's reputation isn't dragged through the shit. I'll write it so no one comes badly out of it, and we can finish this thing quickly.'

The old soldier's head came up. He had cold, narrow eyes with no trace of fear in them, only a weariness that Zarubin, had he been a religious man, would have prayed for fervently.

'What?'

He could have kissed the fellow's bruised lips. What he wanted could be explained with in three words, and he got even fewer in return, and before Sergeant Ahmadov had begun to make his careful way back to the cellars with the teapot and cup the new confession was being written out above the signature the old soldier had scrawled already upon the blank page.

## 33

'You did this to yourself?'

Fischer took the glass and drained it, wincing as the near-pure alcohol seared his throat. 'Not intentionally. I climbed a wall. The descent was much quicker than the ascent. I landed very badly.'

'You were Fallschirmjäger, and you landed *badly*?'

'So, irony lives.'

Kuhn didn't smile. The sight of Fischer sprawled on the floor had applied itself to several hours' frayed nerves and shredded them. He kept both hands clamped firmly to the bottle to prevent the tremble from becoming something worse, like an infarction.

'But you weren't seen?'

Carefully, Fisher sat on a stand chair and let Beulah May anchor his lap with her head. 'I don't think so. I climbed an unlit stretch, and from there to here it's a kilometre at most. It felt a lot longer, but I kept to the rail track for most of the way.'

'Can you eat?'

'I think so. I need to.'

To pass his fraught time Kuhn had cooked that day, an unusual pastime for someone who inhaled most of his nourishment. It was a sort of *bauern-topf*, though meatballs had been excused duties in favour of a surfeit of noodles. The resulting odours had failed to arouse the slightest canine interest, but Fischer ate ravenously while Kuhn picked moodily at his own portion.

'You won't have heard the news.'

Fischer paused with the spoon half to his lips. 'What?'

'It's posted outside on the telegraph pole, new instructions for Germans. The Poles are setting up a transit camp somewhere between Torney cemetery and the Deaf and Dumb Institute. It'll be fenced, so once inside you can't get out except to the docks, or along the railway one stop to Scheune and then on to Lübeck, or south to Marienthal or Helmstedt if the Amis agree to it, which they haven't as yet. And that isn't all of it. The Russians are going to be herding in Germans from villages all over this part of Pomerania and dumping them on the Poles, who'll force them out through the camp. It says the first transports are going to be for women, children and the elderly and sick.'

'The sick? That includes just about everyone.'

'Men below a certain age are to go last, probably so that a final bit of free labour can be squeezed from us, the cheap bastards.'

Kuhn said it unselfconsciously, though he had adeptly avoided every forced labour round up since the war's end. Fischer hadn't been so clever. He still had trouble not recalling the potato harvest of the previous August, when over the course of almost two weeks he had dug what seemed to be tonnes of produce from the unseasonably sodden soil, for which he'd been paid in rancid fish soup and a bunk in a barn with fourteen other 'volunteers'. It didn't qualify as his fondest memory.

'There'll be deaths if they do it this way.'

'I know. The further they march them, the less chance they have. Just like last year.'

Officially, spring was almost here, and if this thing didn't start immediately then the refugees wouldn't be marching through the worst weather. But they would be dragging possessions and a winter's worth of weakness in their bones. First, the old men would drop out, and then their wives, shapeless forms at a roadside to mark the route for the next batch. Russians were sentimental about children, so mothers and pregnant women at least would be treated decently, perhaps even fed a little extra *en route*. As for the rest, as many would reach the railhead as nature intended, and nature had been in a bitching mood this year. Probably, that was why the younger men were to go last - who else would have the strength to bury the dead?

Kuhn spooned more gruel into Fischer's bowl. 'That's done it for me, anyway. I should get out while I can still take more than my underpants.'

'It'll take time. They have to arrange a lot of transportation, decide numbers with the British and put on just enough supplies to make it look like it's a transfer rather than an expulsion.'

'Why would they care what the British think?'

'Because almost certainly the British are going to send someone here to monitor any arrangement they agree to. Do you think they'd allow the Poles just to stuff thousands of typhus-riddled Germans on to trains and send them west?'

'Oh.' Kuhn seemed to cheer slightly at a faint prospect of sterling transactions.

'Don't get your hopes up. Whoever comes is going to be watched more closely than a high-stakes cockroach race. The good news is that when the end comes for Germans in Stettin we'll at least have impartial witnesses. It may make things easier.'

'Still, it's shit, isn't it? We're just cattle waiting for the guys with the sticks.'

'It's what losers face. We shouldn't have taken on the rest of the world and come second.'

Kuhn sniffed. 'I'm blameless. War started when I was sixteen, I hid for most of it and then got the shit kicked out of me by the home side. Someone owes me a pension.'

Fischer leaned back and stared into his empty bowl. The news was both bad and good. The worst of it was too obvious to need stating, but if the Russians were going to evacuate most of the rest of Pomerania's Germans through the Stettin bottle-neck there would be a deal of humanity welling around in a relatively small area. The Red Army wouldn't - couldn't - keep a paper trail on an exodus like that, so a matter of identity could be determined only by the documents that the refugees themselves carried (if any). It would be a confused, messy business, the kind that a man in trouble might pray for.

Kuhn was watching him, waiting politely. 'I should have asked - did you find what you were looking for at the river?'

'I'm not sure. Possibly more than I wanted, less than I need. You deal with Russians, don't you, Earl?'

For a moment Kuhn's face betrayed something, but he covered it quickly. 'For their cigarettes and memorabilia, sure. Anything you want, just ...'

'No, I just need some general information. How many Red Army personnel are based in Stettin?'

'Hard to say. It isn't a fixed number and most of them tend to stay in the Control Zone, the Poles being sensitive about the parts of Poland they haven't yet settled into. In the town area, perhaps eight hundred, a thousand. In this part of Pomerania, I'd guess a couple of thousand more. The Free Poles are further east, so that's where most Soviets units are, trying to root them out.'

'A thousand men would be battalion strength. It seems a small number, to have a general officer commanding.'

'They don't.'

'What?'

Kuhn's face was open, guileless. 'The garrison at the Control Zone has a Lieutenant-Colonel, name of Konnikov. He's their commander.'

## 34

'I added five percent, like we agreed. Is that alright?'

For a man with two large bodyguards (both ostentatiously armed), Achym Mazur seemed strangely nervous. Beulah May Annan might have accounted for some of that, but Kuhn had locked the apartment door and she was snarling despondently behind it while several hundred kilos of fresh Pole and a couple of bony Germans stood on the steps outside, shivering. There was a slight but definite twitch in Mazur's left eye; Fischer recalled something like it from their encounter at Trassenheide labour camp, when he had interrogated the Pole on a matter that, even now, seemed prudent to leave undisturbed in its shallow grave. Back then he'd had good reason to be nervous, being a Pole, facing the lawful authority of the Third Reich armed only with a stinking horsehair blanket over his fever-wracked body. But times had changed, tables had turned and Otto Fischer, even with Earl Kuhn acting as his unconvincing henchman, wouldn't have troubled the most fraught constitution. It couldn't be about the money.

'Really, interest isn't necessary. It's only been two days.'

'Crap. This is business, you have to take it.'

It wasn't worthwhile to argue the point. Fischer took his dollars from the Pole without removing his eyes from the lower slopes of Wojciech, who was caressing a gun handle protruding from his waistband. The monster was even more intimidating wearing a close copy of Mazur's uniform - leather jacket, black sweater, pants and boots. The other fellow - Fischer didn't recognize him - was dressed in the same manner, so clearly it amounted to a statement of belonging. That sort of gesture didn't happen unless a point was being made or resisted.

Mazur swallowed visibly. 'I, um … need a favour.'

Fischer held out the hand that had taken the money.

'No, a real favour, it might be dangerous. Well, it *will* be dangerous.'

The strange Pole swore under his breath, something that needed no translation.

'That coal deal we did, it was bad. I mean, we were …'

'Fingered? Stiffed?' Earl Kuhn brightened slightly, as he always did when tasting American slang.

'Like when you walk into something like a country dolt?'

'Both, yeah'

'Well then, both. We've managed to keep clear for now, but the crew of the *Beatrycze*, they were arrested and handed over to the Russians for abetting the theft of war reparations. You can guess how bad it is for them.'

'Who was it?'

'Who do you think? The fat bastard who came to me with it in the first place. It was a …'

'Sting. It was a *sting*.'

'Thanks, Earl. He must have thought it a low-cost way to climb the greasy pole, rid Szczecin of a part of its social problem *and* push his tongue up the Reds' arses. It worked sweetly, too. We sold off our share of the stuff behind the old Art Gallery in less than three hours and went home to celebrate. They had a *milicja* squad waiting for us, hiding in doorways on Kuśnierska … I mean, Pelzer-Strasse.'

'How many dead?'

'None, I think. The rest of our guys watched them arrive from some top floor apartments we rent. They fired high to keep heads down until we got out. We don't need a new fucking war, do we?'

'So what can I do?'

'Speak to your guy, the Russian. See if you can do something for Miron and his mates before they get put against a wall.'

A woman walked past them pushing a pram filled with wood, and the conversation paused with almost comic abruptness. Fischer waited until she reached the corner and turned into Wolgaster-Strasse

'You're joking?'

Mazur shrugged. 'Apart from my ears I don't have anything he wants. But you do. If you manage it we'll help you find whatever prick killed the girl. Right?'

Wojciech and the other Pole nodded hopefully.

Fischer examined each face in turn. 'Why should you care about the crew? They can't bring you more trouble than you have already.'

Mazur shrugged. 'Miron's my second cousin. He's also the guy who brings in the Czech cigarettes. The rest of them are decent lads. They don't deserve this.'

Lieutenant Zarubin wasn't likely to care. He was NKGB or SMERSH, and probably used to putting bullets into people who didn't deserve it. At the very least he would regard any plea from Fischer as serious denting his pet's usefulness, and incline him to add a name to the arrest sheet, or arrange a playful slapping by way of a refusal. One thing he absolutely wouldn't do was to put his own backside into the sling for the sake of half a dozen thieving Poles.

Mazur was watching an inner conversation going the wrong way, and it took his voice up half an octave. 'The Ivan, he wanted me to tell him what you're doing, who you're speaking to. But I didn't, I swear.'

Earl Kuhn coughed. His face had reddened markedly. 'Me too. I mean, the Russian wanted me to snitch on you. Sorry, Otto.'

Fischer said nothing. Saying nothing had extracted more in less than a minute than anything he'd said for days now, so he kept his lips together, pursed, giving an impression that odds were being weighed and found lacking. In fact, he cared surprising little about offending Zarubin. The man's uncle, the mysterious non-commander of the Stettin garrison, would presumably object to having his surrogate policeman shot or disappeared, so he couldn't just be erased – not yet, at least. But it would be better to go to him with …

'In the meantime, Karol, Wojciech and me are going to find our rat and teach him to swim in divers' boots.'

'No, don't do that. Speak to him, nothing violent. And then give him to me.'

Mazur stared at Fischer. 'Why? The bastard turned us …'

'If I ask the Russian to do something about your cousin and his mates, I need to offer something. How about a pet Pole, a big fellow in the town, who thought that redistributing Stalin's coal was a good idea?'

'You mean have them shoot him instead? Why would …?'

'They wouldn't. My Russian's their anti-Soviet agitation man in this part of the new Poland. We're offering him a pair of permanently compliant ears, tuned to pick up any anti-fraternal sentiments in the council chamber.'

For a moment no one spoke, and then Karol smiled for the

first time, putting his gold teeth on display. 'Cool'.

Kuhn made a noise that sounded like 'copacetic', to which both Mazur and Wojciech nodded.

'Agreed?'

'Yeah, it's a good idea. Just make sure you paint the sleazy fucker as blackly as you can. He has to suffer.'

'I need a name.'

'Wiktor Madeja, he heads the administration's roads department. They don't pay him enough. Before the war he ran a factory for his father-in-law, so he had it pretty sweet. I'll bet he was tempted to keep his share of the coal.'

'A capitalist, then.'

Mazur grinned. 'Yeah, that should do it. When will you speak to the Russian?'

'Today, probably. Soviet military justice isn't likely to take its time with economic saboteurs. But don't be too hopeful.'

'We won't.'

'So where will you go now? Not back to Pelzer-Strasse?'

'No, that's gone, along with the loot in it. There's a cabin we use in Eckerberger-Wald to hide the better quality stuff until we can find buyers. I suppose it can hide us for a few days. It's basic, but ...'

'He means there's no fucking heating', said Wojciech, sourly.

'Or kitchen, and if you want a shit you take a spade into the trees. No one wanders around out there in winter, so it'll be snug.' Mazur smiled for the first time. 'We'll save you a bunk, in case you screw it with the Russian.'

## 35

Fischer was summoned by means of an envelope thrust beneath Kuhn's cellar door, a manoeuvre carried out with such discretion that it failed to wake Beulah May. He went to the Bellevue-Strasse entrance and was made to wait for more than an hour after presenting Zarubin's card to the sentry there. It was raining lightly, and to protect his suit he edged gradually against the archway. Occasionally the boy's shoulders moved slightly to allow his peripheral vision to check whether he might need to use his gun.

Eventually the lieutenant came out to the gate, nodded curtly at Fischer and waved him in. The easy manner had gone; he was frowning, preoccupied, and said nothing all the while they crossed the parade ground. Still, to Fischer's eye there remained something unmilitary about him. Of all the Soviet personnel in sight he was the only one who cared, or dared, to walk with one hand in a pocket, and though he was straight-backed there was little in his gait to suggest he was a soldier. Had this been a German kaserne still he would have been bawled into some sort of conformity, but he moved among his countrymen as if unseen.

Fischer knew enough of the Cyrillic alphabet to reassure himself that the name on the office door they entered was that of his handler. It didn't seem to have been screwed on recently - during the past hour, for example. Beyond it was a small room with a window on to the inner yard, probably a former duty officer's den, more comfortable in winter for having an exposed clutch of heating pipes running through it. The desk had been moved to the window so that its occupier would face inward, his face shaded by the light from outdoors. Zarubin sat, and waved Fischer to a stand chair opposite.

'So, what progress?'

'None, as regards a culprit.'

The Russian pursed his lips and stared at his desk. 'You have ideas, surely?'

'Oh yes.'

'Tell me.'

Fischer said nothing for a few moments. He coughed, scratched his nose and tried to convey an impression of reluctance. It wasn't difficult.

'We aren't going to find the killer.'

'That isn't what I'd hoped to hear.'

'No, I expect not. But look at it logically. The first part you'll have worked out for yourself. If a German killed Marie-Therese Kuefer he may very well be gone or dead by now. A Pole would have friends and possibly abettors, and I couldn't begin to mount an effective search without authority, which you won't give me and the local administration wouldn't recognize anyway, not without someone leaning so heavily upon them that the whole business becomes an open secret. A Russian culprit is of course entirely beyond my power to identify, much less apprehend. This is all obvious, yes?'

'Logical, at least.'

'And that's before we look at the facts, such as they seem to be.'

'She was killed on the night of 7 February, on Berg-Strasse.

'No, she wasn't.'

'What?'

'You told me that she was *found* on Berg-Strasse, not that

she was killed there. In fact, she couldn't have been. The street abuts the marshalling yards, and is lit its entire length by large floodlights that your people erected to keep their precious coal heaps safe from thieves. Someone attempting a crime there would be on-stage in front of a large audience – that is, anyone who cared to peer from one of a hundred windows on the kaserne's southern flank, or one of the patrols that wander the street at night. If it happened in Berg-Strasse a lunatic did it, and there's no need to concern ourselves further.'

'He killed her elsewhere and dumped her there?'

'No, for the same reason.'

'Then how the hell did she come to be there?'

'May we leave that for the moment? It's only our first problem. We also have the method.'

'I see no problem there. It was efficient.'

'Exactly. Murderers don't kill clinically, not if murder's the point of it. She didn't struggle, did she?'

'We found no signs of it.'

'So it wasn't a necessity to keep her quiet, a panic response. This was an execution.'

Slowly, Zarubin nodded. 'Perhaps someone didn't want his association with her to be known?'

'In that case, it would *have* to be a Russian and almost certainly an officer, because no Pole in this town would have had anything amounting to an *association* with a German woman. But I still have a problem.'

'Which is?'

'What Russian - officer or otherwise - would regard himself

as being damaged or exposed in some way by his use of a whore? Are there wives on this base?'

'Of course not.'

'Well, then. Most of the millions of your countrymen who've had a German girl during the past year didn't bother to ask permission first or pay afterwards, so something as legitimate as a regular financial arrangement with one would hardly constitute an offence, would it?'

Zarubin shrugged. 'A minor disciplinary matter, perhaps, if it was flaunted.'

'Then it's something else.'

'What could it be, apart from sex? Excuse me for saying this, but she wasn't anybody.'

'I know, but even nobodies can be dangerous, if ...'

'If?'

'If she knew something, perhaps witnessed or overheard a matter that someone was anxious to keep out of sight.'

'How would you begin to test this theory?'

'I wouldn't. I don't understand anything of what happens in your Control Zone. I have no access to files, to people or even to basic information on who comes in and goes out, and why. To pluck a motive from the air would be just that. I could spend a lot of time on this and then tell you with equal certainty or error that Private Ivanov, Chairman Stalin or Hedy Lamarr was the culprit'.

The sounds of soldiers making their indelicate way through the rest of the building didn't stifle the silence that fell between the two men. Zarubin chewed his lip and stared at a point on his desk that almost certainly he wasn't seeing while a finger tapped out a monotonous beat at its edge. It all looked more like disappointment than anger, which would have been the correct response.

'What if I gave you access?'

For a few moments the words made no impression upon Fischer. He had braced himself for trouble, or at least a frank appraisal of his investigative skills. He had hoped at a minimum for dismissal, to return to his own business of caring about nothing but what he had and had not. He didn't want tolerance of his failures and certainly not a second chance, an extended opportunity to chase his bespoke ghosts. Most of all, he didn't need the threat of *access*.

It couldn't be a trap. Why would Zarubin bother to bait one when he need only draw up a charge or cast an accusation - any accusation - to have Fischer sent East or to the firing post within an hour? He surely couldn't believe that a friendless, unconnected German was the only man for a job he could have no interest in seeing through, or that its resolution would cause the slightest stir when millions of civilians were starving, dying or disappearing as a cruel new world rose upon the bones of the old. Was it a pleasantry then, an opportunity for the Russian to display his trademark wit? And if it were, wouldn't he have sought a wider audience than just the butt of it?

'Why would you do that?'

The answer occurred as Fischer asked, and made the other possibilities attractive. It was mad that Zarubin had chosen to use him, whatever his uncle's affections for Marie-Therese. There was a bare logic to involving a friendless outsider, but it had to be a risk. The Russian's superiors could hardly regard such a wild diversion from protocols with equanimity or favour, and if it became even slightly problematic - something that Zarubin had no means of judging in advance - then the subsequent train eastwards might well be carrying two transferees. It only made sense if there was a prize or menace here that required a grope into darkness, and for want of something better he had chosen Fischer to be his stick.

The laconic smile had returned. 'Because you're right - this is a dead end otherwise. I didn't want it taken on in the first place, I told you that. But my uncle's a persistent fellow and I want the pestering to end. Also, he has friends I wouldn't wish him to call upon if it seems I'm not trying.'

Zarubin raised his hands and opened them, inviting Fischer to understand just how it was with elderly general staff relations who happened to have survived the purges with acquaintances who had done the same. It couldn't have been luck, and certainly not any quality of innocence. The old man was either a Central Committee favourite or a military genius, and Fischer didn't think it was the latter.

'How could you possibly arrange for me to speak to Soviet personnel without it all falling out immediately?'

A German wandering the Control Zone with a pen, paper and lively curiosity would be regarded in much the same way as a rodent in a bakery, only it wouldn't be a flying clog that did for him. Yet Zarubin, even if he were dangling Fischer with the keenest disregard for his health, presumably wasn't trying to waste his own time. There was no logic here, only a sense that enlightenment was unlikely to arrive earlier than a body sheet.

One of the lieutenant's half-outstretched arms waved away the matter as if it were a trifle not to be entertained.

'Not difficult, once you're in the proper uniform.'

Fischer was beginning to dislike the smile profoundly, but he said nothing. The Russian, expecting a line that would play to his banter, waited until it was obvious he was going to be disappointed, and then the smile slipped off his face. He had a clever man's inability to hide frustration, and there was no playfulness in the question.

'The other thing?'

'Which thing?'

'If she wasn't killed on Berg-Strasse, and she wasn't dumped there, what happened?'

It would have been far more sensible to keep something dry in the pouch, but Fischer was tired of being played. 'Obviously, someone put her there very carefully. She was meant to be found, to be noticed.'

'Why?'

'I have no idea, nor interest in knowing.'

He shouldn't have said it. Without leverage a closed mouth was his only asset, and the look on Zarubin's face told him immediately that he'd stepped into something that wouldn't support his weight. The man was actually smirking now.

'Then you had better become interested. I doubt you care much for your own skin, but what about your friends, your fellow criminals?'

'I don't have any friends.'

The Russian picked up a single sheet of paper and flicked it across his desk. Its contents were entirely in Cyrillic script.

'Let me give you the bones of it. Theft of Soviet state property - specifically coal, three-point-five tonnes. Mandatory death sentences all around I would imagine, and at least four of those men have families. I know that you were with them, and I don't need to prove the point.'

'You can do something for them?'

'They belong to me, or will do. What they did falls squarely within NKGB interest, and in Stettin I *am* NKGB. What would you suggest?

'Let them go. It's a tiny amount, about what falls into the river when they load the big vessels. And technically it was still Polish coal when it disappeared.'

'A novel argument. Presumably you're joking? I can never tell with German humour, it's so straight-faced.'

'You wouldn't be dangling them if you weren't prepared to give them up.'

Zarubin shrugged and said nothing. He didn't need to.

'Alright, I'll carry on with this pointless exercise. What did you mean by the *proper uniform*?'

'Not a uniform as such, obviously. Even NKGB can't induct Germans into the Red Army. I'll give you the authority to question a *few* men, where you feel it's absolutely necessary. Naturally, this must take place in my presence.'

Fischer stared at the Russian, trying to read the bland, open face. 'Well, we're of the same mind about something, at least.'

'Really? What is it?'

'I need to know about her paying customers, so we both hope it's a *few*.'

## 36

'I knew there was going to be trouble. I *knew* it.'

'How?'

For a few moments Kuhn said nothing. Tenderly, he was removing money of several denominations from his coat pockets and placing it on the table with the three small bags of cash he had stacked there already. Fischer couldn't recall having seen so much of it since before the war ended, and then only in quartermasters' offices.

'It was when the referee trotted onto the pitch in a Red Army cap. I think the Poles had doubts about his impartiality, but they needn't have worried. By the final whistle the only man he hadn't ruled offside was their goalkeeper. I got out before it blew, obviously.'

'The final whistle?'

'The explosion.'

'What was the score?'

'Fourteen-nil at least. The Poles were down to seven men when I left. I think he sent one of them off for having red hair. At least, I didn't spot any other offence.'

Fischer had worried needlessly about the threat to Zabelsdorf's remaining German population. The riot had contained itself to the stadium, and needed both Red Army units and most of Szczecin's police force to quell it. For the moment the area was heavily patrolled, almost a safe haven.

Kuhn sighed contentedly. 'Every pack. Every. Pack. It would have taken weeks to get rid of them on the street. I really owe

Achym for this.'

'He's taking ten percent for doing nothing. What's to be grateful for?'

'Me and my boys weren't bothered by anyone. You'd think we'd had the exclusive franchise, except for a couple of guys who were selling to the Russians at the other end, which is fine. And when we left no one tried to redistribute our wealth. Achym really must have put the word around.'

Kuhn lit one of his few remaining cigarettes, did a half-shimmy to the gramophone, slid a record from its sleeve and loaded the weapon. Fischer suppressed a wince. It was only a little consolation that the fellow with the guitar sounded as unhappy about it as himself.

'Blind Lemon Jefferson', said Kuhn, as if to explain things.

'What ails him?'

'He's asking for his grave to be kept clean.'

'He's dead?'

'Well, it's a looking-ahead kind of song, but actually yes, he is. He was poisoned by a lover.'

'A music lover?'

'Oh, very amusing.'

At least it was slow, not the sort of locomotive cacophony that Kuhn usually favoured. Until he moved into the cellar Fischer had never really had cause to dislike Americans - he hadn't faced them in battle or had a comrade shot by one during an attempted surrender. But he was coming around to Stalin's view of the race, nudged by a daily aural bombardment from platoon-strength ensembles that made Parsifal seem almost musical. It had been an effort to keep his opinion from his landlord.

'So, can I see it?'

Fischer took it from his pocket and passed it across the table. Kuhn pushed his cigarette and ashtray to a safe distance, carefully unfolded and inspected it with a connoisseur's eye. 'What does it say?'

'I have no idea. Apparently it allows me in and out of the Control Zone without let, hindrance or a good kicking. You'll notice it's stamped.'

'I do', said Kuhn, reverently. 'Three times, in red.'

'Soviet officialdom is very emphatic.'

'You realise that for what this could buy it might as well be signed by the Governor of the Bank of England?'

'Yes, but there's nothing I want, not in Stettin.'

Kuhn sighed. 'A pity. It would more or less guarantee my supply lines to the Ivans - no more hiding in ditches, waiting for the right military vehicle to come along, hoping that I don't wave down a fucking patrol.'

Fischer held out his hand before the vision became too compelling. 'Of course it may well say that the bearer of this pass should be regarded as an enemy saboteur and shot immediately. That's the thing about trusting a Russian - it requires too much faith.'

'How will you start?'

Zarubin says he'll try to get a full list of men that Marie-Therese ... knew.'

'How?'

'She only ever met them at the kaserne, so she was signed in and out each time, a precise record of her visits. He should be able to match that to duty rosters and narrow the field.'

'No one's going to be admitting to it. How will he encourage them to talk?'

'NKGB deal with foreign subversion, so perhaps he'll tell them that Marie-Therese had links with anti-Soviet activities in Stettin. They'll want to clear themselves of any connection with *that*.'

'Yeah, but not to a German.'

'Actually, that should be easier. Zarubin can always say that I'm a Red spy, an informer, a …'

'Fink?'

'Yes. Who would know otherwise? It's his job to run scum like me.'

'So how will you do it? Is there something in a killer's eye you can make out, or will he just fall to pieces and admit everything?'

'You enjoy detective fiction, Earl?'

'Yes! Strictly *hard-boiled*!'

'Well, don't believe any of it. No one's going to give himself away, or confess. And I have no idea why she died, so how can I start on establishing a motive? At best, when we've spoken to her customers we might be able to say who didn't break her neck.'

'So why do it?'

'I'm not.'

'Really?'

'It would be futile. I agreed because I look willing by doing so. But it would be a joke, breathe wasted. No-one will admit to anything other than putting their cock in her, something I'd rather not hear. If it *was* one of them who killed her Zarubin would know or suspect it already and have done something about it or not. He's letting me talk to them because they can clear themselves and he can then push me in another direction.'

'Push?'

'Think about what's happened since I started this. You were told to watch me and then got beaten up by way of an encouragement to try harder, our only Polish assistance is neatly disappeared and Mazur's sailor friends are set up and then shown the firing post. It's like we're in a long corral, and at each point he's waiting with a prod.'

'How does he do it? I mean, how does he know?'

'There are only two sources that could account for all that's happened. You're one of them, but we can pass on that. So, unless Zarubin speaks to God he must be getting his information from one of the Pelzer-Strasse gang.'

'Shit. How do we tell Achym?'

'We don't. It's far better we watch our mouths than flag it to Zarubin by exposing his fellow. It doesn't matter now, anyway. I've agreed to do what he wants, his way.'

'You don't imagine he's going to just shake your hand once it's over, do you?'

'It depends on what this is all about. The least likely possibility is that he's being truthful, and only wants to keep his uncle happy. If that's the case I may get out of this with a bottle of vodka. More likely is that he's playing at something, officially or otherwise, and that I'll be a loose end when it's over.'

'I don't like his smile.' Kuhn shivered.

'It's nice, isn't it? But you, Earl, you have your money and no more cigarettes to sell. You should leave, go West.'

'I don't know; I don't know. I tell myself it's time, but something keeps grabbing my collar. It can't be the town - it's all-to-shit now, and my memories of when it wasn't aren't too golden. It isn't my love life either, that's for sure. I suppose it's just better to be where you already know the worst rather than walk into it. You're right, of course. I should get out before I get thrown out.'

'If you wait until then there's no way to guarantee you'll leave on your terms. They'll probably strip search you and pocket the cash.'

'Yeah.' Kuhn sighed and rubbed Beulah May's head. 'Where to, girl? Heidelberg? Vienna? Biarritz?'

'That one might be expensive.'

Another, deeper sigh. 'No, it wouldn't.' Kuhn pushed back the small, ragged carpet with a foot, lifted a ring-catch beneath and pulled open a small trap, about twenty centimetres square. From the hole he drew out a long, snake-like package, its outer layer a waxed cotton wrap, tightly bound. He didn't untie it.

'What is it?'

'Swiss francs - fourteen thousand, seven hundred and fifty-eight US dollars' worth at last month's exchange rate. And some pink sapphires.'

'Christ, Earl! You made this from cigarettes?'

'No, I spend all of that on bribes and living expenses. *This* is from General Raus.'

'Raus?'

'Yeah, I think so. Who else but a General would be moving

that sort of cash? And it was his train ...'

'The story's true, then? About the train?'

'You've heard it? Me and the Fourth International got word that it was stopped, broken down or bombed, about a half-kilometre outside Gotzlow. I wanted us all to go and have a look but the guys said no way, it was too dangerous. So I went on my own, belly-crawled the last half-kilometre and waited. In the afternoon the soldiers guarding it started to argue about something and then half of them marched off. When it got dark I came out of the woods and hid under one of the carriages, counting legs. At dawn the rest of them had another argument, only this time I could hear it. One of them said he didn't fancy a Siberian holiday just because *General Raus* needed his Gastein pension, that he was fucked if he was going to wait for a relief locomotive that wasn't coming anyway. Some of his mates started talking about duty, but they got laughed down as arse-kissers. Then one of them said anyway, he's a fucking Austrian and I've had about as many of those as I can take. *That* got them going again, but just when I thought they'd start their own war someone else obliged. A Yank Mustang strafed the train and they ran like greyhounds.'

'All of them?'

Kuhn shrugged. 'I didn't see anyone in the carriages I crept through. In the third one I found a strongbox, broke the lock, grabbed the first thing in it that my hand touched and then bolted. Someone took a shot at me but by then I was in the tree line. When I got back to town I was going to share it with the comrades, naturally. But that was the day they decided to fuck off West or wherever, so I was left with the guns *and* the money.'

Fischer regarded the slight, vaguely apologetic figure with amazement. He'd known comrades in *Fallschirmjager* 1 Regiment who would have refused to take the risks that Kuhn seemed to think were a normal part of getting through life. And having seized the reward of those risks he was now sitting on his badly-hidden pile of assets in the middle of a lawless town, letting the moment when armed thugs steal it all from him creep forward unmolested.

'This isn't the best place for it, Earl.'

'I know.'

'That hole, and the one in the back hallway - they'll find them in half a minute.'

'I know.'

'Money in the ground isn't working for you, Earl. It should be ...'

'*I know!* Jesus!' Kuhn groaned and dug his hands more deeply into Beulah May's neck muscles. She shifted her tail between his feet, happily oblivious to how her retirement fund was underperforming. 'It's just that ...'

'When you start to move, you'll be vulnerable.'

'Who could I ask to help? As soon as we discuss money, he - they - might decide to cut out the banker. I don't trust *anyone*. Well, except you, Otto.' Kuhn looked up. 'You're the only guy I've ever met who doesn't care about money, it's just too strange. But what can I do? I think about it every day and nothing happens. I just sit on my arse, hoping the right idea comes in time.'

'It would have to be a way that didn't put you through a gate, so ...'

'No transit camp, no railway stations, ports, airfields, I know. It's going to be a fast car on back roads - I can't drive, by the way - or a slog through the woods. But what if all that goes well and I get to the West? Who do I trust *there*? I'll be just like every other poor bastard who's been kicked out of Pomerania, except for the fatal bulge of my money belt.'

'You'll still have Beulah May, won't you?'

'But I have her here. *And* four good walls, *and* an arsenal, *and* an idea of what's around the corner. It feels safer, even if it isn't.'

Home - how many people had it killed in war, that fatal pause, the illusion of sanctuary, autonomy? Fischer had thought about it often as he crawled through ruins, looking for an enemy and finding only dead householders, their open, surprised eyes fixed upon a fled chance of safety. To remain in the familiar or run to the unknown – they'd twitched between the two options like a blinded rabbit and gone nowhere, and then it had become no choice at all. He had never answered the question to his satisfaction. He assumed in every case that he would have made the sensible decision, but he was someone who'd last had a *heimat* in short trousers. Other folk had ties, a sense of belonging to something more than its physical presence - really, he couldn't say that their dead eyes hadn't seen more than his ever would.

He noticed that Kuhn's gaze was upon him. For a man in his situation, it was almost hopeful. 'Otto, we could get out together, you and me. I'll hire you to watch things for a month or two, once we get there.'

'There?'

'Wherever. We can find a place that's not too bombed but not too untouched either, somewhere with plenty of Allied wallets. It could be sweet!'

'I doubt I'd be much of a bodyguard, Earl.'

'With that face you'd scare a jeep. Anyway, it isn't muscle I need but eyes, the ones I don't have in the back of my head. What do you say?'

'That there's a lot of rubble between now and the moment we get the chance to leave, any piece of which could make plans for a future pointless. Zarubin isn't going to let me just walk out of Stettin, is he? And even if I managed it, Mazur's friends would go to the wall.'

'He wouldn't do that, would he?'

'I doubt he makes paper threats. Keeping them alive would be the difficult choice, given the charge against them. Besides, I don't want to leave without having a chance to solve this.'

'Who killed your girlfriend?'

'No, why anyone other than me should care. And why a Russian's being careful to keep me looking at other Russians, not Poles or Germans. Now, start making plans to leave.'

'I told you, I won't go alone.'

'I don't mean town, just the cellar. We need a safe safe-house, and this is a death-trap.'

37

In three days, Zarubin compiled a list of eighteen officers, all names on the duty roster on the evenings Fischer knew Marie-Therese to have visited Soviet Headquarters. Most were junior men, but a major and three captains had been present also. Eight were adamant - even under Zarubin's earnest questioning - that they had no connections with German prostitutes. A further three admitted to the hobby but claimed not to recognise the woman in the photograph shown to them. Seven men readily acknowledged their acquaintance with her.

Seven. Fischer couldn't get the number out of his head. He hadn't met any of them but he saw them all, shadows in a variety of fornicating positions, using her, satisfying themselves upon her body. He wished that it were merely jealousy, rather than despair that he was being obliged to delve into the minute detail of what most defined his impotence.

According to Zarubin's notes, none of the seven had ever been disciplined for mistreating civilians, but that meant as little with regard to the Red Army as it had the Wehrmacht. It was difficult to imagine an offence that might attract notice, much less sanction, from their own. Nor were any of them known to possess atypical sexual tastes, and Marie-Therese had never hinted that she was more than earning her fees with certain customers. All seven claimed to have *liked* her enough to make the effort to give her repeat business in preference to other local whores, and again, Fischer's tortured imagination dwelled upon what she might have done to generate such consistent satisfaction. Mercifully, Zarubin hadn't asked them for details.

None had an obvious motive to harm her, absent a known taste for inflicting pain. Only two were married, and even they had expressed amusement and produced their standard-issue condoms when Zarubin commented upon the morality of using a German woman. All were regular army; all had a respectable collection of campaigns and wounds medals (as Fischer had suspected, most personnel in the Headquarters building were drawn from a convalescent regiment), and two had been awarded the Order of the Patriotic War, First Class for conspicuous bravery in the field (in the margin Zarubin had scribbled 'the Killing Many Germans medal!'). Three had been - officially - in the building on the night of her death, but Fischer considered them his least likely suspects. She hadn't been killed in passion, therefore the perpetrator was not likely to have provided an obvious trail.

He didn't want to speak to any of them, didn't want to put faces to the act. In fact, he wanted to wash his hands of any of Marie-Therese's paying friends. But that wouldn't work for Zarubin. He had placed himself firmly upon NKVD's toes by questioning these men, and if it was taken amiss his next posting might be to a place where the year was measured by ice-floe migration. It added to Fischer's curiosity that the thing had actually been pushed this far. When he was summoned back to Bellevue-Strasse he had half assumed that it was so he could be arrested more conveniently.

'What actually happens here?'

Zarubin had been signing papers, playing the in-my-own-time game with his guest, but the question roused him. 'What do you mean?'

'Here, in this building. It's generally referred to as a headquarters, but of and for what?'

'It manages the Stettin Control Zone, obviously.'

'Your export business, you mean?'

Zarubin laughed gaily. 'If you like. In fact, whether or not you like. Staff here coordinate, administer and protect the onward transfer of war reparations from Brandenburg and Upper Silesia.'

'No active operational function?'

'Not military, no. The Free Polish Army - or recidivist instruments of International Capital, if you prefer - are well to the East, jumping in and out of the woods like rabbits, imagining they can get Lithuania back.'

'So, no military secrets. What about Intelligence?'

'Well, I'm here.'

'Yes, but that's unusual, surely? There can't be need of a formal presence at Stettin.'

The Russian didn't seem surprised or offended by the question. 'Of course there is. Until the last German is scraped west of the Oder-Neisse this part of Europe regarded as an oddity, something that is, yet at the same time isn't, an occupation zone. We can't have you all wandering around unobserved, can we?'

'And yet your staff comprises a single secretary. There's no way I could check this, but I doubt that there's an official NKGB or SMERSH establishment in this part of Poland. Do you report to Moscow directly?'

'If it's necessary to know, my immediate chain of command passes through SVAG, in Berlin-Karlshorst. You *are* a curious fellow, Fischer. Are you thinking of applying for a salaried position?'

'It's about *why*. This wasn't a sex crime, and it certainly wasn't an argument over the price of a fuck, so it must be something else. If a member of the Red Army did it - and that seems likely, otherwise you wouldn't be doing this - he either has an ugly hobby or a good reason. So, I need to know what you all do here.'

'Sturdy procedural reasoning, Herr Kriminalkommissar. What may I help you with next? Would you like to interview any of the men who *knew* your young lady?'

There was a mockingly innocent quality to the question that Fischer wanted to correct with a fist. He calmed himself by imagining Zarubin's pretty head in a crossfire.

'I doubt that the man who killed her would admit to an acquaintance. If one of the eighteen officers on your list is the man, he's far more likely to be found among the group who deny any contact with prostitutes. And no, I don't want to speak to those either.'

'Why not?'

'Because I wouldn't know what to ask. At the least, I need to have precise details of what they do here. But of course I can't access their service records - if you keep such things - or the details of their correspondence. You need to give me more before I can begin to look at - to know if there *are* any - Soviet suspects.'

Zarubin was scribbling on a note pad, and Fischer watched closely for a hint of emotion. He had asked the impossible and it hadn't managed to curl a single hair on the Russian's head, much less coax out a blunt refusal or laughter. Either he was about to be given a fantastical degree of access to the Occupying Power's classified information or be pushed, head first, into a gin-trap. He kept his face straight, playing it as if the two of them were arranging no more than a mutually convenient date to inspect Stettin's surviving iron water-pumps

The Russian capped his pen. It was a *guilloche*'d Otto Hutt, a popular reparation among the Red Army's officer class. 'This may take a little time to arrange.'

'I have time.'

'Perhaps not as much as you might hope for.'

'You mean I won't be able to do this from Lübeck?'

'Oh, your forcible removal isn't likely. We're keeping our *valuable* Germans, at least for the short term. I was referring to the quality of my patience.'

It was nice to have it confirmed. All across Pomerania and Silesia embittered refugees were on the move, kicked out of their homes, robbed or cheated of their heritage and despatched on foot to a staggeringly uncertain future while Otto Fischer, a man with ties only to his boots, had his feet nailed to the ground.

Zarubin stood up, terminating the meeting. 'You know already what I have by way of disincentives to your making a dash for the West. So please don't.'

'I wouldn't think of it. But I'll need some accommodation for me and Adolph Kuhn, whom you know I believe. Our part of Zabelsdorf isn't safe for Germans anymore.'

'Why Kuhn?'

'He knows everyone, more or less. He's useful to me. And I can give you something in return, a small triumph to put under your anti-agitation hat.'

'What?'

'An arsenal of personal weapons - they were hoarded by a Fourth Internationalist cell that intended to shoot it out with the fascists. Wisely, they left shortly before you liberated Stettin. Kuhn inherited their guns when he occupied their cellar. You'll appreciate that disposing of them has been difficult.'

'He's willing to hand them over?'

'He'd be delighted, providing you don't pin it on him.'

The Russian shrugged. 'Alright. I have an idea where to put you.'

Fischer wondered for a moment if he had been too clever. But then he thought about the twists of this business, the curious direction in which gravity or some other force seemed to be dragging him, and his anxieties faded. There really was only the single possibility.

'May I ask where?'

'Certainly. Among your own kind, where you'll be safe.'

## 38

Three uniformed members of the Citizen's Militia came to Bernhagen on a Sunday as the German church emptied (the Polish residents had their makeshift Catholic church at an abandoned farmhouse at the other end of the village), and read out instructions for the upcoming movement of non-resident aliens. While they hadn't held divine service as such - the congregation lacking a pastor still - Bernhageners regarded the timing as disrespectful, even profane. No one thought to mention this, however, as the offending gentlemen carried side-arms and seemed the type to use them if provoked. Bernhageners had become very adept at not provoking Poles.

They were told that they had just three days in which to prepare for evacuation *to Germany*. Monika could see that the man who wasn't Clausewitz took profound exception to this; fortunately, Amon Stemper stood beside him and managed to smother the detonation with a frown and a finger to his lips. They were told also that some means of transport might be provided but that only light luggage, amounting to a maximum of two suitcases per family, must be taken. No amount of frowning or fingers could have quelled the explosion that greeted this detail, but for all that it moved the three militia men it might have been directed at the moon. Their leader waited until most of the louder complaints had subsided and then continued as if he were delivering a sermon. Food would be provided at several points between Bernhagen and their initial destination Stettin, but it wouldn't be much and evacuees should bring whatever foodstuffs they had. Those with medical conditions should come forward and make themselves known (fearfully, every Bernhagener with a bad back, hip or foot kept his or her mouth firmly closed), and might, if facilities permitted, be allocated a seat in a cart. However, no horses would be available, so it would be up to the healthier evacuees to decide who would pull the same, if necessary.

'Where are we to sleep?' cried Amon Stemper. The militiaman ignored that question too, though his eyebrows rose very slightly to indicate that folk shouldn't imagine that his hard-pressed time was to be wasted; that if the journey from Bernhagen to Stettin was not going to take more than two days even on foot it was hardly likely to be another Brünner Death March so they had no right to make a fuss about it. He continued, emphasising that any provocations on the part of evacuees - such as destruction of property they considered to be theirs prior to departure, or aggressive behaviour *en route* to Stettin - would be punished condignly, without recourse to prior arbitration. Though most Bernhageners understood only a few of these words, no one had any doubt about what they meant.

When he had finished, the militiaman carefully refolded his instructions, stepped back, saluted the villagers, shouted 'Long Live Poland' in German (which his audience considered rather spiteful), and then he and his two colleagues got into their car and drove off on the road to Zampelhagen, to give that village's folk the good news of their impending fate. Monika watched them disappear, putting off the moment when she would have to turn and meet the expectant gaze of almost everyone present.

If only Marienwalde had survived the winter, she thought. His natural authority had far exceeded any imagined status she enjoyed, which would have left her the burden only of saying 'we should ask Albert, Ritter von Marienwalde' whenever her advice was sought. She had no doubt that, in all the villages of his patrimony, someone like her would be an unwilling prophet on this day, asked to dispense wisdom they did not possess regarding a business they had no way of anticipating.

She spoke before a question could be put. 'It's no good arguing. We should get ourselves ready.'

Expecting a Bernhagener not to argue was futile of course, and she said it only to make a point to which she could later refer sternly when they had wasted an hour or two. Her mouth was hardly closed before they were at it - remonstrating with fate's whims, imploring God's mercies, lamenting their many misfortunes and, yes, arguing the meat and bones of what they were powerless to influence. She sighed and looked around for her familiar, Erika, who could be trusted at least to say nothing that wasn't necessary. The girl was stood a little behind her, watching the general hubbub with a cast to her face that Monika had not seen before - an impatient glare, the sort a parent might give someone else's unruly children. She was murmuring something too quiet to be heard above the din, but Monika knew that it would be a song, one of only three she knew, mantras she chanted to herself when she became agitated. They had just three days, and there were a hundred things to be done - shoes and boots repaired, secret pockets stitched into clothing to hide what money and jewellery they still possessed, food scavenged, begged or bartered from their Polish neighbours, labels prepared for the possessions they'd be allowed to take, and - for Monika at least - farewells to be said over the long and recent dead, whose graves would lie untended forever now.

She returned to her house with Erika, knowing that the others would follow when they'd worked the flies from under their collars. Her own preparations would be as sparse as her worldly wealth; she would wrap three old photographs, her bible, the altar tablecloth and the three christening spoons that had welcomed her and her two brothers into the Church. What Erika possessed she didn't know, but it could hardly amount to an inheritance. Less would be better; whatever the militia had promised by way of arrangements and protection, Monika wasn't reassured for a moment. As soon as they were on the road they would be refugees, under no laws but those of nature and chance. They had all tasted the experience in the previous year when their part of the world had been Germany still, and even then they had been obliged to leave their dead by the roadside. What was coming might be worse than that terrible trek if someone decided to take a last chance of vengeance for the crimes of other Germans.

And yet she had a feeling almost of relief that the pause of the past year was ending. What had they to look forward to until this moment, other than more of the same fearful expectation of a future that couldn't be guessed at? Perhaps there might be a new life after all, for those with time enough still to make something of it (she excluded herself from this fortunate element, naturally). Even if the coming days and months were to be uncertain and filled with strangeness, Bernhagen's former residents would be somewhere that Germans could live in the company of their kind, rather than be cursed as artefacts of a gone age. And if the very worst were to happen upon the road to Stettin, wouldn't that be an ending at least, of everything that had fallen upon them?

Monika glanced anxiously at Erika, who was sitting in the window seat she had annexed, staring out into the small, neglected garden. She wondered sometimes if the power of her fatalism allowed it to be carried in the air like a sneeze, to infect others with bleak expectations. She hoped not; it wasn't right to visit it upon the young, even a girl for whom life had so far offered little prospect of better.

But Erika was in her usual, faraway place, singing softly about things that had meant something to her before meaning was excised. She was a template of this and other, similarly cruel ages - scarred, remote and yet offering frail evidence that what had been stamped upon might bear intact seeds still, a promise of life. Monika wondered if *resilient* might be putting it too optimistically. Fourteen was too young to be done with hope.

She was perfectly aware that the girl visited her daily for more than companionship. She lived with her father's brother and his family, good people who had taken her in willingly and who treated their own children with no more love and attention. But her heart was hers to give, and it seemed that she had chosen an old spinster to fill the hole excavated by her parents' deaths. It wasn't clear why. Perhaps she found comfort in the still hours they spent together, not speaking, not worrying about anything larger than their stitching. It wasn't something to be discouraged, but Monika feared that she was too old, too beyond her time, to become necessary to someone.

'We should think about what we'll take with us, when we go West.'

Erika turned and smiled vaguely, and for the first time Monika felt a great disquiet, a fear for more than abstract things. The girl was becoming a beautiful young woman in a world that punished beauty hideously. Fourteen was too young to marry, too old to discourage a man's baser instinct - it was an age at which girls were prone to be mistaken for something else. She had been *mistaken* already in every sense, and the journey from Bernhagen to Stettin might bring a further testing.

Distracted by the thought, she was about to repeat herself when a fist rapped once on her front door and Amon Stemper walked in. Without invitation he sat down heavily upon a lower stair step (other than an armchair and truckle bed, Monika had by now converted all of her furniture to firewood) and sighed.

'They want to know if you'll draw up a list for them, of necessary things.'

'No, Amon, I won't. If they don't know that they need warm clothes, food and water then there's nothing to be said or read.'

Stemper squirmed slightly. 'You're right, of course. But I think it would be good for their spirits if there was seen to be some *process* that remained in our hands, rather than the Poles'. Even if it's an illusion, it would make it seem that we were doing things *together* still.'

Reluctantly, Monika acknowledged the point. Fears amplified when one faced them alone. If Bernhageners – or whatever they were about to become – could convince themselves that there was a plan, or at least that attention was being given to the means by which they would get from here to there, they might be less inclined to panic when the moment came.

'But we can't list the two most necessary things they'll need.'

'What are they?'

'Courage, and strong hearts.'

There was a twinkle in Stemper's eye. 'We'll write them anyway. But you have to sign it, Monika. They expect it from you, not me.'

## 39

Though he had known it was coming for months now, Earl Kuhn didn't take easily to being a displaced person, a refugee. He and Fischer had almost a full day in which to evacuate the cellar, and it passed largely around an argument about how much of his trove he was allowed – or likely - to take with him. The guns he was glad to be parted from, particularly without penalty for having given them a home for so long. His money was of course very necessary, and with great care they managed to construct a money-belt that gave it a home without making Kuhn look unconvincingly portly. But his gramophone, record collection (almost a hundred discs) and original concert posters of Jazz Giants were inevitable victims of the move. He resisted this obvious fact strenuously.

'They're everything to me!'

'You can replace them all, eventually. It isn't as though they're collectors' pieces, is it?'

'Can't we sell them, at least?'

'Who would pay? We'd be taking them to where the Ivans regard everything as theirs. And if they decided to help themselves to your goods, would they stop there or move on to a full body search? It's better not to tempt fate.'

Kuhn's eyes narrowed. 'You're glad about this. You hate great music, or black men. I can't tell which. Both, perhaps.'

Fischer sighed. 'Really, I don't care. Look, we can tell Zarubin that you've left some stuff for him to sell off, if he wants. It might bring a little goodwill, and we can use some.'

'Well, Beulah May's coming. You know that, right?'

'I suppose so. We'll need to take the rest of the *eiserne* portions, then.' It was a crime that in a starving town such nourishment was being reserved for a four-legged processing plant, but Fischer didn't know how to make the point without causing offence. The debt he owed to Kuhn for having taken him in wasn't insignificant, and even to hint that he might consider executing his best friend in the cause of food economy might be considered ungracious. What the Russians would make of her he didn't know. *Ragu*, perhaps.

Zarubin had offered no suggestions regarding their method of transfer from Zabelsdorf to the Control Zone. They were to turn up at its Vulcan-Strasse gate at 7am the following day, where they would be shown to their new accommodation and given instructions (which, Fischer assumed, would comprise a dogged iteration of *don'ts*). That particular section of the Zone was only a half kilometre from Kuhn's cellar, so the risk of being intercepted by the wrong sort of Poles *en route* was slight. Still, it gave them at least one good reason for keeping Beulah May on staff.

Despite his disappointments, Kuhn retained an unreasoning faith in life's capacity to improve. As he re-packed his money and few remaining cigarette packs, he kept up a steady monologue on the opportunities a smart man might seize.

'I hope you held out for a two bed apartment, Otto. With a view, perhaps?'

'Obviously. I particularly stressed that we wanted a Swedish kitchen and roof garden. Also porterage, a functioning lift and an attractive concierge who regarded hand-jobs as part of her service contract.'

'Sarcasm isn't necessary. There's little point going through this if we don't step up.'

'We aren't switching lifestyles, just getting out of a trap.'

Kuhn had been saying a tender farewell to his copy of *South Side Swing 1934 - 1935*. He waved it at Fischer. 'You realise it's going to be a hundred times more difficult to spring ourselves from the Zone? Here, we could just walk into the fields and then race for the border. There ...'

'I know. But there isn't a way for me to go west without Zarubin's blessing. If I ran he'd have me picked up somewhere in Mecklenburg, or he'd shoot Mazur's cousin and his crew, one by one, to let me know how disappointed he was. It's a matter of getting him to want me gone, gently, like it's his idea not mine. If I can manage that then the journey's going to be a great deal safer for both of us than hopping from farm to farm in the dark.'

'Yeah, you're right.' Kuhn sighed. 'A night run wouldn't work. She'd be pissing every hundred metres, or chasing every twitch in a bush. Wouldn't you girl? Yes, you would! Yes, you would!'

'So, for now we become good Germans. You know you shouldn't mention your Fourth International friends?'

'I'm not stupid.'

'Who *are* the good commies, in the Ivans' opinion?

'Ulbricht's gang, the KPD. It's their collective tongue that's tasted the most of Stalin's arse. But they're the ones who spent their war in Moscow. The *kozis* who stayed here and kept their heads down aren't trusted.'

'Well, we don't have time to study doctrine. Call everyone comrade and keep smiling.'

For the rest of the evening Kuhn played selections from his collection, tapping fingers in time to the beat, glancing morosely at Fischer every so often in case his sense of betrayal wasn't obvious. At eleven they turned off the lamp and tried to sleep, but a gun battle several blocks to the south and Beulah May's horsemeat-induced flatulence kept them awake until it began to rain steadily, causing the corrugated roof of the kitchen area to emulate several of Kuhn's favourite rhythm sections. Fischer, tired but comfortably relaxed on his sofa, thought of Marie-Therese and the unlikelihood of their relationship, playing with a different ending and how he might have dealt with it. He'd just about tired himself with it when the springs under Kuhn squealed.

'Otto?'

'What?'

'Do you think about her?'

He was too beaten to be surprised at this feat of telepathy.

'Every day and night.'

'Of course. Sorry.'

He wanted to say nothing more, to push it as far away as possible, but his morale was no more immune to darkness than anyone else's. It came out before the words were clear in his head.

'The days are fine. I'm thinking of her because I'm looking for her killer, it's just a practical thing, my job. But I don't get a say about what goes into dreams.'

'Bad?'

'And without sense. She's always there, and always different. I see her with any one of the faces of girls I used to know, or of female work colleagues – anyone, they only have to have been pretty. But I don't see *her* face, never hers. It's like I'm ashamed of what she was. Yet as soon as I'm awake again I see her as clearly as if she were bending over me, asking if I want a cigarette for breakfast. I must enjoy the pain.'

Kuhn turned again somewhere in the dark. 'Or the

schoolboy guilt. You couldn't protect her. Goodnight, Otto.'

At least there was no possibility of bad dreams now. He lay wide awake, wondering what had brought him back to Stettin of all places. A man looking for an escape usually chose a blank sheet, a place without memory, a bullet. Here, even before Marie-Therese, he had stored up enough shit to …

'Earl?'

'Mmm.'

'This is Poland, yes?'

'They can't fool you, Otto.'

'But as far as the Russians are concerned they'd like it still to be Germany, in one sense at least.'

'Which sense?'

'The *how much can we grab* sense. The Poles are inheriting an empty shop.'

'Serves them right for losing, just like us.'

'But when, exactly, did it become Poland?'

'Eh?'

'A decision was made. When?'

'I don't know.'

'Nor me. The British and Americans were against it, weren't they? Didn't they want the 1939 borders restored?'

'Joe didn't like that idea.'

'So they agreed the *principle* at Potsdam, but even the Russians weren't sure it was going to happen. Everything was confused. They talked about the Oder-Neisse line, but most of Stettin's on the West bank of the Oder, so I doubt it was originally intended to be part of the new Poland. Why else would they have kicked out the Poles and re-instated a German administration at Stettin?'

'That lasted ten minutes, didn't it?'

'Yes, but that's not my point. I want to know when they became convinced that it was definitely going to happen.'

'Find a working 'phone, call the Kremlin.' In the darkness, Fischer heard Kuhn turn over in the decisive manner that signals the end of a conversation.

'That would be my first choice. But what other evidence is there? When did the Soviets hand over real administrative powers to the Poles here?'

'The first time they gave them bullets to shoot Germans with.' Muffled by a pillow, Kuhn's voice was hardly audible.

'I think the Poles brought their own.'

'*Christ!* Wouldn't your Russian boss know?'

'Possibly. But he'd want to know why I want to know. And that might be fatal'

A sofa creaked somewhere in the dark. 'So you're not going to ask him?'

'Of course not, not in so many words. But finding some way to raise it might …'

'Might what?'

'Give me a better idea of what he wants.'

'He wants you to get your girlfriend's killer.'

'No he doesn't. He wants something that might be helped along by my finding the man, but the death of a German woman can't be of any interest to someone who's built a career on killing Germans.'

'Does it matter, knowing?'

'It'll give me a better idea of whether I'll be walking or floating away from this.'

## 40

Achym wondered if Napoleon had felt the same after Leipzig. The Emperor had been as Polish as any Corsican could be so they had a certain affinity, a brotherhood. On the matter of betrayal they were almost twins.

Even Wojciech was making the wrong noises, whining about how his arse was always freezing, how his navel was rasping on his spine and shouldn't they be making moves to get back into the Game? The others hadn't complained, not a whisper. They'd just waited until dark and then, one by one, fucked off. Everything he'd said about how they should bide their time and make the smart move at the right moment had gone in one ear and out the other, unhindered. Four days of country living, and it had broken them.

It wasn't as though he was their leader as such. This was a fraternity of like-minded businessmen, only the bit about minds had turned out to be blind optimism and the fraternal part a poor joke. He felt worse about it than he should. It wasn't as though their calling called for honour and integrity - in fact, thinking about anyone other than Number One was asking for trouble. But any way Achym looked at it, it hurt like a thumb under a hammer, or a breech delivery.

The salt in the wound was that they trusted him enough to leave the goods here in the cabins, knowing he wouldn't stiff them. Perhaps he had an aura, an invisible label, that said *Pliable*, or *Prick*. There were cases of cheap (now priceless) French brandy, almost a thousand tins of herring, pilchards or other oily fish, bales of fine wool cloth, a matching pair of Mauser hunting rifles with enough ammunition to depopulate the Black Forest, a case of Darjeeling tea (Achym had tested it on several old ladies to check that the British hadn't tainted it with industrial-strength laxative) and more PX ration packs and cigarettes than could be counted – all apparently safe in the increasingly lonely hands of a man they wouldn't trust with a strategy. No doubt they expected to come back in their own time, take their share, say thanks Achym and fuck right off again. So when he woke to find them gone he'd opened two tins of herring, just to make a point. The gesture made him feel a little better, but it wasn't going to be enough to keep Wojciech sweet. The man needed four meals a day just to stay conscious.

Napoleon got his men back eventually, but Achym didn't have time to do *eventually*. He couldn't wait to let the idiots find out how much they needed him, not with Szczecin threatening to become like every other town in the new Poland. He needed a fresh idea quickly, something that even they could appreciate. But it couldn't be just another hit and run thing like the coal; this had to as close to legitimate - to be lucrative *and* safe - as his limited experience of straight business could conceive.

'Girls', Wojciech suggested, as he always did when asked. But prostitution invited unwanted attention both from potential competitors and upright citizens, and the overheads were huge - Achym had been perfectly honest with Fischer about that. Besides, pimps were *people* people, and he wasn't sure he could do that much retail. The other obvious option was to intensify their cigarette business, but that would put them right up against some of least well-adjusted people in Szczecin, and in any case the market was being swamped by American product and they had no way to influence that supply. Tinned food was good but low profit, and alcohol – other than the type that removed organs – was being chased by everyone. Besides, he trusted neither his men nor himself with the product. The gold standard was medicinal products, obviously - demand so outstripped supply that a tenfold mark-up almost counted as charity. But Achym had no military hospital contacts and the Russians were uncharacteristically upright about not short-changing their own sick and wounded.

His head was beginning to hurt worse than the cold in their unheated cabin when the thought occurred to him. For a few minutes he doubted its simplicity and looked for the hole in his logic, the large fly in the pudding. But other than require an unpleasant degree of straight-dealing and even integrity it was perfect – a new (or at least renewed), untapped market for which he already had some product and could find far, far more. Best of all, it wasn't he or his men who would have to do the work. All they would be responsible for was supply and distribution.

He decided to tell Wojciech about it. Naturally it wouldn't appeal to him, but that was the point – if he could convince the colleague who least wanted a career in the legitimate business world, how hard would it be to bring in the others?

It took a while to calm him enough to explain the whole thing – the initial contract (a quick sale, no complications), the second phase (in which they went into a partnership arrangement with the very last people in Szczecin who'd want to speak to them), the formal agreement and onerous registration hoops they'd have to jump through and then the pay-off: a steady, profitable, honest business that would have the Straights calling them Polish patriots. Hell, if it went sweetly he'd probably be invited to join the fucking Rotary Club.

At first, Wojciech's face imitated a clubbed pike's, and what had taken Achym a few minutes to work through in his head required considerably longer to hammer into his lieutenant's (and yes, there'd have to be a chain of command now, not just Achym coming up with great ideas and hoping the rest of them latched on); but by the time they were ready to attack another few tins of herring he had a firm *yes* in his pocket from the biggest, most intimidating member of the former Pelzer-Strasse/ulica Kuśnierska gang. The rest of them would agree to the idea, he was certain. When it came to making long-term decisions, to showing a degree of initiative beyond the momentary impulse, they were as likely to go their own way as piss in a steep gutter. He wasn't worried about them; it was the other party to the arrangement that needed persuading – firstly, not to kill him and then to swear eternal brotherhood, or at least articles of association.

Wojciech's air of despondency had evaporated. He planted his massive fist into the table top, a blow that would have sent a man into a coma. 'When do we move?'

Achym preferred to take his time, think things through, look for the possible turds. But this was a Man of Destiny moment, and though he was far less familiar with them than Bonaparte he rose to it with a shrug that looked a lot more nonchalant than it was.

'Tomorrow morning OK for you?'

'Fine.'

It would still need to be arranged, and a hundred details might cack themselves in the process, but Achym suddenly felt much better for having conceived a plan. Even sat in this sty in the middle of a damp, charmless forest he felt he had a slightly stronger grip on his destiny than only a few moments earlier. The cold still scoured his bones but he no longer felt it; the lack of anything to do other than stare at the walls was less onerous than before (he could at least re-re-count their merchandises and comfort himself with what they were going to buy); even the overcast evening – a raw, thin, unseasonal evening - had lost most of its power to oppress his spirit. In fact his mood was as good as he could recall since he first came to this town. It was a pity then that the polite but firm knock on the hut door almost brought on the sort of seizure that had done for his father and two of his three uncles.

41

Fischer had wondered how Kuhn was going to deal with the matter, but in the event it couldn't have gone more smoothly. When one of the guards shook his head and began to slip the rifle from his shoulder, Kuhn told Beulah May to sit and then shouted *Умереть за товарища Сталина!* She groaned loudly and toppled over, and the Russians on the gate laughed so hard the tears flowed down their cheeks. The one with the rifle waved them in, pointed them at a hut that served as a duty office and actually thumped Kuhn's shoulder as he passed by.

'What ...?'

'I told her *Die for Comrade Stalin*. It was the only trick the guy I bought her from taught her before he decided she'd work better as calories.'

There was paperwork on the duty officer's desk that identified both Fischer and Kuhn. The man glanced at the dog without interest and in heavily Byelorussian-accented German told them to follow him. At the end of what had been Arthur-Strasse stood a group of small warehouses, most still showing heavy shell damage. The officer took them to the door of one of the larger units that had the luxury of a roof still, nodded and walked away without further ceremony. The door was open; Kuhn nudged Beulah May in ahead of them.

The single space inside was large but had been partitioned into roofless rooms, their wooden walls rising to the height of a man. A central aisle separated the east and west sections, across which were hung dozens of string-lines, most of them hung with drying laundry. A glance at it told Fischer that there were plenty of women and children here; a second glance – at the many faces that peered fearfully from the rooms' openings – confirmed it.

Slowly, a small crowd of people assembled in the aisle, advanced cautiously and stopped a few metres from the new arrivals.

The men among them were dock workers – it didn't need a harbour master's eye to identify the stevedores' clothing or the characteristic tattoos on their thick arms. Their women and children seemed tired, fearful, but all of them were in much better condition physically than the average Stettiner. Fischer scanned the faces quickly and found a familiar one – Gottlieb. He got a slight, unwelcoming nod.

Fischer's own face would have bred anxiety in the hardiest adult stomach, but the lure of Beulah May was too strong for the children. Four of them shuffled forward slowly, and the bravest hesitantly held out a hand for her to sniff. With infinite care she examined the scent, made a half-play at a lick, and was immediately engulfed in a stroking frenzy. The atmosphere loosened slightly.

'Germans?' Kuhn nodded at the lady who asked and offered his Lucky Strikes to no one in particular. They were gone in a moment, the final strand of his American connection parted.

Once they began to speak it was hard to stem the flow of questions – about the world outside, the rumoured new war between the Allies, the annexations of what had been German provinces by neighbouring states. One woman wanted to know if it was true that Bavaria was now part of Czechoslovakia, and had the turncoat Austrians helped themselves also? Another seemed to think that Churchill had given sanctuary to Admiral Dönitz's government in London, from where it was urging Germans to assist the Americans and British against the Soviets. Fischer found it hard to believe that the Control Zone was so tightly sealed that such stories could have gained purchase; but then, these were people who made an effort not to antagonize their new masters. Unless they were in the habit of going over one of the high fences at night (a feat Fischer had only just survived), their daily contacts were with Russians and the occasional Polish crew. Why wouldn't they have taken a twisted version of events about which no one could yet be certain?

When the conversation died the mood chilled once more. They wanted to ask why the two men had come to this place, but a wall had been raised around more than their home. Kuhn saw it, too. From one of the two large bags he had dragged from Schwartzkopff-Strasse he pulled an *eiserne* ration. 'We've brought food, if you're hungry. There's plenty.'

They looked doubtfully at the tin. One of the men coughed.

'Thanks, but we have food. Would you like breakfast?'

Accepting someone's hospitality never increased mistrust, so Fischer, already fed, nodded. They were led down the aisle bisecting the partition-village to the far end of the warehouse, to a mess area with tables and two wood fired stoves.

'Jesus', said Kuhn, and Fischer's nostrils caught it in the same moment - oatmeal and almost-real coffee.

They sat, surrounded, while a woman brought two bowls and an old man a coffee pot. Kuhn hardly had time to blurt his thanks before he was into the porridge. Fischer sipped his coffee and tried to make eye contact once more with Gottlieb, who was hanging back as far as didn't seem like indifference.

One of the other dockers pushed his way to the table.

'You're the one asking questions?'

It was hardly likely that Gottlieb hadn't given them a detailed description. In any case, Fischer wasn't here to deny anything. 'I am, yes. But I'm not a spy, and we're not here to spoil your arrangement with the Russians.'

None of them seemed convinced by the claim. No doubt they had a list somewhere of what would get them all shot or shovelled East, and it was unlikely to be a short one. They only way that they could be absolutely certain of not getting into trouble was to say nothing to Fischer or anyone else who wasn't family.

'Why, then?'

'It isn't safe for us out there. One of the Russians arranged it. We won't be here for long.'

'So you're not going to be asking stuff?'

'To be honest, I will. But it's been cleared by the Russian. Look ...'

Fischer took his authorization from a pocket and held it out. The docker took it and passed it to one of the women, who read it carefully. When she had finished she nodded and handed it back.

'We haven't done anything wrong. We do what they say.'

'I know. It isn't you I'm interested in.'

'We don't know anything, either. We don't watch and we don't listen. We just load and unload, or whatever else they set us to.'

'Yes, I understand. Actually, what I want is the very opposite of what might get you into trouble.'

'What's that?'

'Specifically, I want to know what you don't know.'

42

The General had made his staff wait for almost an hour now, freezing off their arses at the edge of the field while he talked the *Izvestia* correspondent through what he could recall and the adornments he had attached over the years for want of a sharper memory. He was glad the time was dragging, and of the several opportunities it gave him. His men were discovering just who they worked for, and why, and how very much harder the soldiers of his time had been than the milksop academy boys they put into officers' uniform nowadays for no better reason than their parents' Party connections. If his own arse wasn't getting numb he would have been happy to keep it going all day, giving them a break occasionally to run off into the trees to piss icicles.

The reporter was trying to keep the eager expression on his face, but the rattle of his teeth gave him away. That was fine; the General wasn't the sort of vodka warrior who needed the warmth of adoration to tell him he was alive still, and he'd given the boy about as much of the story as he could usefully print. After all, it hadn't been a victory - just a single, lonely piece of competence in six days of colossal fuck-ups.

He glanced around once more, this time for his own benefit. Twenty-five years ago that long tree-line had hidden his cavalry battalion, the last cohesive unit of the disintegrating 16th Army. His men had been foaming as much as their mounts, dying to ride into the flank of the advancing enemy, but he'd held them back long enough to make sure that the Poles weren't supported by any of the armour they'd managed miraculously to scrape together. It had been messy, confused, hardly the sort of thing that anyone lost or won; but it had checked the bastards long enough for the battalion to withdraw across the Bug looking like it was part of an army still (even if it wasn't). They'd not shamed their uniforms, unlike so many of their compatriots – including one snotty young chancer, name of Josef Vissarianovich Stalin, who'd goaded his Army chief into breaking off the advance on Warsaw to attack fucking Lwów of all places and then proclaimed their inevitable failure as proof that the world revolution wasn't going to happen. *Prick.*

The General caught himself and silently begged fate's pardon for his ingratitude. That business had saved his own life seventeen years later, when Snotty realised that a certain whining, self-justifying letter he'd sent to an old friend immediately after the debacle had been carefully preserved and hidden away. Otherwise, he'd have been retired to a lime pit along with all of the Boss's other unfinished business.

His men had stopped stamping their feet and were trying to stand to attention. They thought he was staring at them but he was seeing himself still, shivering in the trees, waiting, shit-scared of ordering yet another failure. A quarter of a century ago; it sounded like an age when you said it, but Christ, look how far they'd come since then, from abject failure to absolute mastery in twenty-five years exactly, and they'd smashed the finest army in the world along the way. *Second finest* - he corrected himself (it was shit, of course, but a good soldier didn't even think heresy). For that he had to give the Boss credit, even if he was entirely wrong about what should happen next. Two centuries had taught them that they couldn't hold on to these people, not without weakening the centre. Better to rob them blind, shoot the likely troublemakers (plus a few more), force them to sign eternal friendship and then pull out smartly.

*I'll be dead, it doesn't matter.*

It wasn't for him to care about other men's futures - he was done with all that, ready to accept his lot. A rear-echelon division wasn't much to round off a career, but better than the shallow grave that most of his generation had found waiting for them. Really, he wasn't ungrateful; he had a nice apartment in Minsk, a fat pension he'd arranged for himself on the sly, a housekeeper who'd perform favours for an old man as readily as bake his favourite pie and the satisfaction of knowing that the Boss checked his General Officers list at least once a month in the hope that one of them had died. A man could be happy with far less than that.

It was a pity he couldn't leave it at *that*. He didn't want another job, another obligation that wouldn't let him be at peace with himself. He wanted to go home and spend his final days drinking, eating and looking down occasionally upon his housekeeper's busy head, knowing that when the time came he could put the barrel of his Nagan in his mouth and neatly avoid decrepitude. But there it was, one thing more holding him - a heavy, painful duty, and when it was over he would have to face the only man he had ever loved and explain himself, beg forgiveness. Who wouldn't want to avoid such a thing, to put it off until death made the matter moot? He'd let it prey upon him, wished fervently for the strength to let it go. But a great wrong had been done, and it had to be put right.

The *Izvestia* hack closed his notepad and was saying something, offering his obsequious appreciation. Distracted, the General nodded, shook the clammy, cold hand.

'You'll send me a copy.' It should have been put as a question but there wasn't one, of course. It would arrive the very day after publication, with a complementary bottle of vodka, or a jar of preserved pears, or some other means of sweetening an enigma, someone whom no one had expected to survive so long. He loved this system - it kept everyone frightened by what they didn't know, which was more or less everything.

It was the tree-line and its memories of decisive action that did it, that made him decide to face the business. Until now he had made up reasons to deal with other matters, been too sentimental about things; but he had no way of knowing how much longer he'd be in this place, and a twenty-five-year-old letter was no guarantee that he'd be allowed to deal with matters in his own time. *Soon is better than later* he told himself and waved to his adjutant, the only other man who knew already what needed to be done.

The rest of his staff caught the gesture, jumped into their cars and started them up, delighted to be leaving finally. The day was bitterly cold and this was just a field, a barren, featureless stretch of Poland that had some unknowable resonance for an old man who hadn't held a fighting commission for years. Its tree-line seemed to fascinate him, but so what? Trees meant nothing to the modern Soviet Army, nor anything else that made for bad tank country.

## 43

'It's a shame.'

Gottlieb shook his head sorrowfully. In a world of *shames* it didn't seem a particularly striking one to Fischer, but then he wasn't a river man.

'Right now, she's the *Nekrasov*. I don't know what she'll be next week, but she used to be the *Kaiser*.' Gottlieb away turned from the vessel moored directly across the Oder at the mouth of the Bredower Graben. 'She was built right here, at Vulcan, in 1905, the first German ship ever to be fitted with steam turbines. It's unusual; we don't get many Stettin-built ships through here anymore. I've seen just two others since the war.

'She's definitely the one?'

'No doubt about it. For the past week we've been working on her under the Poles, so it looks like the Ivans are going to hand her over, or perhaps lease her. She's only nineteen hundred tons, so I suppose they don't need her in the long term. The old girl must be sick of being passed off - after the First War the British took her as reparations but sold her back to us. I doubt the Poles will do the same. Anyway, the Ivans have been using three vessels regularly for the reparations transfers that go from here. She's one of them.'

'But isn't she's a passenger vessel?'

Gottlieb shrugged. 'She was, once. A mine-layer more recently. And a barracks ship.'

The *Nekrasov* was a pretty vessel, the sort that had carried well-heeled Germans around the Baltic in happier times. But her early history didn't interest Fischer nearly as much as the very recent past and probable near future. The dockers had been ripping out fittings, making large spaces from small ones, so they assumed the Poles were going to use her to transfer displaced Germans to the West. She had been designed originally to carry about a hundred and thirty passengers in four-star comfort, but she was becoming a far more practical, one-star flesh mover. If they didn't bother with sleeping arrangements, perhaps six hundred each trip.

'So, 8 February?'

'Yeah. We'd all been loading for three months by then. I mean, *nothing* but loading. Mainly machinery and chemicals, delicate stuff mostly, so they needed us. All of that stopped on 8 February. Two days earlier we'd sent off the old *Wangoni* (she's the *Chukotka* now) to Memel with a hold full of Nobel Dynamit's lathes. Then the *Nekrasov* arrived and berthed in the Hafenkanal. Naturally, we were expecting to load her too, but the Ivans shipped us all across the Oder – men women and kids, everyone – to Arthur-Strasse, and told us we were going to be clearing wreckage from the Vulcan dock. They even gave us new lodgings. One minute we were on Lastadie, the next, here. But it was all shit. Two days later they started shipping half the men back to Lastadie each day for loading work, just like before. Only *Nekrasov* had gone by then. And all the clearance we've done here, it's been for nothing. They don't even use this part of the Zone.'

'So they wanted you off Lastadie, but only during 8-9 February.'

'Looks like it. As far as we can tell, there wasn't a single German on the island for forty-eight hours. And I'm betting no Poles either.'

'And none of the Russians have said anything since?'

Gottlieb shrugged. 'We don't socialize. A mate, Gunter, he was being ferried back and forth sometime after 8 February and spoke to one of the friendlier guards in mid-river. Asked if we'd been demoted or something. The Ivan didn't even grunt, like

Gunter wasn't there at all. It was a hint I suppose, and we took it.'

'And this has never happened before or since?'

'We started working for the Reds a few weeks after the surrender, once they decided to use Stettin as their main port for Silesian plunder. From then to now, that was it, the only time.'

Why would a group of river workers, the defeated enemy, be dangerous witnesses to whatever happened during those two days? Fischer stared across the Oder, willing the *Kaiser* or *Nekrasov* to offer up a hint. She looked to be unguarded but all of the island was secure, so even if her secrets remained baked into her flaking grey paint he couldn't get close enough to discover them. And he still wasn't sure that he needed to. Only the timing was right - Marie-Therese had died in the early hours of 8 February, but her body had been found almost a kilometre from the vessel, and all but one of the bridges that linked Lastadie to Stettin were down still. It would have been a risky, pointless distance to have carried a body, even for someone who had the authority to move between the two areas at night. It was only a possibility, a faint coincidence of events, and in a normal world he might have let it drop, looked elsewhere. But Zarubin had been pushing him towards this since he'd first been dragged into the business, and that meant something. A disinterested party might have allowed his investigator to follow leads among the town's large Polish criminal element, but Fischer's only potential source of information at Town Hall had been surgically excised within forty-eight hours, a dead-end closed off neatly. A Russian wanted him to look only at Russians, and had not only colluded in sabotaging the trial and swift execution of Miron and his fellow coal thieves but used them to keep Fischer on the leash, pulling hard. Asked to provide accommodation, Zarubin had promptly brought his unwilling employee into the Control Zone itself, the only Soviet enclave in this part of what had been Germany, the conduit through which Stalin's industrial plunder passed unhindered by auditors, international observers or God Himself.

Fischer didn't bother to wonder whether he should be nervous about any of this.

Gottlieb nodded at the far shore. 'She's fast. Not as much as she was, but she can keep up twenty knots all day. From here to Memel, say, no more than sixteen, seventeen hours. Less, if it was Königsberg.'

'And there's nothing on the eastern Baltic that isn't Soviet.'

'The Poles don't have anything yet. The Finns, fishing smacks perhaps.'

'So if something sensitive was being transported, it would be the safest method, storms allowing.'

'A tank column might be safer, but more eyes.'

'All the way through Poland, it would be very difficult. They'd have to clear a path ahead of them.'

'Very noticeable.'

'Public, even. By air?'

'Depends on what it was.'

Of course it did, and they had no way of knowing. Documents could have been in Moscow in hours by aircraft, but a … weapon? Fischer thought of Peenemünde, a place he'd hoped to forget. Where had production of the A4 gone after the bombing? Somewhere in Thuringia, they'd said, now in the American Zone. But there must have been other secret programmes, other technologies that Germany had tried to develop to rebalance the odds. If the Russians had found something, would they want their supposed allies – or anyone else - to know about it? Another possibility; another wild guess.

Gottlieb took his arm. 'We've been staring long enough. They'll notice soon.'

Looking in every direction he couldn't see a single Soviet soldier, but that wasn't reassuring. They seemed to do security very well, in his experience. The two men moved away from the shoreline, back along the shipyard's principal wet dock. It was filled with almost clear water now, the collapsed superstructure lifted, sectioned and stacked neatly at the rear of the dock.

'You worked fast.'

Gottlieb followed his gaze and shrugged. 'The Ivans brought in acetylene torches. It wasn't too difficult. I'm sorry I couldn't tell you more about …'

'No, that's fine. I didn't expect more. It's why Earl Kuhn's with me.'

'Your friend with the dog? Does he know ships?'

'I doubt it very much. But he knows some Russians.'

Monika told herself not to be a fool, but the feeling persisted, a small, inappropriate sense of pride in herself and her fellow Bernhageners. In fact, for the first time she could remember she felt quite *German* without fearing what the consequences of that might be. A year earlier they had fled their village as wartime refugees do – terrified, lost and helpless in the tide that swept them up. Now, their number more than halved, their possessions a pitiful fraction of what they had taken with them on that earlier flight, their few remaining carts without a single horse or ox to pull them, they were showing their strange new world a proper, dignified face.

The schedule helped of course, even if it was one that would remove them from their homes forever. A date and a process put walls around uncertainty, even if they could have wished for neither. A goal was something to aim for, even if it was of necessity, an ordained end. They had become used to nothing, emptiness, and this was at least a path into some sort of *next*.

No one had been more surprised than her by the behaviour of their new Polish neighbours. They had accepted nothing in return for food and blankets, and a few had even expressed a form of regret for what was happening (though Monika knew that this could be no more than politeness, or Christian pity, or the empathy of folk who themselves knew what it was to be displaced). It was made clear to the German villages that, while they were not expected to be allowed ever to return, they could be satisfied that the new owners would treat their land and homes with respect in memory of those now going. Monika wasn't sure how much of a balm this would be once folk started thinking about it, but for the moment it offered an illusion of continuity, of having left a footprint in the world.

So, with a little Polish goodwill and Amon Stemper's

practical help she had organized her willing disciples. Their clothes now contained more secret places than a smuggler's cove, where Bernhagen's few remaining heirlooms could be kept hidden during their march. She had also been urging them all to walk regularly, if only for a kilometre or two around Bernhagen's roads and fields, so that when the time came their bodies would not be too shocked by the novelty of it (she was fairly certain that only a few of her congregation had found this particular commandment amenable). Most urgently, she had impressed upon them the importance of presenting a compliant face to the men who would herd them to Stettin. While their own Poles had proved to be decent folk, there were probably many who yearned for a chance to settle debts, and to give that sort an excuse would be to add to their present woes wilfully.

But preparations could do only so much, and Bernhageners had been eating too little for too long to be ready for any substantial trek. Monika comforted herself as best she could with the thought that the past year had been an efficient sieve; that those who remained alive were best able to make do with least. Looking at what they had become she often wondered if others found it ironic also, that defeat was doing more to achieve the goal of a stronger, more resilient species than anything the Party had attempted. Still, she couldn't deny that when others reminisced wistfully of the old days, of beer and sausages, *fettkuchle*, *hutlesbrot* and *zimtsterne*, her stomach growled no less than theirs. Think of Lübeck and what we'll find there, she told them at such times, more certain in her voice than heart.

But when the morning came her flock assembled quietly and efficiently. Even those who had never before suffered fate's elbow without bending its ear didn't complain, or sigh, or roll their eyes with unspoken cause. Quietly, they brought their little handcarts to the junction outside the church, formed a line with the least hearty folk in the middle (much, they imagined, as British convoys did in the oceans) and waited, each man and woman performing a silent audit upon their immediate neighbour's dress and manner, looking for signs of despair, dereliction or omission. Old friends caught each other's eye and nodded as if they had not kept company the previous evening, as if to say well here we are then, let it happen. It could hardly have been more unlike the panicked prelude to the previous year's march.

As befitted a general and her *aide de camp*, Monika and Amon Stemper arrived after everyone else, having first checked all the emptied houses to ensure that there were no stay-behinds or overlooked potatoes. Erika had assigned herself to Monika's handcart by the simple act of placing her tiny hoard of possessions into it and wheeling it off to the church before its owner could have a say in the matter. For the moment she formed the column's vanguard, and had a face ready for Polish officialdom that occupied the thin edge between defiance and insolence, a face that her aunt watched anxiously and asked her husband several times to try to persuade away. He was too busy arranging his own estate to oblige her, but Erika's attitude softened to merely officious as Monika arrived and required helping through the appellant mob.

Their escort had not yet graced Bernhagen with its presence, so Monika had time to be led down the entire column, to give her opinion on whether this could be done a little better, or if that was quite what she had in mind (and if not, what?), or whether there room for a particular piece of furniture that a great grandmother had bequeathed and would cause the lady to stir in her grave should it be left to plunderers. To each entreaty she offered the same response – that it was entirely up to the supplicant whether this, that or whatever should be moved, abandoned or loaded, and no matter what he or she did the Poles might have a different idea about it. This was not what they wanted to hear but no one said so; the day was going to be one for surprises and shocks, and they realised that even Monika Pohlitz's wisdom had to make a little room for the indifferent tide of events.

By eight am (checked surreptitiously on a watch that emerged from and was promptly re-concealed in a hidden pocket), a slight sense of deflation was beginning to infect the Israelites, who had hoped that the authorities might take the business as seriously as they.

'Perhaps they're having a leisurely breakfast' suggested Ellie Bontecou, with a loud sniff that put everyone on notice that she didn't care who heard her. A few of her neighbours nodded wistfully, recalling that lost pleasure of better mornings. Amon Stemper asked one of the girls to watch from the church tower to give them all warning of the Poles' approach (and him time to calm the more turbulent tempers), and two others to bring water from the pump to ensure that the trek didn't commence upon the back of a general thirst or half-emptied bottles. But the girls had only begun to collect pans for the task when a truck appeared from the direction of Zampelhagen, belching dark exhaust fumes as if announcing the fate it presaged.

An officer of some sort emerged from the passenger side. No Bernhagener was sufficiently familiar with Polish military traditions to be able to identify his rank, though the absence of any gold braid on his uniform was a little disheartening for those who had hoped to have their expulsion marked by a little ceremony. Unerringly, the young man identified Amon Stemper as the competent authority and saluted him quite smartly. Amon use his halting Polish to introduce Monika (as she had feared and expected he might), and offered to translate instructions as best as he could. These took a while to deliver across the barrier of language, but it became clear very quickly that the protection promised to the villagers was going to be more moral than practical. Though the Government of the new Poland was determined to make a start upon its German problem the resources it could provide were hardly up to the task (the officer apologized for this, as though his victims had a right to expect more *Germanic* arrangements). So, armed guards would be available but only at the concentration points where the refugees would assemble along their route to be fed and allowed to sleep. Otherwise, the young man hoped to be able to organize a flying column of troops to deter attempts by unruly elements to make an unpleasant experience even more so.

Amon asked if it was known how many Germans were going to be converging upon Stettin during the next days. The young man apologized once more for his lack of precise information on this point, but was quite certain that it would be several thousand from this *voivodeship* alone, so if Bernhageners wished to remain together during their journey they might be required to wait some hours once they reached the main Naugard-Stettin road before being able to join it. This disappointing news was offered with such obvious regret than no one felt they could make a fuss about it, particularly when the officer reassured them that no penalty would be incurred if some refuges arrived at their concentration points behind whatever schedule might or might not have been determined.

Monika listened to this with a heart that mirrored Amon Stemper's falling face. The others seemed a little relieved that their exodus would be less rigorously policed than they had feared, but she was quite certain that slipshod arrangements weren't in their best interests. Really, if they had to leave it should be organized like a military campaign, with every eventuality anticipated before it occurred rather than being left to luck, God and the whim of roving gangs of pillagers who fancied a last shot at the departing German population. She didn't say so, of course. No one needed less reassurance than they had already, and complaining about it would change nothing.

The officer handed a piece of paper to Amon Stemper. It was a map, showing the route that Bernhageners and Zampelhageners should take. For the first time the young man put a little iron into his voice when he explained that this was not a suggestion but their designated itinerary, chosen to prevent premature congestion. One of the villagers who peered over

Amon's shoulder to confirm to his satisfaction that it was the wrong way to get to Stettin shook his head contentedly and shouted to the rest 'We're going west, not north.'

Monika took the map while everyone else remonstrated with the officer. They were to cross country by back lanes as far as Gollnow and join the main road just west of the town. For birds it was the quickest, most obvious route, but humans wanting to make the easiest passage to Stettin tended to head north and join the road well to the east, trusting to a broad, smooth metalled surface to make up lost time. Naturally, the main tide of German expellees would be on that road already by the time they reached it, so the logic of keeping Bernhageners off it as long as possible was sound enough; but local village roads, never very good, had become a lot worse since the end of the war, so a hard journey had just become a little harder.

The Pole, smiling amiably, let the complaints exhaust themselves, said one more thing to Amon Stemper, shouted *good luck!* in Polish and climbed back into his vehicle. To rub salt into the wound it promptly took the northern road out of the village, straight towards Naugard, the route they would all have taken if given the choice.

Almost every pair of German eyes turned from the Naugard road to Monika. 'Well,' she said in a voice too loud to carry any of the many emotions she felt, 'are we ready?'

Amon Stemper looked at her blankly. 'What ... just like that?'

'You want to ring the church bell? We should go now, use as much daylight as we can. Erika, we can't be in front. Let Albert and his family lead us off.'

Obediently, Albert Foerster pulled his cart to the front of the line. He had two sons, young but strong, and had already promised one of them to Monika to help pull what remained of her family possessions. She nodded as he passed by her and carried on, not pausing, a one-cart *hegira* pointing the way towards Zampelhagen. Once Monika was in her seat Erika seized a shaft and, with Simon Foerster, followed his father's lead. Slowly, the line of carts behind them began to move, their owners' reluctance to leave scoured into every centimetre of the shallow ruts they drew in the dusty road. A few heads turned back as they left the village but Monika's remained firmly pointed to the west, hinting at a discipline and determination she hardly felt. Within five minutes they were out of Bernhagen, passing slowly by fields they had once worked, had once fed their families from, had once called their inheritance. But other men stood in them now, pausing in their work as the column passed by, watching one world pass into another as it had done so often in that part of Pomerania.

That evening, a few kilometres to the west of Zampelhagen, the former residents of Bernhagen (now, irrevocably, *Ostrzyca*) were robbed for the first time.

## 45

The docks had disturbed Fischer. It wasn't the massive, obvious damage done by enemy aircraft and artillery (there could hardly be a German anywhere who wasn't inured to a surfeit of rubble), but the areas that had been cleared and levelled, made pristine for whatever was to come, reminded him starkly that a way of life had been erased. For almost a century, Stettin had filled the Baltic with shipping – trawlers, colliers, merchantmen, pleasure cruisers, passenger liners, ice-breakers, patrol boats, destroyers, cruisers and even battleships (until fashion and the race to outdo the British demanded that they grew beyond twenty thousand tonnes). The Bredower shipyards – Vulcan, Oderwerke - had taken generations of men, fathers, sons and grandsons, and given them a job for life, with skills that protected against both recruitment and recessions. Across the river, the vast Lastadie docks had loaded the finished products with men, manufactures and weapons and sent them across seas and oceans, the palpable proof of unified Germany's explosive rise. Stettin's river trade had created an Imperial boom town, a prodigy, and now it was the precise reverse – a cracked plughole through which trickled the last of a former nation's wealth as it seeped into other hands. To see this place as it had once been required the sort of imagination that could resurrect Babylon.

As a young policeman he had been sentenced to six months' night duty here, his reward for failing to accommodate a local Party official over the minor matter of the rape and murder of a young girl. At the time he had hated every moment of his exile from Augusta-Strasse, but memory softens edges, and now he recalled the Brechtian panorama of his nightly beats almost with affection - the abundance of front-room taverns (unlicensed since the days when Prussia had been one hopeful duchy among many); the corner soup stalls – *goulash cannons* – blunting the worst effects of cheap booze and then greasily assisting its explosive evacuation; the lively business done by whores on Friday night, when the workers left the yards and docks with a little money fattening their pockets and later faced their wives with slurred excuses for its curious disappearance. He could hardly forget the fights - short, savage and sometimes fatal, only ever broken up by brave men (or, in his case, an over-confident idiot who imagined he had one too many testicles), and the charge sheets half written-up then tossed away for want of witnesses . It had been a wen, as full of raw, dangerous life as a laundry chute in a plague ward, and yet he almost yearned to have it back.

'So that's a ship, then.'

'Don't be glib.'

Earl Kuhn had no interest in nautical matters, but having grown up in Stettin and plundered the wrecks that littered the river at the war's end it was unlikely he was unfamiliar with marine architecture. He stared without interest at the pretty lines of the *Nekrasov*.

'What's the story?'

'You have regular contacts among the Ivans?'

'A couple, for cigarettes. It isn't like we're mates.'

'I never asked - you get cigarettes, but what do *they* get?'

'It depends. German souvenirs were big last year, so more or less anything with a label did it. Now, they're more discerning. The last time I bought large they wanted currency, or plate. I found them some porcelain.'

'You must talk about more than business. Don't Russians seal a bargain with a drink?'

'Not in my experience. Usually it's a nod or a grunt. There's one, he likes to talk about his girl back in Volskoe, but that's only because she's not there anymore. A Volga Mennonite, the poor bitch.'

'Ethnic German?'

'Yeah. You'd think he'd have more sense than to get involved with that sort. But at least he has something to be miserable about, and Russians aren't happy unless they're miserable.'

'It's probably what gives him the stomach to deal with you.'

Kuhn flicked his cigarette butt into the Oder. 'Liking Germans? That's what I thought. Anyway, he speaks the language, so I get more than a grunt.'

'He's here in Stettin?'

'Most of the time. He's Rear Services, transportation, so he gets around. But his posting's here.'

'Good. I need to speak with him.'

'You're kidding! Hand over my best supplier?'

'A word, that's all. No one has to know about it except the three of us.'

'You think a guy who's handing himself the death penalty on a daily basis is going to push his head out of the cave and say fine mate, what shall we talk about?'

Fischer extracted his magic authorization. 'You can take this, show it to him. Tell him that I'm not interested in cigarettes, only a little information about a matter that's nothing to do with him. Say that his bosses will be very pleased with him if he cooperates. And give this to him, too. Tell him it's his, whatever he decides.'

Kuhn pulled a face but pocketed the document and ten dollar bill. 'What about you? Without this you can't get in and out of the Zone.'

'Then don't take your time about it, or get shot.'

'You'll watch Beulah May?'

Kuhn was becoming nervous about his dog. The German children were petting her constantly, playing games with her, feeding her on demand (not an easy task) and gradually draining her resolve to be a threat to limbs. If it carried on she'd be no more than a pet, useful only for what her original owner had planned for her.

'I'll be harsh, I promise. And Earl ...'

'What?'

Kuhn slouched, waiting, half-filling the tattered sailor's jacket he habitually wore. Fischer suspected that its previous owner had gone down with the *Ancona*, surfaced and then been strafed heavily as he floundered amid burning wreckage. The refugee look was an advantage on Stettin's streets - it deterred the casual thief and even drew out the occasional act of charity from the more forgiving Poles. But in the Control Zone it invited someone with a gun to ask questions, and Fischer didn't trust Zarubin's authorization to grease every encounter.

'While you're outside, go to Grossmann. Get a half-decent coat, one that makes you disappear.'

'A sailor's jacket is conspicuous in a port?'

'That one is.'

'Otto, I'm not spending my Swiss francs. They're going to buy me a record shop, not style.'

Fischer sighed and extracted one of his three remaining Hamiltons. 'This should get you something decent. You can pay me back in Heidelberg, or wherever.'

'Right.'

'And while you're out there don't forget Zarubin for a moment. The man has eyes in the back of everyone else's head. If you suspect you're being watched or followed, don't meet your fellow.'

'I won't.' Kuhn shivered. 'For someone without staff he's covering a lot of ground.'

'He has informers. These days everyone needs, knows or fears something. His biggest problem is sorting good information from dross, but he seems to know how to work people. And now we're here in the Control Zone with only his authority that lets us come or go he probably won't miss a thing.'

'Bastard.'

'This is the Age of Doctrine, Earl. Men like him are useful.'

'It must have been nice, back when no one cared what you did or didn't think.'

'When was that?'

'Well, before unification I suppose.'

'You mean in the good old sixteenth and seventeenth centuries, when half of Europe slaughtered the other half on the matter of what they believed?'

Kuhn shrugged. 'I don't do much history, as you know.'

'The Fourth International must have tried to put you right.'

'Them and Goebbels were brick fucking bookends in my head. Look.'

A crewman had appeared on the main deck of the *Nekrasov*, just forward of the stack. He was too far away to make out clearly, but the shirt sleeves were rolled up and there was nothing of a uniform about him. From the low, relaxed way he was leaning on the rail he was probably having a smoke-break from whatever was going on over there. Perhaps his eyes were directed to the west bank of the Oder and fixed upon two ragged Germans, flaunting their presence in a restricted area, watching business that was most decidedly not their own. For Fischer, imagination was always a good indicator of inner anxiety. He never seemed to suffer one without the other.

Earl tugged at his sleeve. 'Let's be somewhere else.'

They walked away from the shore, following the southern edge of the Vulcan dock. At its far end Fischer paused and turned to the *Nekrasov* once more. The man was gone.

'Something about that boat bothers me.'

'It's a *ship*, Otto. Even a lubber knows that. What?'

'It's small.'

'Not to me.'

'But to the Ivans? The merchant marine took a pasting, but there must be enough large vessels still floating for their needs. If they're stripping everything out of Pomerania and Silesia before the Poles can lay claim, why slow the process unnecessarily? The other vessels doing the Stettin run are about eight times bigger than her. She's not only small but badly laid out, if moving loot's why she's here.'

'So why then?'

'Gottlieb said she was *fast*. What if that's the whole point?'

'What if it is?'

'That's what bothers me.'

46

It was Amon Stemper himself, dying at the roadside a few kilometres south of Gollnow, who convinced his neighbours that it wasn't murder. He had been stubborn, refusing to relinquish the briefcase, and the young man had little appreciated his own strength. The shove had hardly counted as a deadly assault, but Amon's violent fall into the deep drain ditch had been enough to persuade his weak heart that its work was all but done. They lifted him carefully and tried to make him comfortable. He seemed embarrassed by the attention, the tears.

'It's a pleasant place for it', he told Monika Pohlitz, whispering into her ear so as not to distress the press of Bernhageners around him with the hollow quality of his gasps. And it was, a most pleasing prospect; the treetops of Gollnow Forest loomed directly above him, framing the sky he expected imminently to explore, disturbed only occasionally by the heads of fellow refugees passing by, their numb, traumatized gazes a telling reminder of the situation he was departing. He told Monika that he felt quite comfortable, and it was almost the truth.

A few Bernhageners turned from the upsetting prospect to scan the road in both directions, fearing the consequences of their collective pause. They had lost their place (if *place* it was) in the vast column of refuges trudging southwards, and like all good Germans knew that there were penalties for obstructing official arrangements. But their herders were too few for the job and visible only occasionally, bustling up and down, shouting or shoving when someone tried to rest, or complain, or struggle with one of the many carrion Poles who fell at will upon the passing trade in victims and picked at what remained of their possessions. The protection they had been promised seemed to consist of a small group of mounted policemen whom they had seen just once the previous day, cantering very prettily along the road's western verge, their attention far from the rabble they supposedly guarded.

Monika's knees had hardly begun to lose their feeling when a second, massive infarction seized Amon's heart. His face, already reposed, hardly registered the event; she felt only a brief tightening of his grip upon her hand and then it was as gone as the rest of him. She closed his eyes and climbed to her feet using Erika as a crutch, while Ellie Bontecou began one of her loud, tearful remonstrances against God, the fates and the common fortune of unloved peoples. Hurriedly, she was hushed by a clutch of women around her who were long familiar with what lack of tact accompanied her outbursts. She settled for weeping noisily, the lead voice in a choir of similar.

Respectfully, two men laid out Amon's corpse among the trees and covered it with a thin blanket. No one suggested a burial, and any prayers were silent ones, offered hurriedly as the Bernhagen faction of the exodus reassembled and prepared to force itself back into the lethargically moving stream. From the ditch Erika retrieved Amon's briefcase, abandoned by the thief when he discovered that it contained only documentary evidence of the life he had extinguished. It had no further purpose now, no function without an officially recorded interment, but for want of any other ceremony preserving it seemed the respectful thing to do. Carefully, Monika placed the papers with the artefacts of her own, less substantial life history (a bundle of tattered certificates folded in old newspaper), and nodded at Albert Foerster, who was waiting to lead off their column. His own grief looked to be of the sort that might be eased considerably by someone objecting to their re-joining the flow of refugees. Perhaps it was noticed; in any event the road was wide, and room was made without comment other than the brief, muttered introduction between two carts that found themselves side by side – a *Bernhagen* offered for a *Düsterbeck*. Gradually, the two villages merged into single file.

Amon Stemper's was the third death upon their two-day-old odyssey, all of them heart-failures brought on by exhaustion, or dehydration, or that sublime concurrence of body and mind that things are best done with. The displaced had received no food during that time, and only the streams they'd crossed had gone some way to replacing what had been drunk far too quickly the previous day. Perhaps it was the Poles' famous lack of organisation that was to blame, but Monika didn't think so. It seemed to her rather that she and her fellow outcasts were fading like the histories they represented, dissipating into the air, unnoticed by those who had lives to build here. It was a wonder to her that more had not died, but there was time enough yet. Stettin was another full day away at least.

They trudged on for a few hours more until the sun began to sink over the western horizon, where what was said still to be Germany began. When the halt came it was without notice; along the road ahead of them carts were turned and wheeled on to the narrow strip of grass that kept the trees and road apart. Bernhageners and Düsterbeckers were mingled still as they departed the metalled surface, but by the time they collapsed wearily onto the soft turf some herd instinct had separated them amicably. Up and down the emptying road a few fires spluttered to life, defying the peeling, fading German signs (some upright still) that enforced the forestry rules of another age. A few optimists wondered if by some remarkable turn of fate there was a prospect of hot food, but they were quickly disabused by a number of Poles wearing armbands who walked up and down shouting the same phrase over and over - *Jutro jedzenie, w Szczecinie!*

'Oh well' said Monika, a little too brightly to convince her despondent audience, 'we can last another day.'

'But I'm hungry,' said one Bernhagener, unused to not speaking her mind.

'We all are, dear. But no one's starving yet.'

This was true, and most of her fellow villagers squared their shoulders a little, reminding themselves that they had done very well to come through worse things than a little hunger since the end of the war. Erika - who had laid discreet but firm claim to the vacant position of Village Backbone since her voice returned - stroked the grass with both her hands.

'At least it's dry, and not too cold.'

Again, Bernhageners nodded, allowing that their arses could have been damper than they were, and considerably number. Young Ernst Foerster (who held a great secret and had been desperate to let it go for two days now), glanced imploringly at Monika, and after a brief struggle she nodded slightly. He trotted to his family cart, returned with a large canvas bag and gave it to her. She spoke quietly, hoping not to rouse any attention from nearby strangers.

'There should be enough for everyone to have a piece, if we aren't greedy.'

Stale bread wasn't a traditional Pomeranian delicacy, but not a single Bernhagener rejected this unexpected bounty. With unchristian care they raised their portions discreetly to their mouths and tried not to chew too obviously, though in the fading light it would have been a keen pair of Düsterbecker eyes that made out the transaction.

The new Polish baker in Bernhagen had offered three dozen loaves to Monika before the German villagers departed - his expiation, perhaps, for sins that other Poles had commissioned. She had kept word of this from everyone other than Amon, Erika and the Foersters, knowing that, given a choice, their neighbours would have devoured their portions before the last cart had departed the village. She should have been stronger, waited until heads became lighter for want of food, but sometimes a little raised morale went further than a feast.

Most of them had hardly swallowed their last crumb before they were asleep, fully clothed, their bags for pillows. They had enjoyed the small blessings of relatively good weather, flat terrain and decent roads, but walking without choice was hard work and even Monika was content to let her body's aches have their say while putting all tomorrows from mind. She drifted almost pleasantly towards unconsciousness with only her hand on sentry duty, clutching the edge of the altar cloth she wore as a blanket.

She wakened with no sense of time having moved on. It was already half-light, the air cold and heavy with moisture that passed through the altar cloth, her clothes and skin with equal ease. She moaned, forgetting to stifle it. Around her, several of her neighbours were standing, rubbing feeling back into stiff limbs, mute with misery. A little way from them, Düsterbeckers were gathered around a fire, passing around breakfast, and even the hungriest Bernhageners were too shamed to wander across to see if there might be a surplus. One of the diners noticed the wistful glances and ignited a brief but intense debate. A few minutes later she and another woman entered Bernhagen territory.

'I'm sorry. We have nothing to spare.'

Monika nodded and introduced herself. Anna and Gerda did the same. Anna was a large woman with a ruddy complexion made much ruddier by the cold. She wrapped herself in her arms and rubbed briskly. 'We won't be moving for a while. The Poles came past about a half hour since and said we had to wait.'

'Wait? For what?'

The other woman shrugged. 'I don't know. One of our lads spoke to someone from further up the line. They're saying the Poles have tripped over a dead man in the trees, some big officer, a Russian. But what can you believe? It's probably just someone having fun making us miserable.'

'I didn't know there were Russians here anymore.'

Anna stared at Monika. 'They run Stettin port and the river all the way to the Baltic.'

'We haven't heard much news lately.' Monika shivered. She liked the thought of dead Russians even less than live ones. It would bring trouble for someone, a German or Germans most likely.

Gerda hawked and spat into the grass. 'It was probably the Poles. They hate the Reds more than they hate us.'

'Not the communists. They've been kissing Russian arse for years. They're redder than Stalin.' Anna snorted. 'Hearth dogs to a man.'

Monika listened to this sophisticated exchange with some awe. She knew very little of the world beyond Pomerania (and not much of that either), yet these village women spoke easily of distant things. Perhaps they'd had access to a radio.

As they stood there four mounted Poles rode past at full gallop, south towards Stettin (or the incident), scattering the few refugees who had wandered on to the road. In a moment they were gone again, swallowed up by the mist.

Gerda sniffed knowingly. 'They wouldn't be rushing if it wasn't serious.'

With a nod to Monika the two women returned to their camp fire, which had almost surrendered to the wet, heavy air.

'Shall we light one of our own?'

Erika was at Monika's elbow, shivering. She was wearing a shapeless woollen hat, her first attempt at something other than a scarf. It gave her the air of an unkempt pixie.

'It's too late. We won't find any dry wood now. If we wait in the trees it won't be so bad.'

For once only half of her flock took her advice, as she herself remained on the verge, staring to the south, hoping to see movement. For almost half an hour she shivered in her damp clothes, refused offers of blankets, deflected questions whose answers either were obvious to anyone over the age of five or clearly beyond her power to answer. She was about to surrender to her own suggestion and take refuge among the firs when the view of the road began to close from its further point as refugees streamed back on to it with their carts. Pointlessly, a group of Polish militia were moving north on its western side, shouting in bad German, trying to rouse folk who were fully roused already. They looked worried, preoccupied by something more than their sheep.

The road filled quickly with refugees wanting – for once – to be moving. A few shouted to strangers, trying to get some idea of what had held them there; most busied themselves with their carts, re-tightening cords or shifting loads, checking that their straitened inheritances were intact still. Within ten minutes the column had begun to shuffle forward, creeping once more towards Stettin, or whatever name it bore these days. Monika refused young Ernst's offer to pull her cart while she sat in it and walked with the other Bernhageners, ignoring their low chatter. There was no cause to worry; nothing had happened other than a small delay, a minor ripple in the arrangements that were displacing them, something that someone with no home, no future and a fading past might hardly have noticed. But the feeling remained with her all that day, even when her ankles and knees hurt so badly they should have chased away every other concern - a quiet, pressing fear of strangers and their inconceivable doings.

## 47

For two days Fischer waited, fretting about things he couldn't affect, hoping not to glimpse Earl Kuhn's body floating slowly northward past the Vulcan dock. He had no more questions to ask of the captive port Germans, no lines of enquiry that he could pursue within or outside the Control Zone without his precious authorization to shield him from a Russian bullet. He rediscovered boredom, that wonderful artefact of gentler times.

His hosts accepted his presence as they did that of the weather, without comment or apparent notice. He ate with them, washed in a raw, communal bathhouse segregated only to maintain the proprieties between sexes, slept in a space partitioned for his use and had no illusion as to the unbridgeable distance that lay between himself and every other human being in this strange, not-quite-anywhere. More so than he could ever recall he felt apart, and despite himself began to observe for no better reason that to satisfy his curiosity.

Their past life was gone yet they lived it still, stubbornly, ignoring the vast changes in material circumstance that scoured this part of Germany no less than the rest. At worst they were prisoners, forced workers for an unpredictable conqueror; at best, specimens preserved in some finite medium with no way to test its resilience. Either way, he decided, they should be worried.

Most of the time the men were quiet and dour, worked to a blunt indifference to their situation. But the women were less closed in, and such chatter as he overheard seemed to Fischer no less superficial than that of folk whose walls were much lower. Their children did what children everywhere did, which was to take their environment for what it was and adapt their games to fit. They played at war, and gangs, and hide-and-find, and teased the occasional kindly Russian who would chase them for just long enough to make it interesting. They had even – Fischer didn't know how he was going to explain this to Earl – taught Beulah May to roll over for a tickle within twenty-four hours of her master going back out into the world. It was, in every sense but the literal, an ordinary domestic continuum.

On the first evening of Kuhn's absence, Gottlieb had taken him aside and named the price of his information in the matter of the *Nekrasov*. It was acceptable of course, but it relied upon Fischer's ability to meet it. When he explained the situation the docker shrugged, as if it was a given that any promise was subject to the vagaries of a world in which Germans had no rights of redress. 'We'll wait and see', he'd said, and shuffled away without a handshake or any other token of a bargain struck.

The Ivans came at 6.30 every morning to take away the men to their several tasks. On both mornings that Fischer made the effort to catch the moment the same two soldiers turned up, bored, their weapons shouldered and probably unloaded - like a low-security prison everyone seemed to know and accept their situation. The end-of-shift was less precisely timed, usually between 6 and 7pm. The men returned unaccompanied, because no-one was going to run from everything that was dear to him. In any case, weariness hung almost like a camouflage net over the returning dockers after a day's unceasing labour to load Soviet booty or clean the docks of the shit the Allies had made of it. If anyone *did* try to run, his gaolers wouldn't need more than a child's fishing net to recapture him.

It made Gottlieb's price seem even stranger, but Fischer had little interest in other men's ambitions. He had no idea whether it was within Zarubin's gift to arrange it, though it was hard to imagine that NKGB, or SMERSH, or whatever organization he represented, couldn't do such things if they considered it necessary. The worst of it was obvious – that Fischer had committed himself to being sufficiently useful to the Russians to make it a price worth paying, as he had on behalf of the imprisoned Miron and his boat mates. Slowly, unavoidably, he was acquiring a heavy burden of other men's expectations.

On the third morning the same two soldiers returned for the dockers, trailed by Earl Kuhn. He was limping badly but seemed cheerful enough. Part of his fine mood may have been the fault of his new Grossmann coat, which, strictly against orders, made him anything but invisible. It was a long dark thing, a slaughter-field of pelts that shone subtly when the sun caught it at an angle. In the old days it would have been worn by an impresario, or pimp, or someone wishing to make the sort of statement that offends impressively. In the present age it was a slap to the face of an entire, shattered continent.

'My God.'

'Hello, Otto. You look cold. I'm not.'

'Could you not be more ostentatious?'

Kuhn looked down complacently, moving his hands in the pockets a little to disturb the sea of fur. 'I really didn't choose it. The old man went through his stock until he found something that hid the money-belt properly. He insisted, said he owed me.'

'For putting the Nemitz gang on to him in the first place?'

'Hush.'

'Did you speak to your Russian?'

The fur shrugged. 'I did, but all I got was fuck yourself. Told me we wouldn't be doing any more business if I pushed it. Sorry, Otto.'

Fischer took the authorization and unused Hamilton from Kuhn's reluctant hand. 'How far did you get?'

'*Hello*, more or less. I managed to say that a friend had a couple of questions and would he mind? That got me a blank look, but the piece of paper killed the conversation. I think it was all the red stamps.'

'He can read?'

'Yeah, but some things you don't want to.'

It was what Fischer had expected, but he allowed the disappointment to show. He nodded at the leg that Kuhn was favouring. 'Who did that?'

'Me, and a pothole.'

'You were running?'

'Redeploying, before a militia patrol needed to examine the magic paper. It's cool, they didn't see me.'

Fischer sighed. 'I wasted your time, then.'

'Well ... 'Kuhn took an arm and pulled Fischer away from the barracks, though no ears were visible; 'yes and no. I've been talking to Achym.'

'I thought he was a forest dweller these days?'

'He was, for almost a week.' Kuhn shook his head. 'He's going straight. Would you think it fucking possible? And guess how?'

'I couldn't.'

'The very hardest way. While old Grossmann was fitting me out with this beauty he twitched like there was a worm up his arse. Then he asked me if I knew some Mazur fellow, a gangster *lyakh*. So I said yeah, but Achym's a good guy - I mean, you wouldn't want to buy a car from him, but ... and then Grossmann pulls a face like that's exactly what he's done. So obviously I had to know, and it wasn't like the old guy didn't want to spill it. You won't guess. They're partners now.'

'What?'

'Achym came to him one night, which you have to admit took some guts. He claimed that he could get hold of plenty of fine fabric that a good tailor could make into something profitable. Said it was his for next to nothing, *if* ...'

'An arrangement.'

'Hell, yes. Achym told Grossmann he had no more chance of staying in Stettin than the *schkutzes* if he didn't get himself a Polish frontman. That was when the old man reached for his gun, but Achym got it out quickly that he wasn't going to get stiffed like back in '36. He offered to get it done legally at City Hall and told Grossmann he'd sweeten the right bastards out of his own pocket if they could agree to a long term deal.'

Fischer almost smiled. 'Mazur in the rag trade.'

Kuhn nodded. 'What's the town coming to? More importantly, what's coming to town these days?'

'German refugees; thousands of them, passing through Scheune with ...'

'More than they were told to bring. Family heirlooms, sentimental shit and ...'

'Clothes.'

'So, Achym and his guys are going to hang around the transit camp and do the straight thing, make fair offers. Obviously not market rate, but more than the poor bastards could expect from other Poles. And who among them won't be more interested in eating than looking smart right now? The good stuff Grossmann can alter and patch, the crap can be unravelled and made up into something new. But that's just the short term; Achym says he doesn't see why they shouldn't be ambitious, make it a regional thing eventually. I mean, is there an intact textile factory in this part of Europe? Anyway, he lays out all of this to Grossmann and then says he'll even organize the right premises for when the new company expands and hires!'

'And Grossmann agreed?'

'Hard to say. He hates the idea of getting cosy with a gentile, but he knows he can't carry on with things the way they are. This way he makes as much money as anyone can in a shithole and keeps everyone off his back.'

It was a fascinating story, but Fischer didn't see how it accounted for Kuhn's fine mood.

'But I said I spoke to Achym.'

'Yes.'

'He sort of took the risk that Grossmann would agree, so he wanted to make sure the thing was possible. Before he went to the old man he blew half his stock on bribes at City hall. Wasted most of it of course, but a couple of guys told him they could arrange everything for a small, ongoing percentage. They shook on it, and, well ...'

Kuhn's face was lit up like a child's on Christmas morning.

'Go one, Earl. Surprise me.'

'It's the paper. The authority, I mean. It has spaces for the names and the sort of enterprise, and there's the usual shit about balance sheets, profit and loss accounts, audited books and all the other legitimate stuff. But it's the authority's *authority* that you'll like.'

'Local or national?'

'I don't know. But there's a sort of preamble at the top, laying out how and why it is that the suits at Town Hall can give their blessing. It's all down to an administrative order confirming

Polish political and commercial rights in Stettin, and it gives the date.'

Fischer's stomach lurched. He grabbed Kuhn's plushly covered arm and squeezed, but the revelation was already on its way.

'The tenth day of February, nineteen hundred and forty-six it said, official as you please.'

Only two days after Fischer had paid his first visit to Soviet Headquarters and mortuary, upon the matter of...

'It was just that you asked when it was.'

'I did. Thank you, Earl.'

'So what does it mean?'

'I have no idea. It's the date when Poles got an official say in what happens here. How much of a say I couldn't say.'

'Ask your Russian guy. He knows everything, I'll bet.'

The last time, Fischer had dismissed the option. Now, looking at it from the narrow end of a funnel into which he had been thrust by Zarubin, it seemed unlikely that the Russian wouldn't be expecting the question. The other question was whether he would regard it as a sign that a plan was working smoothly or that his useful German had become too clever for his own good.

## 48

For the third time since his arrival at Stettin, Senior Lieutenant Zarubin stood in the mortuary, staring at cold meat. This one, of course, had more than an orderly for company. Captain Lev Arokh, his NKVD counterpart (a man who didn't rouse himself for anything less than a mass execution, usually), stood at the table's opposite side wearing the slightly perplexed air of a man who was trying to squeeze his arse into an equation to see if any of the variables was going to bite it. Beside him, the commander of Stettin Garrison, Colonel Konnikov, stared down at the business, gratefully practising the regretful but wholly detached look that regular army wore when one or more of the many Intelligence branches expressed an interest. The object itself was beyond caring, though the red tabs on the uniform it had worn less than two hours earlier suggested that it might have demanded a say had the subject been other than itself.

Zarubin had made the formal identification already, before Arokh arrived. NKVD could make as much or as little of a matter as they chose, but only if it was their hand that grasped the lid. By putting a name to what was left of the face he'd ensured that it was already too late for them to bury the corpse, so to speak. On the other hand, there no doubt that this was a potential embarrassment to both agencies, given the *discrepancy*.

He shouldn't have drafted the confession so precisely. Obviously, the General's driver had had no way of knowing just how it had happened, because witnessing the event would have been a terminal error. Prompted, he'd admitted to putting one in the back of his commander's skull because that's how it was done, the Russian way, neat and quick. But the lump of meat lying between Zarubin and Arokh was unhelpfully displaying a temple wound that had removed the right side of its head. Equally quick of course, but not *neat* in the way that Zarubin had anticipated.

NKVD could be very difficult about discrepancies, particularly when their toes had been quite firmly stepped upon. Zarubin had no business interrogating a man suspected of assisting a Russian General's apparent suicide, even had the fellow made a habit of buggering members of the Polish Free Army in his leisure hours. It should have been *their* arrest, *their* interrogation - but then, it would have been *their* mistake also, and Zarubin was hoping that the point wasn't lost on Arokh. After all, the good Captain had done what was expected of him (at least, it had been Zarubin's ardent expectation), which was to have the prisoner shot within a day of his confession and handover. It wasn't the sort of thing that could be undone, now that a further conversation needed to be had.

'You again, Sergei Aleksandrovich.' There was no hint of resentment or exasperation, naturally; either would have been as much as an admission that this was a wagon NKVD was chasing rather than driving. Zarubin nodded formally, giving Arokh his serious, concerned face. 'Yes, sir.'

Konnikov was bending down, looking into the entrance wound as if curious to see whether the opposite wall was visible through the mess. 'Wasn't his posting Swinemünde?'

'Świnoujście' Arokh murmured.

'I mean, he had no official role here, in the Stettin area. Didn't he have some sort of liaison role, with the Poles?

'I understand so.'

'Ironic, really, given what he did back in 1920. It must have been like vinegar in a wound.'

'Things move on. We're allies now.'

Arokh kept a straight face as he said it. Zarubin was mildly surprised; he hadn't suspected the man of having a sense of humour. After a moment to allow the absurdity to ripen in the air he coughed politely.

'It was a Polish militia patrol that found him, wasn't it?'

Konnikov straightened, adjusted his tunic and nodded. 'To be fair, they reported it immediately. And kept the scene cleared until we could examine it and extract the body. Really, our own people couldn't have done it more discreetly.'

Zarubin snorted. 'It's not something they'd want to touch, is it?'

'Still, they couldn't know that some of their own people didn't do it, could they?'

'Are we entirely certain that they *didn't*?' Arokh stared pointedly at Zarubin as he asked.

The difficult bit had arrived much too quickly. Zarubin shrugged with what he hoped looked to be an easy conscience.

'The timing makes it next to impossible. We know that the General departed Swine … Świnoujście on the morning of 20 February. His car, a Packard, was found half-submerged in Szczecin Lagoon the following morning, so a Polish perpetrator would have had to have precise knowledge of Soviet movements *and* the nerve to drive almost forty kilometres in a Red Army staff car after killing his target. In any case, the General's driver, Vassily Boytsov, was tracked to a farmhouse near Wolin, where he was found to be appallingly drunk and in possession of the Packard's keys. Even if one can imagine some deranged motive for a man to admit to a killing he didn't commit, the keys are decisive, I think.'

'But his confession …'

'I know, it isn't entirely correct. But the sergeant who was loaned to me for the interrogation was very … enthusiastic. By the time that Boytsov made his statement it's likely he was confused about some of the facts. We've all seen it before.'

The pasty cast to Colonel Konnikov's face suggested that he at least hadn't seen *it* before, but as it had been he who'd loaned the undoubtedly enthusiastic sergeant Ahmadov he wasn't likely to complain of the outcome. Zarubin was only just beginning to congratulate himself upon this fact when he noticed Arokh's face also. It was moving, twitching slightly, the way a face does when it decides it needs to be elsewhere. This wasn't NKVD business even if it was; they had an important corpse and a written confession, an executed perpetrator and a closed file that neatly attested to the agency's swift and efficient pursuit of what might have been a highly damaging case. There was a single, small discrepancy, certainly; but what did that matter to a man whose job it was to get results and hammer the facts to fit them?

Arokh lifted a finger, and the medical orderly (the same man who, weeks earlier, had retrieved the German whore's corpse with all the diligence of a Khazak rail clerk) jumped like an s-mine. The gurney was dragged away, and with it went the last of Zarubin's more immediate fears for his skin. He'd done it, had played Drunkard's Roulette with every chamber loaded and somehow not removed his head. The only potential exposure was now effectively sealed off, moved sideways, put in a place to which no-one would bother to return, because a system that flaunted its perfection could never admit that mistakes might occur. He was safe, on this front at least.

He might have relaxed a little and enjoyed the feeling, but of the two adversaries he had so wilfully chosen to create, Arokh – and the rest of the NKVD, for that matter - was by far the least dangerous.

## 49

'It might not be as easy as I ...'

Achym thought about what he was saying, and to whom, and started again.

'It won't be difficult. We'll just have to be clever about where. And when.'

His audience remained unnervingly quiet. He hoped they were merely waiting for the details, but indifference, scepticism or outright disbelief often looked the same in his experience. He forced himself to be calm, to not start talking shit in the hope that some of it might stick.

'There are two camps, one at Turzyn, the other about three kilometres south and west on the same rail line, at Gumieñce. I mean, at Torney and Scheune. The Torney camp seems to be the main collection point for refugees coming into Stettin – it's by far the biggest and the authorities have put their registration people there. The other place is a disused sugar factory, very close to Scheune station. We think the refugees are herded from one to the other just prior to being offed to the West. At least ...,' for a moment Achym tried to think of a gentle way to put it, but then he recalled who he was speaking to. 'It's a fucking mess already. They're shovelling them into Torney and then on to Scheune almost immediately, but not enough trains are coming from the British Zone yet so the numbers are building. And the word is that the Poles who guard the Scheune camp are bastards. In the main camp they make an effort, use female guards to deal with the women and children – which is most of them, of course. But at Scheune they're just thugs, *UB* dregs. I hear they strip-search the prettier ones and then fuck the result. Lots of beatings, too. The British have been here two weeks at most, but they're complaining already.'

Old Grossmann coughed. 'The British?'

'Yeah, about half a dozen, a liaison team to make sure we aren't sending them a typhus epidemic. Only we are, apparently - at least, that's what a mate who works at Scheune station told me. The first train that reached Lübeck had to be fumigated. It carried two hundred and fifty refugees; two were dead on arrival, half the survivors needed to be hospitalized and the rest fed before they toppled. That was last week, so things are probably worse now.'

He looked for a glimmer of concern or sympathy in three pairs of Grossmann eyes and found none. 'So my thinking is that we ignore Scheune entirely and concentrate on Torney. We'll get official permission to go in with food and do the business there, where folk still own their stuff. That way we'll be saving Town Hall some expense, helping to keep the British off their backs *and* shining our reputations as good Poles.'

The brothers winced at that and glanced at their father, but there was no reaction. The younger one shook his head.

'A thief shall pay double.'

Old Grossmann laughed. 'I'm sorry, my son wanted to be a Rabbi. Fortunately, there are few rabbinical schools in England.'

Achym swore to himself. If you couldn't trust Jews to stiff Germans, who could you trust?

'Look, we're going to be in the arrival sheds where they search the refugees' luggage for contraband. And contraband is everything they'll think will look better on a Pole than a *schwab*, so it's lost the moment they open their suitcases. But we'll be standing just ahead of the tables, offering something more than a thank you for what we want. That's not stealing, is it?'

'What will you give them?'

'Tinned goods, mainly fish. And PX rations, US Army, almost unexpired. All of it fine cuisine to anyone who's been walking for more than a day, believe me.'

'But the Poles will take that, too.'

'No, they won't. We've got the official paper that says it's a transaction, and those who deal with us get waved through with a chalk mark on their luggage. My boys are big enough to discourage anyone who says otherwise.'

'They'll lose everything when they're moved on to the second camp, at Scheune.'

'Yeah, but not the food. That'll be eaten and crapped out by then. So what we're doing might save some of them, if they go west soon enough.'

Old Grossmann shrugged. It was all one to him. 'I'll show you what we need. And what we don't. Old rags are of no use, obviously. Nor uniforms.'

'Fine. In a month's time you'll be a threads baron, believe me.'

'You said that before. I don't see how. We all know the communists are going to steal the elections this year. What will they do with a capitalist?'

Achym had rehearsed the answer to this question above all others, but he pretended to be surprised by it. 'Of course they are. But by then you'll have shifted your profits to the Bank of Haifa or wherever. And if you want to stay on in Szczecin for old times' sake you can declare your business a workers' collective the week before the election and earn the new lot's undying love.'

'Love?'

'Why not? This town's dying in its cradle because scum are the only ones doing business here – not you of course, I meant me. What it needs is proper, large-scale legitimate industry making commodities and a customer base to buy them. Shit, if you expand they'll probably hold you up as a patriot – or they would, if you weren't a *schwab*, sort of. But even that's workable. They don't make any secret of the fact that they're as desperate to keep their smart Germans as they are to kick out the other sort. Train up some Polish workers to be tailors, pay them decently and you'll be able to stay until your toes curl up.'

The big son shook his head. 'We're going to Judea. Soon.'

He sounded convinced, but his father sighed and shook his head.

'If I want sand I'll go to Berg Dievenow. Send me photographs of my grandchildren, Ephraim. I'll be happy for you all.'

Achym watched the faces of his putative partners as they struggled and failed to find reasons to say no. As upsetting as it was to argue the merits of honest enterprise, he was pleased that old Grossmann seemed to accept that he wasn't being bent over. It really was a sweet arrangement. For a while, perhaps no more than a few weeks, they would have a rich stream of impoverished folk trudging through the town - hungry, tired, ever less attached to that best dress or suit they'd mistakenly imagined would be going west with them and willing to lose them in a moment to fill their aching bellies. At next to no cost to Achym Mazur or Grossmann and Sons, the premises and attached warehouse on Wussowerstrasse were going to fill in double-express time with stock that would need only light alteration to meet the urgent demands of the town's expanding Polish population. By the time the initial supply (and the refugees) disappeared, they'd have the funds to travel into Mecklenburg to tap the equally urgent situation of Germans there. The profits would be tremendous; Achym wondered if this was the sort of deal that constituted the *free* in free enterprise

All that had to be arranged still were new retail premises closer to the centre, but he'd turned an eye – a pocket - to that business already. When the time came, an obliging gentleman at the resettlement office would hand over letting papers for an almost intact shop opposite what used to be the UFA Palast department store before the Eighth Air Force put it into involuntary liquidation. It was tempting the fates to congratulate himself, but really, Achym couldn't recall when an idea had hit so many marks. He might even be able to drop his New Zealand plan (a final resort in every sense) if the town administration spotted the historic relevance of his Clovis moment, a hooligan become pious hero by virtue of a splash of holy water (in this case, the filing of a tax return).

Grossmann's gaze brought him down. The old man seemed mildly amused - dazed even. Achym assumed the idea of partnership with a bent Pole needed some working upon. Or perhaps it was being on the wrong end of a sixty-forty split? No, it couldn't be that. The outlay, risks and leg-work were all his new partner's, so forty percent was reasonable, even generous. Was he seeing a hole that hadn't been considered? Achym could admit to himself that his particular genius wasn't entirely comfortable with lawful dealings, but the only exposure he could see was if they were *too* successful, in which case some snake with better connections might declare himself their lawful heir. But that was for the future, and no-one could cover those odds.

Rafael, the youngest, most pious Grossmann, sighed. 'If we're going to stay ...'

'I'm not.' Ephraim folded his arms at Achym and glared.

'If *some* of us are staying, we'll need friends, even if they're *goyim*. And having paper is better than no paper.'

The elder Grossmann *humphed*, slapped his knees and

leaned towards Achym. For a moment it seemed to Achym that his massive hand was going for the throat, but it stopped at a respectful distance and waited.

'You'd better call me Zev.'

Achym took the hand, pacing himself so as not to seem too eager, and didn't wince as it squeezed his own. 'In that case, Zev, allow me to offer proof of our goodwill.' He took the carefully wrapped, over-franked package from his bag and placed it on the table.

'What is it?'

'It doesn't matter what it is, Zev. It just needs a good home and loving foster parents. Just for a while. You wouldn't mind?'

## 50

'I don't know.'

'Is there any German who might?'

Gottlieb considered this like a bad actor, and Fischer knew the answer was already very obvious to him. He pressed it.

'I don't know how dangerous the question might be, so a Pole or a Russian won't do.'

The docker shrugged. 'Two men. There's a river pilot left here from the old days, but I wouldn't ask him the time of day.'

'Why not?'

'He's a *kozi*, a cast-iron Bolshevik. I doubt that Stalin's as sound on doctrine as he is. Whatever you ask him would go straight back to the Ivans, double time.'

'The other one?'

'The assistant port manager. The poor bastard got his wife and kids west just before our new masters found out who he was. Mostly he organizes the dredging, but if the Ivans want to know anything about how the port area used to work they go to him.'

'Where will I find him?'

'You won't.' Gottlieb pointed eastwards, across the Oder to Bredower Werder. 'He still lives in his official accommodation, just north of what was the Union chemical plant. Nice house, pretty garden and about half a regiment of brown uniforms on his doorstep.'

'But he comes out each day to go about his business?'

'Yeah, and with enough guards to make sure he doesn't run,

ever. They need him badly.'

Fischer shaded his eyes and scanned the island. The chemical plant was a cleared area now, the bombed zone scoured flatter than a parade ground. What might have been a house stood just beyond its northern boundary, one of about half a dozen small buildings near the water's edge and less than four hundred metres from where the *Nekrasov* had been moored until two days earlier. There were no jetties on that stretch of shoreline, an absence that relieved him of any inclination to be stupidly courageous; but to be this close yet as removed from his goal as if it were hovering at five thousand metres was yet another splinter under the fingernails.

*Yet this is where he wants me to be.*

Gottlieb coughed. Any minute now the Russian guards would be arriving to escort him and his mates to work, and he hadn't yet had his breakfast. Fischer nodded and took his elbow.

'The dredging — is it done entirely in the Stettin port area?'

'No, the river silts as far as the northern tip of Gross-Kamel-Werder. It's probably the deforestation of the banks before the war that's to blame. Naturally, the new reefs made by the Allied bombing haven't helped. What the Poles will do when they take over completely here I don't know, but right now the Russians need the navigation clear for ...'

*For* didn't need an explanation. They walked quickly back to the dormitory, but by the time they reached it the other stevedores were shuffling into an imprecise line, and Gottlieb's breakfast was something he could torment himself with for the length of his shift.

'Sorry.'

'No, it's fine. I need to lose some weight.'

Fischer smiled. Was there a German anywhere these days who could say that? He tightened his grip slightly on the large tattooed arm before it could release itself.

'The dredging machinery?'

'An old steam bucket job, mounted on a pontoon.'

'Where?'

'It's moored at the old Toepffers Kanal basin.'

'On *this* side?'

'Yeah.'

One of the Russians was looking at them and slowly slipping the rifle from his shoulder. Gottlieb raised a hand in the universal *yeah, it's my fault* gesture and prised his elbow from Fischer's grasp.

'A name?'

'Frank, Michael Frank.'

The docker trotted to where his mates waited for the order to move out. Without putting any strength into it the Russian guard thumped his shoulder as he passed by and barked an order. Fischer watched them go, trying to recall the route between where he stood and the Toepffers Kanal, whether it was possible to get from here to there without leaving and re-entering the Control Zone. The less he needed to wave his damn permit the better.

It took no more than five minutes to confirm that there was no direct route to the south. This shoreline had been occupied by a collection of shipping and cement industries, all of them pointing west to east, all of whose perimeters were jealously protected by high walls or fences that Allied bombing had only further reinforced as obstacles. He had no intention of being caught climbing rubble by someone needing a little target practise.

He found Earl Kuhn attacking at least a kilo of oatmeal and gave him the news. Kuhn offered to come, but the prospect of placing his Swiss franc-laden midriff in the path of more pillaging hordes made it a weak effort, easily declined. Fischer deposited his remaining twenty dollars with the Bank of Zurich (Stettin branch) and told its proprietor that he would be away for no more than two hours - three, if his luck held.

He departed the Control Zone at the Vulcan-Strasse gate without having to show Zarubin's pass (the same duty officer waved him through with precisely the same degree of bored indifference as four days earlier) and turned south along Schmiede-Strasse. After less than five minutes' stumbling through bombed out warehouses and factories he was overlooking the canal; a hundred metres beyond it, directly opposite the wide eastern extremity of Hindenburg-Strasse, stood another gate into to the Control Zone. He walked up to the nearest guard and presented his papers and permit.

There was no wave-through here. Each word of both documents was checked minutely, and the Tartar eyes of the soldier narrowed further as every line of the supplicant's mutilated face was committed to memory. Only a single question was posed and it sounded like a blunt accusation. Fischer had ready the apology that constituted his only Russian. At least, he hoped it was Russian.

'Мне очень жаль, сэр. Я не говорю по-русски.'

This bought him another few minutes' close scrutiny. The guard's comrade wandered across the few metres from where he had been scowling at most of the visible landscape and took the permit. His expression told Fischer that its contents were only slightly more plausible than a voluntary confession, but he handed it back and tossed his head toward the gate. Smiling, nodding,

Fischer gave them both a half salute and hurried in.

Immediately he spotted the slight flaw in his shrewd plan. He had no idea where Herr Frank might be at any particular time of the day, and doubted whether merely waiting at the dredger for the man to appear would be acceptable behaviour to soldiers longing to kick an idler. He was fairly confident he could plot his course to the Toepffers basin without line of sight to aid him, but the sooner he arrived the longer he might have to linger, too visibly, as out of place as flowers in a barracks. And if he arrived too late ...

This was no good. He moved steadily but confidently and passed only one small group of infantrymen whom he ignored in the manner of a man long used to not being diverted from important business. He wasn't challenged. In far less time than he had hoped to squander he was at the canal, and only a few metres from where it widened into the basin. Two vessels were moored there, a pre-war R-boat commandeered as a river tug and its tow, the pontoon dredger. Beyond them, beside a low, damaged wall at the basin's mouth, a squad of Russians stood or sat, smoking and chatting as bored men do.

*Shit.*

Furtive wouldn't work - he'd been seen already by a couple of them at least - so he explained the pause by pretending to toss a stub into the canal and then walked straight to the R-boat's gangway. He had both feet on it when the first warning reached him, and was almost halfway up its four metre length when his offending feet were kicked away. He had the wit to cover his head with both his arms before the first rifle butt came down.

A plan proceeding as expected isn't always cause for satisfaction. The narrowness of the gangway prevented anyone from swinging energetically enough to do serious damage, but the better half of his face and the smaller bones in his hands and arms were fair game. Fortunately, an occasional boot found his balls, which took the mind off the rest for a few moments at least. During a slight pause in the assault he managed to scramble into a foetal position and prayed that the inevitable figure in authority wasn't going to be late for his shift. That hope had begun to die when everything stopped and a hand grabbed his collar. He was dragged head first down the gangway and deposited on concrete.

Had he the strength he might have tried to kiss the boot that poked him politely. He couldn't follow the conversation above him; it wasn't heated, but one voice had a welcome hint of censure to it that suggested the beating wasn't going to continue on the flat. Two hands grabbed his collar and he was lifted upright. When he met the concrete again he realised that he hadn't been hit, merely released by optimists. The next time they kept a hold and he was dragged into a hut that served as some sort of office. The warming feeling in his testicles mirrored the relief he felt at being in perhaps the least worst place he might have expected, after the canal.

A chair was produced and he was put into it while someone went off to find a German-speaker. Two soldiers stood directly in front of him with rifles levelled. Their commander – a lieutenant - sat on the corner of a desk, rolling a cigarette, watching Fischer with the faintly irritated air of a man confronted by a failed suicide. He was young, in his early 'twenties, marked by enough near-misses to suggest that he probably wouldn't over-react to stupid provocations or his own boredom. Slowly Fischer raised a bruised hand to his breast-pocket and made an obvious mime. He got a slight nod.

The permit was examined once more. There was nothing in it that authorized the bearer to ignore a clear warning or preserve him from the unpleasant consequences of doing so, but Fischer was betting his teeth on the thing carrying enough weight to allow the beating to stand as quits. He couldn't parse the lieutenant's expression; if he was impressed by what he was reading, or worried that his men had gone too far, it didn't show.

He glanced around, hoping that this wouldn't be interpreted as a blatant act of espionage. The hut was barely furnished but obviously used. Two desks held a quantity of paperwork; the chair belonging to one of them was being warmed by the arse of a Russian NCO while a stove, safely located in the precise centre of the floor, was already doing its business for the rest of the room. The wooden walls were covered untidily by notices, circulars, proscriptions and what he assumed to be technical data of some form. The most prominent decoration was a large pilot's chart of the Oder from central Stettin north to the lagoon, marked with outdated depth and shoal contours. Several areas were shaded, and these he assumed to be stretches that had been, or needed urgently to be, dredged. Other, more general hand-drawn markings were less easily interpreted by his still-ringing head, until it occurred that lines marching neatly across topographical oddities could only be administrative boundaries.

He was thinking about this when the door opened and two men entered. One was a standard private soldier, Soviet class, his face wearing the *what have I done* familiar to officers in all armies; the other was a civilian dressed so aptly for his work that an *orpo* on his first day's beat couldn't have missed it. He seemed irritated, as though a pleasant day was being pointlessly interrupted.

Curtly, the lieutenant gave the soldier instructions. The man turned to Fischer.

'Why are you in this restricted … place?'

There was nothing that wouldn't sound weak, so he dosed it with just enough indignation to tempt another beating. He claimed that he was employed by his honour Lieutenant Zarubin, chief of the Anti-Soviet Agitation unit at Stettin, who had sent him to warn of potential saboteurs in the Port area, elements of Free Polish gangs who were thought to have infiltrated the new territories in the past few weeks. As to why he had been attempting to board the R-boat without first having presented his authority, he had failed to notice this office (his glance around the small room managed to accuse it of utter anonymity) and assumed that the vessel, making smoke as it was, was the correct place at which to make his report. As he did not speak Russian he had not understood what had been shouted at him as he stepped on to the gangway; indeed, he had assumed it to be some boisterous soldiers' talk, directed elsewhere. The ensuing violence had been therefore a complete surprise. He assured the officer that he had attempted strenuously to introduce himself even as he was assaulted, though the preponderance of blows to his head, ribs and groin had made this difficult. Finally, he was pleased to inform the officer that he had been resident in the Control Zone – that is, at the German dockers' compound in Arthur-Strasse - for almost a week now. Again, this was at the order of Lieutenant Zarubin.

The officer seemed considerably less than convinced. His hand rested, twitching, on his pistol, and Fischer was certain that Zarubin's pass was the only thing keeping it holstered. He hoped that he'd sown enough doubt to make worthwhile at least the possibility of a quick telephone call, but before his luck swung one way or the other Herr Michael Frank stepped into the line of fire and offered a remarkably clean handkerchief. Gratefully, Fischer took it and applied it to his bloody nose.

The port manager said something to the lieutenant via his translator and received a slight nod.

'Who are you? I mean, your name and rank.'

Frank didn't have the usual cowed air about him that Germans offered their Russian guests. He was a thick-set man with hands that had seen their share of punishment, a man probably raised by experience rather than formal qualifications or favour. The way he'd spoken to the lieutenant suggested that his work for the Russians bought a little more than rations and overly-secure accommodation.

'Otto Fischer. I have no rank. I was a *kriminalkommissar* here in Stettin before the war.' It didn't seem the moment to mention his war service, but then half of his face told that story quite comprehensively.

'And you work for the Soviet administration?'

'As do you.'

'Clearly, I have some worth to them.'

'The officer who provided that document seems to think I have, too. Perhaps if this gentleman were to contact him ...?'

Frank gave all of this to the soldier. His superior listened to the Russian version and asked something.

'Are you a good socialist?'

'No. I don't care about politics. I didn't when it mattered, and I don't now. The Ivans pay me, and I hate Poles'

A ghost of a smile flitted across Herr Frank's face before taking cover once more; the lieutenant's hand wandered away from the pistol, made a half-effort at the telephone, and gave up. The translator got another order, which he transmitted quite succinctly.

'Fuck off. Don't come back here, ever, not without advance notice and a proper escort.'

'Definitely not, sir. And may I apologize for the inconvenience that my improper behaviour had caused the officer?'

It took no more than ten seconds for the soldier to convey this, but Fischer was ready. The two questions he'd needed to ask the port master had, thanks to that quite wonderful pilot's chart, become a single, concise query which he put in a normal conversational voice as he held out his hand to the other German.

The port manager was surprised by it but answered readily enough in a similar tone and before the translator's attention was upon them once more. When it was, all the Russian might have reported was that the suspect was asking his compatriot whether the handkerchief should be returned immediately, or might he take the trouble to have it laundered first? Though discretion was not allowed to any private soldier in the Red Army in anything other than dreams and bowel movements, he decided that this was not a matter with which he need burden Lieutenant Sovurov, who could be a proper bastard on days when his schedule didn't flow as smoothly as the Oder.

51

*Is this how it was?*


Monika had heard the rumours and dismissed them, but as the months passed she had begun to wonder if her disbelief was something else – a lie, perhaps, protecting the self from understanding what the world had become. If the thing were a slander, why was it repeated so often, and by folk who had nothing to gain from it?

It was inconceivable, insane almost; yet she to admit that she hadn't known any Jews, homosexuals or gypsies, and a village had always known how to keep its idiots, its deformities and derangements to itself. She had disbelieved in hope, not certainty.

Here was a sort of proof of her error. If it *had* happened it must have started like this, in a chaos pretending to be a plan, an intention pretending to be something else. Like this, it must have taken with one hand and offered a small, pale hope with the other, if only to maintain the obedience of those it processed. Surely, they would have fought back otherwise? Her own father, dead these fifty years, had it said often - that the strength of any system could be measured by the degree to which its victims accepted their condition.

Monika had never seen so many people. It was if the edge of Pomerania had been seized by vast hands and shaken like a blanket to remove its unwanted skin flakes, but in so precise a manner that they had all fallen here, together, at once. Since entering the town (which was so big she was sure it must be really a city), every street through which they passed had been so pressed in with bodies that they had flowed rather than walked, a slow current of bodies directed by the memory of those who preceded them. At first, Bernhageners had tried to stay with each other, but in this vast churn they had parted like the waters of the Red Sea (an apt simile; the crowds reminded her of a scene from *The Ten Commandments*, a foreign film that she and several other pious Bernhageners had taken the bus to see at Gollnow picture-house almost twenty years past). Her world had got much larger yet at the same time much smaller; now its far horizons comprised Erica's hand, fiercely grasping her own, and the bag she clutched at her other side, wielded to cushion the lurches of their fellow cattle.

Polish militia had halted them briefly on the eastern shore of the Oder and ordered them to leave their carts there. A few folk had tried frantically to unload all of their surviving possessions and drag three, four or five suitcases with them; most were too tired, hungry or dispirited to do more than make a swift choice and say goodbye to the remainder. Civilian workers wearing MZO armbands descended like carrion, dragging the abandoned vehicles and luggage to a vast and growing park on the Altdamm, while the refugees shuffled in a continuous line across a single bridge, much damaged but standing still, ignoring the once-fine views of the town as it rose from the broad river's western bank.

She had been here once before as a little girl, brought by her parents to see what the Second Reich's booming economy had done to a place her father had known as a sleepy little port. She couldn't recall a single detail of her visit; a faded memory lingered - a street café, the fancy chocolate cake she had eaten there - but that might equally have happened here or in Naugard, her other great childhood adventure. Time, like war, stole things.

It was a fine place, or had been. The principal streets were broad, their buildings like something from the guide books she had borrowed from her luckier acquaintances. One of the larger, grander piles had a much-damaged inscription above its broken doors, declaring it to have been a bank. She could hardly believe that money-telling required such a distinguished setting. If Mammon deserved this, what must the town's churches be like?

Erica pulled hard on her arm. Ahead of them, where a side street joined this thoroughfare, a group of Germans had attempted to break away from the column. A line of Polish militia appeared as if the manoeuvre had been weeks in preparation, blocking the hoped-for escape route. It was enough to halt the majority of the breakout in mid-stride, but a few of the younger, more hopeful ones tried to shove their way through. The Poles didn't negotiate the point; without further warning they laid into heads with *schlagstocks*, swinging as freely as the confined space allowed. Monika watched women – all but two of the would-be escapees were female - go down like bloodied sacks, and even those who begged mercy took two, three or even four savage blows before the punishment stopped. An old man rushed up to the militiamen to remonstrate; he too was felled but stood up again, as straight as his age permitted, to confront his assailant. The brute raised his baton to give him more but his arm was seized by a comrade. In a moment the blows became kicks instead, rough but not savage, to tempt the injured back to their feet and into the mainstream. Some managed it by themselves; others were helped up and away by samaritans who risked a beating by leaving the flow. One woman, checked briefly by a militiaman and then by the courageous old gentleman (who signed a cross on his breast as he did it), remained on the floor, unmoving.

*God, let her be childless.* As the press moved her on, Monika tried to turn and keep her eyes on the woman, hoping to see some slight sign of life. But the militiamen stepped forward, over their handiwork, to form a new line much closer to the stream of refugees. Then it was past - another German past, to add to the innumerable rest.

They had an audience. She hadn't noticed it until now, her

attention having been seized by the day's other, bitter novelties. Men and women, civilians, stood in small groups at almost every street corner, paused to watch the passing tide. Some carried bags or newspapers, held their children's hands or gripped pram handles, smoked cigarettes; they looked very much like any other folk distracted by some novelty from their usual business. Monika saw what she took to be an air of *schadenfreude* in a few half-smiling faces, but others seemed subdued and a few even distressed by the prospect of this mass exodus (or at least she allowed herself to think it). Only a few metres separated new and old Pomeranians, but it was as if two worlds were passing each other at a remove - the one an emptied fragment dispersing in a cold wind, the other indistinguishable from the comfortable, mundane place she had known all her life prior to the hideous year past.

She reined in her wandering imagination and concentrate upon her poor feet, which were feeling every inch of their trek. Her old boots were just about done for, bound only by memory now and the congealed blood that had filled them over the past days. With every step she felt more and more of whatever surface she shuffled across, yet even now a persistent, wilful strength kept her on her feet, moving, when all reason told her that she should be at a final extremity, ready to follow Amon Stemper into that sublime peace hoped for by all Christian souls. Even young Erika looked wearier than she felt herself, though the girl's grip was consistently ferocious. She wondered whether it was the power of the girl's need for her that kept her in this life rather than the next.

The grip grew even stronger, and Monika winced. Ahead of them, to their left, stood a high, wide gateway constructed of wood and wire. The road to the front was blocked entirely by militiamen, ranked at least four deep, and as the refugees ahead of her reached this impassable barrier they turned through ninety degrees and passed beneath a sign that slowly revealed itself to Monika. It read *Centrum Przesiedlenie,* for which she needed no translation. Curiously, the reference to a *centre* raised her spirits slightly; it suggested a degree of planning, of some intention beyond mere expulsion. But then she recalled once more what the worse of *planning* could be, and her anxieties washed in again like a spring tide.

She looked into the faces of their captors as she executed the manoeuvre, hoping for a hint of what was coming. All she saw was unreadable blankness, a blind indifference to what passed before them. So she picked a younger, almost baby-faced man who seemed to be looking at her (or Erika) and smiled. He started slightly, and moved his head so discreetly that it might have been a response or a warning. The frown stayed where it was, but Monika didn't take that too much to heart. It was what men in uniform did. She only hoped that …

Then the militiaman passed from her mind. They were at the *centre* of a mad, furious tumble of bodies suddenly, a press of refugees corralled by officials shouting instructions in what might have been German only it was difficult to tell because no two of them were shouting the same thing. The only open route led directly to a low, wide blockhouse with six doorways interrupting its whitewashed façade at even intervals. For those who couldn't be bothered (or were unable) to count them, they were numbered, and it occurred to Monika that the babble had something to do with getting the arrivals into an order that would process them through the doors efficiently rather than as a panicked herd. Before the direction became physical she pulled on Erika's hand, dragging her to the left, through the bodies and luggage to a space in front of doorway one. Perhaps other Germans saw this or came to the same understanding spontaneously, but slowly they separated, streaming into almost regular columns. The guards' stern tone became more encouraging; potential thumps became pats upon the back, and one or two of the female MZO staff even helped gather and return discarded luggage.

When they were all in place and complaints, arguments and vague objections had almost subsided, an officer stepped onto the low deck that spanned the width of the blockhouse and faced them. Monika knew that he was an officer because he wore a peaked cap and riding trousers that closed at the knee, of the fashion that briefly had become very familiar to Germans from newsreel broadcasts at the beginning of the late war. He cleared his throat and raised a piece of paper.

'Welcome to Szczecin ...' (at this a few voices behind Monika murmured *Stettin*, but not so loudly that it carried), '... which is the point of transit for displaced persons from the voivodeships of Pomorskie, Zachodnio-Pomorskie, Warmińskoe-Mazurskie and Lubuskie. Here is accommodation for one, two, three nights before you leave on trains. Or possibly ships. Be obedient to the rules. Food will be provided when available, and always water. First you go in here and be checked for health and what possessions you have brought with you, which must be personal only, and according to the instructions you received before today. Any contraband will be confiscated as property of sovereign state of Poland. Thank you.'

For several seconds following this speech, loud music blared from loudspeakers attached precariously to the blockhouse's roof guttering. From its confident, martial tone it seemed to be some sort of anthem, though few Germans present recognized the tune. The moment it ended, someone shoved Erika roughly and she stumbled forward, dragging Monika with her towards doorway number one.

In a large, bare room, floor-boarded and slat-walled, a line of large tables face the several entrances. At each of them sat a young woman in brown uniform who had charge of two neat piles of paperwork. Armed guards stood behind them, but at a distance that suggested they were intended only to intervene if Germans didn't play by their rules. It was slightly comforting to Monika that examination of the refugees was considered woman's work, but then something caught the left edge of her attention and she turned. Another, larger table sat at a right-angle to the others, and almost surrounding this was a group of quite the most fearsome looking men she had ever seen (not excepting the thugs that had accompanied the first National Socialists to run for office in her home district, twenty years past). Most were dressed in black, like peace-time SS, only their hair was much longer and they wore no indications of rank - which, if anything, Monika found even more unnerving. Not one of them was less than two metres tall, yet several were wide enough across the shoulders to seem almost squat. She dreaded to imagine their role in a place that processed unwanted old men, women and children.

Two of them were sharing some pleasantry with an armed militiaman who graciously accepted and pocketed a pack of cigarettes. This was not how military hierarchies behaved (as even an elderly Pomeranian woman knew) so it seemed unlikely that orders were being given, but the militiaman seemed happy to agree to whatever the black-clad gentlemen were asking, or demanding, or merely saying how this or that was going to be. Whatever their intention, Monika had decided already that a wise person would do nothing to put herself in the way of it. She adjusted her grip upon her old carpet bag and took Erika's hand, intending to deliver herself to the mercies of the young lady at table one; but before her feet could begin to assist this excellent strategy one of the fearsome men who had been talking to the militiaman looked directly at her, raised a finger and beckoned her to him.

## 52

Watching Earl Kuhn was like having a spare face that registered all the pain he was feeling. Actually, *more* than he was feeling; Kuhn was enduring the extra agony of thinking about how many of the bruises he was dabbing were precisely where a cash belt might have cushioned the blows. When Fischer winced at the attention given to a particularly tender spot the face was comically anguished.

'They didn't go easy, did they?'

'They probably did. I couldn't have made it back upright, otherwise.'

'Bastards.'

The water in the pan was bloodied, though Fischer felt no worse than if he'd gone eight rounds with Schmeling's feet. One of his shoulders had done excellent service protecting his head and would need a week or two to work properly once more, but everything else was more or less what a ninety-year-old woke with most mornings.

'Can you do something for me, Earl?'

Kuhn couldn't take his eyes from the damage. 'What, piss?'

'Trains. I want to know which lines coming into Stettin are functioning, and since when.'

'*All* of them?'

'Ignore any that terminate on the west bank. It's the traffic passing directly into the Lastadie complex that interests me.'

'Who do I ask?'

'The dockers, or their wives. It shouldn't be a state secret, but be discreet.'

Kuhn helped Fischer get back into his shirt, a slow and careful process. 'Is it important?'

'Probably not. Like everything else.'

When Kuhn had gone he lay down in his cot and tried to sleep, but the threat of Marie-Therese wearing any face but her own collaborated with his wounds. Besides, it was midday, and he didn't do decadence well. So he went over his beating and wondered if he'd been too dazed in its aftermath to see something that might have been obvious to a fully conscious Otto Fischer. He was surprised still that he was alive, given the offhand manner in which Soviet officialdom usually dealt with irritations. He doubted that he'd stumbled upon a rare, compassionate junior officer, yet given the choice the lieutenant had gone for the less convenient option. It couldn't have been the presence of Herr Franks that had deterred him. A salutary lesson, one involving an entirely expendable compatriot, would have been just the thing to keep a valuable German in line.

He tried to sit up too quickly and fell back, clutching his shoulder. How long had he taken to walk from the Hindenburg-Strasse entrance to the basin? He'd assumed less than five minutes, but worrying about being too early or late often compressed perceptions of time. If the gate guards had had a field telephone they might have warned the lieutenant of his arrival. Was that why he'd been delayed, or was it another call that had detained him? Had Zarubin already put around word of his pet German's presence in the Zone? If he had, the duty lieutenant's late arrival at Fischer's beating may have been either deliberate or the fault of a call that had to be made to Headquarters. He both hated and liked the idea - it was further proof that he was being worked and neatly explained why he hadn't been shot. What it didn't do was tell him whether he had been encouraged further along a path or smacked for stepping down a dead end.

But then he thought of the river chart once more, and his mood lifted slightly. At the very least it had saved him days of putting further questions that flagged where his mind was going to people who might want to stop it with a stave. It also brought home to him how out of the world he and other Germans in this town had become, to be so ignorant of the state of things that were barely a stone's throw from its boundaries. He wondered how ...

'Two lines. They had one cleared, repaired and running by August last year, the second just at the turn of this one.'

Earl Kuhn's head was decorating the top of one of the partition's walls. He peered down at Fischer.

'Into Lastadie?'

'Yeah, both of them, the spur from the main line at Scheune. The last bit into the main station isn't repaired yet. I don't think the Ivans see it as a priority.'

'No, they wouldn't.' It had been exclusively a passenger line, but the spur brought heavy goods and merchandise from ...

He looked up at Kuhn. 'This isn't just about Silesia and Pomerania.'

'What isn't?'

'It's Berlin as well. They're stripping out Berlin, and some of it's coming through Stettin.'

Rail lines into Lastadie came from several directions, but the traffic from Berlin had always been Stettin's principal landward artery. Would it have stopped just because Berlin was smashed?

Kuhn shrugged. 'Does it matter?'

'I don't know. The Allies must have agreed on how much each of them can claim as reparations. But after that, does anyone really know *what's* being pilfered? I doubt it.'

'No one would care. We're fucking beaten.'

'We are. But Berlin's different; it's the only part of Germany where the Allies are cheek to cheek, where each of them can see what the others are doing. If the Russians were taking extra they'd have to be more careful there.'

'Well, it's a strange system they've got, isn't it?'

'How do you mean?'

'That one group of Ivans strips eastern Germany or western Poland, whatever the fuck it is now, and a different lot handles the portion that comes through Stettin.'

'What?'

Kuhn looked surprised. 'You didn't know? No, why should you, you don't deal with them. It's Northern Group of Forces that's doing the stripping out in new Poland, but Stettin's the only part of it that falls under Western Group's control. That's why your lieutenant's line of command runs through Berlin, not Liegnitz.'

Fischer cursed his naiveté. He'd made the fundamental error of looking at an enemy, a threat, in the singular; yet he'd lived twelve years under a regime that had more, and more warring, factions than the Allies had divisions. Why should the Soviet Union be anymore a union than National Socialism had been ... well, socialist?

'I don't suppose they mix much?'

Kuhn shrugged. 'Buggered if I know. I sometimes buy stuff from Western Group suppliers and sell it on to Northern Group customers at a profit. What do you call it?'

'Arbitrage.'

'Yeah, that. So they can't be too much in each other's company, can they?'

Fischer lay back and stared at the dormitory ceiling. This wrecked corner of a wrecked Europe had gathered to itself an infinity of hidden corners; it was the last, God-forsaken rubble heap of the West or the first of the East, a malevolent petri dish, killing off or expelling one strain of bacteria as it nourished another, a sink hole, evacuating the final remnants of a once-mighty economy, flushing out the final symptoms of twentieth century society in favour of an austere version of the seventeenth, a place so removed from understanding that the Russians could play games here even with themselves in a land of opportunity barely four kilometres wide.

It was different here. All across the new Germany, the beaten natives ran eagerly to the conquerors, promising for a little food or patronage to be their eyes and ears. There, it was hard to be unseen - a sleight of hand or booty had to be adept, or what happened in Mecklenburg would be known soon enough in Bavaria and Hesse, and definitely to the wrong people But 'new' Poland was different - the eyes and ears of Germans here were downcast or purposely deaf to matters that did not concern them. Here, a man or men with ideas had a little space in which to make them work, or to erase the consequences of their discovery.

The thing – the very large thing – was, a Russian officer had led him by the nose to understand this, which meant that there was no possibility that Otto Fischer was other than disposable. He rubbed his damaged shoulder and sighed. There were no clear suspects, a hundred possible motives – and a hundred more things that might or might not be motives - and a 'boss' who would have made an excellent sheep dog were his teeth not so firmly lodged in the mutton. There was only one way to go and that was in the direction laid out for him.

'Earl?'

'Otto.'

'You're a resourceful fellow.'

'I suppose I am.'

'Someone who knows how to organize things, if he has to.'

'I can't deny it.' The self-satisfaction in Kuhn's voice suggested he wouldn't dream of doing so.

'Good. I need to find a man. He's probably in Berlin. If he isn't dead, of course.'

## 53

Zarubin read it through a third time, carefully. He realised that this was futile, that he had already gleaned precisely the limits of the discretion it allowed him. These things weren't called *orders* for nothing.

Still, it presented him with a choice. If he pressed on it would have to be at the gallop, and he didn't like doing anything hurriedly. If he decided to stop, to cut his losses and walk away, it would require a lot of squirming and at least one unpleasantness he'd rather not arrange. It was, as always, a question of priorities.

He didn't have to wonder about the consequences of making the wrong decision. A long career shuffling forms around a small desk somewhere north of the Arctic Circle or having a Tokarev scatter his brains around a small glade in foreign woodlands struck him as unattractive prizes, equally to be avoided. It was the avoiding part that needed careful thought.

Ironically, the thing appeared to be a promotion. Had he applied himself only to his work it would have been a welcome (if overdue) recognition, but arriving now it was more in the nature of a lump of metal flung in a moving mechanism. Naturally, he would – by return of internal post - shower Headquarters with his effusive thanks and promise a world of industry to reflect the trust placed in his unworthy talents (he could kiss arse like a toilet seat when necessary), but ...

The timing was what poked deepest into his gut. Was it just a case of the system having turned until his moment arrived, or was someone shoving it along for a reason? Of course, a *reason* needn't be bad – he was, after all, far more talented than his career to date suggested, and even Soviet bureaucracy sometimes forgot itself and stumbled into recognizing merit; but deep, nervous suspicion was the safest response of someone who had tried to bend the system. Until he knew better, this was a bad thing.

And then he almost laughed as the thought occurred. He would be taking the business home - well, as near to a home as it had anymore. Half - the secretive, dangerous half - of Northern Group was probably scouring the region by now, trying to track it down on the urging of a half-lunatic, and Sergei Aleksandrovich Zarubin was about to remove it to a place outside even their power to follow. Had he been an idiot he might have congratulated himself on his good fortune.

Then there was the other small piece of paperwork, a timely little warning from Captain Arokh, presumably a small gratuity for keeping their exalted corpse from becoming an embarrassment. *That* he'd been expecting, because even Moscow wasn't staffed uniformly by fools. The only question was whether their investigation would be merely *rigorous* (in which case an execution would probably satisfy their masters) or *thorough* (a dozen at least, some of whom might actually be guilty). He assumed that a copy addressed to him personally would be arriving sooner or later – there was little point to an announcement intended to loosen bowels and prepare Western Group for the wrath of their Godless Deity if it wasn't universally known. Still, it was good to get advance notice, even if he wasn't going to allow it to spoil a further minute of his day.

But the coincidence of the two correspondences jogged his cautious nature, and it came to him forcefully that things had to be organized so that he wouldn't be exposed. Regarding his 'promotion', informers had to be retired or re-allocated and at least three pending executions signed off by his immediate superiors in Berlin. The Polish coal thieves he could hardly care less about, and he had all but decided already that their release would be a cheap way to grease local good feeling (they had, after all, merely attempted to steal what the Red Army had stolen already). The German ... well, that might yet be a regrettable necessity, but Zarubin comforted himself with the obvious truth that the victim wouldn't care to cling to this world as less damaged souls did. Finally, most urgently, the object had to be ready to be moved at a moment's notice or less.

It would all take time he wasn't sure he had anymore, so he set himself to clearing the docket. For two hours he made calls, signed papers and had short interviews with a number of frightened, compliant Polish and German citizens he dragged into Headquarters to hear the good news of his pending transfer. After that he tried to concentrate on the pile of reports he'd allowed to accumulate on his desk over the previous few weeks, but none of what he read registered. From the moment he'd decided to do the sensible thing and move the object after dark it had been whispering in his inner ear, begging him not to wait, teasing him with the possibility of discovery and loss. The *loss* played particularly on his nerves, because there wasn't a limit to what he was capable of losing, so on impulse (a mode earnestly to be avoided usually) he ordered his usual driver to sign for a car and pick him up at midday.

The drive was long enough to eat into his schedule but too short to calm his nerves. Twice he almost told the man to turn the car around and return to town, but that would have been an admission of fearfulness he didn't want to make. That last part of their journey was the worst; too much had happened lately in these forests for the slow, painful passage down the rutted track to seem other than a metaphor for a bad idea turning for the worse. He swore quietly to himself, reciting obscenities like a prayer.

The large lock that secured the hut's only door had been smashed, and for a moment he thought his heart might stop. Resisting a strong urge to draw his pistol he entered, and it took only a moment to confirm both that the place continued to shelter enough contraband to refuel a stalled municipal economy and that the object was not among it. He took another moment to enjoy the dizziness and novelty of his head being entirely emptied of thoughts, then summoned the wit to take two packs of American cigarettes from the nearest pile to present to his driver when he returned to the car, a part-payment for sealed lips. He had no idea how he managed the small talk he made on the drive back to Stettin, when all he wanted to do was release his bladder.

Over the past half year he'd become quite fond of his little office at Headquarters. It was warm, reasonably well equipped and too modest to attract the attention of senior officers looking for accommodation; but the battalion of Red Army veterans who surrounded it no longer seemed enough to fend off the wolves he'd woken with a stick. Before he locked himself in it he secured a litre of Purveyance Board vodka from the canteen, enough nourishment to help him through the coming night and the infinite possibilities it would puke into his lap.

By dawn, still drunk but thinking clearly once more, he realised that he might very well have to be *rigorous*, if not *thorough*. He was fine with that in principal; it was the challenge of keeping his arse out of the firing-line and name out of the subsequent reports that concentrated his headache wonderfully. At least he need waste no more time parsing his 'promotion'. Once the business was done he had to get out of Stettin as quickly as possible, and the safest sanctuary on his particular Earth was precisely where he was being transferred.

## 54

With deep shame for her unchristian spirit, Monika had waited until the other inmates of their 'dormitory' (a stinking, bare hut) were out of doors before sharing the pilchards with Erika. Afterwards, she washed the tin carefully in the bucket that served for their personal hygiene and placed it into her bag so that no nose made sensitive by hunger would know of it. She had two more tins, and meant not to lose them.

They were receiving one official meal each day, a soup thinner than water almost. So far there had been no bread to ease its offence, and the Polish woman who brought it pulled the same face each time and said something that sounded almost apologetic. Folk were muttering that it was part of a plan intending to kill off as many Germans as the British wouldn't take, but she doubted it. There seemed little that was deliberate in what their Polish keepers were doing - most were as confused as their guests about what was happening, and almost as undernourished. Only the small squads of 'special' men who strutted occasionally through the camp, taking particular care to sneer at everyone they didn't threaten, looked to be lacking nothing. A German had whispered 'UB' at the retreating backs of one such group, in a tone that removed any desire she might have had to know more.

There appeared to be no real order or organization here, no hint of a plan to deal with the great numbers of Germans whose gathering at Stettin had been ordained by great men. Folk wandered around the camp almost at will, seeking word of what was coming or trying to find enough nourishment to keep them alive until it arrived; everyone was thin, enervated, dispirited at having come so far only to reach a new state of uncertainty. Bernhageners' brief, surprising spark of fortitude had dissipated the moment the gates closed upon them, and even their bickerings had subsided to a malaise under which they waited dully for Fate or other competent authority to cast the die and decide tomorrow. Several times, Monika approached a guard (never the same one twice) and very respectfully asked when they might expect to be moved on to the west. Two hadn't understood her; the others had replied with shrugs that might, for their uniformity, have been taught at a school for transit camp overseers.

The men who had bartered the tins of fish for her grandmother's altar cloth returned at least twice in the following days, offering more food to those willing to deal. They said that wanted only good clothes and fabrics, but she noticed that a couple of them often drew individual Germans aside and traded jewellery or other ornaments instead. They bargained hard and loudly, and often walked away when their victim proved stubborn (knowing that hunger would weaken the strongest wills), but at least they didn't take what they wanted by force, which was surprising in a Pole. Erika said that on one occasion she had seen the biggest of them (a truly fearsome creature) put something in an old woman's pocket without taking anything in return. Monika wanted to believe it, but she feared the girl was imagining goodness where none existed.

They seemed to be entirely unconnected with the official staff in the camp, who they kept happy and uninvolved with a quantity of cigarettes that made Monika suspect they ran either a warehouse or a tobacco plantation. Briefly, she wondered if they purchased the product with the fruits of their barters, but then realised that this would have been a very circular and pointless pastime. They were the sort of men that some looked upon admiringly and called *businessmen*, which meant that they were at least partly thieves and probably swindlers too, and regarded the inmates here as their natural prey. Watching them at work them she was reminded of her mother's warning in the days when wandering gypsies (a breed that disappeared soon after the Führer became Chancellor) came to the village - *Never open the kitchen door to a knife sharpener*. What she would have said of these fellows Monika didn't know; they looked as if they could sharpen things by looking at them.

Her courage was gone, fled. Everything – the camp, the men who ran it, the uncertain future – frightened her as if she had some stake in life still. In Bernhagen they had pretended a sort of resignation that felt like stoicism, but here she couldn't ignore the truth – that they were less than spawn in a stream, helpless to move the course of their lives, unable to see or understand the world about them. They might all die here and the event need not achieve the weight of a statistic. It would not even be the natural hurt of war; they were merely what war had shit out.

And the worst of it was that she had no-one with whom to share or ease her fear. Amon Stemper was rotting gently at a tree-line, safe from hurt but beyond saying something wise or witty that would make her feel less alone, less like the widowed mother of her tiny, shrinking nation of Bernhageners. To Erika she dare confide only false hopes of better things to come and pray that the girl hadn't noticed the arthritic gait and weak lungs of those who had been here for a week or more.

Yet she knew that her prayers were breath wasted. Most eastern Germans, even the younger ones, were now familiar with typhus - it had become a regional tradition, tasted too often to count as a delicacy. She wondered if the Poles were aware of what they were risking, bringing together such a quantity of fertile, willing hosts and then letting the result sit, maturing, in their midst. But then she recalled from her schoolbooks that Poland had been entirely spared the Black Death even as her immediate neighbours had lost half their populations to that horrible affliction. Were they immune, or just favoured by a God who, then and now, had so palpably abandoned their German enemy?

No. Even if that were the case, allowing an epidemic would be foolish. She had no idea how the British had fared under the Death, but she doubted that they would welcome trains filled with diseased refugees. Was this then a way of ensuring that displaced Germans neither stayed here nor reached their new homes? *My God, I'm thinking like a Bernhagener* she chided herself when it occurred to her, but the only reassurance she found was even grimmer than the fear. This was the new Europe. Drains, toilets and hospital wards no longer functioned, and fields that should have been filled with rising crops or grazing livestock lay fallow for want of men to work them. Transportation, elected local government, the charity of strangers - all the safeguards of modern life were smashed or gone, while thousands of displaced folk were being herded into concentration zones by new men of authority, hardly yet in their places and thinking only of the next step, of making a nation where their own people would not be refugees. With all of that, and the deaths of uncounted millions still blunting the consciences of decent folk, who had the will to care for what happened in one small part of an insignificant region?

Monika looked around and tried hard to find something to feel better about. The only plentiful things in the camp were lice, water and kindling, so she told as many Bernhageners as she came upon to boil everything – what they intended to drink, their clothes, themselves even (or at least to wash in water as hot as flesh could bear). She urged them not to hold on to any valuables they had managed to hide from their welcoming committee but to sell them for food to the gangsters - it was no good planning for a future in Lübeck if they didn't manage to survive Stettin. Watch for signs of illness among those whose beds were closest, she begged, and warn others in the same dormitory if you seem them. Finally, those who could speak Polish she asked particularly that they listen for hints of what was coming so that everyone would be as prepared as helpless folk could be.

A few of them promised to do their best, but most offered her the shrug they had learned from their gaolers and wandered away quickly to find some other important matter to attend. To her great surprise, Monika realised that their indifference piqued a sense of self-importance she had not thought she possessed. Perhaps she had become comfortable with their trust in her judgement even as she pretended that it was a burden (she wasn't quite sure where one sin began and another ended). And that made her angry - that it was she alone, a woman without any investment in what was coming, who should be carrying Bernhageners' anxieties like a solitary pack mule.

But as days passed her fears, irritations and uncertainties slowly distilled into something more immediate. Twice, Erika had to run from men who fancied easing their days' frustrations upon pretty young meat. The first was one of the UB fellows, who, fortunately, was only half-heartedly aroused and let his mates goad him into groping her as she passed by. The second was an ordinary guard, a man who was probably paid and fed so little that he regarded rape as his just recompense. He was a more deadly, friendly suitor, plying her with compliments and then taking her silence as the necessary provocation. Grabbing a fistful of hair he dragged her towards the nearest dormitory block, using a shoulder to part the small crowd of refugees who didn't dare let their anger show. But they were awkwardly in his way, and Erika kicked his ankle, broke free and ran for the relative safety of the administration hut. She was there still half an hour later, too frightened either to enter or move more than a metre from its door, when Monika found her.

They returned hurriedly to their own hut. 'Cut off her hair. They don't like bald heads, they think it's rickets', suggested an old woman who lived two beds away. Another proposed that Erika bind her small but quite obvious breasts and pass as a boy until the British trains came. Erika herself declared that she intended to escape from the camp that same night and find her own way west, and it took every gram of her uncle's wit and Monika's pleading to persuade her how foolish this would be. In fact, the old woman was forced to ask for her trust, claiming that she had a plan to get them to Lübeck safely. That calmed Erika for the moment but it was a flimsy lie, one that would be discovered all too soon if Monika couldn't put it right. She thought about where they were and wanted to be, and considered her assets - a tired head, a reputation built upon nothing more than knowing who her ancestors were, and (for when she put into action her great strategy and needed to sweeten its path) two small tins of Turkish pilchards. She doubted that the Führer himself could have made much of all that, even on one of his cleverer days.

## 55

In a third-floor office of the *Volkspolizei* Praesidium in Keibelstrasse, Berlin, Unterkommissar Otmar Scholle allowed himself a hearty slap on the back. He took great care not to allow any appearance of it, however, as the Oberrat was notoriously hard on anything that smacked of what he sometimes called *egoism* but more often *fucking smuggery*. So Scholle straightened slightly to attention and reined in his eagerness to please.

The Oberrat was frowning at his paperwork as he always did when obliged to confront it. A slight cough brought him to the surface.

'What is it, Scholle?'

Rumour was that this was a mere affectation, a deliberate ploy to unnerve his subordinates, but the Oberrat seemed to know every one of his men by name. The Unterkommissar coughed again, to give himself a moment to get it right the first time.

'The name you wanted us to listen out for, sir. It's come up.'

The Oberrat's face was back in a report already. '*The* name? We have shoals of them on the books. Be specific.'

Scholle gave it to him, and almost raised an eyebrow. At least he had the man's attention now. 'It was one of my contacts in the rail yards, sir. He said someone had been asking in a way that wasn't meant to attract too many ears.'

It was particularly satisfying for Scholle – other than being the man to bring the news to Keibelstrasse – to be able to remind the Oberrat of his invaluable connections among the proletariat. Like most other members of Berlin's *volkspolizei* he wasn't a policemen other than by grace of his very recent and cursory training, so being useful in the job was by way of a distinguishing mark. At least, he hoped the Oberrat would think so and pass on the word.

He'd definitely teased out some mild interest. 'You were a railwayman, weren't you, Scholle?'

'Stoker, sir. Reserved post.' It never hurt to remind folk that you hadn't been *Wehrmacht*. The Oberrat himself had been a policeman *and* a soldier, but part of the beauty of rank was that old shit didn't stick nearly so messily up there.

'Hm. And what was the question?'

'There wasn't one, sir. I mean, other than that someone was looking for the man.' It was good that he'd been led to the next part, the interesting part. He could hardly be accused of *egoism* if the thing had to be asked.

'Does someone have a name?'

'Only a forename, sir.'

'And might you share it with me?'

Flushing, Scholle did so. If only he'd got everything out at once. Now he had to volunteer the important part and risk sounding like an arse kisser.

'The thing is, he's out-of-country.'

The frown on the Oberrat's face had lightened slightly. 'Out of country? How far out?'

'Stettin, sir.'

'Oh.' Of course, for many Germans Stettin didn't count as the abroad, but no-one dare argue the point. To Scholle (who had never visited the place) it didn't matter one way or the other; it was just a name on a map, now redrawn. But the Oberrat's frown had returned with interest. Had it been a mistake to bring the news at all? Flustered, Scholle forgot himself and volunteered once more.

'Shall I bring the file, sir?'

'What file?'

'On the suspect?'

'There is no suspect. Or file. Forget about it. But let me have the name of your contact in the yards.'

'But you ...' Scholle clamped his lips, too late. His little triumph had become a waking nightmare, or at least the sort of dream one suffers after a surfeit of bad cheese. The Oberrat was giving him the stare he usually reserved for prisoners on whom the damage had to be hidden - an appraising, technical stare that measured the most pain a man could take and remain conscious. To be a member of the *volkspolizei* was to live by rules, of which the most numerous – just – were laid out as regulations. The others were the ones a man sensed, or learned by the example of his peers. Not sticking out like a hard-on was one of the most obvious, and yet he'd forgotten it in his eagerness to please (another definite Don't). For a moment, all he could see was a future in traffic management, but then the Oberrat made it worse. He smiled.

'Thank you Scholle. You've been very ... *assiduous.*'

Scholle staggered out of the office, needing urgently to lose his breakfast. Had he found the courage to test his boss's loathing of *fucking arse-kissing* by turning and thanking the man for his time and attention he might have felt a little easier, or at least allowed a vista of motor congestion to fade a little. The smile had become a broad grin and was perched atop a body that was attempting for only the second time in its life to dance *a solo*, a remarkable graceful effort given its size, brutish build and the tin leg that shared duties.

## 56

Fischer had noticed that Kuhn could hardly be parted from his new fur coat. When he wasn't wearing it or in the latrine he draped it over his knees and stroked it like the several cats it may once have been, seemingly unaware that he was nurturing a habit. Beulah May had made several playful attempts to dismember the thing when first it intruded into their relationship; now, she used it as a luxurious pillow whenever hypnotizing Kuhn into feeding her.

They sat on the low wall separating the German dock workers' home from its neighbour. Kuhn was applying himself to his coat with nervous persistence. Several times he opened his mouth to start something that didn't quite make it out of the blocks. Fischer waited, content to let weak sunshine do its work upon his shaved head.

'This ...'

The shipyard odours rising from the drying ground were dragging his mind back once more to the pre-war town. He wondered how long they might endure. Some smells were virtually indelible of course, and not all of them foul. It was pleasant to imagine that whatever emerged here might have more than the fled memories of ghosts to mark its past.

'... was a mistake.'

'Which bit of this?'

Kuhn must have been warm, but he was shivering. 'Here. Coming into the zone. We're like stuffed rabbits on a fairground range.'

'We didn't have a choice. At least if we die here it'll be on orders.'

'That's a comfort?'

'I'd hate it to be by accident.'

'We're being watched. I can feel it in my joints.'

'Probably. Zarubin wouldn't have put us in here and then forgotten about it.'

'It doesn't worry you? That you might just be a ...'

'Piece of cheese in a trap?' Fischer got it out quickly before he had to endure *patsy* or *stooge* once more.

'Yeah.'

'In Stettin a German is whatever someone else intends him to be. At least our lieutenant *wants* something, though he's being coy about what, precisely. Did you manage it, by the way?'

Kuhn stared down at his hands and said nothing.

'Earl?'

'Shit! Sorry, Otto. Yeah, I managed it. He'd dead.'

Fischer closed his eyes. The pain was duller this time, stretched to allow him to savour its slower, more brutal effect. He hadn't allowed himself to hope because that would have been almost to will the worst, but unreason had whispered that the chaos of a war's end might have left room for a small, impossible thing. It might have, just.

'Are you sure?'

'Too sure. For once I'm glad we're not living in Germany anymore, because I've really kicked a can in the dark. Hell, it's actually official.'

Kuhn passed a crumpled piece of paper to Fischer. In a rough, hurried hand someone had pencilled a short message.

*Herr Holleman is dead. Fucking dead. Oberrat Kurt Beckendorp of Berlin Volkspolizei made me write this exactly as he said it. Aloise.*

'Poor Aloise. I've dropped him into a vat of it.'

To Kuhn's intense surprise this observation seemed to raise Fischer to a state of mild euphoria. For a while the man couldn't speak for laughing – not the sort of laugh raised by a decent joke but a quiet, abandoned convulsion that brings as many tears as a bereavement (which this was news of, of course). And then there was poor Aloise, a mate, whose guts had probably messed a section of wall by now, and that was all at Kuhn's door. He appreciated a black sense of humour as much as any man, but this was …

'No, Earl …' Fischer struggled for a moment, slapping the wall to bring himself to order; '…you haven't, really. Ah …'

He wiped his eyes and then gave the ground between his feet some attention. Kuhn wanted to make a start on getting the full story, but he recognized the distance in the other man's face and waited with uncommon patience.

'Aloise is a friend?'

'Yeah. We used to jump the trains as kids, got as far as Britz once before the BzP caught us and dragged us back to Stettin for a slapping. I grew out of it but Aloise loved the railways. When he left the orphanage he got a job as a wheel tapper and then transferred to Berlin and somehow managed not to get dead. Until now.'

'Aloise isn't getting dead. He's just found a second job, courtesy of the *Deutsche Volkspolizei*.'

'As a kicking-post?'

'A letter-box.'

'The Oberrat? He's ...?'

'Freddie Holleman, yes.'

'Jesus.'

'Not even close, fortunately.'

'That's good, yes?'

'That he's alive *and* police? Of course. Whether it helps I don't know yet. It depends.'

'On what?'

'On what he knows. More importantly, on what he can find out.'

Fischer smiled as he said it, and again Kuhn wondered at his sense of humour.

'But that's going to be dangerous for him, isn't it?'

'Almost definitely. And fascinating, too.'

'What is?'

'That Freddie ... sorry, Oberrat Beckendorp, and our dear friend Lieutenant Zarubin, report to precisely the same address in Berlin-Karlshorst.'

'Which is?'

'SVAG. Or SMAD, if you're German.' Fischer looked at Kuhn almost with affection. 'Which you are.'

'That would make it *fucking* dangerous, then.'

'Possibly. But he has advantages. Even Zarubin can't know who he really is, even if by some chance he's heard of Kurt Beckendorp, which I doubt. And then there's the luck side of it.'

'Luck?'

'Freddie makes his own. If you're ever in front of a tank assault, try to stand behind him, it's the safest place.' Fischer paused. 'No, not you; you're the same as he is. How you've managed not to drink Oder until now is beyond me. I'd put it down to your lucky fur coat, if you'd had it longer.'

Kuhn flushed, carefully folded the item and put in on the wall next to him. 'I don't believe in luck, good or bad. Stuff just happens and you're either in the way or you're not. Me, I had no parents, no connected friends, no fucking options. So I ...'

'Made your own *luck*. You should be serially dead by now but you're not. It's the same with Herr Beckendorp, except that after every dodged execution he rises a little more, as if God's being given the finger. An Oberrat, it's just too ridiculous.'

'How did he do it, do you think?'

Fischer sighed. 'I have no idea. Perhaps the Russians really are as stupid as the Führer used to tell us. Or they have a wonderful sense of humour. But we'll test his luck this time.'

'Will he help?'

'Of course, if he can. Tell Aloise that I need just one more thing from him and another from the Oberrat.'

'What are they?'

'Actually, they're the same thing. A day in February.'

## 57

Gregor's eyes, staring directly into Zarubin's, crossed that most private of thresholds, from awareness to eternity. The other man noted it dispassionately and managed to turn his head far enough to the left to focus on his watch, a much closer and more difficult subject.

*A minutes. Ninety seconds, at most.*

All of his head hurt, as if the bullet had taken much more than a slice of his ear. It was the precision of it that worried him the most, an insult that carried one of two messages: either *behave yourself, little Sergei* or *this is all that we think of you; we need you to know before – immediately before – we exact the price.*

The cold bastard had taken his time, taunting Zarubin with his driver's death, knowing that he wouldn't have the nerve to run or try to counter-attack, and then marked him with the sign of the troublesome serf. He'd been close by – close enough for his second victim to hear the bolt action that ejected the empty cartridge and reloaded, adding to the terrible anticipation.

But he was still breathing, and it had been five minutes now at least. He had to move, to do something; above all, he had to rouse his ringing head, to make it earn its rations. He had a problem to deal with, either a large one - his death - or the small but very necessary matter of cleaning up the crime scene. It was the nature of the system that it required almost as much of its victims as its perpetrators, and Zarubin didn't need that sort of attention.

He staggered towards the car, stumbled and fell, his already tender head slamming hard into the fuselage. Gregor didn't seem to mind, though usually he was fiercely protective of his vehicles, to the point at which he would tut and pointedly polish away fingerprints that Zarubin thoughtlessly deposited upon the paintwork. Today, he just sat behind the wheel, eyes wide, taking in the pretty woodland view, oblivious to the blood he was leaking on to the leather and the small dent he would never be required to explain to the motor-pool.

His boss cursed, dragged himself to his feet and politely requested the use of Gregor's handkerchief, which he stuffed into the fuel intake, removed, reversed, and re-inserted.

'Where do you keep your lighter, Gregor? Don't tell me I'm going to have to rummage in your pants.'

Zarubin stood well back when the handkerchief caught. The fuel tank ignited with a soft sigh, and in two minutes the car was engulfed. He waited just long enough to ensure that the most delicate detail was burning robustly and then stepped back into the small safety of the dense undergrowth.

It was a shame about Gregor. They'd been together now for a year almost, and the man had been admirably mute in the face of several egregious pissings upon regulations. Doubtless he'd thought Zarubin a black-marketeer and expected his return in due course (he'd see enough contraband, certainly). He had a wife, apparently, and children, which made it a greater shame; but then Zarubin considered who, other than himself, had known about their previous visit to this place, and suddenly his sympathies were considerably diluted.

He knelt down in the undergrowth, willing himself small, and tried to think it through. The mystery was how he'd been caught. At most, the assassin had been given an hour to put things into place, and although the route might have been anticipated he couldn't have done it without resources. Yet he was still alive (a provisional conclusion), so it may have been improvised, a chance taken quickly, without definitive orders. That was the most sense his ringing head made if it, anyway.

He'd need to move soon. No-one was coming to help, and it was possible that his assailant would change his mind and return to finish the job. His pistol was in its holster still, but – it was too embarrassing to contemplate – he hadn't thought to load it.  What would have been the point, when all he'd intended was an almost friendly chat with an employee?

He lay under a canopy of leaves, trying to calm himself, to put it into perspective. It was to do with the object, of course. Misplacing it had made him as safe as a punishment battalion's carrier pigeon, but he'd misread the other party's peculiar taste in old fashioned revenge. He'd expected the knout, applied by an expert hand; he hadn't thought it might be an erasure, quick and clean. So what did it mean?

Never mind. Clearly, his plan had been peeled, or enough of it exposed that the consequences of *this* rather than *that* could be weighed. It was a slight comfort that the execution had been handled so discreetly - at least the other party believed that there might *be* dangers still, when in fact Zarubin had already emptied his bag of magic beans. If he'd taken the head-shot today he doubted that anyone would look for him, much less regard the deed as falling under one of the Red Army's staggeringly long list of recognized offences.

*Fuck.* Even if he got out of the undergrowth without collecting further holes it was at least a six-kilometre death-march back to the only building in this entire region in which he stood a chance of reaching nightfall other than as fertilizer. If he kept to the treeline he might be fairly confident of reaching the northern fringes of Stettin, but once on the streets it would be blind luck alone that kept him alive. And really, he didn't believe in luck.

He timed himself, allowing another hour. Lying among the odours of earth, life and decay it passed quickly despite his tormented analysis of vanishing options. He was tempted to wait until dusk before starting back, but if he did he'd probably blunder into an uncleared minefield or a Waffen SS reunion. An hour – if the fellow hadn't returned by now he was probably on his way back to his operational area, putting distance between himself and questions. Zarubin sighed, spat over his left shoulder three times for that thing he didn't believe in and dragged himself out of the undergrowth.

He was almost upright when he heard them, and it took a great effort of will not to run. Carefully, he sank back into his hiding place and wrapped himself into as small a space as he could manage, clasping his legs and burying his face into them as he used to do when playing *priatki* with his schoolmates. In his head the thud of his heart echoed like a jackhammer judas, drowning the birdsong above him. He squeezed harder into himself, trying to smother the bloody thing.

The rustle of parting undergrowth grew louder, and it was obvious that they were making no attempt to disguise their approach. No doubt they expected panic to flush out their game, a bottle of vodka and boasting rights to the one to react first and bring it down. They were talking, chatting even, as if the world and its business was going on as usual, undisturbed by its imminent loss. It was as if his mortality was being undersold, and he felt almost cheated. He wondered if his own victims had ever had similar cause for resentment. He hoped not; he'd tried always to be efficient, never cursory.

The sound of their voices resolved into words, and for a moment he couldn't make sense of it - not the sense of the words themselves, only that he was being required to translate. And then he realised that at least one thing had gone to plan today, though the degree to which circumstances had changed made even that comfort a thin one. Slowly, he released his legs, allowing blood to return to them, and tried not to think of the consequences of making the next decision. It was easier to move that way.

## 58

Achym's band of brothers bickered, complained and made the usual threats, and ignored all of it. He was irritated beyond – well, irritation, so he realised that he must be something else. Wasn't this all so fucking typically the sort of shit-slide that had chased him through life to date - setting aside, that is, recent and seemingly hopeful passages aided by what might almost have a following breeze?

What was that Greek bastard's name, he wondered – the one who'd rolled a rock uphill through eternity and watched it roll back down again just before it reached the summit? It had almost come to him when Wojciech stumbled, and the obscenities chased it away. In any case he needed a better exemplar, one who didn't just shove his own rock but those of a bunch of infants in men's bodies who were full of it when things went well and second-arse-useless when they didn't. *Limpets*, he decided, not caring that he was emptying his metaphorical quiver. *Fucking limpets.*

What could go wrong, he'd asked himself when his master plan first came to him. That had been stupid, obviously, because Mazur's First (and only) Law of Serendipity - formulated during his long, flea-infested vacation at Trassenheide holiday camp - clearly stated that Everything could not only go wrong all the time but might well invite a friend to help with the kicking.

Someone with sense would have taken the hint and walked away, not towards it. But it had been *his* work of genius, and to admit now that it was a steaming pile on the cobbles would seal his reputation forever. The limpets – those who managed to avoid the militia in days to come - would entertain their grandchildren with tales of Achym the Vain, or Achym the Half-Wit, the man who managed to turn gold into … well, rags.

Old man Grossmann had laughed – actually *laughed* – when they showed him their magnificent collection of German couture. Worse, it hadn't been a sneering, contemptible laugh, the sort that usually prefaced some hard bargaining, but one that genuinely appreciated a good joke, expertly delivered. *Oh dear*, he'd said, wiping his eyes and lifting a number of items to share the jest with his two sons while some of Szczecin's hardest bad fellows stood around with hurt, puzzled expressions on their dim faces and a growing cold, empty feeling in their pockets. They'd struggled uphill all the way from town with approximately four hundred items of bartered clothing in their carts; Grossmann *père et fils* took just nineteen of them.

Outside, on the Grossmanns' stoop, they'd all given Achym the same look, the one that said something between *what now* and *fuck your mother*, and all his razor wit managed by way of balm was *no, it's fine*. It was testament to his standing among them, he supposed, that they'd accepted this as a deposit on a new plan rather than kicked him the length of Wussowerstrasse and back and then walked away.

The trouble was, he hadn't since been able to come up with a viable answer to *what now*, which is why they were stumbling back to their hut in Eckerberger-Wald (or whatever his countrymen would get around to renaming it) to pick up even more of their precious stock of cigarettes and tinned fish to trade for even more worthless refugee crap that would probably entertain Grossmann even more enormously. Like a sucker who'd bet on black six times in a row and lost it all, Achym was trying to convince himself that it had to come right this time - that some lost colony of Eastern German nobility was about to stagger into Stettin with matching leather trunks stuffed full of silks and fine linen, all of which they'd happily tip over for a few tins of pilchards and a pack of *Detvas*. As a strategy, it ranked with playing the stock market according to how a pet monkey scratched its arse.

So he was preparing himself for the mutiny. At some nearing point, one or more of the limpets would notice how much smaller their pile of valuables had become and decide to detach himself from the hull of their joint-stock company. The rest of them would follow immediately of course, and at best Achym would be left with a tenth part of the loot (if they were sufficiently forgiving not to just leave him unmarked), which was about as much wealth as he'd managed to scrape together before coming to Szczecin. That counted as going backwards, his least favourite direction. Worse, his reputation as a leader of men would be lower than a pimp's, so his future was going to be a lonely, one-man business. His mind's eye had already made out an older, seedier Achym Mazur, standing on a street corner, dealing prophylactics out of a suitcase while a snotty kid (occasionally rented out to his more regular customers) kept watch for the law.

What he needed was yet a new idea – a sound, commercially promising idea that was proofed against Fate's whims – to astonish his associates and restore his juice among Szczecin's entrepreneurial class. It shouldn't have been so elusive. After all, this was a new town in a way, without resources, an infrastructure or adequate police force; a place where initiative could gain more in a year than a lifetime's graft in the civilized, ordered world. It was also the end of a war - and not just *a* war but a bigger, bloodier, more destructive war than the wettest fantasy of military minds could have conceived. He should have been able to think of *something* to fill his small part of the largest hole in human history.

'Why does it need all of us to do this?' Wojciech had his surliest face on, the one that usually needed a fight to soften (or a plank to remove).

*Because I say so* wouldn't work anymore. Achym sighed. 'What if someone's found the place and just a couple of us walk in?'

'Who?'

'I don't know. That's the thing about nasty surprises.'

Achym looked back down the short line of his expedition. A few had overheard and were removing their pistols to check the magazines once more. It wasn't really likely that someone had just wandered this deeply into the woods and discovered their hideout, but the way his luck was turning he didn't want to test its limits. As far as he knew there was only one other person who knew about the hut, and that was …

One of the rearmost limpets called out plaintively. 'Can anyone smell burning?'

Achym's mouth opened to deliver something crushing and remained there. The last time he'd been so surprised, so utterly winded, was a warm night in August 1943, when the RAF had unloaded tons of ordnance upon the slave camp in which he and several thousand other poor bastards had imagined they'd already reached the limits of their awful luck. The guy's name and face had been right there in his head, ready to receive some ripe ordure for the way he'd inserted himself into Achym's already very complicated life, and the very next moment, barely three metres in front of this hapless column of dolts, up he rose from the woodland undergrowth like a fucking elf. A bruised, whipped and severely kicked elf.

Achym managed to grab Wojciech's wrist before he could aim. He wasn't sure that it was the right thing to do, but his gut told him that when in doubt in this dangerous new world it was best not to drop a Russian officer without first considering alternatives.

'I was looking for you.'

'You found us. And someone else, apparently.'

'Guerrillas, I think. Probably Free Army.'

They looked each other in the eye, politely pretending that wasn't nonsense. The Russian was wobbling slightly, trying to keep a balance that wanted to be elsewhere; there was a bloody notch in his ear, a gash on his head that ran into the hairline, staining the front of his pretty blond hair, and his uniform looked as if it had spent time with playful wolves. If they decided to shoot him now no one would think it was anything other than a wrap-up, a loose end tied by unknown parties, and Achym's head began furiously to work on the possibilities.

Zarubin's smile, like that of any intelligence officer, looked as genuine as Moldavian caviar. 'Obviously, I'd be grateful for your company back to Szczecin.'

*Grateful* could be taken two ways — either 'I'll owe you, comrade' or 'thank God I won't have to think too hard of a way to get you into Soviet HQ'. Achym moved an inch closer to the Wojciech solution (as he liked to think of it, rather than the *borrowing Wojciech's gun and doing it myself* solution), but he returned the smile and said 'My pleasure.'

This was about the *thing*, of course. Achym still couldn't be sure whether it had been a simple — even simple-minded — test of his loyalty or a bear-trap wrapped in plain paper. It had to be the reason for Zarubin's day out from the office, but the reason for the reason escaped him. Was the test ended, or was it time for the trap to be sprung? He glanced around at the faces of his associates as if revelation might be found in various shades of befuddlement. Other than Wojciech none of them knew about the item, and he hadn't been tempted to tell them. The first thing they would have wanted to do was get to the bottom of it, very possibly a fatal urge.

*Damn.* Someone wanted the Russian dead, but Achym didn't know enough to make a sound judgement. If he finished the job here and now there was no way of anticipating whether the reward would be a shower of gold and influence or a nice shallow trench somewhere nearby. Perhaps the *thing* itself was deadly; perhaps it was keeping them both alive.

*Well, that helps.*

Achym gave the battered Russian another smile and offered his handkerchief to help stem the trickle of blood onto the uniform that was telling him to bide his time and do nothing until he had no other choice; that the only sensible decision was to continue to dance until the band ran out of music or some half-obvious next step revealed itself.

## 59

Fischer and Kuhn reached the outskirts of Köstin (now Kościno) just after 8am. The Russian soldier remained in his battered Ford truck, lovingly examining the A-11 wristwatch Kuhn had slipped to him before departing Stettin's Control Zone. They crossed the fields to the rail line unobserved other than by the local fauna, until a lone Polish guard at the unmarked border halted them with a half-raised rifle. Fischer had his NKGB pass ready; deploying an ingratiating tone, Kuhn explained it to the man (who spoke neither German nor Russian) and lost two packs of cigarettes.

'I promised we'd stay in sight.'

Fischer rubbed his shoulder. The day wasn't cold but moisture rising from the ground did what it always did to his damaged joints. 'And if we don't? Two Germans going west? He'd probably get a commendation.'

Kuhn glanced around the near-empty landscape and shrugged. 'Yeah, but it's still a border, sort of. Poles seem to be sensitive about them.'

'One wonders why.'

They stood on the track, waiting. Fischer thought about how he would come, how he *might* come. Were trains running again in Germany other than at the whim of the Allies? And even if they were, there had never been a direct route from Berlin to Kostin. No, driving would be easier option, unless the Ivans retained their love of checkpoints. And if they did, what power did the uniform carry? He had been out of his country for no more than a year, yet had no greater idea of conditions there than he did of the Near East. It might be getting better; it might be hell still.

Logically, a man would leave his car east of Grambow, where the road crossed the tracks, and walk along the line from there. But with just the one good leg? Fischer smiled. He pitied anyone coming along for the company and a day in the country. The language was going to be terrible.

The tree trunk had been removed from the track in the two weeks since he had sat in an over-pressed rail-carriage here, waiting to become a refugee, so the bit where New Poland ended and Whipped Germany began wasn't evident. Presumably, their border guard would get twitchier the closer they came to it. Fischer smiled at him and nodded to indicate he understood the rules, hoping that his face didn't spoil the message or the man's breakfast.

'Is that someone?'

The trees to the west were darkening whatever emerged from them (the line included). Kuhn shaded his eyes as people do when trying to see further than their sight allows. Fischer resisted the urge to do the same. There was something moving at the point where the rail lines converged to a blur, but it might equally have been men in *volkspolizei* green or saplings caught in a breeze, and he had no intention of bringing on a headache trying to anticipate which. He pulled a flask from his coat pocket and nudged Kuhn.

'What's in it?'

'Almost brandy.'

Kuhn took a swig, coughed, and then another, longer pull. When he returned the flask his eyes were watering with more than tiredness.

'This police friend of yours. Does he have anything against businessmen?'

'Black marketeers, you mean?'

'Well, yeah.' Kuhn squirmed a little in his fur coat, He was probably thinking about his money belt, armed strangers and an international border just a step to the rear of a spur-of-the-moment decision.

'He's broken just about every law known to National Socialism, but he's not on the make if that's your itch. The last time he had spare money he took the lads out for a drink that cost two days we'll never remember. Or fully recover from, probably.'

'A *mensch*?'

'Solid. You're right, it's definitely someone.'

The movement on the line ahead of them had become too regular to be natural. At first Fischer made it to be three, possibly four uniforms; but as they approached they resolved themselves into one small and one very large, limping man. Even at a distance, it was obvious that conversation was taking the form of a monologue.

'... as twice-shat dumplings!'

The big uniform came to a stop two metres from Fischer and Kuhn, so unless someone had an unusually precise sense of place one party had probably entered another country. The smaller uniform (his shoulder tabs made him a kommissar at least) sniffed and nodded towards the Polish guard, who had come to full invasion posture. 'I'll fuck off over there, then. For a smoke.'

'Right.'

The big one watched him safely half-way to the guard post and then turned to the two waiting men. Kuhn got a quick glance that didn't care to hide how unimpressed it was. Fischer got something else.

'Hello, Otto.'

Kuhn could count one close friend in his life to date, and that had been a fellow swing boy with whom displays of affection would have been unthinkable, a betrayal of their code. So he watched the two men hugging each other with growing discomfort. The disparity in their respective builds made it easier to think of it as a mauling, so he tried that instead. Eventually – much too eventually - it ended.

'What the fuck are you doing abroad?'

Fischer laughed. 'It's a rest-cure.'

The big man snorted. 'Well, come on, let's go home. We've had a word with whatever passes for the authorities here and they won't make a fuss.' Kuhn got another withering glance. 'You can bring your mate, too.'

This was it - every problem they'd foreseen in moving two bodies and several thousand Swiss francs across a border melted away like frost on a hot-plate. Not only could they cross into Germany unmolested but would have a gold-standard reliable police escort who seemed to think the world of one of them. It wouldn't be any trouble to make some safe, short-term arrangements in Berlin – they'd need a few days to rest and look at the situation, make an informed decision on exactly where in the west to kick-start the recorded jazz market and then move slowly, surely and safely towards a beautiful, bourgeois future. Kuhn almost whimpered.

'Thanks, Freddie. But we can't, not yet.'

Kuhn whimpered.

Friedrich Holleman sighed. 'You daft arse.'

'I know. What do you have for me?'

'Four trucks, all Fords. Karlshorst to Pankow-Heinersdorf, dawn, 7 February.'

'Why those in particular?'

'You said something unobtrusive. These were G8Ts.'

'One-point-five tonnes.'

'Yeah, couldn't carry a heavy fart. But they moved in the company of the best part of a battalion of motorcycles.'

'Was that unusual in Berlin, back then?'

Freddie shrugged. 'Not particularly. The Ivans make locusts look like fruit flies. They'd have stolen the fucking roads too if they could have prised them up intact.'

'So why these, then? It's the right date, but …'

'Think about from where to where.'

'Karlshorst is Soviet HQ in Germany, but Pankow …'

'Was the closest station in on the Stettin line that still worked, back in February.'

'A fair distance.'

'About twelve kilometres. And that's the thing.'

'What?'

'They closed it down. Everything. Roads, s- and u-bahns, rubbles paths - everything. They deployed almost a full division to make sure that nothing, including us, got anywhere near what was moving from A to B.'

'And no word since on what it might have been?'

'Nothing, and I'm not asking too hard. But if it went in four G8Ts it wasn't hardware, not unless we invented a wonder pistol in the final days.'

'And you spoke again to Aloise?'

'He says no-one was allowed into Pankow-Heinersdorf that day, not even the signalmen. The Ivans brought their own. The next day was just like any other, as if nothing had happened.'

'Anything else?'

'Yeah. According to Aloise it was units of 94th Guards Rifles who shut down Heinersdorf. But I know the transfer was handled by the 32nd.'

Fischer understood nothing of current Soviet formations. Like OKW, Red Army's High Command seemed to enjoy breaking up and reassembling their toy as a child did a construction kit, and about as often. But he was fairly sure that dividing a single, tiny operation between two Corps was taking security – or discretion – to an extreme. The authority to do that would have been stratospheric.

The man generally known as *Oberrat der Volkspolizei* Kurt Beckendorp glanced sternly around while Fischer absorbed the news, as if assessing what the Poles had made of what used to be Germany. Kuhn, by now quite terrified of the man, tried to put a shine on any opinion that might already have been pinned to himself.

'Aloise, he's a good mate of mine. We were kids together.'

The Oberrat sniffed. 'He seems a good sort. I've put him on the payroll.'

Kuhn was aghast. 'A snitch?'

'A what?'

'An ... informer?'

'Why not? New Germany's just like the old one, only it's Nazis we're sticking it to now. Aloise jumped at the offer. He's got three kids and they need feeding.'

Fischer struggled out of his reverie. 'Freddie, thanks for doing this. You're covered?'

'Yeah. I'm pretty snug with the bosses. This is a lead I'm following, no need to ask questions, I'll be back by mid-afternoon. You know the routine.'

'I meant to ask how the hell you did it.' Fischer's gesture took in the entirety of the green uniform.

Holleman grinned. 'Did you know that I was lucky?'

'Christ, yes.'

'Who arranged the papers that got me out of Berlin back in '43? You?'

'A contact at WASt, put me on to Hamburg. All I needed was some Luftwaffe name unlucky to have been on home leave when the Brits hit the city. Up came Beckendorp and family. It wasn't hard to adjust the casualty list - God knows, it was long enough.'

'Well, thank you Otto. When the Ivans arrived I was shitting my pants, wondering what they might have against Beckendorp. Not that they were looking for excuses. They tore up the Spreewald, did you know that?'

'There was some heavy fighting down there.'

'You could say that. I think the tin leg saved me from a quick one in the back of the head, but after a week dodging patrols they pulled me, Kristin and the kids into an interrogation unit. That's that, I thought.'

'And?'

'We didn't get fed for two days, and all the while a couple of Mongolians were eyeing Kristin like their cocks were already busy.

But then a Captain or something turned up smart as you please, invited me into an office and kissed me on both cheeks. Hell, Freddie, I thought, your arse is going to get it before the wife's. But he turned out to be some sort of Intelligence, had a file on me.'

'On you?'

'On Beckendorp. Kurt did stuff before Luftwaffe got him, apparently.'

'What?'

'Killed policemen. To be exact, four policemen, over a period of twelve hours on 23 October 1923.'

'The Hamburg Uprising?'

Freddie Holleman laughed aloud. 'He was fucking KPD, a hard core *kozi*, from one of the few groups to crawl out of the rubble last year that the Ivans didn't put against a wall for being the wrong shade of red!'

'So you're a communist now?'

'Loud and proud. How ironic is it, that a man whose only experience of police was to shoot them now wears the uniform, while Freddie Holleman, a life-long *orpo* who couldn't spell *communist* if he tried wouldn't have got a first interview for the job? Fucking idiots. And not only is our Kurt an Oberrat, he's been asked to stand at the next election, the one Uncle Joe's already rigged.' Holleman pointed to a small badge on his lapel. 'Wilhelm Pieck himself put that there.'

'Who?'

'Doesn't matter. Think of it as the key to the cake shop.'

As far as Fischer could recall, Friedrich Holleman had never admitted to holding principles, so to move merely from blackness to white probably hadn't put a strain upon his conscience. No doubt there were many Germans similarly making the leap of conviction demanded by absolute defeat and praying that the past kept its mouth firmly closed, but Fischer doubted that many had marched so brazenly from one state to the other and ended up with boots that smelled of lavender.

'How are the boys?'

Holleman was patting his pockets. Quickly, Kuhn offered a cigarette and lit it.

'Thanks. They're fine. This time last year they were *Hitler Jugend*, now, they're *Freie Deutsche Jugend*. Different uniform, same ditches to dig or fill, same seeds to plant. They don't seem to know how things have changed, or they're young enough not to care.'

'And Kristin doesn't mind you being a *kozi*?'

Holleman's eyebrows rose. 'She eats, we have a roof. What do you think?'

*Why am I so curious?* It struck Fischer suddenly that it was he, not Holleman, who was the oddity here. Everyone had a plan, or dream, or hopes for something better than what they suffered as their present penance - everyone except the sole inhabitant of Planet Otto, where time and tides stood frozen to attention, parade-smart, waiting hopelessly to be sent off on other duties. He was out of phase, self-exiled, waiting upon nothing, and for the first time that he could recall he was experiencing envy for something else - a spirit that could live in the times rather than break against them.

Holleman and Kuhn were watching him carefully, expecting more than they were going to get. Both wanted him to be sane, to turn and walk west with them while the kommissar kept the guard talking; to take up a future while it was being offered on a gilt salver. And he wanted desperately to be able to please them.

'This thing isn't going to last much longer. It can't, can it? I'll come then, Freddie.'

Blank-faced, Holleman beckoned his subordinate. 'Has it helped?'

'Yes, I think so. It fits more than it doesn't, at least.'

'I assume this isn't just a new hobby. Who's on you?'

'SMERSH, I think, or NKGB.'

'You silly bastard!'

Fischer laughed again. 'That's all my headstone will need.'

'Anyway, they're both MGB now.'

'Who?'

'NKGB, SMERSH, they've been rolled up, amalgamated into *Ministerstvo Gosudarstvennoi Bezopasnosti*.'

'You speak Russian now?'

'A little. It's necessary. If they tell us Fetch we need not to sit and wag our tails.'

'Is it bad still?'

'Better than last year, just. They're not as brutal as we were with them, but that's not saying much. They prefer us to fuck our own, rather than go to the bother of doing the fucking. For the rest, it's all fraternal brotherhood if you stay in line and a trip east if you don't.'

'And you're at the head of the line.'

'Yeah, my Aryan forefathers would weep. You should eat

more, Otto. You never could keep flesh on those bones.'

'I eat what everyone eats over here. Can you do one more thing for me, Freddie?'

'Jesus! What?'

Fischer gave him the name. 'Just a yes or no, so the answer can be sent via Aloise.'

'Well, I'm not limping down to the fucking countryside again, that's for certain.'

They shared another rib-straining embrace while the kommissar and Kuhn looked on. No one said goodbye in case it stuck.

The green of the uniforms had almost blended with the trees before Fischer thought of it.

'Go with them, Earl. Freddie would ...'

'Nah. I forgot about Beulah May. She'd never forgive me.' Kuhn glanced around. 'I'm glad we came. There's plenty of cover here. This could be as good a place as any when the time comes.'

Fischer shook his head. 'No roads, no rail. Not without someone who can turn eyes away, make it safe.'

'We'd better get that tunnel started then.'

They re-crossed the fields to Kościno, and found a space where their ride had been.

Kuhn cursed quietly. 'Eight fucking kilometres!'

It felt much less than that. The weather was fine, the road flat and almost straight and no one challenged the right of two Germans to be moving in precisely the wrong direction. Their conversation in particular was fertile, and by the time they reached the hamlet of Schwarzow some two hours later, Fischer was profoundly grateful that Kuhn had refused the offer of flight.

## 60

The young Polish woman had a kind, sympathetic face, and though she wore a uniform with an armband (it bore the letters PUR), the blouse beneath it was a pretty, lace-edged thing, obviously home-made, and fastened demurely at the throat. This was strong evidence of propriety, and Monika decided to trust her.

The woman – a girl, really - had entered their hut with an armed guard, but a single glance had told her that there was no threat here, and the man – a slouching, untidy fellow - had been dismissed with a nod. She took up a position in the row that divided the beds, cleared her throat, and spoke in perfect German.

'You are all to go to Lübeck very soon. Before that you must assemble at the Gumieñce holding area, which you call Scheune. Please gather your belongings today, as you must go this evening or tomorrow morning.'

An old man who looked as frail as anyone might and still be in the world raised his hand tentatively. 'Is it far to walk, please?'

The girl smiled. 'Less than three kilometres. And along the rail-track, which is very regular and easy. A meal will be brought for you before you leave.'

When she had gone Monika considered the news. There was nothing in it that could have worried her. Their expulsion from this part of what had been Germany was inevitable, as even the most obdurate refugee understood, and the fact that there was clearly a timetable for it was reassuring. Here, at Torney, there was hunger and a risk of mistreatment from men who allowed lust or vengeance to seize them seemingly at a moment's whim. Whatever future Monika could or couldn't anticipate, it would be better to be gone, soon.

Yet the feeling of dread in her heart persisted. She was certain that the girl had been entirely honest as far as she understood the truth, but what did girls know of the world? For days now they had watched folk being moved out of the camp, along the rail line, orderly evacuees with their luggage and name tags attached to coats, Many seemed anxious, unwilling to go; others were hopeful, glad to be out of the camp and on their way west. They couldn't send back word of their treatment or fate, of course, and despite herself Monika imagined many variations of an unknowable worst – their abandonment or mistreatment, murder even; the indifference of the British if they managed to reach Lübeck unmolested; the antagonism of other Germans forced to take in more hungry mouths to share what little there was. All of it seemed depressingly likely, more so than any fortunate outcome.

And though no one had returned to Torney once dispatched, there were rumours of what awaited Germans who were obliged to wait at the Scheune 'holding area' rather than board trains immediately. Some claimed to have overheard Polish staff criticising the quality of their counterparts at Scheune - an old woman swore that they were no better than criminals, spared their just desserts and stuffed into uniform, brutes who starved, robbed, raped and beat their charges to punish them for the pittances they received from the Polish government. There, the seeds of typhus that were evident at Torney blossomed terribly, and the trains that went west carried as many dead as living Germans. All this, said the old woman (though known to be a gossiper, her testimony suspect), she had heard with her own ears.

Monika tried to reassure herself that they *had* to go, it was necessary. The camp was filling up, hundreds more displaced souls arriving every day, and there was a definite order in which sections of huts were allocated for emptying. That to which Bernhageners and others had been assigned on the day of their arrival was neighbour to the last to be cleared, so there was no need to ask *why us?* Again, the fact that someone among the Poles knew how to plan things almost calmed her anxiety that their fate was being determining upon a whim or a change in the wind. But the old woman's words lingered in her mind, making her fear that the final hurdle in their wretched odyssey would be the highest of all.

She forced herself to be busy that day. Her small empire was packed in less than a minute, and Erika's even more quickly. Then she went to find the rest of Bernhagen, to discharge her final duty as their seer. The villagers were scattered between several huts, yet almost every one of them wore the same, weary *Oh God* expression on their face as she approached. In each case she ignored it and came straight to her only point – *when we're moved along to the next place, stay together with your fellow Bernhageners. If there's any trouble, no-one else will help you.*

Even the most stubborn of them conceded the point and promised to do this, but Monika feared that a degree of nagging was going to be necessary. Her consolation was that Erika was growing a healthy wasp's tongue and would help goad them into some sort of sense, or at least obedience. It wasn't much, the will of a girl and an elderly woman, to preserve what remained of their village against all that might stand in their way, but if God had preserved them so far it had to be for some purpose, surely?

That argument sounded weak even to Monika. Relying upon God's love, Polish forbearance and British goodwill to speed them through Scheune wasn't a plan but a sincere admission that she was helpless. She imagined her far ancestors, the struggles they must have faced in their new, strange land, surrounded by enemies, burdened by ignorance, disease and want yet made strong by the same necessities, and wondered if she deserved their blood in her veins. Mere acquiescence – even to God's will – wasn't what was expected of a Pohlitz.

In the afternoon the leather-clad gangsters returned to the camp, and for almost an hour she followed them as they approached newcomers to offer food for possessions. They seemed less confident now, almost subdued, but plenty of deals were agreed and sealed. Eventually, she felt sure that she'd identified their leader, the one who said yes or no to some unusual item offered and sent one or more of the others to fetch more of their currency when the tins of fish were gone. When he was alone except for an elderly German man from whom he was trying to tease an overcoat, she walked across and cleared her throat.

Achym Mazur was struggling to keep the smile on his face, when what he longed to do was strip the old goat and use his arse as a flower pot. He'd offered three tins of fish for the coat (once an elegant garment, now a tired, stained travesty of fine tailoring), but this, apparently, was an insult to the memory of Gerda, the wife (God rest her soul) who'd searched half of Insterburg's commercial quarter one Saturday afternoon twenty years past to find a suitable Christmas gift for her devoted husband. At this point the bereaved spouse introduced himself as one Eric Formann and insisted on shaking hands, cunningly pressing upon Achym a moral obligation to deal fairly and forcing him to put down the tins of fish and the suitcase in which their brethren resided. It had been an effort to take the hand and not make a fist instead.

This was about his twentieth haggle so far today, and the admirably resilient Mazur morale was close to breaking. It was all shit, a disaster, a humiliation for a man who prided himself on skirting the edges of bourgeois society, to be putting himself in the way of creatures like Herr Formann. He was in a mood to walk away and keep walking until he reached his trombone and one of the gang's pair of Mausers, fill a rucksack with necessities and choose an open road at random, to find new opportunities where a man's enterprise was not punished by God, Fate or other comedian. But some craven need to see a thing through kept him here at the blunt end of grey commerce, wheedling at folk for the chance of a rag windfall. It *was* shit, as bad as any he used to hang over in the communal latrine at Trassenheide.

Remarkably, he felt his resistance crumble, and before Herr Formann could make good his threat of producing a photograph of fucking Gerda he held out a further two tins. Apparently this improved offer entirely rubbed out the stain of his earlier insult. Herr Formann removed the precious item with no noticeable heart-searching and stuffed more food than he deserved into the pockets of his jacket. For a moment he paused, touched its lapel and raised his eyebrows hopefully, but Achym was already turning away, coat over his arm, dragging the suitcase to its next disastrous rendezvous.

An old woman blocked his path. Obviously, he couldn't strike her to the dirt, but the moment tested his respectable middle-class upbringing sorely. She was indistinguishable from most other adult females in this place – thick-set peasant stock with weather-beaten features and a healthier moustache than his own (not that he envied her that), and he was certain she was going to offer him some filthy piece of nineteenth-century fustian in the hope of smoked salmon or a pork chop. Apart from a small, tattered leather bag she carried nothing, however, and momentarily his hopes rose at the prospect of jewellery, a family heirloom, a small but perfectly wrought silver cigarette case.

She took his arm, and he resisted the urge to snatch it back (she'd have to release it anyway to open her bag, so the ordeal was bound to be short). When she lifted her face, he quickly held his breath before her own could reach him.

'Young man.' Definitely a Pomeranian, but he knew that already – why else would she be here? The bald statement hadn't been a question yet it hung in the air, and with a sinking heart he realised he had a walk-on part in this ordeal.

'Yes, mother?'

'Do you believe in God, our Saviour?'

## 61

'But why didn't you tell me?'

'Otto, don't go on. It's just something he wants keeping safe. You know how Russians are with private reparations – it's probably going to buy him a farm back in wherever.'

Fischer rubbed his forehead with a knuckle, deeply, trying to reach his brain. With an office, one or two telephones and a small staff who understood the nature and value of facts, his sense of helplessness might have been a passing thing, a mood that this tiny revelation could have teased away. Instead, it applied itself as a needle did to infected flesh.

'You didn't think it might be worth mentioning?'

Kuhn shrugged. 'Why should I? Half of Europe's stealing from the other half. Well, from us. What's interesting about it?'

'Oh, nothing. The man who holds my balls between two pieces of glass-paper – why should I want to know what he's doing?'

'That's just ego … something. He's an important guy, probably got a hundred snitches working the streets for him, tracking down the anti-Reds. Why should any of it be to do with you?'

'I can't say that it is, Earl. I can't make any judgement about it, one way or the other. Do you know why?'

Kuhn's face reddened slightly. 'Because I didn't mention it.'

'Never mind. What is it?'

'I don't know. Neither does Achym. The last thing he's going to do is open it. It could explode in any number of ways.'

Reluctantly, Fischer had to agree. No one with a gram of sense would have agreed to take on the 'favour' and then chased for details. 'When did he take it on?'

'After his coal scheme cacked, I think. Just about everyone's balls were in the mangle then, so the Russian must have known he'd say yes.'

'Have you seen it?'

'I've seen the package, yeah.'

'Show me.'

Kuhn made a shape with both hands. They held a space the size of a small chocolate box. 'Achym got nervous, though. The Russian probably knew he was keeping it in the woods – that's where he handed it over. So Achym broke the lock on his gang's hut to make it look like a robbery and then moved the thing into Stettin on the quiet.'

'Where?'

'He asked old man Grossmann to look after it for him. He's probably the only guy in town who's not on Zarubin's books.'

'Grossmann agreed to it?'

'Well, he didn't get the story, obviously. He just thinks it's some loot of Achym's. Anyway, now he's really worried – Achym, I mean, not Grossmann. Something's happened.'

'What?'

'He won't say. But he's got the feeling that Zarubin might be being too clever. Or not clever enough. Or he's playing some fucking game ….'

'So, anything?'

'Just about. Anyway, he took the package back from Grossmann greasy-quick, because he's changed his mind.'

'About what?'

'About having the thing. *Now* he thinks that if there's one thing worse than having it it's having Zarubin think he hasn't. Did that come out right?'

'I think so. Obviously, I need to speak to him.'

They were standing at the dusty junction of Storbeck-Strasse and Stephan Allee in the hamlet of Schwarzow (the signs now said Swierczewo), the point where fields gave way to the western suburbs of Stettin. A kilometre to the east, at Torney, much of German Pomerania was being crammed into an area the size of ten football pitches; here, not a single person or vehicle disturbed the conversation.

Kuhn stroked the front of his coat, flagging his anxiety. 'Is that clever? Why be closer to it than we need to be?'

Fischer found a wall, a moss-covered perch overlooking an open field-drain, and sat down. 'Earl, think about it. I've been dragged, pushed, herded like a market-day heifer by the man who apparently wants me to find my girl's killer. Other than write a series of notes for me to follow he couldn't have been more blatant. At the same time he's corralled Mazur, a small-time black-marketeer who just happens to know me from the good old days and placed with him an object or objects that might have nothing to do with what I'm looking for. Yes?'

'Yeah.'

'No, Earl. Absolutely not. Why would he use Achym?'

'He knows how to hide stuff ...'

'Not that well. In fact, if it weren't for your lack of a

gossiping gland I'd have known about the thing within a few hours, and if Zarubin doesn't realise that then he's a dolt. And he isn't. So this is another prod, another shove, by proxy. It isn't subtle, but I doubt that it was meant to be. The only curious thing you've told me is that he appears to have nerve-endings.'

'Curious?'

'Worrying, then. If something can hurt him it can hurt us too. And we have no idea what it is.'

Kuhn's face brightened. 'Or hurt him before he can dangle us.'

Fischer flicked a stone into the field drain. 'This is why I need to see inside his package. It's the only way to begin to understand the threat, where it's coming from. And, perhaps, put Marie-Therese to rest.'

'Are you anywhere with that? I mean, we go places, you ask questions, get kicked, told to fuck off and I don't know what, and I can't see that you're any closer now than a month ago.' Kuhn removed a hand from stroking duties long enough to dismiss himself with a wave. 'Not that I'm an expert, obviously.'

Surprised, Fischer realised that he hadn't yet asked himself the same thing. Following the forms had kept him moving instead of lying down and waiting for the next truck to hit the bump in the road. He'd been honest about not caring who had done it or why, but the process of reducing odds, of siphoning the possibilities, had a way of validating itself, of making answers seem necessary even if they weren't.

'I think I know where she died, and when of course. *Why* isn't difficult to guess. *Who* could be anyone, I suppose.'

'You know all that? How?'

'Without a police department behind us it's a matter of

establishing what's impossible – or at least improbable - then applying common sense. Marie-Therese was found on Berg-Strasse, just about the most dangerous location in all of Stettin to dump a body. The Americans say *dump*, don't they?'

Kuhn was impressed. 'Yeah, they do.'

'So it's reasonable to suppose that she was there for a reason. The obvious one is that she died in the building and was pushed – or placed – out on to the street.'

'Why not just wrap her in a tarpaulin and drive her into the woods? That way no one need know even that she was dead.'

'I assume that someone wanted *someone* to know that she was dead. And in such a way that it couldn't be ignored.'

'Who?

'Me, for one. Who else I can't say.'

'You? Who'd give a shit-and-a-half about you? You're German.'

'Someone who wanted to involve me, for whatever reason.'

'*Zarubin* put her there?'

'It's likely. If he couldn't investigate it himself and didn't want the thing smothered, who better to take it on than the victim's ex-policeman boyfriend?'

'So she died in there.'

'Or was brought to the building from somewhere else and then pushed out.'

'Christ, Otto! You've just narrowed it down – don't widen it again!'

Fischer shrugged. 'That's what police do.'

About a hundred metres from where they were sitting a man emerged from a field and crossed the road. He was carrying a lamb over his shoulder, holding it as if griping a baby. He didn't see or chose to ignore the two strangers. The lamb gave them a single bored glance and went back to nibbling its ride's collar.

Kuhn watched wistfully as they entered a cottage garden and went indoors. 'How is *why* not difficult to guess?'

'The timing. She died on 8 February. Too much else happened that night, or within the same forty-eight hours, for it all to be coincidental.'

'The thing in Berlin?'

'And then here, the *Nekrasov*. It was something so sensitive that the Russians took care to keep it from the Allies, the Poles, Germans, even other Russians.'

'How do you know that?'

'They closed off half of Berlin and, on the same day, ejected all non-military personnel from Lastadie and Bredower. That's a hint, at least. But the most interesting thing's the timing. Remember what you told me about 10 February?'

'You mean the Poles getting to wipe their own arses from that day?'

'The transfer of authority, yes. Two days after *that* something else happened. I wouldn't have known about it, but Herr Frank the assistant port manager was very helpful. Prior to 12 February the Ivans controlled the navigation of the Oder from north of Gorlitz to the Baltic, but on that date the Poles took responsibility for all the east bank except the Stettin security zone itself and the Stettin Lagoon – Swinemünde stretch.'

'That's important?'

'Since 12 February, anything leaving Stettin on the river could be observed all the way from north of the town to the lagoon. I think what happened in Berlin, and whatever was loaded into *Nekrasov*, was timed to beat that deadline, to keep it all very, very discreet. It narrows down the possibilities.'

Frowning, Kuhn examined the sheen of his fur coat. 'So it wasn't the usual stuff. Reparations, I mean.'

'Not the usual sort, no. The Ivans don't seem to care what anyone thinks about their light fingers, so it wasn't industrial plant – unless it's something secret, in which case we'll never know – and definitely not people, who could be removed in any number of ways. What if the nature of the thing means it *had* to go by water?'

'Poison? Gas or germs, perhaps?'

Fischer considered this. 'That's not bad. But the problem is Marie-Therese. If I'm right she came too close to the thing, but I don't see how a ... whore could do that if it was any kind of weapon. What about art?'

'Paintings, you mean?'

'Or statues. Something fragile, that a thousand-kilometre road trip might not be too good for?'

'Why would the Ivans try to hide that? They've stripped every front parlour in eastern Germany. Why care about the public stuff?'

Fischer sighed. 'You're right, obviously. I can't get excited about what was in the *Nekrasov*, but it seems to be the key to what happened to her. At least, Zarubin wants me to think that it is. So this package ...'

'Yeah, I get it. But Achym's more likely to join the Communist Party than let you take a peep inside.'

'I know. But speak to him, tell him it's in all our interests if we know.'

'How will I get back into the Control Zone?'

'You won't, for the moment. I'll come out for you tomorrow. You have somewhere to stay?'

Kuhn scratched his chin. 'There's Andrzej the cop, he still owes me for not being Jewish anymore. But what his wife's going to say about having a German guest …'

'Charm her, Earl. Take a bottle of wine, if you can find one.'

'*Wine*? Why would I part with currency?'

'For an evening in an almost normal world? What price could you put on that?'

## 62

Zarubin was devoutly glad that he'd taken the time to repair the visible damage. It was a formal investigation, so formal that they'd brought a stenographer. And it was *they*, a plurality, not some overworked, middle-ranking Internal Affairs official who would ask a few questions, shake the right hands and shoot off back to Moscow to write some creatively self-absolving crap and deep-file it thereafter. Like most intelligent men in any Soviet organization, Zarubin didn't doubt their ability to be thorough.

Fortunately, he kept his spare uniform in his office, so there was only the ear-notch and light facial bruising to explain if anyone asked (for once he could claim that it had been he, not a suspect, who'd missed a step in the stairwell). He'd been given an appointment sometime in the early afternoon, and he had plenty of time to wash, dress and practice an appropriate mood. His defence was the simplest - he knew nothing, had heard nothing and therefore suspected no one – but, as always, correct appearance spoke as loudly as testimony. Obviously, he wouldn't be so naïve as to pretend surprise or indignation; in this sort of investigation such a response was tantamount to saying *I did it*. No, an open, concerned attitude, conveying the sense that every fibre of his being eagerly hoped for a swift resolution and condign punishment, was the only prudent approach. He had nothing to fear; everyone above the rank of sergeant was a potential perpetrator. Hell, he *was* innocent in a way. Almost.

Of course, it was all a waste of time (unless the point of it was a confession rather than a resolution). They knew only what he'd revealed to them, and it wasn't enough to point a finger in anything other than a vague direction. With an entire Ministry's resources they couldn't begin to follow a trail involving thousands of men and hundreds of potential opportunities. He smiled to himself. They had no suspect, and everyone – *everyone* - had a motive. *It would be time better spent to head east, pick up a spade and start over.*

The first thing he'd done was to take a look at the schedule. As he'd suspected, Captain Arokh had put himself first in line. No doubt he'd make the offer, try to be indispensable. If he could control the Stettin end it would attract attention, grease his path to something better. It occurred to Zarubin that he hadn't thought to do it himself, though he'd anticipated – expected - it from others. But that would have been too clever, wilful almost. He wanted to come out of this well, not as yet another impediment to local river navigation.

His turn came at 1.30pm. He hoped that hunger hadn't stirred their peevishness. He'd been present when too many arbitrary decisions had been made to the sound of rumbling bellies; attended meetings whose conclusion had greeted the lunch bell with uncanny precision. Logically, his intelligence role would incline them to regard him as half-inside, an ally like Arokh, but he wasn't so optimistic as to assume that there wouldn't be at least one difficult bastard trying to cement a reputation for impartial rigour. He hated that type. Invariably, they blended native stupidity with a whimsy that would seem cruel in a cat - you couldn't let your reputation speak for itself because its ankles were being gnawed already.

He was admitted by a civilian. They had commandeered the old officer's mess room, where Prussians had once imagined themselves part of the historic furniture. He counted eight behind the table, none of them military, with two uniformed flankers occupying the table-ends. He appreciated the deployment. A man told to sit in the chair opposite, already moist-handed, wouldn't be able to keep them all in sight simultaneously, and if he turned to answer a peremptory question it would be a moment before he could determine who had asked it. He'd never have the chance to settle down, to think what to say before he said it.

He was nodded to the chair. Usually, a man could discompose himself while his interrogators' names and rank were offered, but not today. A heavily-jowled fellow with *committee* etched into his very anima coughed and offered a single name. It was more than enough.

'Thank you for attending. We report to Minister Kaganovich.'

In an ordinary world, Zarubin might have raised an eyebrow and asked what the man responsible for the nation's building materials could possibly find interesting about this matter. But the Soviet Union didn't follow conventional political protocols. With admirable economy, they had let him know that this was now family business, and absolutely the worst possible family at that. If Lazar Kaganovich had taken it on, then the General Secretary himself was an intimately interested party.

*Shit.*

How had it come to this? Was it the scale of the thing, or did *he* somehow know more than the bare detail? Zarubin chided himself. The man was a cunning beast but no more omnipotent than the non-existent God he'd replaced. The message was merely that someone had gone much, much too far and when this was over its only legacy would be several stains on a cell floor. The prospect was intended to be terrifying, and even Zarubin's bowels shifted slightly. But then, hadn't he made every effort to see that it would come this far?

Once he'd steadied himself the interrogation went well enough. The questions were imprecise and the implications half-hearted; all he could be accused of was a broad geographical proximity to the crime and a level of authority which might have allowed him to obscure the evidence trail. It amounted to nothing, as he'd expected. Of course, when they'd finished with him he offered to put the full resources of his office (ha!) at their disposal, and promised all possible diligence if they chose to accept. They thanked him and made a comment about his proper attitude. It all was rote-stuff, as expected as the back of a priest's hand during a catechism recital.

Afterwards he found Arokh and tried to get a sense of how long they'd remain in Stettin, but *Kaganovich* had worked its dark magic upon the captain as it had on everyone else. The only sense he got was that no-one in NKVD Stettin would so much as fart without filing a report in triplicate upon the event, which at least reassured him that Arokh wouldn't be using his own initiative to delve deeper into this business. When the Boss took an interest it was never clear whether industry would be rewarded or dismantled and shipped east.

Paralysis was the wisest course of action, and Zarubin had to force himself not to be wise. If the matter dragged on they might stumble into a half-sight of the truth, and he might find himself on that cell floor, counting his teeth from a distance and mumbling his thanks for a roomier mouth. All the attention he'd ever sought had now been roused, so *now* pressed its case keenly. Until twenty-four hours earlier it had seemed that he held the initiative; now, with half the leadership of the Soviet Union and an angry bear snapping at his arse, he wasn't so sure.

63

Achym Mazur arranged to meet them at the Rose Garden just after 9am. It was as public a place and time as Szczecin could admit to, and Fischer wondered why he'd thought their business was best conducted in the light. They watched him approach around three sides of the square, navigating the suits, uniforms and prams carefully, as much a part of the scenery as a *spucknapf* in a tea-salon. When he arrived they got the barest nod.

'I haven't brought it.'

'But you said ...'

'I know, but it needs more thought. Or more information. As it is, the thing's a bomb, and we don't know if it's live or not. So until someone can say to me Achym, this is how it is, I'm not opening it. For anyone. If it can harm the Russian, what will he do to an audience?'

Fischer had several arguments ready, and each would break against the high wall of common sense. Mazur was right, of course. None of them could say how dangerous it was.

'Sorry, Hauptmann.'

'No, it's fine. I'll think of something else.'

Mazur glanced around, counting nearby ears. 'While we're here, do you know anything about holy books?'

'Holy books?'

'Well, bibles then.'

'A little. My school's pastor was uncommonly engaged.'

Mazur delved into his bag and removed a parcel. He handed it to Fischer. 'What about this?'

Carefully, Fischer unwrapped the item and opened it at the frontispiece. 'Have you read it?'

'The bible? You're kidding. Why would I ...'

'No, I mean this page.'

'Should I have?'

'It tells you everything. This was printed in Zurich, in 1531, at the sign of the ...'

Fischer stopped, and tried to recall his church history. Being a German it wasn't simple. 'Good Lord.'

'Ha, yes.'

'Look at the printer's name. It's a Froschauer.'

'Wow.' Mazur was trying to look more impressed than dumbfounded.

'And a 1531 Froschauer.' Quickly, Fischer flicked through to Genesis. 'It's probably the *Kombinierte* Bible.'

Kuhn coughed. 'I'll give you a good price for it, Achym.'

Expertly, Mazur noted the wide eyes, the too-pale, bad poker complexion, and gave the only reasonable answer. 'Fuck off, Earl. So, the date - that's good, yeah?'

'It was the first Swiss-German translation, at least the first to be produced in a single volume. But there's something wrong. It's too small.'

'It should be bigger?'

'It *has* to be bigger! At least quarto, and more usually folio.

But this is, well, octavo. And ...' Carefully, Fischer leafed through the book; '... it isn't illustrated.'

Mazur's face fell. 'Still, it's old. It must be worth something?'

'No, I mean it should be illustrated, copiously, but it isn't. It should be about forty centimetres long, but it isn't. I don't think it's a forgery, so ...'

'You're murdering me!'

'A one-off, a special production. Look at it. Exquisite!'

'Someone's handwritten a lot of shit at the front and back.'

'But they didn't deface the text. Do you know what I think this is?'

Mazur's face said that he needed rhetorical questions as much as a new navel. 'Do you know, I don't.'

'An evangelist's personal copy - a man who was going somewhere dangerous and needed to be able to hide it. There's no point to a small bible otherwise. The larger the text the easier it is to read, and most copies of any vernacular bible would have been display pieces, for use in the family home or chapel.'

'Is it valuable?'

Fischer shrugged. 'I'm not a book dealer. But if I'm right about it being a one-off, it must be priceless. Especially on the American market.'

'Why? Because Yanks are richer?

'Because this is as much a part of their history as ours. Their early Dutch and German settlers took printed bibles from Zurich or Geneva with them, but much later editions. This, they'd probably regard as an ur-text. If it *is* the *Kombinierte* it was mostly written by Zwingli himself. You've heard of Zwingli, I hope?''

'Jesus!'

'Only the later chapters.'

'Oh, very funny.' Mazur was almost hopping from one foot to the other, and his fingers twitched visibly. Tenderly, Fischer re-wrapped the book and returned it as if he were removing the fuse from 250 kilogram general ordnance. 'An obvious question, but where did you get it?'

'Never mind.'

'It was a German refugee, wasn't it? What did you pay, a couple of sardines?'

It was too much effort for Mazur to seem affronted. With a priceless artefact-filled hand he waved away the accusation. 'Actually, I gave her exactly what she asked for.'

'Which was what?'

'Information.'

'Just information?'

'It was that or sardines. She wants to get her folk to the west alive. I told her what was between here and that.'

'Which is?'

'If they're lucky, a few days' kicking empty tins around the camp and then a quick rail journey. If not, the sugar factory.'

Fischer's long-dormant kripo's memory stirred. 'At Scheune? The Ketzin Salzwedel place?'

'That's what the sign says. You know it?'

'From a couple of robberies, back in the 30s. But it's hardly more than a warehouse - no water, no toilets, no windows even. The Poles are actually keeping people in there?'

'About two thousand at a time. If they don't get moved on quickly they die on the premises or head west with a little gift for the British.'

'Typhus.'

'Yeah. That poor old bitch and her fellow villagers were heading there yesterday.'

'And you took her bible anyway.'

Mazur reddened slightly. 'I threw in a few tins, told her to make them last. They'll do more than prayer will.'

'That book's no use to you here. Either you trust someone in the west to sell it for you or you go yourself.'

'I know. Shit! I don't speak English.'

Kuhn was doing it now, glancing around to determine whether anyone was close enough to have psychically sponged up the business opportunity. 'I do, Achym. Even Otto does, a little. Why don't you come west with us, be a partner in our music shop?'

'Thanks, Earl, but I don't do people. I've tried it recently, and it's made me unwell. I'd sooner retire hungry.' He half lifted the bag and looked hopefully at Fischer. 'You wouldn't ...?'

'Of course. I'd be happy to assist yet another plunderer of German culture to get a good price for his loot. Or would I perhaps hand out the cash in handfuls to starving German children? It's a difficult question.'

'Alright, alright! I'll go west and hire a translator. They can't be too expensive right now.'

'Are you going to return Zarubin's package or run with it?'

Mazur shook his head. 'The thing's a grenade. Why did he

decide that *my* arse was the best place for it?'

'Because he wanted both to keep it from someone and to let me to know it existed.'

'Fine. On the day I fuck off you can take it, return it to the Russian and he'll call you his best boy. Then everybody wins.'

'It may not be safe.'

Kuhn frowned. 'I don't get that, Otto. He obviously wants the thing badly, so where's the problem?'

'The timing, the contents. Who knows about the package? Who's watching? If the wrong people see me return it, does that help us get out of Stettin or put us in the river? Will having it make Zarubin think I've gone a bit further than he intended?'

'For God's sake!' Mazur's arms half-lifted and dropped helplessly. 'It's just a *thing*, an object! We don't even know *what* it is! Just tell him you've got it and ask politely how, where and when he wants it back!'

Fischer smiled. 'I'm already in the shit, so more can't hurt?'

'I didn't mean … alright, yeah.' Mazur shook his head. 'It puzzles me how men like you make a death-wish seem like optimism. Don't you care?'

'I fall in and out of it. Lately, more out.'

'You're not working something, are you? Getting an edge in a sweet deal?'

'In Stettin? There are no sweet deals for Germans, only the boot or a bullet. My problem is working out which is for the best.'

'So …?'

'Keep hold of it for now. I'll think of a way to defuse it.'

## 64

On the evening that Bernhagen came to the sugar factory, Monika Pohlitz's heart, which she had begun to fear was stronger than a Hinterwald bull's, finally broke. They had walked the rail track from Torney to Scheune with no greater hindrance than the taunts and insults of their rude, ill-bred guards (who might have had the sense to learn enough German to make their insults intelligible to their victims), and the day itself, warm and dry, had done as much as it could aid their tired joints. But at the end of their short journey the full measure of what Germans had become laid itself out plainly.

They were robbed at the factory gate, a thorough shearing that made previous outrages seem like polite misunderstandings. Bags were slapped from hands, and faces got the same if the hands didn't open quickly enough - an old man, frantically clutching a gilt-edged photograph of someone lost to him, was brutally felled with a rifle butt and the object requisitioned; children, trusted to conceal their families' last scraps of worth in the hope that human decency might preserve them, were made to strip as if they were urchins, thieves caught bothering respectable folk. Infinitely patient, the line from Torney passed slowly through this ordeal and was unburdened of the final shards of its heritage.

And then the real outrages commenced. A small gang of uniformed thugs took their pick of the women in the factory yard, dragging them away to places where urges could be satisfied. A son, daughter or rare, live husband who tried to intervene got an elbow at best but more often a proper, painstaking kicking that left them half-conscious on the cobbles, bleeding, their heads not quite up to understanding what had put them there. One young girl, a teenager, beautiful beyond her years, was graced by the attention of three men in turn, and preserved only by her pallid complexion and hacking, lung-deep cough that warned her suitors of what they might expect in return. After the last of them went away to press his affections elsewhere an old woman helped her to her feet, but the girl shrugged it off as if such things came like the weather. She adjusted her dowdy, tattered clothes, and with a gesture that even a keen eye would hardly have noticed checked that four small tins of fish were undisturbed in their secret pockets.

When they had been properly robbed and violated the dazed refugees were herded into the dark, dank building and the doors closed on them. Monika was surprised that the guards themselves didn't enter to continue their entertainment; but then her eyes became accustomed to the small light that penetrated the broken roof and the reason made itself horribly apparent.

The place was a charnel-house filled with what seemed to be a nation's bones, though these were dressed still and moving in imitation of life. It was a high-roofed space, and the cathedral acoustic echoed with wracking coughs, dragged out of the dark corners to which the weakest had crawled to suffer privately. A wretched congregation clustered in the central space around two small fires, trying to will warmth into the building's cold, moist air while the remainder of its inmates shuffled aimlessly past them like pilgrims fulfilling a debased version of *Tawaf*. But Monika's attention was forcibly dragged from what she could see by the overwhelming odour of vomit and excrement. She gagged dryly, covering her mouth instinctively as if to ward off what was airborne in the effluvia. Others newcomers failed to exercise self-control, and added fresh foulness to the stale.

She turned around. Bernhageners had gathered behind her, clustered close for mutual protection. She waved them in closer. 'We need to keep to ourselves. This won't last for long, so be patient. Don't wander off to find food or anything else.'

Ellie Bontecou, her face was almost lost in the vast scarf she used as a guard against the world, pushed her way forward. 'But what about water? We can't just do without it.'

She was right, of course. Even two days languishing here (and Monika fervently hoped it wouldn't come to that) might kill off half their number if water wasn't made available. Surely, no one would abandon them without *any* provision?

'Wait here. All of you.'

Monika returned to the broad doorway through which the refugees had been herded. It was closed and locked, but a hatch at eye-height (well, the height of a man, at least) allowed her to stand on her toes and peer out into the factory yard. Three militiamen stood a few metres away, smoking and chatting. She cleared her throat and tried to sound stronger than she felt.

'Excuse me, sirs. We need water, both to drink and to wash with.'

The one who was speaking interrupted his story and half-turned to the door, flicking a butt that almost caught her nose. *'Spierdalaj, babcię!'*

A translation was hardly necessary. Monika frowned as if at a naughty schoolboy's cleverness.

'I'm sure that one of you young men understand me. Without water we can't boil our clothes, and there's disease here already. If it spreads, who will be safe? If you have to empty this place after we're gone or dead, will *you* be safe? And all for just a little water?'

They laughed at her but it was forced, pretending indifference. She closed the hatch, hopeful that they would at least speak to someone with the common sense and authority to act, and quickly. They had been told that this was merely a collection point, a place where the displaced waited for the next available train to take them west. But what did available mean, when they couldn't put a time - or, God forbid, a date – to it? Monika didn't fear death, but she feared a meaningless ending ordained by no greater force than the indifference of stupid men's half-arrangements.

She returned to her folk. They had moved a few metres, to where a collapsed partition wall had deterred anyone from occupying the space beneath. They were clearing bricks and making a low wall of them, and Monika, for the first time in recent memory, was impressed by their initiative.

Erika placed a brick carefully and straightened up. 'We'll have a room, almost. Just for us.' Her carefully-rehearsed cough had disappeared, though her complexion was still stained by the ash that she and Monika had applied hurriedly in the moments before they departed Torney.

'Fortress Bernhagen!'

Monika didn't see who said it, but she frowned. That sort of talk reminded her of the laughable claims they'd heard on the radio during the last days, of German towns that would be made impregnable by diktat, high hopes and children armed with *panzerfausts*. And look at what had happened to them, all of them.

For the next hour she directed the work, urging it on when hunger and tiredness slackened the pace. When their barrier began to look too much like a rampart she made them topple and scatter it, making a rubble course that blocked idle visitors just as effectively but drew no attention to the space it protected (they needed not to offend or make others think that Bernhageners had anything – particularly food – to hide). It was a pitiful thing, something that would put two metres at most between them and infection, but as with all efforts it cast an illusion of purpose. The builders smiled at each other, winked, moved a little less like the lost souls they had been.

Night came quickly to their half-world, bringing deeper fears than the adult Monika had ever known. Coughs, retches and moans amplified hugely in the absence of light and were joined by the howls and sobs of the half-demented and bereaved, for whom darkness sharpened the panorama of their new world wonderfully. One voice in particular, a high, keening thing, almost constant in its agony, seemed to carry around the factory as if its owner were constantly moving, a messenger lamenting the fate of everyone. Despite her best efforts to sleep it stayed with her all night, her mind isolating it from the generality of torments.

At dawn the factory's population roused itself gradually. Someone had organized latrines in a sectioned-off area, probably the old office space, and queues formed lethargically outside it. It was necessary of course, and quite deadly - impossible to avoid for more than a few hours yet a highly efficient nursery for the affliction that would kill them all within days. Monika tried to think of alternatives that wouldn't offend decency, but all that came to mind was the inaccessible outdoors.

She was still thinking of plumbing when the minor miracle occurred. The main door was unlocked and opened, and a militiaman's head appeared, seemingly disembodied, to one side. He shouted something in Polish. When this elicited no reaction from his dumbfounded, anxious audience he repeated the phrase, and an equally disembodied arm joined the head to reinforce it with a beckoning gesture. Both then disappeared so promptly that they might have been on a spring mechanism.

The Bernhageners' enclosure being so close to the door, Monika and Erika were the first to emerge from the sugar factory into the courtyard. Two long troughs had been placed in it since their arrival the previous day, and a lorry-tanker stood immediately outside the yard, its hose passed through the railings into one of them. A forlorn collection of old pans and kettles were piled close by on the cobbles (Monika wondered how it was possible that she hadn't heard their arrival), and a quantity of wood, old skirting boards from their shape and size, was stacked behind them.

From outside the railings their shy militiaman whistled through his fingers and tossed something into the yard. It was a single matchbook; Erika ran to pick it up before the day's early moisture ruined it and handed it to Monika.

Still confused by the events of this early Christmas morning, she was staring at its *Haushaltesware* label when a heavy thought occurred. She turned back to the factory. Several dozen pairs of eyes were upon her, some dulled by despair, hunger or loss, others with a quality of expectancy she had come to know well and fear. Only a few of them belonged to Bernhageners.

Monika sighed. 'We need water for three things – to drink, to wash ourselves with, and to wash our clothes. We boil all the water we drink, and we use boiling water on our clothes, to kill fleas. If they continue to let use the yard we'll keep this trough for washing ourselves in because it's against the wall and allows a little modesty. The other is for clothes. We light fires over there. I wish we could do something about the latrines but we can't, not without lime and disinfectant. We must hope that we go from here soon.'

A woman, a stranger to Monika, stepped forward. Her face was the same cold grey colour as the yard's cobbles. 'But *will* we go soon? Who would want to take us as we are? They want us to die here, and there be fewer Germans in the world.'

There was a terrible plausibility to what she said, and Monika struggled to think how to deny it. They *were* dying, so how could it not be true? She shook her head, bracing herself to lie.

'No, it's just that they don't care. They want us gone one way or the other, but I think that if the British will take us they'd sooner we went. Who would want to empty a plague pit? Who would want to risk their new town that way?'

An old man pushed his way to the front and pushed a finger towards Monika. 'Madam, you don't know how they feel about us. I come from Danzig, and I can tell you that we treated our Poles as badly as we did the Jews. In '39 most of them were shipped off to forced labour gangs or the camps and none of them ever returned. Why shouldn't they repay us in our own coin?'

Dumbfounded, Monika stared at the finger. This was a revelation, and she wondered why. Had she deafened herself to it? 'But ... why?'

The old man shrugged. 'I don't know. The Führer said it was necessary. I don't recall that any of us wept for them, at the time. No, we were glad that Danzig was German once more. And what we did in the General-Government ...' he turned away, shaking his head.

That this might all be God's justice upon Germany filled Monika with despair. How could a sinner begin to be penitent when her crimes – terrible, inhuman crimes - had been committed by proxy, in her name? What saving grace could ease such offences?

Her audience waited. Some of them looked remorseful (or so she imagined); others shook their head, denying the possibility of what they'd heard. Most of them stood dully, beyond consideration of the recent past and their part in it. This was a new world, in which the history being written was of their ordeal, not that of mere anecdotes, of the ghosts of a regime that had been obliterated.

It wasn't fair. A woman whose own world had been bound by a clutch of fields and friends, a woman born before Germany even *was* Germany, shouldn't have to be the brass chalice into which poured every fear, expectation or regret of strangers. She was denying truths, defending the unknowable, discounting awful anticipations, and with what? A wisdom founded upon an education that hadn't lasted even into her thirteenth year. It was too much. She raised her hand.

'Well, what happened can't be undone. I would think that those wanting vengeance for such things have probably taken it already, during the terrible times before and just after the surrender. These people are crude and some are cruel too, but a bullet would be far quicker way of telling us how they feel if that's what they're about. We all know the Poles can't organize themselves, much less anything else - it's their nature, like it's ours to be careful, and thrifty, and hard-working. They aren't trying to kill off Germans, even if some of us deserve it. What was our land is theirs now. They just don't want to share it.'

Monika had never made a speech to strangers before, and didn't know how they would take it. She prayed that they'd think her a fool, a rattled old bat best ignored, and wander away. But even though she could have convinced only a few of them, they stayed, mutely packing the doorway and the space behind, trusting to a head that would think for them all.

So she repeated what she had said about the water and organized them into parties, each with a single task, making them too busy to dwell upon what their situation meant. Erika was happy to be her lieutenant, and the girl's fearless disregard for offending anyone, as much as her beauty, ensured that no one thought to question the arrangements. Monika watched, and said something occasionally when it was necessary, but for the most part she concentrated on not entertaining the scandalous thought that had wormed its way into her mind while she was trying to raise their spirits.

*It isn't an opinion they want, or advice, or guidance. It's another Führer.*

## 65

'Otto, come on. This isn't clever.'

Kuhn's radar was on full battery power, sweeping through 360°, ready to identify and relay any bad news. He'd forgotten to light the cigarette in his mouth, and it was threatening to leave at every nervous twitch. Directly beneath it, Beulah May watched intently, half-hypnotized by its jerking progress and the small circles her owner's knuckle was tracing in the middle of her brow.

Fischer heard the noise but not the words. He stood, one foot on the low basin wall, leaning into it, his forearms crossed on the elevated knee. Directly ahead of him, across the Oder at the mouth of the Bredower Graben, the jetty where *Nekrasov* had moored was empty, though he could see brown-uniformed movement around the warehouses that surrounded it. To his extreme right on this side of the river he had a partial view of the entrance to the Toepffers Basin, a prospect that still made parts of his body ache in fond memory of the beating he'd taken there. There was no traffic on the river today; from the broken bridges and bombed, half-submerged piers in the town centre to the furthermost visible northern reaches, where the remaining forest on Gross Oderbruch gave an impression of primeval wilderness, not a single craft disturbed the smooth, slow flow northward. Technically it was a fine view, but to Fischer the panorama delineated the scale of his frustrations. All of what he could see was Poland now, but Russian rule lay absolutely upon it. He stood at one edge of the Control Zone and couldn't see its other limit - he wasn't even sure what constituted a *limit* here. Somewhere within it a dark pantomime was being played out of which Marie-Therese's murder had been a brief, insignificant entr'acte. After several weeks exercising the last of his kripo's skills he knew nothing of the plot, or of the entertainment's duration, its logical conclusion, its purpose. He could guess at certain things the way a poor mind-reader stumbles upon occasional truths, haplessly; but his tiny audience seemed more amused by the puppet act, the absurd movements of pulled strings. He'd allowed himself to be used, to be played as Kaspar. It was hardly reasonable to resent it after the fact.

But he found that he did, intensely. Had he been ignored, passed over by Zarubin in favour of some other performing fool, he might have flushed the grief out of his bones by now, probably gone west (or south, to Berlin) to fall into a new half-life, a getting-by scramble that most Germans seemed familiar with now. Had it been Berlin perhaps Freddie Holleman would have found him a quiet little clerical slot in the *Volkspolizei*, where a man's police experience could be put to legitimate use cataloguing the anti-social crimes of folk who weren't quite familiar yet with the new rules; where he might savour his bowel-twisting guilt in trachten'd comfort and anticipate a pension just big enough to keep a stomach quiet. Here in Stettin, end-of-service would probably mean the same for him as it did a broken nag.

*They might eat me too, if the harvest fails.*

From the moment he'd first been summoned to Soviet Headquarters, this thing had been worked as closely as a ten-mark shave. He'd known it since his discovery of the Russian officer's tunic button in Marie-Therese's handbag yet had continued to allow the hand to shove him along, correcting his course when it wandered even slightly from true. Did he put so little value in initiative, to be this complicit?

Beulah May whined, pushing Kuhn to do the same. 'Otto, we'll be seen, and then …'

Then what? If a man didn't know the rules of the game, all he could be certain of was that he wasn't going to win. He'd performed as adeptly as he knew how and had discovered precisely what Zarubin wished him to discover – things of which the Russian must have been perfectly aware already in order to herd his victim in their direction. Two days before Marie-Therese died, something important left Berlin on its way to ... he couldn't say, but it had come through Stettin, and while it was here an event occurred to make her death necessary. The thing came when it did because the Russians (or someone in Western Group at least) didn't want other Russians, Germans, the Poles, anyone, to know that it had come. That was it, the lot. The big questions – why Zarubin should need him to know this, why no one else could deal with it, what the consequences of this half-knowledge might be, what might constitute a resolution – weren't capable of being answered, not by him. He had gone as far as it was possible to go in every direction except one, the very probably fatal one.

So he had a decision to make. It was one that would affect him, Kuhn, Miron and his imprisoned crew, the German colony in the Control Zone, possibly Achym Mazur and the Pelzer-Strasse boys and God alone knew who else. Absent the baggage it wouldn't have been difficult, at most a toss of a borrowed coin. But this was more a case of Moses come to the point of 'Is it left or right here?'

That was the other irritation, the obligation. He'd come to Stettin as unburdened as any man could be in this life, charged only with a chemical will to survive the avalanche that bore down upon every German, destitute of ties, resources, even expectation and most content to remain so. A year later only his pockets remained empty, while the rest of the Fischer fundament had filled like ... his imagination failed him. Probably, there was a maritime cliché about clean hulls and barnacles, or trawlers and tangled nets. But he'd been Luftwaffe, and things that tangled with 'planes invariably brought them down.

He turned to Kuhn. 'Earl, you should go west - today if possible but tomorrow at the latest. Bribe your Russian to get you as far as Berlin, then go to the Oberrat. Tell him I'm asking, as a friend.'

'Jesus, Otto, don't say that!' Kuhn's free hand clutched the coat with ardent strength. 'We can go together, shoot off like sprouts from a plate. The Russian won't even know we've gone before we're safe. What's to think about?'

'Everything that isn't you, me or Beulah May. You know how it is - stuff brings complications. Wasn't life simpler before you had the money, the dog and that arsenal in your apartment? When it was just Earl Kuhn and his underpants against the World?'

'No. Yes, but ... fuck your mother! Who do you think's thinking of *you*? What if you do just what the Russian wants and then he offs everyone anyway? Why would he want complications that can be removed easily? Achym's cousin and his mates are dead already, you can't stop it. Ach!'

Fischer hadn't seen Kuhn angry. He looked like he wanted to hit something but didn't know how, hadn't been genetically primed for it - an innocent afloat in a sea of spilled blood and guts, most of that innocent too. With a visible effort of will he had another go.

'Otto, if it's guilt, remember that you're German – you're guilty of *everything*.' Why swallow more than your ration? Just bank your half-face, the shoulder you don't have, the funny bird's claw you pick your nose with and all the people you could have killed on a whim but didn't and call it quits, account settled. You're not too old or even too ugly to get another chance, not when everyone else is looking for the same. Please!'

A shrill siren sounded across the water, from the island. It might have warned of heavy plant moving, or of a shift ending, or of men attempting to escape from their bonded service – a very new or very old form of slavery that pretended to be an arrangement between parties but wasn't. The noise didn't seem to arouse the brown figures at the docks' edge. Perhaps they were used to it, or relaxed about the fact that nothing was going to get off Bredower unless they said so. Perhaps it was just time for the Israelites to eat, or to have an ersatz coffee and an authorized bowel-emptying break. He wondered why normal things were the last to occur to him, and what it meant about the place where his head lived.

'It's not *just* guilt. I have to know, Earl.'

'But how? How will you do that?'

'By making Zarubin talk.'

## 66

Even by the usual standards of a bad idea put into action, it didn't go well. He produced his authorization at the kaserne's Berg-Strasse entrance and was allowed to proceed by the sentry without even a disapproving frown to send him on his way. He managed to cross the old parade ground (still a Soviet lorry-park) and enter the twin doors of the administrative reception. There he was brought to a dead halt by a captain of …. well, he couldn't say. The tabs seemed similar to Zarubin's, but then the Red Army was notoriously limited in its taste in trimmings. The man said something in Russian, but the hand thrust beneath his nose was quite intelligible. He removed the authorization from the inside pocket of his Grossmann once more and offered it. It was read, briefly, and then torn into pieces with theatrical emphasis.

Fischer wasn't surprised. Every time he'd held out the thing to a Russian he'd expected to lose it, or at least have someone seriously question the absurdity of its residence in a German pocket. But its sudden retirement as he stood in this particular building felt like a life-vest being ripped away in a Force-Ten, and the prospect of ever seeing Berg-Strasse again (other than face-first, in a chair to which he was still attached) receded rapidly. He tried to stand to attention and say *Lieutenant Zarubin* without a trace of anything that might sound provocative. To his relief, the captain stood out of the way and nodded him on.

The tiny office was a mess, but in an orderly way. Boxes sat on every available surface, filled to greater or lesser degrees with paperwork. Zarubin was perched on the window-sill, sifting through yet another pile on his lap. He didn't seem surprised or offended to see Fischer, and the news of the encounter didn't get more than a slightly raised eyebrow.

'You've just met Kadurin, my successor here.'

'You're leaving?'

'Soon. A new posting. Obviously, Captain Kadurin is going to do everything by the regulations until he's measured the lay of the land, and that piece of paper definitely wasn't regular. No doubt he's composing an official note as we speak, complaining about the idiosyncratic nature of my methods.'

'You don't seem worried.'

Zarubin shrugged. 'Anything that happens in this town can be explained by reference to the situation.'

'Which is?'

'God Himself can only guess. The longer I've been here the more evident it is that that we're chin-deep in a cultural, sociological and political slurry from which we can only hope that something recognizable will emerge. Thankfully, a bureaucratic hand has helped me out of the mess. I'm going to Berlin, to Karlshorst, where real business is conducted.'

The name strengthened Fischer's resolve. 'You probably know why I'm here.'

The Russian ripped apart a report and threw it into a box. 'It's likely to be one of three things. You want to tell me you have nothing, or that you want to leave Stettin, or that some irritation needs scratching. As you've told me the first already, and the second we can assume you'd have arranged without my permission, it must be the latter.'

'Marie-Therese was killed because she knew about something, something that commenced in Berlin-Karlshorst on 7 February this year and ended three days later when it departed Stettin for ... somewhere else. You knew of the business, of course. You also knew that the perpetrator was a Russian, otherwise you wouldn't have so neatly led me away from Poles, Germans and any other race. But you also must have known that I could do only so much, go only so far, even with that piece of paper you gave to me. If a Russian – any Russian – doesn't want to speak to me he won't. If he decides he's offended by the question he can just shoot me and choose from a range of valid reasons for it. You put a German upon one of your countrymen's arses, in a town owned by the Red Army and pretend-owned by the Poles, an exercise in futility. So this was never any sort of investigation intended to come to a resolution, and you must have known that I'd realise it, sooner or later. So you teased – or deflected - me further, with a package.'

Zarubin's face was unreadable. 'Did I?'

'Mazur says you gave it to him because you wanted it kept safe, which is nonsense. A man in your position can make a hundred bodies disappear from history, and this is something the size of a jewellery box. Rather than hide it you wanted to flaunt it, in particular to me. Therefore I have to assume it's connected to, and perhaps responsible for, Marie-Therese's death. At least, it opens the door upon the rest.'

'Then perhaps you should have opened it?'

'Mazur won't let me see it. He's scared that it's a death-sentence, and he has enough friends to dissuade me from asking too hard. He just wants to be rid of it. Why don't you ask politely for its return and then you can decide whether I see it or not?'

'It may surprise you to hear that circumstances have altered, to the point that I quite earnestly want it back. But your Polish friend took me at something of a disadvantage recently, and I think it frightened him. Since then he's managed to elude my shrinking staff.'

'And you can't requisition more resources, can you? Because that would ring a bell you want kept smothered. So one of two things happens now. Either you decide that this damn business has gone as far as possible, somehow reclaim your package, put me in the Oder and walk away, or you give me enough to do whatever it is you had in mind when you knocked on my apartment door. I can't offer an opinion on which would be the wiser option, obviously.'

Zarubin closed his eyes and rubbed his forehead, and Fischer wondered if he'd pushed too strenuously for the Oder option not to be singing loudly. When a man had no possible worth, how could he be indispensable?

The lieutenant opened his eyes and hands together. The smile that irritated Fischer intensely had returned, as if warning that was coming would be a *divertissement* for only one of them. 'Alright, Major. What can I tell you?'

'Let's begin with something easy. Who broke her neck?'

'I did.'

## 67

He threw with his right, the damaged arm, rage compensating for its lack of muscle tissue. Zarubin went down heavily, his head striking a rare uncluttered space on the wooden floor like a dropped boot. By the time his hand found the holster it was already empty, its contents in Fischer's hand. He was aiming carefully, forcing down the desire for something slower, more drawn-out.

The Russian pulled himself to a sitting position and nursed his head as if it and he had any future together. He didn't look up.

'For a cripple, you ...'

'Shut up.' The shot would mark time – the entire time remaining to him in the world, less than an athlete would need to break the 100 metre tape. He found that he didn't care. An offer of amnesty, his freedom and a cartload of gold to sweeten his path wouldn't begin to weigh against this one, perfect opportunity - two bullets to end two problems, and Captain Kadurin would have the perfect start to his tenure here. The trigger pin tightened beneath his forefinger.

There was something wrong with the way Zarubin was taking it. Debasing himself would have been ugly and pointless; but a cursory, half-hearted plea, a shout or lunge for the gun was the least a man in his predicament might have attempted. It wasn't as if he had anything to lose, yet his shoulders hadn't even tensed in anticipation of what was about to make their load considerably lighter. Fischer eased the pressure slightly.

'You asked the wrong question.' The voice was steady, unafraid, like that of a man too stupid to understand the situation. 'And you won't do it.'

'Why? Because I'm scared of the consequences?'

'Because I'm your fucking saviour.'

'I have no use for being saved.'

Zarubin sighed. 'Yes, you do. Here.' He placed a hand on the floor, levered himself to a kneeling position facing the barrel, and his hand disappeared into the tunic. Fischer didn't waste his breath telling him not to be stupid because there was no longer any choice that would constitute sensible, but the trigger finger stayed where it was. He wondered suddenly if he had the stomach even for this.

It was a piece of paper, folded, creased like it had been there for some time. Zarubin held it out, putting it between his face and the Tokarev. Probably, it wouldn't stop a bullet.

'It's yours.'

'There's nothing that I need.'

'You need this, very badly.'

'A pass out of here? No thank you. I'm beginning to like Stettin.'

'Take it.'

It was a matter of continuing a pointless conversation or ending it efficiently. Fischer took the paper, rubbing his thumb and forefinger together to open it one-handed. It didn't take long to read. After that he stood quietly, letting the room move around him. In the pause Zarubin climbed unsteadily to his feet, gently took back the pistol and gave some attention to the blood that pumped from his nose.

Eventually, Fischer tried to speak. 'How?'

'You're an investigator. Tell me.'

It was obvious, humiliatingly so. He'd seen it a hundred

times (though not carried to such a perfect degree of misdirection), which made the part he'd played doubly painful.

'Dislocation. Suggestion. Timing.'

'Yes. I knew that it was possible. Still ...'

A conjurer only had to find the perfect mark, lead him to the business and let the inertia of shock to do the rest.

'You broke her neck.'

'You asked the wrong question.'

'You didn't kill her.'

'No, of course not.'

'But you made sure the angle ... I would have needed to lift her head to see the face properly.'

'Or walked around the gurney.'

'I might have done that.'

'Yes, you might.'

'Or tried to examine her.'

'Possibly. But in your state, doubtful.'

'I might have *known*.'

There was a cast to Zarubin's expression that in any other man might have been taken for sympathy.

'In which case I should have apologized for my mistake, congratulated you heartily upon your good fortune, wished you good day and devised some other stratagem. But you didn't. You saw a woman, dead with all the swollen disfigurements that death brings, dressed in your girl's clothes. The corpse was soaking wet also, and this too disguises things, particularly hair colour. I had told you already that Marie-Therese Kuefer was dead and you believed me because I am who I am and this is Stettin, where such things are not only possible but expected, and therefore I merely made real what you deeply feared already. As a *kripo* you know that the Bereaved look as little as possible, and through lying eyes. Under the circumstances it was only necessary that she had a proximate likeness.'

'How did you find her?'

'I didn't. The perpetrator has certain ... tastes in women. He knew them both, quite intimately. In fact, they were in each other's company that night, as requested by him.'

A tart layer-cake. Fischer closed his eyes and let the pounding in his head do its business. The last time he had seen her alive she had hugged him, kissed him, told him she'd be careful. And then she had gone off to satisfy some bastard's urge for crowded sex.

'How did the girl die?'

'Suffocation, I believe. He likes to hurt. Affection he saves for his dogs.'

There was something in the way Zarubin said it that rang an alarm, but Fischer wanted to keep his mind out of that or any other bed.

'And Marie-Therese was there? She saw it?'

'Yes. She fled, obviously. Fortunately for her I was on duty, and managed to get her into my office.'

*Why would you do that?* 'It was she who had the package.'

'What's now in the package, yes. Let's call it the object. She was wearing it - actually, it was *all* that she was wearing. A fancy of her client's, perhaps.'

Fischer winced. 'Why did you help her?'

'Because I think very quickly. *She* wasn't thinking at all or she'd never have said a word about it, just run as far and as fast as possible. She handed herself a death sentence by talking to me, but I commuted it because it placed something very valuable into my hands. She gave me the means to damage the man.'

'It was the general.'

'Yes. Dear Uncle Feodor.'

'He thinks she has it still.'

'He did. Now, I'm not sure. I've made mistakes.'

Fischer opened the paper and read it once more. He noticed now the British Occupation Forces postal frank. He'd seen only *Lübeck* the first time, and that had been blurred by the contents. It was addressed to Zarubin personally, at Soviet HQ, Stettin. He wondered what the British had thought of it, why they'd allowed it to proceed.

'You sent her west.'

'On the very first displaced persons train out of Stettin, two days after the incident. She was, I believe, the only non-pregnant woman among many.'

'You're playing your own uncle? Why?'

'I want him against a wall, knowing that I put him there.'

'He's blood kin.'

'He's a murderer.'

'Of German whores? You're not serious.'

'A thief also.'

'A vice he shares with every other member of the Red Army who crossed the Vistula. There's something else.'

'It's not enough?' Zarubin sounded slightly disappointed. 'What must a man do to offend a German these days?'

'Offend me with the truth.'

'Of his other crimes you'd be safer not knowing. For myself, I despise him.'

'Good. Why?'

'He's my uncle.'

'That's a reason?'

'It is when he's my father also.'

'How is that possible?'

'Rather more easily than one might have hoped. The man I call father – who would have raised me, whose name I carry – was a hero of the Revolution despite his privileged social rank. Unfortunately, his vision for the new Russia diverged from that of the eventual victors.'

'A Menshevik?'

'A socialist-liberal, at least. He believed in continuing the war against Germany, so he managed to get himself killed in action during Operation *Faustschlag*. My uncle, his brother, was by contrast a man of no principles whatsoever. As younger siblings often do he followed my father's example, but only until the Bolsheviks' victory persuaded him of his tactical error. He then threw himself enthusiastically into their cause, one with which he had not the slightest affinity. Between these two states of belonging, however, he managed a brief visit home to Petrograd to offer my mother his heartfelt condolences upon the death of her husband. Remarkably, he conveyed them by means of rape.'

'His brother's wife?'

'Appalling, isn't it? His record suggests that he's always had difficulty deciding whether forced sex or polite conversation are more appropriate to an occasion. Perhaps Mother asked for it – she was in mourning after all, and had a figure that black flattered wonderfully. She kept this sordid detail from me of course, and built an entirely conventional mythology of a perfect family life marred only by my father's early death at Daugavpils Junction. Years later, following her own death, I came upon an old letter from her sister, a horrified response to the news of it. Nothing graphic, obviously; just when, how and by whom. The date, regrettably, coincided far more neatly with my eventual birth than did that of my titular father's last home leave.'

'So you have a motive.'

'I hardly need more, do I? And yet strangely it didn't move me as it should. I suppose it's a flaw of youth, to see the past as a closed door behind which both good and bad lie untroubled. The old beast helped me when necessary with money, the right word in influential ears, arranged my transfer to Counter-Intelligence, and I came to regard him much as one does any difficult relation. I have to admit that it took a moment of melodrama to effect the necessary moral boot up the arse.'

'The girl who wasn't Marie-Therese.'

'I wonder what it says, that I was able to snap the neck of the person whose death resurrected my conscience.

'Nothing good, probably.'

Zarubin laughed mirthlessly. 'No. It's not that she reminded me of mother, only the proof her death offered that time hasn't moved Uncle Feodor either into a degree of humanity or a deserving grave. I realised that some sort of push was necessary.'

'I don't see how I could possibly play a part in that.'

'It was important that he didn't, either. Had he done so it wouldn't have taken much to remove the problem - a quiet word to one of his old comrades in Western Group and parts of you would have turned up in stray-dog-shit all over Stettin. He only had to know was that you were ex-police with good cause to do what we wanted.'

'I was looking for her killer, so I'd be bound to find her?'

'Obviously not, but he didn't know that I'd extracted her.

Like many senior officers he owes his success to single-mindedness, not a surfeit of intelligence.'

'You hid the object, got rid of Marie-Therese, set her German boyfriend to find neither and … what? Blackmail him? But you removed all the evidence that could hurt him.'

He has nothing I want, except his pain – to see one of his many pasts return to piss on his prospects of dying in bed. I just needed time to arrange it so there was no possibility he could avoid the drop.'

'So how has it got to this?'

Zarubin rubbed his chin. 'I indulged my cleverness, unfortunately. The plan needed a stick to keep my uncle distracted so I involved one of his oldest, dearest friends, whom he promptly executed in the forest. I didn't think my fingerprints were on it, but it made him suspicious. I'd been insisting that the business was closed down, kept between the two of us and a fugitive whore, so either I was incompetent or lying. Soon after that he returned to his division, but I was nervous. So I made another mistake by trusting your friend Mazur.'

'You shouldn't put any faith in men you've already fucked.'

'You're right, obviously. It's a weakness in those who employ weakness in others, to think ourselves omnipotent. But you see now why I couldn't be more open about this? If the Pole discovers who wants the object he'll certainly try to negotiate, at which point the last reason for my being alive will excuse itself.'

'I feel your pain.'

'You should. It's yours also.'

'To be frank, if I have to take a bullet I'm indifferent to who does the job.'

'Why would you say that?'

'Because I can see no point to your keeping me alive. If you succeed I'd be the only rain-cloud over your picnic, threatening to spoil it. Why on earth wouldn't you tidy things?'

Zarubin pulled a face. 'One can wipe as well as sweep. If you go far enough west it's as good as a deep grave. I never asked, but you wouldn't try to stay, given the choice?'

Fischer lifted the folded paper. 'Not with this, obviously.'

'Would you wish to return? I mean, ever?'

'I could say no, of course. But can you afford to trust me?'

'It's a matter of reason, not trust. You no longer have even a slight incentive to stay. In a year this town will be one hundred percent Polish - apart from the Control Zone, obviously. A German would have to be a fool to imagine there's any kind of future here. I need to know you're not a fool.'

Fischer slumped into the Russian's chair. He felt as if his soul's battery acid had spilled entirely, its chamber pierced by a small, sharp shard of hope that had leapt out from its dark corner. For as long as he cared to recall he had waited for nothing, hoped for nothing, looked only to have the peace of nothing, nothing at all. And now he was being told that *nothing* was a game, a subterfuge to achieve something, a ploy. The humiliation was easy to bear - Germans had become scholars of abjection, eager to demonstrate their understanding of the role the new world had prepared for them. But an offer of more than that, even a little more, levered off the fragile carapace that hopelessness had woven. Ridiculously, he felt fragile now, a broken toy adrift. He wondered if she felt the same.

'If I go, I won't return.'

The bloodied Zarubin brightened. 'So, you know what I

need. Can we do this?'

'Without deaths?'

'Without regrettable deaths, certainly.'

'Not even Mazur's?'

'Why would I do that? The Poles are our fraternal allies, even the corrupt bastards among them. In any case I can hardly raise the enthusiasm to hurt a man who merely wished to keep his balls out of the fire. If we can persuade him to be sensible, that is. And quickly.'

'I also need something.'

'Safe passage, obviously. That isn't ...'

'Something more. Can NKGB or whatever you are now organize internal exiles? Relocation of enemy nationals?'

Zarubin looked blankly at Fischer. 'Obviously, to a point. Within reason, and with good reason. I can't empty a city.'

'The Red Army's going to be done with its German port workers soon, isn't it? Once the river's dredged and the shipyards cleared they'll be ... what? Let go? Sent somewhere else?'

'I don't know. Typically, skilled workers are retained for as long as they can be useful. '

'That's what I thought. So this shouldn't be too difficult. They *want* to be useful, and they know where they can best be that.'

'Where?

'Memel.'

'What? But it's now ...'

'Lithuania, I know. But you'll never stop needing the best harbour in the Baltic, will you? The men I spoke to in the Control Zone swear that you're going to be expanding its facilities massively in the coming years, and they know the port as well as any. They want to go there when they're finished here. With their families.'

'Why, for God's sake? Why not their homeland?'

Because they have no faith that Germany isn't finished, and I don't blame them. They want to know they have a secure future, even if it's as guest workers. Wages would be appreciated, naturally.'

Zarubin shook his head. 'The Ministry of State Security isn't an employment agency.'

'Would it be too hard to convince someone that you've had a brilliant idea how to continue to utilise highly skilled men for the good of the Soviet Union *and* neutralize a constituency that traditionally breeds some hard, politically troublesome bastards? Is Democratic Germany – the new front line - really the best place for that sort?'

'You owe them this?'

'Don't be coy. You pointed me at them for a reason. They just did what you needed them to do.'

'I can't set a timetable.'

'No. But if you made the case soon it would acquire a certain inevitability by the time a decision had to be made. At the least, it would allow the right people to convince themselves that *they'd* had the idea. And there's no cost, is there?'

Zarubin considered it for a few moments and shrugged. 'And you? Will you be lost among ten thousand other refugees?'

'Is there a better way to get to Lübeck?'

'I don't know. It isn't straightforward.'

'Why not?'

'Most west-bound Operation Swallow trains are stopped in the Soviet Zone of Germany, where further undesirable elements – the sick, destitute, petty criminals - are loaded and gifted to the British.'

'Operation Swallow?'

'Their name for the agreed transfer process. We're acting in bad faith, obviously, but the British almost invite it. Eventually, the economy of their Zone – what economy there is - will collapse under the weight of its wretched, diseased population'

'And when the train is stopped, we're vulnerable.'

'Adolph Kuhn's money-belt will be, certainly.'

Something in Fischer's face made Zarubin laugh. 'It's not difficult to spot, to practiced eyes. My 'eyes' tell me he has a bad habit of checking it too often, and tenderly. Don't worry, every one of them's a German, and wouldn't dare try. I can't say the same about Soviet troops boarding a refugee train. They are, after all, quite adept at finding German chattels.'

'I told him that road or rail would be too dangerous.'

'I can get you to Berlin safely. Then it's your business where you go.'

'That would be … good.'

'Excellent. I suppose I should spit on my hand at this point, but it's such a meaningless gesture.'

'Then I must trust you.'

'So how will you do this?'

'I won't. You must come to the funnel's tip and do it yourself. Come to Scheune Station. And you'll need to bring something. Something very large.'

# Scheune Station

For possibly the first time in their long association, Wojciech had good news for Achym.

'He's called Dariusz, and he's a ferret. Looks like one, too. But he's fleeced some good stuff from folk who looked to have had their last fleecing already.'

'Why us?'

'He's scared. Town Hall's getting hard on pillagers – well, on those that wear their uniform at least. They say the militia's giving everyone a bad name and it has to stop. He could deal with the *UB* thugs, but that's probably more dangerous than offering it to the Ivans. So he thought of me, his mate.'

'What's he got?'

'Small stuff, easily hidden - watches, some jewellery, tie-pins, cigarette cases. Says he's willing to take half what it's worth.'

'Sweet. When can he get here?'

'He can't. He works the Scheune sugar factory shift, and they're all officially quarantined. We have to go there, or he thinks of someone else.'

'Fuck.'

'It's cool. They're well separated from the poor bastards in the factory.'

'Your ferret isn't, or he wasn't. Not if he's been managing to rob them.'

Wojciech frowned. 'Oh. Yeah.'

Achym sighed. 'What are the chances of strong, well-fed types coming down with it?'

'No idea.'

'Want to risk it?'

'Definitely.'

'Find Karol, tell him where we're going.'

They walked along the rail line, adding their footprints to the thousands that had passed the same way in the previous days. Wojciech glanced around continuously, keeping one hand on his gun and the other on a cigarette; Achym kept both of his tightly upon the shoulder bag in which resided two objects, one with the power to put him in a hole, the other his passport to middle-class oblivion in the west. He was certain that some small part of his psyche regretted his failure to tell his colleagues about the latter item, but he hadn't yet located it. A fortune split ten ways would be something else - a shame, mainly.

They were almost at the sugar factory when they heard it.

'That changes things. Dariusz'll be at the station, loading them in.'

Achym stopped. 'It's too public. The place will be crawling with militia, probably *UB* too. And the British, probably.

'Well, *they* can't do anything, can they? Anyway, we can get him into a carriage before they load up and do the business there. Come on, Achym, we won't get another chance. It'll be sweeter than a month's worth of fucking rags.'

This was definitely true, but typhus *and* a chance of hiding a bullet were beginning to weigh heavily against the sweetness of the deal. Achym tried out his sigh once more. 'Alright. In and out.'

Scheune station was a shivering mass of wretched

humanity. Hundreds of weary, filthy refugees had been herded the short distance across the sidings from the sugar factory and squeezed on to a single platform. Achym scanned them anxiously, looking for signs of disease. They were all on their feet still at least (except the odd one who had retained his or her suitcase and could use it as a seat), but the confused cacophony of orders, curses and pleas had a back-chorus of wracking coughs that made his guts clench. Miraculously, he'd emerged from Trassenheide without having contracted more than the shits and an infection-fever; it would be the worst irony to succumb to the labour camps' disease of choice here, voluntarily, in new Poland.

His nerves were lighting up but he noticed another irony – or perhaps a deliberate gesture by his countrymen, a final bucket emptied upon the heads of the imminently-departed. The locomotive that had dragged fourteen carriages into the station was German, a battered class 52 that must have spent the final months of the war cowering under a tree to have escaped the Allies' attention. A Polish flag almost covered the red star that betrayed its new ownership, which was about as cutting a metaphor for what both Germany and Poland had become as Achym could imagine. He grabbed Wojciech's arm before the idiot could launch himself into the mass of flesh in front of them.

'Spot your man first, *then* move.'

'Why?'

'So we spend less time wearing infected *schwabs*.'

'Right.'

Less than ten seconds later Achym wished he'd kept his mouth shut. They were almost surrounded by militia uniforms, but Wojciech shoved his way to a metal stump that had once supported an elevated walkway and climbed it. His 100-kilo, leather-clad frame stood out like a surplice'd hard-on, almost begging official Poland to take an easy shot. Astonishingly no-one noticed, even when he put two fingers into his mouth and whistled with enough force to drop a dog. He waved at Achym and pointed helpfully to the far end of their platform.

*Shit.*

Clutching his shoulder bag, Achym followed his lieutenant, trusting that the man's broad frame would attract the shorter-sighted germs. Fortunately the militia were using their shoulders, feet and rifle butts to impose some sort of order upon the press of refugees, who sullenly formed into a six-rank-deep honour guard along the length of the platform. As the view ahead cleared Wojciech stopped suddenly, and Achym's nose met a muscular back.

'That's odd', said Wojciech, mildly.

'Ow. What is?'

'Them.'

He moved aside, giving daylight a chance. A small group of militiamen stood in front of them, about ten metres away, in the clear space between the waiting passengers and their ride out of Poland. They were arguing the pleading way, using their hands rather than fists at something that was obviously unpleasant, or inconvenient, or against orders. The two men on the receiving end seemed unmoved - or rather, the Russian officer did. The other man, a civilian carrying a war's-worth of old wounds, was looking around, indifferent to whatever was being said.

Achym's stomach tried to turn and run a moment before the rest of him.

'Come on.'

He plunged straight into the crowd of waiting refugees, taking his chance with whatever they hosted. The hard-learned deference of Germans carved a path for the two men, though enough of them had been left in possession of their luggage to make it difficult going. Twice, only the larger man's iron grip kept Achym on his feet, and it saved him from falling onto the opposite track when they reached the platform's edge. To the east, back towards Torney, the track was clear and inviting; to the west …

'There's Dariusz', said Wojciech. 'Oh, fuck.'

Achym looked, saw instantly what *oh, fuck* was about. Their Polish militiaman was standing on the track, leaning against the platform edge. He was receiving what looked to be at least three packs of cigarettes from the hands of a man dressed in an exuberantly plush coat, a man one might have mistaken for top of the bill at a music theatre had this not been Szczecin, 1946, a half-smashed railway station.

They climbed down on to the track. The militiaman's peripheral vision caught the movement and he turned, started, and clambered frantically onto the crowded platform. The music hall act remained where he was.

'Hey, guys.'

'Hello, Earl', said Achym, mildly. 'Paying off your man?'

'Yeah. Sorry.' Kuhn didn't look as scared as someone in his situation – directly beneath the north-face of Wojciech – should have been. 'Had to get you here. Otto's orders.'

'You're handing us over to the Russian?'

The hurt in Kuhn's eyes made would have made a rock apologise. 'What, stick the knife in? Me? Shit!'

'Zarubin wants his package back?'

'Yeah. And Otto found a way to do it neatly, so you don't put your arse in his sights.' Kuhn nodded at the mass of Germans crowding the platform. 'Give it to one of them and point out the

Boss. Easy. Might even do you some good.'

'What if I just take your money-belt and fuck off with it?'

'You wouldn't. We're businessmen, not wild boys. Anyway, what would you do with Swiss francs? The first time you tried to turn them into spending money you'd have half of Stettin on your arse. The very worst half.'

There was a slight tic in Kuhn's eye as he said it that hinted at a degree of uncertainty, but his voice was steady. It was true enough; all the Pelzer-Strasse boys together, forming a circle with the wagons overturned, couldn't fight off the local interest that hard, steady currency would arouse. Achym took a grip on Wojciech's arm, just in case. Kuhn noticed it and got a little paler.

'But I can give you *something*.'

'What?'

'It's about Grossmann.'

'What, he's Jewish?'

'He's sticking it to you.'

'You mean he isn't buying our stuff? We're sort of suspecting that already, Earl.'

'No, it's something else. You've got him his business registration, the one thing he didn't have. Now he's officially resident. But it isn't clothes he's interested in.'

'A tailor isn't interested in clothes?'

'I had a few drinks with my mate Andrzej the ex-Jew the other night. I mentioned Grossmann and he nearly choked, came on all shifty. So we had a few more and he decided I was kosher. He told me that the old man and his sons are the underground railway in Stettin. They smuggle in German papers for Jews, to get them out of Poland, into the British Zone and on to Palestine.'

'What Jews?'

'Yours. I'm still trying to work out how twisted it is, that the safest thing for a Polish Jew is to be mistaken for one of us.'

'He *used* me?'

'Yeah. In a good cause, I suppose.'

Achym gave the rail-line his attention. Not only was he a failed businessman but a mark also, a professional victim, a … *rube*. It stirred a sudden, profound sense of awe at the quantity of luck he must have been riding, to have stayed upright for so long with all his front but only half a brain. He caught the soft groan to his left side. It had to be worse for Wojciech; he'd given up a profitable line in the intimidation market to tie himself to what he'd thought was an up-and-comer, and the reward was a mountain of rags that would have looked bad on eight-week-dead corpses. He hoped that the man didn't carry grudges.

'Thanks, Earl. Give me a minute.'

He found her in less than three, because he was looking for her granddaughter, or niece, whatever she was. The girl's hair was a beacon, something a wiser German would have cut off to spare herself the attention, but he supposed that kids everywhere were equally stupid about things like that. He climbed up on to the platform directly behind her. The old woman was holding her hand, tightly. He touched a bony shoulder.

'Hello, mother.'

———————

Startled, Monika turned. The leader of the hooligan-gang was towering over her, and behind him his even bigger friend stared down fiercely, as if he wanted to do harm to an angel. She felt a terrible fear rising from her gut.

*Oh, God, please, not now.*

The hold on her shoulder tightened slightly and turned her around. The gang-leader pointed a finger through the several ranks of Germans that stood in front of them, towards the train. He had to move her sideways a little, to give her the view he wanted.

'Do you see that man? The Russian officer?'

She nodded, not trusting her voice.

'Good. I want you to do something for me.' He reached into his bag and removed a small parcel, heavily wrapped in brown paper and tied with string.

'Will you give this to him? Don't worry, he's expecting it. I imagine he'll be grateful. But don't point out who gave it to you. Yes?'

Monika nodded. What else could she do? If they turned on Erika ...

She released the girl's hand and stumbled forward with the parcel clutched to her chest, begging pardon for the feet she trod upon, for the elbow she used. When she broke cover a nearby militiaman threatened her with the back of his hand but she kept moving, her concentration wholly on the young man who had been pointed out to her. It was futile; he stood at least a dozen metres away, and the militiaman's hand was already on her hair, forming a fist, clutching it. He began to drag her backwards, towards the press of humiliated flesh she should never have had the presumption to depart; but then the man standing next to her officer turned around, and she forgot even the pain in her head. It was the most terrible face she had ever seen, a monstrosity, at once the victim of some evil and an embodiment of it - a *krampus*, a *nachzehrer*. The apparition looked right at her, into her, and turned again, back to the officer. He took the man's arm, and his other hand – a claw, rather – rose slowly and pointed one skeletal finger directly towards her. She felt all the strength in her legs fail, her ears fill with the roaring, emptying torrent of her infected blood, and toppled forward.

---

The girl wouldn't move. Achym hadn't told her to stay or held her, and he didn't see the sort of fear that paralysed legs. Had he thought about it all he might have expected her to turn and run after the old sow (they seemed almost conjoined, after all), but she remained, standing in front of him, staring right into his eyes like her boyfriend had a knife and friends.

She was a beauty, no doubt about that. The first time he saw her in Torney camp he'd had to remind himself that she was a girl still. In a different age she'd have married early for sure, been sold to the highest-bidding suitor in her district, bartered for whatever pretty girls served as currency to acquire - it was what everyone from farmers to royalty had always done. Now, there was no ticket price attached, no perceived value in buying what could be taken. Once, she'd have been a prize; these days, no more than a spa for jaded cocks. She didn't seem to have been broken by it yet.

It came to him slowly that the stare was about something other than admiration for his startling good looks. It was pointed, even expectant, and naturally he had a *fuck off* ready for when he tired of it. But then he saw something else in it, something familiar, and his half-brain began to search its far corners. He had a sense that this wasn't going to turn out well, but before he could turn the dial and lose the signal it was already there, the ghost of a day, his long-dead mother stroking his head, whispering of her great pride and love for him. He had no recollection of the detail, only that the young Achym had carried within him some aspect, some greater promise than his older self, a quality that his mother knew – *knew* – would carry him above life's shit-smeared cobbles. And this girl was stirring the dust of that fond illusion, but *why* he couldn't …

He moaned. *Oh, Jesus.*

The Beauty's big, oval eyes welled slightly (as if they weren't working on him enough already). 'We ate the fish. I'm sorry.'

He rubbed his own eyes before they watered of their own accord. He tried to think but there was nothing – no plan, no clever strategy for putting him a kilometre away instantly. The girl had pushed in the scalpel and found the precise place where the doomed, Good Achym had made his nest before he was marched off the premises. If it had been a better day he might have seen it through, found the necessary indifference, perhaps pointed at something and then ran off when she turned to see what it was. But he was on the ropes already, groggy from the one-two of having been set up by a smart Russian pretty boy and a smarter German Jew.

'No, it's fine.' He lifted the matter slowly from his bag and put it carefully into the girl's hand.

'Tell her it's unlike any other, anywhere. Tell her to find a bookseller, if such men exist still in the west. Tell her not to take his first offer, or his third. Tell her Poland says sorry …' he waved a hand around him, not needing to put detail to it, '… but only today.'

She took it, and then his hand, and Achym was beginning to feel almost good about himself when a fist in his back almost toppled him. Wojciech was pointing back down the track, towards Torney.

'Trouble.'

---

Monika realised that she was being held, had been saved from the ground by two old men, refugees like her, who had forgotten their place and rushed forward to grab her. She thanked them but pulled free hurriedly, anxious not to disobey the instruction she had been given. The Russian officer and *Krampus* were standing as before, watching her, ignoring but not moving away from the militia officers who remonstrated with them. She tested her legs for a moment, reassured herself that they would obey, and approached them.

Closer to the monster, her revulsion lessened. His wounds were old, half-healed into a sort of twisted relationship with the undamaged flesh; this close, he was merely odd, uncomfortable to look upon for more than a moment. The Russian by contrast was quite handsome, the sort of blond boy the Waffen SS used to take and spoil. But he was frowning, as if her presence was an irritation, while the wounded one wore something that might have been a slight smile. He raised that claw again, and beckoned her. She cleared her throat.

'Sir, I was told to give you this.'

Her hand moved from its tight press upon her stomach, revealing the parcel. The Russian's eyes widened slightly and his hand twitched, as if making an effort not to snatch at the object. He mumbled something that might have been a thank you.

The wounded one put his good hand on her shoulder and spoke more loudly than necessary, as if he were deaf or making a point.

'And where are you from, madam?'

Given the circumstances, the question almost begged a little defiance. 'We're from Bernhagen,' she said firmly, emphasising the name so as not to play down the injustice of their not being there any longer; 'in the county of Naugard.'

'You have family here?'

'I have my village here. What's left of it.'

'Then perhaps …' He looked at the Russian, who hadn't been able to take his eyes from the modest brown parcel.

'What? Oh, yes. Yes, of course.'

He turned and spoke German to the senior Polish militia officer. 'Load her and her people first. Put them in a carriage with a stove.'

The officer breathed hard. 'But this is not on the schedule. Nor is it…'

'I don't care. It's *my* train, and you people say you want Germans out of Stettin. So, do you?'

'According to the arrangements made by the Population Transfer Commission, there is a staged process to be observed that …'

Zarubin took one hand from his parcel and wagged a finger at the officer. '… is already several weeks behind its intended schedule. Furthermore, arrangements for the refugees, particularly at the sugar factory, are entirely inadequate. Several cases of typhus have been reported by the British here and at Lübeck, and whatever we may think of them their cooperation is necessary. Otherwise, what are you going to do with your Germans?'

'Fuck the British. They've agreed to the operation.'

'To *an* operation, not to this calamity. Captain …?'

Reluctantly, the officer offered his name.

'Captain Orlik, do you know how difficult it was for me to arrange this train?'

'That isn't my …'

'It wasn't, at all. In fact, Garrison Commander Konnikov praised my initiative as he signed for it. Your people are scraping up every German east of the Oder and bringing them here, or to Kalawsk, with the intention you say of sending them west. But this …' Zarubin waved at the mass of refugees around them. '… it's like you've eaten several large meals and then decided to stick a cork up your arse. As far as I know I'm the first Soviet officer to examine the conditions here, and if I report what I see then I can almost guarantee that responsibility for the Szczecin end of Operation Swallow will be very quickly assumed by Red Army personnel.'

The Captain blanched.

'Obviously, that will include supervision of the two camps, which I believe are significant sources of income for your men. In fact, what they acquire there stands in lieu of wages, does it not?'

The long silence that followed shredded Monika's nerves. She had understood all the words and almost none of their meaning. She had no idea what a *swallow* was, though obviously it was important enough to christen an operation; she didn't know why Russians and Poles should be arguing about Germans, when both wanted them gone from here; she didn't know why this horribly disfigured German should look so at ease in the company of his persecutors, or why he was trying to do a good turn for a village he had never known. But with all her heart she hoped that the Russian would be obeyed, and Bernhageners loaded onto the train, today, to be removed from this filthy place.

Captain Orlik scanned the platform. True to their orders his men had emptied the sugar factory the moment they heard the incoming train, herding the refugees across the sidings at as much of a distance as they could keep and still be effective shepherds. He had hurried from Torney and found the station packed already, and if he wanted a *fait accompli* here it was. If he tried to get them all back into the factory there'd be trouble – enough to require the boot and rifle butt, which meant that in three days half his men would be exhibiting symptoms of the German disease (as he preferred, optimistically, to think of it). And the threat of Red Army intervention …

'But the British Repatriation Team must inspect them prior to boarding.'

'They can't. They aren't here today.'

'The British say they won't take any trains unless they meet their standards.'

'Oh dear. Then they'll have to be disappointed.'

'We're required to dust the displaced persons with DDT powder, but supplies haven't …'

'It doesn't matter. I'll arrange for that when the train stops at Teterow.'

'We 're supposed to provide two days' rations, and we have none until tomorrow at the earliest.'

'Again, provision will be made at Teterow. They can manage for most of today without rations. Captain, this train must depart, within the hour if possible.'

Orlik rubbed his chin and glanced up and down the platform. 'Very well. We need to appoint carriage supervisors to account for the good behaviour of the rest. I can't spare men to guard them.'

The Russian officer shrugged. 'Look at them. They're going to make trouble?'

As Orlik organized his militia Monika scanned the platform, trying to locate all her villagers. Without constant nagging they were as difficult to herd as cats, and she doubted that the Russian's benevolence would stretch to a lengthy wait while she tried to assemble them. At least they were here, and Erika was as good as a long rope when necessary ...

People around her began to shout and she didn't know why - she tried to see what the matter was but she was held and couldn't move. The monster's face loomed over her, close enough to touch, and now that she could see his eyes clearly, the pain in them, she felt a great pity at whatever ordeal had fashioned him. She realised that he was holding her, his arm under her shoulders, and she saw the claw come down towards her. It disappeared from view but she felt it on her chest, pressing, though she felt nothing of the bullet that nestled deeply beneath it.

———

Several hundred people, all trying to dodge a second bullet in their own way, hampered Fischer's efforts to find its source. A long time ago he'd had a necessary instinct, something similar to a bird's compass, that pinned a threat almost precisely; but he seemed to have lost it along with every other martial quality. He was fairly certain the shot had come from the east and a little to the south; a group of damaged siding sheds and signal posts some three hundred metres away was excellent cover and the likeliest location, but if the man was a professional it might have travelled further. He was certain it hadn't found its intended target.

He realised that he was on his feet still, while most of the rest of the station's guests had become as horizontal as the impediment of other bodies allowed. Next to him Zarubin was also upright, carefully scanning the same terrain. His gun remained tied down.

'Did you see ...?'

'No. But there ...'

As Fischer pointed, his view was partly obscured by a young girl walking calmly towards them, picking her way over and around her prone compatriots. In different circumstances he might have appreciated her beauty, perhaps pitied her parents the constant anxiety they must be suffering. But today, strangely, all he noticed was the object she carried – an object which, despite the cloth that covered it, he recognized immediately. It was hard to believe she hadn't prised it from Mazur's dead fingers.

Neither Zarubin's uniform nor Fischer's face seemed to impress her. She knelt by the old woman's side, stroked her head, spoke quietly to her. The flow of blood was less than it might have been, a chest shot that had missed the heart. Fischer considered the other possibilities and came up with nothing good. A rib deflection would have put it somewhere else, a lung or the liver, both equally devastating to an old, worn body. He braced himself, trying to recall a comforting form of words, and put a hand on the girl's shoulder.

She looked up. Her eyes were pale blue, unnervingly clear, dry.

'Monika can't die.'

He'd heard something similar any number of times during the past hellish years, but the way she said it - not the desperate plea of a frantic loved one to an absent God but as a statement of a thing understood, almost serenely – surprised him. He didn't try to argue the point. Two minutes more and he wouldn't need to.

The old woman stirred. Her breathing was loud with an unpleasant rasp to it. *Lungs*. Feebly, her hand closed upon the girl's.

'Put Bernhagen on the train, Erika. Quickly.'

'Monika, get up.'

'No, dear, I can't. I'm done, thank God. Amon was right, it's very comfortable.'

'No, look.' The girl opened the cloth and removed the *Kombinierte*. 'You aren't in the book yet and I can't do it for you. I'm not a Pohlitz.'

The old woman gasped and tried to reach for the bible, but the girl pulled it back, teasing like someone might a dog that wanted its biscuit.

'Get up, Monika. They won't follow me, only you.'

Fischer watched, astonished, almost forgetting to assist the girl as she painfully manhandled what should have been a corpse to its feet. The victim moved with infinite fragility, as if her stolen death had taken a large tithe in compensation; she said something, too breathlessly for it to make sense, and then stood for a moment, hand on her wound, sucking in air that damaged lungs wouldn't have been able to process. She coughed once, and a bloody mess splattered the platform at her feet.

'Ach. Don't let me dirty the book.'

Carefully, Erika released her grip and picked up the bible. 'I'll look after it. The man told me it's very valuable.'

'Then it can feed Bernhagen.'

The old woman swayed, and Fischer took her arm to steady

her. She looked into his face, searching the mutilated and whole flesh, the soft, stretched tissue that joined the two, and for a moment he thought she might reach out to touch it, to give her fingers a sense of what he was. She didn't seem to be revolted by any of it.

Another cough, a slight, normal noise. 'Have I ...'

'What, madam?'

'Are ... are we spirits?'

He almost smiled. 'Would we choose to stay in *this* world, if we were that?'

She looked around with no apparent joy at this revelation. He noticed that her wound had stopped bleeding. It was a remarkable thing; it made him think about himself, about wilfulness, or miracles, or the blind, unknowable luck of those who didn't expect it. She took and held his injured hand with her own bloodied one and turned to Zarubin.

'I'm sorry sir. May we get our people together?'

The Russian had been watching the near horizon, still trying to divine the meaning of a second attempt that hadn't happened. He glanced down at her with milder curiosity than she deserved.

'Please do so, mother. As quickly as you can.'

———————

'Who do you think he is?'

'I have no idea. He's too well-fed for a Herman, so a Pole or an Ivan, probably.'

'Bastard.'

Achym looked up from the dying man. 'We don't know that. He might have had good reason.'

'What, to shoot into a crowd? Fucking assassin.'

'Yeah, well, this kind of thing doesn't have any good side to it. Lose the knife and we'll do a quick one back into town.'

The former signal box was a mere shell, its surviving walls a metre high at most. But some of the outer surface's whitewash was intact still, and the dark form passing in front of it, climbing into it to use it as a firing point, was what had caught Wojciech's eye. It had been lucky for someone, perhaps; not for this fellow. Achym watched indifferently as the eyes emptied. The weapon next to the body was as good as nondescript (a Tokarev SVT-40, of which more than a million were in circulation), and the civilian clothes … he knelt and checked inside the jacket … were stripped of any identifying mark. So Wojciech was right, an assassin, and Achym would have bet his last tin of processed fish on the intended victim being someone other than one of the hundreds of wretched refugees cramming Scheune station.

Wojciech nodded. 'Someone's coming.'

'Then we're going.'

'What about his pockets?'

'They find his stuff on you and it's a death sentence.'

The big man looked down, nudged the body with his boot and sighed. 'Is there *anything* in this fucking town that's worth the trouble?'

———————

Fischer and Zarubin stood over the corpse. The Russian's good humour seemed to be upon a point of something more than his botched execution.

'Do you know him?'

'Know him? He's family, almost. Major, say hello and goodbye to Semyon, my dear uncle Feodor's faithful adjutant, driver, personal torturer, executioner and drinking comrade.'

Behind them, Captain Orlik coughed. 'Not our business, then?'

'Not unless you want it to be. And you don't, of course. But you might 'phone garrison headquarters and ask for NKVD Captain Arokh. Tell him to come as quickly as possible. Say this may be the swift resolution to a particular problem we have.'

Orlik couldn't hide his relief. 'Yes, immediately.'

Zarubin watched until the Pole was halfway across the rail-tracks, then turned and held out his package. 'It would be a pity not to know.'

The knots were tight and his fingers shook slightly, but Fischer had an unusually burning curiosity. Inside the several layers of brown paper it was wrapped in only a single layer of thin gauze. He removed it with infinite care and held it to the light.

'Have you ever seen it?'

'Yes. Just once, before the war. In Berlin, of course - the Altes Museum.'

'So you know what it is.'

'I believe its designation then was the small diadem.'

'A modest piece, but from King Priam's horde.'

'Perhaps. Some archaeologists insisted it may be older, but what would I know? Your uncle stole it?'

'Not commanding a fighting division, he missed the Great Pillaging - that, and the rapine. He must have felt particularly victimized.'

'It was the gold of Troy that went into *Nekrasov*.'

'It was. Apparently, we found it in Zoo bunker and relocated it to Karlshorst, until its transfer became a matter of urgency.'

'Why? You haven't bothered to conceal any other thefts.'

'You don't know that, obviously. But yes, this is a special case. Victorious nations take their prizes, but enemies don't remain so forever, do they? If we're to beat the Americans we need not only to remain in the west but keep the friends we make. As the Boss has decided that the Troy horde is too valuable to return it would be better that its fate were not to be known, ever. The destruction of the last days in Berlin was helpfully comprehensive, so ...'

'Very neat. You'll be returning this to your uncle?'

'That was my intention. But I think Semyon can be the vessel, now that he's volunteered.'

'But won't they believe that he's the thief?'

Zarubin laughed. 'No, Major; there'll be quite definite proof to the contrary.'

'What proof?'

'The proof of desire, of my uncle's persecutors *wanting* him to be the guilty party. The article itself is an irrelevance.'

'But it's the only thing you have against him, surely?'

'Of the crime of theft, certainly. But senior Red Army officers aren't put against a wall for mere theft. Were that the case, we wouldn't have a General Staff. The … what did you call it?'

'The small diadem.'

'… is just the excuse that will allow a façade of legality to finish off the old bastard.'

'It can't be the girl's murder.'

'Hardly. The theft, though nothing, would count for more. No, *this* will be the cause.'

Zarubin removed an envelope from his tunic pocket. With a handkerchief covering his fingers, he delicately opened it and produced a second, smaller envelope, browned with age, its red seal broken in half.

'You don't read Russian?'

'No.'

'A pity. This is an historical artefact. It is, in a way, the confession of one Josef Stalin.'

'To what?'

'To more or less single-handedly fucking up the entire southern thrust of the advance into Poland in 1920. Foolishly, he believed my uncle to be a comrade, at a time when his position in the Politburo was by no means secure, and confided matters he should have kept to himself.'

'Surely he's secure enough now for this not to be a problem?'

'As secure as any human possibly could be, but it's a matter of reputation. What if, in a whimsical moment, Uncle Feodor had arranged to get it out to the west, to be paraded by the World's Press? The Boss would never again dare show his face to Truman or Churchill.'

'How the hell did you get it?'

'By Armed Forces Post, actually. From a dear old friend, a woman I regard as my only surviving female relative. My uncle's housekeeper, Elena.'

'She's betraying him?'

'Think of it as notice to quit her employment. She's now almost fifty and tired, I think, of sucking Uncle Feodor's cock on demand. And I fear it's always a *demand*.'

'How long have you had this?'

'Half a year, almost. I brought on a dozen migraines trying to think of a non-fatal way to use it, but nothing occurred.'

'Until the incident with the two women.'

'Yes. It's a curious thing, but my uncle might be a Cossack for all his suicidal disregard of consequence. One of his old cronies happened to mention the Troy treasure, its transfer from Berlin into the *Nekrasov*, so he simply turned up and helped himself. He had the small wit to pick an article he could hide easily, but the very same evening chose to parade it upon a whore. In Soviet HQ Stettin, for God's sake!'

Fischer held out the diadem. 'She wore it. A girl who'd never touched anything finer than brass, wore a legendary queen's trappings. I wonder what she thought of it.'

Zarubin took it gently from his hand, kneeled and placed it in the dead man's coat pocket. 'Would it be too painful to ask, when you see her next?'

'Like dying from a gut wound.'

'Then leave it in the far past, where it belongs. Here, take the letter, put your fingerprints all over it, then seal it in the outer one.'

'Why?'

'It's both the ticket and price for your escape, you and Adolph Kuhn. You'll post it from somewhere in the Allied sector of Berlin.'

Fischer looked at address on the outer envelope. It was a Cyrillic script, and he understood only *Mockba*. But the envelope itself was a franked American item.

'Military Intelligence Service. It won't be intercepted. And you won't ever return to embarrass me, not with *that* against you.'

'Of course. How will we get to Berlin?'

'Very easily, in my car. We'll make a day of it, perhaps have a light lunch on the way.'

'It had better be a large car.'

Zarubin's face dropped. 'You're joking again.'

'Herr Kuhn says she's non-negotiable. Besides, it'll give you a good reason to stand down a curious driver and take the wheel yourself. And one might assume that any roadside security checks are likely to be cursory with her in the back seat.'

Slowly, the Russian smiled. 'Will there be enough food in the Allied Zone to sustain her?'

'If not, you'll have added your bit to the war against

capitalism.'

'True. Go on, get out of here before Arokh arrives. I'll wait just long enough to make the identification and congratulate him on his brilliant success and imminent promotion. Find your friend, tell him to be ready to move.'

'When?'

'Today. By this evening we'll be in Berlin.'

*Berlin.* A near-atomized city, the former capital of a former state, a charnel-house, dissected and apportioned between conquerors who had imposed a greater sense of the World's iron truths upon their subjects than anything the Mongols had ever managed. A city without hope yet without walls also, and Fischer couldn't quell the perverse murmur that pushed through his composure like a steel prow breaking ice.

He stumbled out of the signal box. Across the rail-lines refugees were clambering into train carriages, jostling or helping each other, shouting, crying, trying to secure and organize those fragments of belonging still permitted to them. The prospect had all the formless desperation of any unwilling movement of peoples, of History happening. Like them he had no feel for what was coming, no idea what possible accommodation there could be in an already desolated land for the vast tide that poured westward into it. On only a single, inconsequential point did he pin what a man of less melancholic disposition might have called an expectation, a far sight of one possible country. He paused and removed the folded paper from his pocket, staining it slightly with the blood of an old woman, savouring the hurt the words made in his chest.

*Otto. Come Soon. M-T.*

———————

Wojciech's mouth struggled to close.

'You mean, *really* straight?'

'Woj, it's a wise man who accepts what he's shit at, and I'm shit at this.'

The big man stopped, stared around, shook his head. 'What about the lads?'

'They'll do better on their own – *you'll* do better. I can't help feeling I've held you back in particular.'

'How?'

'Girls. You've always wanted to run some, and I kept saying no, it's too much trouble, or too many overheads, or something else to put you off. You should seize your dream, mate. Make me proud.'

'Christ, Achym! What will you do?'

'Did you know I have a degree from Warsaw University?'

'What use is *that*?'

'I'm going to make an appointment to see our beloved Mayor Zaremba, who's always trying to make something more of this town than the midden it is. I'll wear my most serious expression, my almost respectable clothes, and I'll tell him that I've seen the future.'

'What's in it?'

'A college, to begin with. There's nothing like a few hundred people doing fuck all that's useful to give a place some class. And I'm going to tell him that there's no surviving acoustical engineering expertise in Poland, so there's a good place to start.'

'What did you study at university?'

Achym looked at Wojciech with affection. He'd met walls with more brains, but none had been nearly as endearing.

'I might teach trombone as a side line - make a little extra cash *and* keep my hand in. Jesus, I'll probably invest in a family eventually, grow a few roots here, become a town councillor, or whatever the commie version is.'

'That's just … tragic, Achym.'

'When is the future not? Szczecin may be a turd, but it's going to get shined any year now, and it's better not to be in the way of the spit and polish. Anyway, I'm thirty next birthday, and that's far too old to be dragging around suitcases full of stuff that everyone wants to fight me for. Even if I was good at it. And I'm not.'

'Fucking Grossmann!'

'Yeah. But fucking Russian officers too. And fucking horribly mutilated Germans. And fucking fate.' Mazur paused, turned his face upward and caught the first few drops of rain. 'And the fucking weather. It's no shame to be outnumbered. Come on.'

'Where?'

'To find a still. I've got about a dozen tins of fish left in this bag. They'll buy two heroic hangovers, at least.'

## Author's note

The post-war expulsion of the *Volksdeutsche* from long-established and more recently annexed regions of eastern and southern Germany has been described as the greatest ethnic cleansing of the twentieth century, the Holocaust excepted. Between 1945 and 1947, the official phase of the process - sanctioned by the Allied Powers and implemented by the Polish, Czechoslovakian and Soviet governments - displaced millions of civilians, most of whom were women, children and the elderly. Of these, hundreds of thousands died in transit - victims of hunger, disease or deliberate mistreatment. There is no need here to revisit the hideous crimes of the Third Reich, or to seek to explain or excuse the actions of those who had suffered at the hands of its servants and who sought to exact retribution. But what many of the policy's architects saw as a necessary measure to preserve those threatened by such retribution became, in effect, the most spectacular example of collective punishment imposed upon a conquered enemy in modern times.

'King Priam's treasure', the gold hoard excavated at Hisserlik by Heinrich Schliemann during the 1870s, was smuggled by him out of Anatolia and sold in 1881 to the Royal Museums of Berlin. During the latter stages of World War II it resided in the Zoo Bunker. Removed by the Red Army following the defeat of the Third Reich, its fate remained unknown until 1993, when it was re-discovered in the Pushkin Museum, Moscow. Though agreement was reached to return the treasure to Germany, Russian authorities have since leaned heavily upon (1998) legislation which treats loot pillaged at the war's end as legitimate reparations and prohibits its return. Modern archaeologists are satisfied that the hoard pre-dates the reign of Priam by a millennium.

The Jewish 'underground railroad' through Stettin/Szczecin

existed. The city's border location made it a concentration point for surviving Polish, Byelorussian and Ukrainian Jews attempting to flee to Palestine (one newspaper estimated that there were some 25,000 Jews there by mid-1946, when this novel concludes). It was the sharpest of ironies that their method of deliverance was to secure documentation identifying them as Germans, thereby ensuring their swift deportation to the west.

In 1946, an Engineering School was established in Szczecin. It comprised three faculties, one of which had an acoustical engineering department.

The Thin Man        Dashiell Hammett

Hercules Poirot's CHristmas

The Corpse in the Snowman
                        Nicholas Blake

An English Murder      Cyril Hare

The Long Shadow        Celia
( THe hours Before Dawn )    Fremlin

The Ice Harvest        Scott Phillips

A Fatal Grace          Louise Penny

The Mistletoe Murder        P D James
      + other stories

Printed in Great Britain
by Amazon